A WAY BACK TO HAPPY

OLIVIA SPOONER

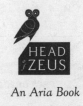

HEAD
of
ZEUS

An Aria Book

First published in the UK in 2021 by Head of Zeus Ltd
This paperback edition first published in 2021 by Head of Zeus Ltd
An Aria book

9 7 5 3 1 2 4 6 8

A CIP catalogue record for this book is available from the British Library.

ISBN (PB): 9781800249486
ISBN (E): 9781800249462

Head of Zeus
5–8 Hardwick Street
London EC1R 4RG
www.headofzeus.com

Print editions of this book are printed and bound by CPI Group (UK) Ltd,
Croydon, CR0 4YY, on FSC paper

MIX
Paper from
responsible sources
FSC
www.fsc.org FSC® C020471

To Mum and Dad, for everything x

PART ONE

BEFORE

ONE

TEN WEEKS BEFORE

"I hate Mondays." Lily slams my front door closed, throws her handbag on the couch, and flops down opposite me at the breakfast bar. I pause from chopping carrots and wordlessly slide a glass of chardonnay towards her.

"Please tell me your day held at least a glimmer of excitement," Lily says, raising the glass to her lips.

I try not to smile. "Does exhuming goldfish count?"

Lily's mid-gulp when she snorts, spraying my face. "What?"

Wiping the mist of wine off my cheeks, I grin and nod. "Freddie's goldfish died. God knows how. Honestly, I followed every instruction in that book." Grimacing, I yank a rogue strand of hair from my mouth. "I buried them under the lemon tree, because I was sure Freddie wouldn't want to see them all bloated and dead-looking, but when he got home from crèche he lost it. Said he didn't have a chance to say goodbye."

"Please don't tell me you dug them back up?" Lily asks.

"In the pouring rain. I washed them off and put them in

a shoebox lined with tissue paper. We had a little service. Freddie said he'd never forget them."

"I thought you only bought those fish a couple of weeks ago?"

I put my knife down, reach for my glass, and stare at my friend over the rim. "We did."

Lily bursts out laughing. Her short black hair bounces up and down, and wine spills from her glass onto the bench. "Em, I love coming here Monday nights, 'cause you always make my days go from fuckin' ordinary to hilarious."

With my eyes fixed on Lily, I take a long sip and swallow. "Sukkie ate them," I say, levelly.

Lily stares at me, her mouth open. "Fuck off," she whispers.

My eyes throb with pressure. I can barely get the words out. "I was giving Freddie a hug and when we turned around, Sukkie had her head in the box. I yelled, she looked up, and there was a goldfish tail hanging out of her mouth."

We lock eyes and then we start to piss ourselves. Seriously, we are a blithering mess. I have to sit down on the kitchen tiles to recover some sort of equilibrium.

"Oh my God, Em," Lily squeals. "You make my life worth living." She staggers into the kitchen gripping her sides, and slumps down next to me. We lean our backs against the fridge.

Wiping at my tears, I take a deep shuddering breath. "Freddie's going to be traumatised for life."

"He'll need years of fucking therapy," Lily says, still grinning.

I don't swear nearly as often as I used to, and I've never sworn as much as Lily. I wonder if she'll curb her profanities in every sentence once she has kids of her own. I doubt it.

We lean into each other and wait till we can breathe properly again.

"Does Paul know?" Lily asks, resting her head against my arm. She's really short. We once worked out, after too many drinks at the pub, that the top of her head is exactly the same height as my nipples. And I'm not all that tall.

My laughter drains in an instant. "Not yet."

Lily stands, reaches for my glass, and hands it to me. Then she retrieves her own, and sits back down.

"Where's Freddie now?"

"Playing in his room."

"Should I go see him?"

"Nah. You're bound to say something completely inappropriate." I nudge her with my shoulder.

"True." Lily pauses for a drink and picks a piece of lint off her black tight-fitting pants. She's in her usual work attire of black on black. I swear the woman must have the most monochrome wardrobe in the universe. If it's not black, it's grey. The one time she wore a pale blue shirt I barely recognised her. Lily claims dark colours make her more badass. While she has most people running scared with the belief that she is, her close friends know better. She looks at me and raises her black-painted eyebrows. "Are you still going to leave Paul tonight?"

There is a moment when the room around me sways, then I blink, and it steadies itself. "Yes," I whisper.

"Promise?"

I don't look at Lily, even though I know she's staring at me. Instead I glare at her black shiny Dr Martens. "I'm going to do it this time, Lils." My voice wobbles like I'm scared, which I'm not. I've never been more determined in my life. It's because of Freddie I keep chickening out of leaving my husband – at least that's what I tell myself. If I go – when I go – Freddie is coming with me. Which means I'm tearing my son away from the only life and the only house he's ever known. I'm trading his comfort and security for a chance at getting my happiness back. It feels so incredibly selfish.

Lily squeezes my thigh and leaves her hand resting on my leg. "I was thinking on the way over here, it's third time lucky, Em. Those first two attempts, they were just bloody practice runs."

"Like the high jump?"

"Exactly," Lily says loudly, slapping my leg. "The last jump is the one that counts."

I hear a jangle of keys and scramble to my feet as the front door opens. Lily stays on the floor.

Paul fills the doorway. "Daddy's home," he yells. His eyes glance off me as he surveys the open-plan living room, dining room, and kitchen. Every time I see him these days, which thankfully is less and less often, I'm sure he's put on more weight. I wasn't kidding about the filling the doorway part. It wouldn't surprise me if soon he has to come in that door sideways.

My husband wasn't due home for another two hours. He's supposed to have a meeting till seven on Mondays. Lily's usually gone by then.

"Daddy." Freddie runs into the room and throws his arms around his father's legs. "Flip and Flop died."

"What?" Paul lifts Freddie up and I wince as Freddie wraps his thin little legs and arms about Paul's body. Freddie loves his dad the way a child does – unconditionally. I can't seem to love Paul regardless of the conditions.

Picking up the bottle of wine, I fill my glass to the top. As I lift it to my lips, I meet Paul's narrowed gaze. "Your cat ate them," I say firmly. Still refusing to look away, I tip wine into my mouth.

"Did you feed them to her?" he spits.

I hear Lily getting to her feet. "Hey, Paul," she says, coming to stand beside me. "Good day?"

Paul looks from my glass, to Lily's, to the bottle on the bench.

"Starting the week as you mean to go on are you, ladies?" His smile is faker than the plastic pot plant on the hall table beside him.

I'm annoyed at the way my hand holding my glass has started shaking. Hopefully Paul is far enough away he can't see it. "It's been a traumatic day, Paul," I say quietly. "Freddie's been very upset."

Paul scowls and reaches up to gently stroke Freddie's strawberry blonde hair. "Come on, Buddy," he says, his voice calm. "Let's go get Daddy changed out of this suit and you can tell me what happened."

I watch them disappear down the hallway.

"That went better than I expected," Lily murmurs.

"Yeah." I sigh and pick up the knife. "Better get this dinner on."

Lily is silent and still as I start chopping again. "Should I go?" she asks.

"Probably."

"Will you be okay?"

I nod. "Course I will."

"Em?"

I'll need to try harder to convince her. I grin, and wink. "He'll be so focussed on defending his cat's honour, he'll barely even register the fact that I've told him I'm moving out."

For the past five years I've made myself smile, crack jokes, and act as if everything's fine. I've become an expert; it's got to a point where acting this way doesn't feel fake anymore. Just empty. Like I have no idea who I am anymore.

Lily puts her arm around my waist and squeezes. "The spare room is all ready for you." By spare room, she means the pull-out couch in her tiny downtown apartment.

"Thanks," I croak. Clearing my throat, I resume my chopping. Lily knows my life is less than ideal. She agrees Paul and I should never have married when I found out I was pregnant with Freddie. She knows we argue; that we can barely be in the same room with each other. But she doesn't know Paul the way I do. No one does.

———

Dinner is hell with a tasty Spaghetti Bolognese on the side.

Freddie's thankfully unaware of the tension at the table. Being four years old, he's too self-absorbed to pick up on much. As long as Paul and I continue to talk to our son with a well-rehearsed smile on our face, Freddie's fine. Especially when I mention the new caramel-flavoured ice cream in the freezer; it seems to eliminate all thoughts of dead goldfish from his developing young mind.

Sukkie has been forgiven too. She's curled up on Paul's lap. It's perfectly acceptable for us to eat at the table with her on *his* bulging legs, but on the rare occasions when Sukkie jumps ship to land on Freddie or me you'd think a cardinal sin had been committed. Eating naked, using nothing but our bare hands, would be less disgraceful.

Chewing on my pasta – which, by the way, is one of my least favourite foods on the planet, but since Paul loves the stodgy stuff, I have to keep cooking it – I wonder when I became so bitter and negative. It makes me feel so ugly. Correction: uglier. I used to be an optimist, and now I struggle to have a single positive thought about anything. Hard to imagine Dad used to call me 'Little Miss Sunshine'.

I'm so exhausted from pretending to be relaxed and happy that the second I give Freddie a kiss goodnight and turn out his light, I go into my bedroom to lie down. Paul is on the couch watching his favourite show. Some CSI crime thing I can't stand. He's addicted to it. Refuses to miss an episode. He's already onto his third beer, and I wouldn't be at all surprised if he's polished off the packet of crisps.

My suitcase is packed. It has everything I can think Freddie and I will need for the next few weeks. It's in my wardrobe. I haven't even attempted to hide it. If Paul opened the door, he'd see the suitcase straight away. Not that he's likely to look; unless my husband has suddenly decided to become a cross-dresser, which I very much doubt, as he's about the most conservative person I've ever met. Plus, he wouldn't fit any of my clothes. I've lost track of the number of times Paul's told me I'm too skinny; that I need to develop some more curves. He used to call me petite, affectionately. He'd grab me round the waist with one arm, lift me off the ground, and kiss my neck over and over while I squealed and begged him to put me down. It's impossible to believe that version of Paul ever existed.

I'm still in my leggings, T-shirt, and trainers because I'm determined to go through with it. I just need to make sure:

1. The stupid programme is finished,
2. Freddie is fast asleep.

Once my son is sleeping, nothing, and I mean nothing, can wake him. I could pick Freddie up and carry him to the car with a monster screaming in my face and he's guaranteed not to stir.

While I wait, I prop myself up on the bed and flick through Instagram on my phone. I spend a lot of my spare time following inspiring females around my age. I'm sure the photos are carefully executed and edited but they appear effortless.

It's not just Instagram I have a minor obsession with. I spend at least an hour a day reading blogs. Mostly I follow lifestyle bloggers – the ones who make sourdough bread from scratch, grow their own vegetables, or give up their corporate career to teach yoga. These gorgeous women – they are always insanely attractive – are committed to nourishing their perfect bodies with wholesome food. They inspire me to get into the kitchen and create interesting things like coconut chia pudding, or quinoa porridge. I'll admit to feeling a little disappointed in the end product and the general lack of boost to my wellbeing after eating it, but I don't think I'll ever stop marvelling at everyday people following their passion. They're free to make decisions. To choose, instead of being yelled at by a controlling, overweight husband. I imagine not one of them feels trapped, paralysed by their lack of self-worth.

My absolute favourite blogger – who also posts the most incredible pictures on Instagram – is Harriet Galway. I love her. I feel like we are the best of friends already and I've never met her. I'm not a complete freak; we have at least communicated with each other. I've commented on a few of her posts and she's personally replied to me every time. She has two adorable little curly-haired angels, a husband who is constantly surprising her with little romantic gestures – a beautiful cane basket full of plump lemons, a thick, gnarly piece of ginger and a jar of local honey when she was sick in bed with the flu is my all-time favourite – and she writes the most wonderful, inspiring words. She works from home as a food writer, photographer, and stylist, and has recently moved out of the city, as she wanted her children to have more space to roam. They now live in a wee cottage by the sea her husband is slowly restoring. They have their own chooks, and vegetable garden, and can walk through their property of native bush to the beach.

I don't even want her life. Not exactly. I can't imagine moving out of Auckland to some remote place where the nearest café is miles away and I never see my friends. I like being able to walk to the shops, or Freddie's crèche, or a wine bar. There's comfort in having people going about their everyday tasks around me – mowing the lawn, emptying groceries from the car, hanging out washing, pushing their child on the swings at the park. I envy Harriet for going after her dream. She's taken risks, refused to be afraid. Said to herself, 'this is what I want' and gone for it.

Harriet's latest blog post is about taking her two-year-old to a mother and child yoga class. I'm slightly disappointed Harriet is getting on the yoga bandwagon, but I should have known it was only going to be a matter of time.

For a while I got all excited about yoga myself. Every blog post I read kept telling me it was the answer to everything. I dragged Lily to a class with me one Sunday afternoon on a rare occasion when I could convince Paul to take care of Freddie. We were useless. Plus, we kept cracking up at inappropriate moments. I mean really, can you blame us? I challenge anyone to lie on their backs, bend their knees out wide and hold their feet in the aptly named *Happy Baby* while rocking from side to side, without wanting to let out a nervous giggle.

The hardest part of the class was the last agonisingly long five minutes. We had to lie still, focus on our breath, observe our thoughts. I hated the way it made me feel – exposed and on edge, to the point I started to hyperventilate. I haven't been back to a yoga class since.

It's astounding how many thirty-year-olds manage to live such fulfilling lives. If only I hadn't fallen pregnant and married a wanker. There's no way I'll ever start a blog because no one in his or her right mind would want to read it. I guess the goldfish story might appeal to some, in a humorous, slice-of-life kind of way. And I make a pretty mean blackberry crumble; which I guess I could try to photograph artistically. I'd struggle to dredge up anything else in my life that was Insta-worthy. Plus I'm simply not attractive enough.

Paul walks in and shuts the door. Instantly nervous, I close Instagram, and place my phone on the bedside table. Surprisingly, Paul sits down on the edge of the bed next to my hip. The bed sags with his weight and I resist the impulse to move away. When we met he was trim, extremely well-built, with muscles he wasn't backwards in displaying, and so full of energy I had a hard time keeping up. Now he won't even walk the three blocks to the park. As for kicking a ball around with Freddie in the backyard – forget it.

"We need to talk," he says with a sigh. I swear he makes even talking to me look effortful.

I frown. "Okay."

Paul runs a hand through his dark hair and I concentrate on the crisp crumb on his shirt. "We don't make each other happy," he says, quietly. "We haven't done for a very long time. Not since Freddie was born."

This is not what I expected. When I look up, Paul's expression is gentle, wary even. He hasn't looked at me that way in months. I clear my throat and open my mouth but I can't talk.

Paul sighs again. "I'm leaving you, Emma. I've tried to make it work. For Freddie's sake. But I can't do it anymore."

I blink over and over again.

"I've met someone else," he mutters.

My voice returns. "You what?"

"Through a friend at work. No one you know." He pauses for a second. Shuffles his big shoes on the carpet. Why didn't I realise something was up when he changed out of his suit into a shirt, jeans and leather shoes? Paul usually goes barefoot and wears baggy shorts and a T-shirt in the evenings. "I'm moving in with her," he says, his voice firmer, angrier.

My body starts to shake, my teeth chattering as if I'm cold. I stare at his shiny brown belt, poking out beneath his shirt. He polishes that belt every Sunday night without fail, along with his shoes. He's a stickler for routine, rules, regulations. This is not some spur-of-the-moment act. Paul will have been planning this for months.

"I still want to see Freddie, be involved," he states. "Every second weekend or something. I can't take him of course, not with the hours I do."

I nod. It's all I'm capable of. Paul lifts his arm and for a moment I think he's going to reach for me. Instead, he rubs his hand on his leg, sighs loudly, stands, and walks to his wardrobe. As he lifts out a suitcase, he grunts and I can tell it's heavy. I wonder how long the suitcase has been in there. Waiting.

"You packed already?" I croak.

"I'm sorry, Em." He won't look at me now. "I'll call you in a few days."

He leaves the room, staggering with the weight. I listen to his lopsided walk down the hall. Then I hear the front door open and close with a bang.

The house is silent with my husband no longer in it.

"Holy shit," I whisper.

Climbing off the bed, I move on stiff legs into the lounge and stare at the front door. I walk up to it and place my palm flat against the wood. Turning my head, I catch sight of my reflection in the hall mirror. My ordinary brown shoulder-length hair frames my ordinary pale face. My ordinary brown eyes are wide, startled. The thirty-three-year-old woman in the mirror begins to smile. I smile back, and raise my clenched fist. "Yes," I hiss, before my knees buckle and I collapse to the floor.

TWO
NINE WEEKS BEFORE

"Mum you don't need to keep doing this." I stand back and open the door wider.

"Of course I do, you're my daughter. Who else is going to help you through a crisis like this?" Mum grips my shoulders with her long, bony fingers and kisses the air next to my cheek. "Leave the door open. Your father's parking."

Sighing, I watch my mother stride towards the kitchen in her favourite stilettos – she's the only woman over the age of sixty-five I've ever encountered who wears stilettos every day except Sundays (being a day of rest, Mum says). I thought she might stop wearing them when she retired from teaching last year – how impractical is it, by the way, to run after a bunch of eight-year-olds in pointy heels? But there's been no let-up. And she's not once complained of sore feet. How is that humanly possible? I wear heels for an hour and my feet and calf muscles start screaming in agony. That's if I haven't already rolled an ankle. I'm a comfort first, fashion second kind of girl, much to Mum's dismay.

Mum's head nods this way and that, assessing the

surroundings, looking for signs of weakness. She's desperate to pick up the pieces of her daughter's tragic life. Tell me all the ways I've gone wrong.

"Where's Freddie? How's he coping? Has he asked about his father again? What did you say?"

"Mum, you asked those same questions yesterday. Nothing's changed. Freddie is in his room playing with his train set. He's fine. He's used to Paul not being here for days on end."

Mum frowns. "You're not letting him think his father is just away on some work trip again?"

"No, Mum. I'm not." I've been deliberately vague with Freddie. I simply told him his dad was having a bit of time to himself and would be back to see him soon. Freddie was very happy with my explanation, but I know Mum won't be quite so satisfied.

I'm thankful to hear Dad's footsteps coming up the path. "Hey, Dad," I say, brightly. "We've got to stop bumping into each other like this."

Dad is wearing his usual uniform of beige pants and navy polo shirt. His shoes are the same scuffed loafers he's worn for years. Dad smiles and shakes his head. "Your mother's idea, not mine."

He hugs me tightly and I inhale his familiar scent of peppermints, coffee, and MDF wood. I used to love visiting Dad at the warehouse as a kid and watching kitchens being built and loaded like giant puzzle pieces onto trucks ready to be assembled in someone's house. Dad started the business himself when he was twenty-eight years old. He had a background in building and thought there was a gap in the market for kit-set style kitchens. Turns out there *was* a gap, only Dad wasn't the only one to see it. Business boomed for a few years, then competition grew tighter and tighter. Dad doesn't seem to stress when he has a few quiet months – not that he lets on to me, anyway. Mum on the other hand is convinced they'll be destitute and on the streets if they don't get some orders immediately. It's even worse now Mum is retired and spends a few hours a week sorting paperwork at the warehouse. Dad and I have gently suggested she go back to teaching part-time but she says she wants to be on-hand to help me with Freddie. Not that I want her help. Or have ever asked for it.

"I'm doing fine you know," I say.

Dad releases me. "Oh, I can see that. Your mother is the one who needs convincing." He winks at Mum then wanders down the hallway in search of Freddie.

"Did you hear back about the job?" Mum asks, opening the fridge. She glares at the contents and closes the door. Nothing in the world would get in the way of me and a fridge full of food. Half the neighbourhood could be struck down with the plague and I would still risk a trip to the market, or Jack's Grocery Store. It's proper food too, none of that pre-packaged, ready-meal rubbish. If I hadn't married Paul and had a baby, I imagine I'd be posting arty photos on Instagram of my cardamom ginger waffles and receiving 10,000 likes from my avid followers, with requests to please, please put the recipe up on my blog.

"Not yet," I mutter.

I've stretched the truth a little. I haven't had a job interview as such, but I've mentioned to a few of the local cafés that I'm available for work. They seemed receptive, asked me some questions and took down my phone number, which is practically the same thing. I've been letting Mum think I'm trying to find a job in journalism or copywriting again, but I'm not. Paul was the one who encouraged (more like pushed) me into that sort of work in the first place. Now is my chance to do something I actually want to do. Just because I studied English and History at university doesn't mean I have to work in a job related to those subjects. I don't want to sit at a desk all day busting a gut to meet a deadline, or write some bullshit drivel about the value of owning a dark red lipstick. The one thing I know about myself is how much I love food. Not just eating it, but seeking out fresh, seasonal ingredients, cooking with them, experimenting with different flavours and coming up with my own unique dishes. When I'm in my kitchen, I lose track of time. It's the one place where I feel a sense of peace. I even told Mum once, many moons ago, that I'd like to run my own café one day, but it's like she didn't hear me. She nodded vacantly, smiled, and changed the subject.

Mum raises her eyebrows. "It might pay to be proactive, Emma. Give them a follow-up call about the job."

I love my mum, but there are occasions – and this is one of them – when I wish she wasn't living in the same suburb as me, or the same city. Make that the same country.

"Freddie and I have eaten already, Mum." I close the front door. "If I'd known you were going to pop round we would have waited. There are plenty of leftovers. It's chicken curry."

Mum waves her hand in the air, and places her shiny black leather handbag on the kitchen bench. Her nails are perfect as usual. She never misses her weekly manicure. I, on the other hand, still bite my nails, and the last time I had them painted was the day before my wedding.

"We've eaten, darling. Wouldn't want to turn up and create more stress for you." Mum unzips her bag and pulls out a business card. "Betty gave this to me today. It's the name of her therapist. Lovely man apparently. Thought you might find it useful. I know you find it hard sometimes, opening up, but I really think it's for the best, darling. A way to process what's happened."

Mum's eyes dart from my nose, to my chin, to my forehead. She does that when she's anxious. Anything but look me in the eye. And I know she's trying. We've always had a funny kind of relationship. I guess because we're so different to each other. I'm way more like Dad. He and I naturally band together, out of necessity more than anything. The more neurotic Mum gets, the more laid-back we're forced to be. Dad and I don't do dramatics. We leave that up to Mum. Growing up, I often wished I wasn't an only child. A brother or sister might have taken the focus off my failings. The weird thing is, I've had several people tap me on the shoulder over the years simply so they could gush and carry on about how grateful they were to have Mum as their teacher. They said she was the best teacher they'd had: fun, supportive and encouraging. From all reports, Mum was a different person in the classroom to the parent she was at home.

"I'm not sure I need to see a therapist, Mum. I feel good. It's a relief more than anything."

Mum tips her head to the side and purses her lips. "A relief? That your marriage has broken up, and you're a thirty-three-year-old mother without a job?"

I shake my head, forcing a smile. "Lily says thirty is the new twenty. And I'm working on the job thing. You know I wasn't happy with Paul, don't you?"

Up till now, Mum's been holding out the therapist's card between us. Now she slams it down on the bench. "Of course I know you weren't happy. I felt helpless and…" she trails off, her face stricken. I'm surprised how badly Mum has taken my recent split from Paul. She never appeared to like him much. Well, that's not true. Mum adored Paul when she first met him. Probably because he was a fellow kiwi and there wasn't any risk of him whisking me away overseas as Edward (otherwise known as the ex-boyfriend who chewed me up and spat me out) had done. I met Edward when I was a student in Dunedin. I was in my final year of a Bachelor of Arts degree and still didn't have a clue what I was going to do with my life. Edward was backpacking around NZ and happened to stumble into the Irish pub I worked at on Friday nights. He was terribly British and terribly charming, and I fell for him within seconds of him shaking his dirty blonde hair in my face and asking for a pint. Three months later I abandoned my degree, abandoned my friends and family, and abandoned my country to follow Edward to London. Mum was devastated of course: her only child dropping out of university and moving to the other side of the world. I felt guilty every time she phoned and asked when I was going home.

What I didn't say was that I had no intention of ever leaving the UK. I was going to stay in London – a city I adored – continue to work in the café off Oxford St where I had landed a fantastic part-time job, get engaged to the love of my life, Edward, and spend long weekends with his very British family at their very British grand estate in Surrey. Instead Edward broke my heart into a million pieces by shagging his flatmate who I thought was a lovely girl until she confessed they'd been having sex for nearly a year and she thought it was about time I pulled my head out of the clouds (her words). I was on a flight home to Auckland within a week.

Even now, all these years later, just thinking about Edward gets my heart pounding. He was like a wild horse, borderline crazy, and the most self-absorbed person I'd ever come across, but by God he was fun to be with. He lit a fire in me that burnt out of control.

Paul certainly helped douse the flames. When he came up

to me and introduced himself at a party I'd been dragged along to with Lily, I was immediately absorbed by him. He was so calm and assured. Smartly dressed, organised. Paul had everything and everyone completely under control. There was no sign of any wild streak. He was opposite to Edward in every way, and I thought he was the exact person I needed. Someone to make me feel like I wasn't adrift and on fire anymore.

Mum loved the way Paul encouraged me to get a proper job, a decent haircut, and a more sophisticated wardrobe. He booked and paid for me to attend a journalism course. Since I'd studied English at University, he said, it made perfect sense to find work in a related area. He wrote my CV, sent it out, helped me decide what to wear to the interviews. And when I was offered a job writing copy for an advertising company, Paul was far more excited than I was. Dad was the only one who expressed concern. When he asked me if it was really what I wanted to do, I laughed. Of course it was what I wanted. I loved pleasing Paul.

It wasn't long before Paul and I were buying a house together, and shopping around for the best deal on a fridge, and a vacuum cleaner, and insurance. It took months before I realised that I hardly ever saw Mum and Dad anymore, or my friends. Whenever I suggested we have them over, or meet up for a drink or a meal, Paul said he was too tired, or too busy, or he simply didn't feel like seeing them. Then I fell pregnant, and we went from shocked, to Paul planning our wedding in the space of twenty minutes. It was too late to do anything, though my friends tried to tell me I needed to think about what *I* wanted, not what Paul kept telling me should happen. I knew they didn't like him, but he was the father of my unborn child, and everything was organised. How could I back out? It was going to be fine.

Mum sniffs loudly. "Before you married," she says, her lower lip shaking, "you were this vibrant, happy, beautiful person, and then… you disappeared, Emma. Something in you just *died*."

I quickly look away from Mum's eyes, shiny with tears. Her outburst is not something I can handle right now. Walking to the couch, I sit down, and tuck my shaking hands between my thighs. "It wasn't that bad," I murmur.

"Darling." Mum comes to sit on the couch but doesn't try to hug me. Thank goodness. "All I want to do is help."

Taking a deep breath, I meet her eye. "I know, Mum."

"What can I do? Name it, and I'll do it." Mum squeezes my leg. It takes every ounce of willpower to stop myself from collapsing against her. I need to get out.

"My friends are catching up for a drink tonight down at Morellis. I said I couldn't make it, but if you could maybe stay and babysit? Only if it works for you, Mum. I don't have to go, it was just—"

"Go," Mum says quickly. "It's a great idea. Get out. See your friends. Go for as long as you want. Your father and I will be just fine with Freddie."

"You sure?"

Mum stands. "Absolutely. We haven't spent nearly enough time with our grandson. Now go and get dressed."

"I wasn't planning on getting changed."

Mum looks at me like I've grown another head. "Emma Tilssen, I insist you get out of those jeans. They've got rips in them for heaven's sake. And that sweater is the same one Freddie used to throw up on as a baby."

Standing, I hug Mum briefly, swallowing over the lump in my throat. "Okay, okay. I'll get into something fancier, just for you."

I let go and quickly walk towards my bedroom. *My* bedroom, not *our* bedroom. Not anymore.

———

It wasn't a lie about my friends catching up. The get-together had been planned for weeks. It was the only date that worked for all of us, and I'd planned to go and have an absolute bender. I was fully prepared to get home at 3 a.m. to face a disapproving husband. In fact, I think that was part of the motivation.

But last night I phoned Lily and pulled out. They knew Paul had left me — they were the first people I told. I simply wasn't ready to face their analysis of the situation. Not yet.

We've known each other since university days. Lily, Mags, Trish and I flatted together, and we had a crazy time. Our grades suffered, due to the fact we rarely made it to any lectures, but that was the least of our concerns. Well, Trish was fine, of course. She can survive on three hours sleep and is naturally the cleverest person I have ever met. She's also the dumbest blonde on the planet, which makes no sense, until you meet her.

Those friends of mine are the most important part of my life (excluding Freddie and my parents, of course). Even looking at them now, with their heads huddled together in our favourite booth at Morellis makes me smile. Thank God they all ended up living in Auckland. Mags moved back in with her parents in Wellington for a couple of years to save money, and Lily got a job in Christchurch for a while, but for the past six years they've lived within a thirty-minute drive from my place, and though I haven't seen much of them since Freddie was born, it's been reassuring knowing they were nearby. It's silly to think I've been so afraid of seeing them since my husband walked out.

"Oh my God," Trish squeals, spying me at the door. She leaps up and runs over. "I didn't think you were coming." Her gigantic boobs press against me. "We were just having a drink in your honour."

With one arm over my shoulder she guides me towards the others. "Last minute babysitter turned up," I say with a shrug.

"It was your fucking mother, wasn't it?" Lily asks, standing up to hug me.

I laugh, pleased beyond reason to be here. "She practically pushed me out the door. Reckons you guys will be able to support me in my current tragedy."

Mags snorts. "Tragedy my arse. Best thing that's happened in like, *ever*." She shuffles out of the booth and lifts me off the ground. She's a solid girl, Mags. And the softest, kindest, saintliest of us all. She has four cats she would do anything for, and usually does. And more male friends than you could throw a stick at. As far as I know, she's had two one-night stands and not a single boyfriend. She deserves better than that. Out of all of us she deserves Mr Fucking Perfect.

"I'm getting us some proper drinks, ladies. None of this cheap plonk." Mags picks up the bottle off the table and waves it in disgust. "Sit Emma Dilemma, we are celebrating." Mags nudges me into the booth and heads towards the bar.

"So," Trish says loudly as she sits down opposite me. "Has the sleaseball darkened your door yet?"

I shake my head. "Not a whimper."

Lily slaps the table. "Leaving you is the only good move that man has ever made, Em. I've been on a high all week. I'm pretty sure my boss thinks I'm on drugs."

It feels so good to laugh. "How is the dashing Darryl?"

Lily sighs dramatically. "Still dashing I'm afraid."

I've never met the man, but Lily has had a serious crush on her boss for over a year. She takes secret photos of him on her phone from her desk. I've seen a lot of angles of his backside and I have to agree with Lily: he wears suit pants extremely well.

"How's Johnny taking your latest separation?" Trish asks Lily. "And your infatuation with your boss, for that matter."

Lily screws up her nose. "He turned up yesterday with another bunch of roses. I've told him I don't even like roses, but he seems to think they're the only flower that can buy your girlfriend back."

"Oh, Lils," I say, smiling. "You give him such a hard time. He's so lovely."

"Yeah," Lily says with an exaggerated sigh. "That's the whole problem."

Lily and Johnny have been on/off since they met at university. Neither of them can go longer than five months before they decide they have to try again. I love Johnny – he has the patience of a saint when it comes to Lily and her tendency to fly off the handle about everything – but even I thought they would have decided enough was enough and gone their separate ways after nearly ten years.

"Well, I'd take a bunch of roses any day over a meat pie," Trish says.

Lily and I look at her and say, "What?" at exactly the same time.

"Elliot turned up at work with a mince and cheese pie for me. Said he hoped buying me lunch meant we could spend the night together again."

Lily turns to look at me, and we burst out laughing.

"Holy fuck, Trish," Lily squeals. "He bought you a fuckin' *pie*."

Trish nods, her flawless porcelain face serious. "I told him he'd have to do better than that if he wanted me to put out. Though I have to say—" Trish pauses to brush a hand through her dead-straight, white-blonde hair – "it was a fantastic pie."

I love listening to Trish giggle. It reminds me of when Freddie was one and had just discovered the joys of farting. "I thought Elliot was long gone," I say, recovering my breath.

"Oh, he is. We've just been tying up loose ends."

I expect Trish has been tying up loose ends with a lot of men over the past year or two. Ever since she broke up with Pete – the man she was convinced was the love of her life; as we all were – she's been spreading her wings, so to speak. It's going to take a long time before Trish lets anyone near her damaged heart again.

"Ladies, Tina's here." Mags is back already, a woman I recognise from the bar at her side. "I've told her about Emma's husband leaving her for some floozie, and she's going to make sure we receive extra special attention tonight."

Tina wears her regular uniform of black apron, black shirt, and black trousers. Her face is a tight maze of worry lines, and as usual she sports the worst regrowth I have ever seen. We reckon customers take one look at her and want to buy another drink. She's been working here for nearly a year, and we've been slowly softening her up. Trust me when I say she needs it.

"Which one of you is Emma again?" she asks, placing a tray of colourful drinks in martini glasses on the table.

I raise my hand.

"Well, Emma. Congratulations. This one is on the

house." She places a bright blue drink before me. "Anything you need, ladies, just give me a wink."

"Thanks, Tina," we all chime in unison. Our buttering up is clearly paying off.

I swirl my bright pink swizzle stick and take a sip. "Jesus, Mags. What didn't she put in here?"

Mags grins and I move over so she can sit. "I told her no tequila. We don't want to have to peel you off the floor."

The four of us laugh then Lily raises her glass. "To Em. May she never get accidently pregnant and marry a fucking arsehole ever again."

"Here, here," Trish and Mags shout.

We drink in silence, my eyes watering.

"So, before you arrived, Em, we were talking about your tragic lack of a hen's party." Lily shakes her head and frowns at me.

"Well, I was breastfeeding a five-month-old at the time."

"Exactly. Trish was saying, and I agree, it feels like we let you down. Obviously, you didn't feel like a big party at the time, but we think we should throw you one now."

"Yeah," Trish says. "None of us have come close to the marriage thing. God knows if we ever will." She rolls her eyes. "Not throwing you a hen's do was an opportunity wasted."

"Totally," Mags says.

Before I went overseas we used to discuss which of us would get married first. Mags was number one on the list; it was a total no-brainer. Lily was next, then Trish. I was last. We all agreed I was not the type to ever settle down, get married, have kids. I was the one who refused to think beyond the next day, who was always taking off to explore random places, and never liked to commit to anything in case a better option came up. Boys were handy for a good time. But settling down? No way.

I look around the table. "You want to throw me a belated hen's party?"

"Yes!" they all yell. A handful of patrons at the bar turn to look at us.

Lowering my voice, I whisper, "Don't you think it's a little hypocritical? Considering getting married was the worst decision of my life."

"All the more reason to have a fuckin' awesome hen's party, Em. So you can take something positive out of this," Lily says.

Closing my eyes, I lean my head back against the cool leather. "What exactly did you have in mind?" I ask, keeping my eyes shut.

When no one speaks, I raise my head and glare at my friends. "Guys?" I hiss. "What's going on in those demented brains of yours?"

Trish grins. "We're not telling, Em. It's going to be a surprise."

"A surprise hen's do?"

They nod.

"You know how much I hate surprises, right?"

Again they simply nod.

"I must be more traumatised than I thought," I mutter.

"Why?" Mags grips my hand, concern painted across her face.

"Because it sounds like the best idea ever," I say loudly, raising my glass.

When we all start whooping, every single person in the bar turns and stares. Tina is standing near the door. She catches my eye and gives me a huge thumbs up. I grin and tip my glass in her direction.

THREE
EIGHT WEEKS BEFORE

I'm so nervous getting ready this morning I keep dropping things: the soap in the shower, Freddie's lunchbox, my phone. It's not as if I'm heading off to some highbrow corporate office job (thank goodness). All I have to do is shove some bloody vegetables into a box. But I haven't worked in nearly five years, and I want to make a good impression. I feel like this is the start of something worthwhile, and I don't want to mess it up.

It's a beautiful, clear, still day and I announce to Freddie over breakfast that we're going to walk to crèche. Since Paul left we've fallen into the habit of driving there, mainly because I've been struggling to even get out of bed. But this morning I feel energised, and Freddie must pick up on my enthusiasm, because he's the most animated and talkative he's been for weeks. He skips along chatting, and whenever we need to cross a road he grabs my hand without me having to remind him. When we reach crèche, I'm sure I'll have no trouble leaving him there, but he clings to my legs. My heart sinks as he starts to cry and I instantly wish I could pick him up and take him home. Eventually, when he's distracted by the bubble machine, I manage to extricate myself.

Trying to shake off my guilt, I briskly walk the three blocks to *Jack's Grocery Store* and knock on the door. I've loved this place on the corner of Victoria Ave ever since it opened three years ago. While I always make a point of going to the markets on Sundays – it's the highlight of my week – if there's any fruit or vegetable that I can't find at the market, or that I run out of, I go to Jack's. I don't care that he charges more than the supermarket; in fact I'm glad he does. His produce is so much fresher and better-tasting, people should pay more for it. Plus, I know he really cares about where the food he sells comes from. He's committed to it being either organic, or spray-free. And one of his missions in life is to support the small, local growers. He doesn't want to have anything to do with those big food producers.

For thirty years Jack was a crop farmer and he's convinced his wife died because of all the sprays he used. He once told me his current business is his way of atoning for his sins. Jack's wife, Alice, has been dead for twenty years and he still mentions her to me every time I see him, like she's just popped out for milk.

"Welcome, Emma," says Jack, opening the door. "You're early."

I smile at his long, grey hair tied up in a ponytail, his skin deeply tanned and gnarly as bark from so many years of working outside.

I couldn't believe my luck when Jack offered me a job last week. "Sorry. I hope that's okay."

He waves me into his darkened store. "It's fine. I was boiling the kettle, if you'd like a cuppa?"

"Ah… okay, thanks."

We sit on upside-down empty crates in the storeroom at

the back of the shop and sip our drinks. It's so quiet and cool. My nerves dissipate into the air as I breathe in deeply. "What a wonderful smell," I sigh.

Jack nods, pleased. "Nothing like the aroma of fresh fruit and vegetables."

"These broccoli are gorgeous," I say, nodding at the crate beside me. "They're so green they practically glow."

Jack and I have become friends over the past couple of years, to the point where I'd often stop in to say hi, even if I wasn't intending to make a purchase. I'd sit Freddie on the little stool by the door (Jack would insist on giving him a new season peach, or a little bowl of peas to pod), and we'd chat about all sorts of things. Mostly Jack would talk about his wife, and I'd be happy to listen. I imagine Jack gets pretty lonely. He has two children who are never around. The son is a high-flying CEO who lives a two-hour flight away, and the daughter married young, got divorced soon after, and seems to have decided it's best if she keeps moving from country to country to avoid any risk of being domesticated again. I think she's in Bolivia at the moment.

It was during one of my regular chats with Jack a few months ago that I suggested he try offering a weekly fruit and vegetable box. I was sure the boxes would attract customers. I told Jack people were so busy they'd love to have a selection of fresh spray-free fruit and vegetables delivered to their door. Unfortunately, I was wrong. Presumably people would rather buy tasteless cucumbers wrapped in plastic from the supermarket.

"I was so sure the boxes would be a huge hit, Jack."

"Ah, I haven't given up on them yet. I had another person sign up for one yesterday."

"Still, I was sure you'd have hundreds of orders by now. Not forty."

"Truth be told, I don't want too many, Emma. Some more would be great, but my growers can only supply so much. Plus, I don't want to have to take on more staff. I'm glad to have you, but I've always wanted this to be a small business."

"I hope I turn out to be helpful. You mustn't keep me if you can't afford it, Jack."

I'm not sure if Jack created a job for me when I mentioned I was looking for work, or if he genuinely needs an extra set of hands. I'd like to think it's the latter.

"It was perfect timing. I've been thinking about getting someone to help for a while now, but I've been too lazy to look."

I laugh. Jack is at the opposite end of the spectrum to lazy. He never stops. His energy is endless, and he's got to be at least seventy. He puts my sporadic twenty-minute jogs around the block to shame.

"Have you thought about doing some more advertising?" So far, Jack's only form of advertising has been a small sign in the window and word of mouth. "Maybe I could make up some flyers for you and drop them in letterboxes?"

Jack stands and winces ever so slightly before placing a hand on his lower back. "That would be grand, Emma. I knew it was right to give you a job before someone else snapped you up."

Smiling, I stand too, and give my legs a good shake. "How 'bout I make a start," I say, reaching for an empty cardboard box.

"Heavy things first," says Jack, pointing at the bunches of beetroot.

I reach for the piece of paper with the list of produce Jack wants me to pack and scan the room, mentally ticking things off.

"I'll leave you to it, Emma," says Jack. "It's time I opened up. Sing out if you're unsure of anything."

"Thanks, Jack," I call. I'm eyeing up the new season pears, already picturing the fruit crumble with fresh ginger I'm going to make tonight.

An hour and a half later, Jack suggests I have a break and I wander into the shop. I've only heard customers' voices a few times and I don't want to ask but I suspect it hasn't been a busy morning. Looking out through the large windows, I notice the leaves on the plane trees across the road are turning a golden yellow. Autumn is my favourite season, mostly because the weather is so settled, the days warm, the evenings cool; but also because there's a kind of wistfulness in the air, a knowledge that winter is going to eventually drown autumn out. There's a tiny little park beyond the line of trees with a bench seat and a patch of lawn. Freddie and I often stop there on our walk home from crèche. Soon it will be too cold and wet to sit cross-legged on the shady grass and eat our ice creams. Freddie is mildly obsessed with ice cream.

"Coffee?" Jack asks.

"I'll make it," I say, veering into the tiny kitchen-cum-office and filling the kettle. It's like I'm in the right place, doing the right thing. I've not had that feeling in years. I wonder if all the fruit and vegetables around me are giving off some sort of chemical, like a pheromone, that's making me feel so good.

My phone rings as I'm pouring coffee from the plunger into two chipped, tea-stained cups. I unzip my jacket pocket and check who's calling. I've switched Freddie to longer days at crèche now that I've started work, and I'm worried it's going to be too much for him. Not that I'm working full-time or anything. Jack very kindly asked what hours would suit, and we agreed on Monday to Wednesday, nine till three.

I'm relieved to see it's not crèche calling me, it's Lily. Probably triple checking I'm still up for the hen's do this weekend. She's convinced I'm going to pull out at the last minute. Truth is, I can't wait. I don't care what my friends have in store for me. I'm going to make sure I enjoy every second of it.

"Lily, I'm at my new job," I whisper, tucking the phone between my shoulder and cheek while I look for milk in the tiny fridge. "It's not a great impression if I keep getting calls."

"Hey, you didn't have to answer it." Unlike Lily, who only ever answers her phone if and when she feels like it, I have to answer if someone rings me. It's impossible not to.

"You knew I would."

"Oh, keep your knickers on, I'm just letting you know I've arranged for your mum and dad to have Freddie all weekend."

"What?"

"I know you said Paul was going to have him Saturday night, but I didn't trust him. He was bound to pull out with some lame excuse at the last minute. So I rang Eric and he's going to pick up Freddie Saturday morning and drop him at crèche Monday."

"But Dad has golf on Sunday. And Mum has her coffee group."

"For fuck's sake, Em. They don't care about missing those things. They want to spend time with their only grandchild. They haven't had much of a chance till now."

Lily's right. Paul was determined to show my parents, and everyone else we knew, that we didn't need anyone's help. Our perfect little family didn't need a hand from anyone.

"Paul will never go for it—"

"He already has, Em."

My voice temporarily dries up.

"He sounded relieved to be honest," says Lily. "I think his new girlfriend isn't so keen on his having offspring."

With shaking hands I add a splash of milk to each cup. Jack comes into the office and sees me on my phone.

"Gotta go, Lils."

"No worries," she says brightly.

"Thanks. Big time thanks."

"See you Saturday, Em."

I hang up and give Jack an apologetic smile. "My friends are throwing me a very belated hen's party this weekend. It's ridiculous really, considering, well, you know." I've given Jack a brief version of recent events. And I suspect he's picked up on a few signals over the past couple of years.

Jack takes the cup from my outstretched hand and blows on his coffee. "Sounds like fun. You deserve it."

I can't believe it. I'll have all weekend to myself. No Paul. No Freddie. In the past four years, there hasn't been a single day when I haven't been responsible for taking care of someone else, or trying to meet someone else's expectations. It's hard to imagine my life getting better than it is right now. I have a gorgeous son, supportive parents, fantastic friends, a job I know I will actually enjoy, and I'm free of Paul. It's almost worthy of a blog post. Almost.

FOUR
SEVEN WEEKS BEFORE

Trish grins as I rush towards her. She's waiting in the taxi pulled up in front of my house.

"Ready for the best fake hen's party of your life, Emma Dilemma?" she says as I stumble into the backseat beside her.

"I'm too old for this," I say. "How am I supposed to know what to wear when you won't tell me anything?"

Trish throws an arm around me and laughs. "Trust me, this is going to be one of the biggest nights of your life."

"Whatever," I grumble. An hour ago I was scrambling about under Freddie's bed looking for some rogue piece of Lego he couldn't live without.

"Will this do?" I gesture at my outfit already regretting the decision to go with my white lacy maxi-dress. I look like a bohemian try-hard.

My friend raises her eyebrows. "It's nice you went with the bridal theme."

"Shut up," I say, punching her lightly on the arm. Just because she looks completely gorgeous in tailored pants and a caramel silk top.

"It doesn't matter anyway." Trish gives me a secretive look. "You won't be wearing it for long."

"You're enjoying this aren't you?" I mutter.

The taxi deposits us on the corner of Albert St next to the giant multiplex cinema where Lily and Mags are waiting. They grab my arms like giggly schoolgirls and we head off down the street.

"Can't believe you still own that dress," Lily says. "Didn't you buy it at university?"

"Maybe." I did, of course. And they all know it. Back then it fitted with my freestyle ways: bonfires at the beach, smoking joints in the back of some club, dancing to indie folk bands.

Lily steers me towards two giant glass doors with brass handles and gold etchings that read 'Epoise Day Spa'.

I let out my breath and slump into Mags. "Thank God," I whisper. "I was worried we were going sky-diving or something."

Mags looks at me in horror. "Why on earth would we do something as idiotic and terrifying as that?"

"You deserve some decent pampering," says Trish, heading towards the perfectly made-up woman at the front desk.

We don fluffy white robes, drink champagne, have our nails done, our bodies oiled and massaged, makeup expertly applied, and our hair fashioned into designer locks. I haven't spent so much time staring at myself in a mirror since I was a teenager. Initially, I keep trying to avoid my reflection, but as the champagne hits the mark, I don't look away quite as often. Usually my shoulder-length brown hair either lies limp and flat, or is yanked into a high ponytail, but now it's got some body, and the way the stylist has swept it loosely into a messy bun makes my face look less narrow. I don't know what miracle product they've used, but they've managed to make my hair shine like melted chocolate too. The eyeliner and mascara accentuate my dark brown eyes, and I have an attractive healthy glow with the help of some wonder bronzer the beautician keeps raving about. The woman staring back at me in the mirror, with a slightly surprised look on her face, is more beautiful and confident-looking than she's been in… well… ever. It's hard for me to reconcile with the fact that person is me.

Woozy with champagne, the girls take me to some fancy boutique on the High St where we have a hilarious time trying on outfits and pissing off the shop assistant. Finally, everyone settles on a new look, the hefty price tags are removed, and we exit the building fully transformed into gorgeous babes. Trish refuses to let me pay for the satin blue dress, or the strappy gold sandals. This hen's party must be costing my friends a bomb.

As we head towards some trendy new bar in a converted warehouse by the wharf, Lily pulls a flimsy gold tiara from her bag.

"Oh no," I say laughing. "Don't make me wear that."

"It could be worse," says Mags. "I wanted to make you wear a pointy Madonna bra."

I snatch the tiara and put it on my head. "I'm happy with this option."

We enter the close-to-full bar and nab a table in the far corner. Then we proceed to drink our way along the top shelf, skipping the tequila of course. I keep catching sight of us in the mirror behind the bar and thinking that even though we're on the older side compared to the other twenty-something bitches in the room, we hold our own. As Lily says more than once, "we look fucking hot".

As the night goes on, we get louder. Everyone we speak to

is convinced it's my genuine hen's do and I feel younger, bolder. I enjoy imagining I'm engaged to Gennaro, an art dealer from Rome who fell desperately in love with me. We plan to marry at his family's villa overlooking Lake Como.

At midnight – and I swear I don't know where the hours went – we head to some club Lily's boss, the dashing Darryl, has been raving about. We nearly don't find it and get lost twice. It's down a dark alley, behind a plain black door. You have to press a bell and then this huge guy in a suit takes you down a lift padded in forest green leather with a chandelier hanging from the ceiling.

The club is heaving. It's ridiculously loud, stifling hot, and so dark you can barely see the person next to you. But that's fine with us. We're beyond the capacity for coherent talk by this stage.

We've been dancing non-stop for almost two hours when Mags drags us into a room behind a revolving door.

"I wish I'd known about this earlier," Trish slurs, fanning her dress in and out.

"I wish I'd discovered it earlier," says Mags, wiping sweaty hair from her face.

The room is quieter, and much cooler. It's long and narrow with a glittering black bar along one wall, plants and fairy lights hanging in a line down the middle of the room, and dark green velvet booths along the other side. We instantly collapse into an empty booth and kick off our shoes.

"I'll get water," Trish says, heading to the bar.

"Do you think she might get asked to leave because of her bare feet?" Mags wonders.

"Not in that dress," Lily says. "Every man in this room is looking at her."

I glance around. It isn't as dark as the noisy cave we've just emerged from. There are a number of couples and small groups in the booths. At one end of the bar stands a group of men. All of them but two have their eyes firmly glued to Trish's ample chest.

Giggling, I slide out of the booth and walk towards them. "Evening boys. Couldn't help but notice you ogling my good friend over there."

One of the two men who wasn't imagining Trish naked but was intent on a phone call, hangs up, and smiles. "Nice tiara, Cinderella." He's tall and lean, with broad shoulders. Smart jeans hang low across his narrow hips and the dimples on his cheeks scream gorgeous. He's how you'd imagine the boy next door you spent your adolescence lusting after would be like once he was all grown up and on steroids. Shame he looks like he's just had his twenty-first birthday.

I raise my eyebrows. "Cinderella?"

He glances at my bare feet. "It is after midnight I suppose. But..." He slides his eyes slowly up my body. "You're still wearing the hot dress."

Maybe he isn't as young as he looks. Or maybe I no longer care. Since Paul left it's as if I've been let out of a cage and all I want to do is let loose. With this guy.

"I'm Finn," he says. He has an accent, Irish or Scottish. It's exquisite either way. My body tingles as our hands meet for a polite shake. We stare blatantly at each other and I swear we both have the same thing on our minds. My groin hasn't felt this alive in years.

Lily appears next to me and puts a possessive arm around my shoulder. "Actually, this is her hen's do."

Finn blinks and his eyes lose their lustful look. "Congratulations," he mutters.

"Lily?" A man moves to stand beside us. "Look at you."

"Darryl," Lily gasps.

I reluctantly look away from Finn. "So this is the famous

Darryl," I say loudly, holding out my hand. "I've seen – I mean heard – so much about you."

Lily elbows me in the ribs.

Darryl shakes my hand but only glances at me fleetingly before returning his attention to Lily. "I thought you were on a fake hen's do tonight."

Lily sighs dramatically. "I am you idiot. Now you've just given us away."

Finn laughs and slaps Darryl on the back. "You might as well come clean too."

Darryl shrugs. "I thought it was such a good idea, I decided to throw a fake stag do. Finn here kindly agreed to be the man of honour, since he tends to break out into a cold sweat at the mention of marriage."

"Really?" I ask. "Not keen on the tinkling sound of wedding bells?"

Finn screws up his nose. "I don't think I'm the settle-down type."

I stare at Finn's lips. "Excellent news," I murmur. The last thing I want is to get into another relationship now. But if I could have a night of drunken sex with a sexy stranger and never have to see him again? I could get onboard with that.

"Interesting response." Finn steps closer and rests a hand lightly on my arm.

Mags and Trish arrive then and I quickly down the full glass of water Mags hands to me, relishing the cool rush in my throat. The room begins to sway slightly less.

There are introductions, handshakes, how-do-you-dos. I move around, chatting to one bloke, then another. They're mostly colleagues of Darryl's from work, many of whom Lily knows, with a few random tag-alongers. There's never a moment when I don't feel the presence of Finn. I know exactly where he stands, where he looks, how he moves.

Which is why I know he's standing close behind me before he speaks. I want to lean back, press my body against his. "Would you like to dance, Emma?" he whispers in my ear.

I nod and we move side by side towards the other room. When I head through the door, I feel his hand on my lower back. He leans over and kisses the top of my shoulder. "Has anyone ever told you, you have the sexiest shoulders in the history of the universe?"

I shake my head and refuse to look at him. "Is that the best pick-up line you can come up with?"

He runs his hand up my back. "I'm out of practice."

We enter the throbbing, dark room and make our way onto the dance floor. I slide my hands up his chest and he places his hands on my hips. We stare at each other without moving as everyone around us carries on with their berserk dance moves.

I lean close and yell above the music, "I have never wanted sex with a guy more in my life." I'm stunned I've said those words. Stunned and thrilled. I'm in charge of my life now. I can do and say whatever I bloody well want.

Finn's eyes widen and his hands move down my hips and over my bottom. Then he presses me firmly against him. "Do you want to get out of here," he growls in my ear.

So we call a taxi, head back to my place, and the rest, as they say, is history.

Stick that on your blog and smoke it.

———

When my alarm goes off at 6 a.m. on Monday, I am so deeply asleep I think Taylor Swift is inexplicably singing in the background of my dream. It's already a weird dream:

about a cat sleeping on my chest. As I slowly rise out of the fog of sleep, I'm relieved to realise Taylor Swift has not infiltrated my dreams, but instead has kidnapped the alarm on my phone.

In the next split second – before I open my eyes – I register the weight and warmth on my chest and wonder if my dream about the cat was real. Maybe Sukkie has somehow returned from Paul's new lair.

I open my eyes to see not a cat, but an arm. A muscly, hairy arm, attached to a muscly, thankfully-not-too-hairy man. He's lying beside me on top of the covers, face down, his head turned away, and he's naked.

My body is bereft of clothing too. Truth is, I've been pretty much naked since we got home from the club at 3 a.m. on Sunday morning.

Lying as still as I can, I inch a hand out and grip my phone. After a couple of jabs at the screen, I finally manage to silence Taylor's voice.

"Thank God," murmurs a gravelly voice from an otherwise motionless body. "Please tell me you are not a closet Taylor Swift fan."

I clear my throat. "'Fraid so. I've downloaded every song. She's my idol."

Finn lifts his head of dark ginger hair and turns his eyes towards me. "Now I know you're joking."

I grin at the dimple on his left cheek. His smile is honestly the sexiest I have ever seen on anyone. There must be a permanent gaggle of women chasing after him. It's still hard to believe he wanted to come home with me.

"I'm thinking of having another fake hen's do this weekend," I say. "Since the last one was so successful." Looking deliberately at his arse, I run my eyes slowly up his body to his face again.

"Really?" He props himself onto his elbows.

I want to duck down and kiss the smooth tanned spot just below his collarbone. Then I want him to roll on top of me. I'm like some over-sexed teenager. Since Saturday night we've had sex on the couch, the coffee table, the kitchen floor, and in my bed. Twice. On top of that, I managed less than three hours sleep Saturday night, and only about five last night. I should be a complete wreck, but I'm not. I should feel guilty. I don't. I feel amazing. Better than amazing. I feel fantastic.

Reaching up, I place one palm on his chest and run my hand slowly round to his back, pulling him towards me. "Before you go." I kiss him on the lips and brush my tongue against his teeth.

He groans softly. "I thought you needed to go to work."

Smiling, I push him away, straddle his hips, and drop down on my elbows, my breasts an inch from his mouth. "Oh, this shouldn't take long."

He chuckles and I feel the heat of his breath on my nipples.

FIVE

SIX WEEKS BEFORE

"Freddie, what's wrong?" I race up to my son who is curled up on a large cushion next to the art table.

He lifts his tear-stained face. "You're late," he whimpers.

I flop onto the floor and pull him onto my lap. "I'm sorry, Fredster. I was delivering the fruit and vege boxes for Jack, and with all the new orders it took me longer than I thought it would."

He sniffs and rests his head against me. "I was worried."

My heart beats furiously. Guilt is seeping out of my every pore. I lift his hand and kiss the top, the palm, and each finger. It's what I do whenever he's upset, and every night before he goes to sleep. "I promise I won't be late again, okay?"

"You're only five minutes late, Emma." The lead teacher, Jill, walks over and crouches down beside us. "Freddie was fine standing at the window with me, until he saw you coming up the path." She gives me a pointed look. "I expect the tears are for your benefit."

"Oh."

"You're not the only parent to arrive a few minutes late. In fact, you're due a late pick-up or two."

I smile at Jill's relaxed, open face. Her expression is permanently calm and I've yet to hear her raise her voice. "Thanks," I mutter.

"He's very happy here, Emma. You're doing a great job and I know it's a difficult time for you."

If only she'd stop being so nice. I swallow over the lump in my throat. Can she tell just by looking at me that I've had the week from hell? Do I really look that bad?

To make up for my tardiness and to avoid having to go home just yet, I take Freddie down to the waterfront. We sit at a café overlooking the harbour and share a hot chocolate – when I say share I mean Freddie eats both marshmallows and drinks three-quarters while kindly permitting me the odd sip. Afterwards, we walk to the end of the wharf and sit on a wooden bench to watch the fishermen casting and recasting.

"I used to go fishing with Grandpa nearly every weekend when I was a little girl," I say. "Till he had to sell his boat."

"Why did he sell it?" Freddie asks. "I want to go fishing in a boat."

I shrug. "He just did."

Freddie shivers and leans against me.

I put an arm around him and rub at his jumper. "You getting cold?"

He nods.

The temperature has dropped dramatically since the sun dipped low over the water. It's only five o'clock but already it feels like shorter winter days are encroaching. I'm freezing myself, but I'm reluctant to admit it, or the real reason I'm avoiding home. "Want to go?"

"Yes," he murmurs.

I get to my feet and carry Freddie back to the car.

When we pull into the driveway, lights in the house have been turned on and Paul's car is in his regular spot in front of the garage. He obviously thought it was okay to turn up early and let himself in. I turn off the engine and take a deep breath. "Give me strength."

The second Paul opens the front door Freddie leaps out of the car and runs towards him. "Daddy," he yells.

All I can think about is restarting the engine and driving away. Instead, I slowly climb out of the car and walk up the path. "Hey, Paul," I say.

My husband ignores me. He picks up Freddie and hugs him tight. "Buddy, I missed you. Your hair's longer, and I swear you've grown taller."

"Mummy said you don't want to live here anymore," Freddie says.

"Did she?"

I look away from Paul's angry expression. "I didn't exactly use those words," I mutter, "But you did leave me to explain the situation to him."

"I thought we would talk to Freddie about it later. The three of us."

"Did you? I assumed our conversations were to be conducted via your lawyer."

His eyes are narrow slits. "I was giving you a few weeks to get used to the situation. That's all."

My throat hurts with the effort of speaking in a calm voice. "You could have at least phoned him." It's been difficult coming up with excuses for why Freddie hasn't heard from his dad.

Paul turns and carries Freddie into the house. "Hey, Buddy, I got you something." He grabs a present off the table and sits down on the couch, Freddie on his lap.

I stare at them, my body frozen outside the door. As

Freddie tears at the wrapping paper, Paul kicks off one shoe, then another. He's wearing his favourite brown striped socks. The ones I accidently placed in my drawers instead of Paul's once when I was putting away the washing. He was in a complete flap until he found them and the rest of the evening was variations on the theme of how useless, irresponsible and untrustworthy I was. Since Paul left, I've let my defences down. Seeing him sitting on the couch is like being punched in the guts.

Walking quickly down the hall, I shut myself in the bathroom, and lock the door. Dropping to the floor, I slump against the bath, and with shaking hands pull my phone out of my pocket.

"Lily," I croak. "I need you to come over."

"Em, what's going on?"

I can't speak.

"Is Paul there?"

I nod but I still can't make any sound come out of my mouth.

"Fuck," Lily states. "I'm coming right now."

Hanging up, I stare at the shower. A week ago I was standing under that showerhead with Finn. He was rubbing his soapy hands all over me, and we were laughing, kissing, talking. It feels like a lifetime ago. Someone else's lifetime. Not mine.

Lying down on the tiles, I curl up into a ball, close my eyes, and wait.

———

"Em, it's me. Open the door, sweetie."

I'm not sure how long I have been lying here, but my hip

is sore, my shoulder too. Gingerly, I stand, and unlock the door. Lily bursts in, her eyes fierce. "What did he do?"

"Is he still here?" I croak.

"No, I told him to leave."

"Where's Freddie?"

"Mags is reading to him. He's fine."

"Mags is here?"

"I rang her. Sylvie too."

"You rang Mum?"

Lily nods. "She's on her way. With Eric."

We stare at each other.

"He bought Freddie a present," I whisper.

Lily snorts. "Course he did."

"There's things I never… he said things and… I never told anyone. I acted like I could cope, but…"

Lily is silent. Then she sighs and tears swell in her eyes. "We didn't know how to get you to open up, Em. You kept on with this crazy charade, but we could see what it was doing to you."

I know I'm going to break then. It's like something inside me is splitting open and it hurts like hell.

As my eyes blur over, I hear a high-pitched wail. I know it's me making the sound, but I don't know how; where it's come from. And I don't know how to stop it.

Lily throws her arms around me and I collapse against her. "I got you, Em," she murmurs. "I got you."

Feet pound down the hallway. "Emma!" Mags throws her arms around us both. "Emma, we're here. It's okay."

They help me into my room, lie me on my bed. I curl up on my side and sob so hard I think my ribs are going to crack. "Don't let Freddie see me," I gasp.

"We won't, Em," Mags says. "I promise. He's engrossed in something on TV."

I hear murmurings then someone climbs on the bed behind my back. They wrap one arm around me and pull me close. "Everyone who loves you is right here, Emma," Mum says firmly. "We aren't going anywhere."

I take a deep shuddering breath, reach down, and grip Mum's hand. "I'm sorry, Mum."

"What for?"

"For not being strong enough."

"You are the strongest person I know," Mum stammers. Then we are both sobbing, and I don't know if I will ever stop.

———

The day after my fake hen's do I didn't feel hungover or embarrassed about bringing some stranger home. I wasn't at all concerned I'd been shagging someone other than my husband in the matrimonial bed. Even weirder, I felt sexy. It was perfectly natural to be stark naked in front of Finn, and the way he kept looking at me, well I can't describe it really except to say, he made me feel invincible.

I think I may have still been drunk.

We didn't just have sex, though I'll admit that was our main focus. When we got hungry, I cooked. Finn raved about everything I fed him. From the porridge with poached pears, to the prawn and rice noodle salad. He seemed to think they were the best dishes anyone had cooked for him. When I told him they were meals I could make in my sleep, that I wasn't even trying to impress him, he laughed, lifted me off the floor, and carried me back to bed.

We talked a fair bit too. I told him in rough detail about Freddie, Paul, my new job. In his lilting voice he mentioned his dog, Leroy, his love of fishing and tramping, and his childhood spent roaming the Scottish Highlands. He told me he moved to New Zealand from Edinburgh on a six-month contract and was working for a friend of Darryl's as a business analyst (whatever that was). Finn hoped to return to Scotland and start his own business; preferably something to do with the outdoors. It's the main reason he came to New Zealand. He'd heard so many people raving about our national parks he decided to come and check them out for himself. He's already seen more of the country than I have. The fact he made a five-day hike, carrying all your supplies (including food), and sleeping in basic huts, sound as appealing as staying in a five-star hotel in Rome, says a lot. I could have listened to him all day long.

On Monday morning Finn dropped me at Jack's on his way to work. Jack could tell I wasn't functioning at 100% as I stumbled in late, apologising and feeling like his delinquent teenage daughter. The lack of sleep and excess alcohol consumption was starting to infiltrate, but I did my best. Once the fruit and vegetable boxes had been delivered, Jack suggested I head off early and I didn't object.

Having not seen Freddie for two whole days I was desperate to lay eyes on him, so I dropped in to pick him up early. It was great to see him, and I could tell he was thrilled to see me. The best part was realising the little break had been good for us both. Freddie didn't stop raving about his time with Mum and Dad. He even asked if he could stay with them again. And I was reminded I had the cutest little boy on the planet; well, in my humble opinion anyway.

Tuesday was when my life started to go pear-shaped. I'd promised to catch up with my friends in the evening; mainly to go over the now infamous hen's night in more detail, but when I plucked up the courage and rang Paul to ask if he might consider having his son for the evening, he bit my head off. Said he was Freddie's father, not some on-call babysitter, and hung up.

I thought about asking Mum, but felt too guilty since they'd already looked after Freddie all weekend. When I rang Lily to explain I couldn't make it she said it was fine, but I could tell she was annoyed. Lily could have suggested they come to my place rather than meet at Morellis, but she didn't. It probably never crossed her mind.

I tried to let that feeling of separateness between my childless friends and me go as I got Freddie ready for crèche. We were running late so I had to drive, even though Freddie kept demanding we walk. Unfortunately, when I dropped him off, he had one of those awful mornings – they seemed to be happening more and more often – where he didn't want to stay. He clung to my neck, and screamed when his favourite teacher tried to take him. Even her suggestion of building a volcano in the sandpit – his favourite thing in the world – didn't distract him.

Eventually, I managed to extract myself and walk to the car with my son's screams reverberating in my ears. It took me three attempts to get my key in the ignition I was so upset.

Work wasn't much better. In the space of three hours Jack and I fielded seven phone calls from disgruntled customers. They were unhappy with the apples we packed in the previous day's box. As one irate woman put it 'unsightly blemishes are bad enough on pimply teenagers'. I did my best to explain they were simply a result of the apples being bred for taste, not appearance. Without sprays our produce was going to show signs of imperfection and this was to be celebrated.

"Have you tried cutting off the little bumps and eating one?" I asked the woman.

"I wouldn't dream of it," she said.

Jack did the only thing he could do in the circumstances and offered the customers a free dozen eggs in the next week's box. But it hurt not being able to make people understand.

The day was slow which didn't help matters. As well as feeling guilty about leaving my upset son at crèche, I could add to that guilt from feeling like excess baggage at work.

My low mood didn't improve after I picked up Freddie and was told he stopped crying and was perfectly happy seconds after I left. Nor did it lift when I made sticky glazed pork ribs with a carrot and ginger mash and Asian sesame greens – which meant I was seriously not a happy camper, because normally that would have had me buzzing. And my mood well and truly plummeted after I finally got Freddie into bed, and opened the mail.

There was a letter from some law firm I'd never heard of stating my husband was requesting a divorce; that in order to divide our assets, the house and contents needed to be sold as quickly as possible, and that Paul would allow me full custody of our son, with visiting rights one weekend a month. It went on to say Paul would not be required to pay child support, as he was currently unemployed, and I had exactly seven working days to respond.

What the fuck? Why didn't Paul speak to me before seeing some damn lawyer? And since when did he not work?

The next day, after dropping Freddie at crèche, I got a puncture and had to buy a new tyre; only my credit card wouldn't work. I ended up leaving the car at the garage and walking four blocks down the road in the pouring rain to the bank where some plonker in a suit said the account had been frozen. Apparently, my husband had the right to stop any funds being withdrawn from our joint account.

I did the only thing I could think of. I phoned Dad. He was the maddest I've ever seen him. Even angrier than the time I drove home from some party drunk when I was eighteen and smashed into the garage door. "What kind of man is he?" Dad fumed.

Of course, Dad bailed me out, sorted the car, helped me to open a new bank account and transferred in some funds. We both agreed it was best if Mum didn't find out. At least for the time being.

As a distraction, I spent the evening designing a flyer advertising Jack's fruit and vegetable boxes on my computer. Then I proceeded to use up all the paper and ink in the house by printing out three hundred copies. When I showed Jack the next day, he was thrilled. He was even more thrilled when I suggested – since the shop was so quiet – that I deliver them around the neighbourhood. There were only so many cups of tea, staring at the empty shop, we could take.

And so the weekend arrived, and with it a vomiting bug. For two days, I alternated between cleaning vomit off my son, his clothes, the couch, and the carpet; and running to the toilet to purge some little microbes of my own.

I spent all weekend without one person ringing me, or one concerned friend showing up at the door. To be fair, I didn't tell anyone we were sick, because I wanted to prove I could handle it. But still. It would have been nice if someone had checked on us. And though it was stupid to think Finn might call me, or that the previous weekend had been anything more than a shag-fest, I still ached to hear his voice for some crazy reason. Maybe it was the realisation that I really was on my own. I was glad Paul was gone, but the euphoria had disappeared, replaced by the biggest sinkhole of failure ever imagined.

When Paul rang this morning and said he was coming

over after work to discuss things, I tried to put him off. I told him about the vomiting bug; said Freddie and I were still recovering. He didn't budge. Which was why I spent all day with a rock the size of Africa in my stomach. From experience I know that when Paul is determined to talk about something, it's not about a family trip to Disneyland.

———

"Why didn't you ring us?" Trish asks. "I thought you probably wanted a quiet weekend with Freddie. Especially after last weekend's bender."

It's two in the morning. Mum and Dad have gone home now that I'm able to go longer than ten minutes without blubbering. I'm on the couch with my fourth mug of tea and Lily and Mags either side of me. Trish is cross-legged on the carpet. She's looking up at me like I'm her preacher.

"I didn't want to spread the bug around," I whisper.

Lily snorts. "Bullshit, Em. You were trying to be fucking Wonder Woman again."

I've freaked them all out. I'm supposed to be the laid-back one. The one who makes a joke about any situation, no matter how dire. It was the only way I could cope.

"Sorry, guys," I mutter.

"For what?" Mags asks.

"For losing the plot earlier."

"Jesus, Emma, we've been waiting for this to happen." Trish shifts onto her knees in front of me, and lays her hands on my thighs. "You tried hard to fool us Em, but we could see how mad things were. We just didn't know how to get you to talk."

"You're not big on emotional outpourings," Lily murmurs.

"I don't know how to… how to talk about this sort of stuff," I stammer.

"Maybe you just need to start," Mags says softly.

I nod and take a sip of my tea.

No one speaks for several long seconds.

"Did he tell you? Why he came over?" I ask.

"No." Lily scowls. "Just that he wanted to see Freddie."

"He said he had to talk to me about something. I assumed it was about the letter. From the lawyer."

"What lawyer?" Trish asks, instantly alert. She used to be a practising lawyer, before she decided to work in IT. She doesn't trust a lawyer as far as you can drop-kick them.

I dip my head in the direction of the hall table. "It's over there."

Everyone in the room is silent as Trish retrieves the letter and reads. "Bastard," she hisses. "He's just trying to scare you, Em."

Taking a deep breath, I stand. "I'm okay, guys. Thanks for coming over but I'm shattered and all I want to do is crash. We've all got work tomorrow. You should go home. I'm fine, honest."

"You seriously think you should be going to work?" Mags asks.

I look at my friends, wondering why they seem to have suddenly aged. "Yes. I do. The last thing I want to do is stay home."

I know they're watching me as I walk down the hall to my bedroom. All I can think about is sleep. I'm craving oblivion.

SIX

FIVE WEEKS BEFORE

My doorbell rings as I'm dishing up dinner. Freddie's sitting up at the breakfast bar opposite me, banging his feet against the stool. The lamb took longer to cook than I expected and he's told me how hungry he is at least eight times in the last ten minutes. It's only twenty minutes past our usual dinnertime.

"Here, Freddie, you start." I place a plate in front of him and head to the door. I'm assuming Lily's work dinner was cancelled at the last minute and she's come round for our usual Monday night catch-up.

When I open the door, I get such a fright I can't stop the words from spurting out of my mouth. "Holy shit."

Finn's smile wavers. "Sorry. I know this is unexpected."

I grip the door and try to smile, but fail. This is not something I'm remotely prepared for. "What are you doing here?" I whisper.

Finn blinks and shuffles his feet.

"Who is it, Mama?" Freddie yells.

I don't answer.

Finn glances behind me into the house. "Sorry," he mutters. "Shouldn't have come."

In an instant I'm no longer embarrassed about my unwashed hair, old jeans, and faded blue T-shirt. How dare he just turn up like this. "You knew I had a son," I snap. "I never made it a secret."

Finn stares at me with bloodshot eyes. His face is tense, and, well, he looks older. I think he told me at some point between shags that he was twenty-eight, but now I wonder if I heard wrong. "Sorry, Emma. I... I didn't realise you were eating. I'll go."

He turns away and my heart gives a weird flutter. "We have dinner early," I murmur.

Finn turns back. "Sorry?"

I shrug. "We eat at five-thirty."

For a moment we look at each other in silence. I'm thrown by Finn's presence, but I'm thrown even more by how different he seems. What happened to the confident, sexy man I remember? "Are you okay?" I ask softly.

Finn sighs. "Not really."

I want to reach out and hug him. Instead I touch him lightly on the arm. "Is there something I can do?"

"Thanks, Emma." He glances down at my hand. "I've been driving around and around for ages and I don't know why, but somehow I ended up here."

I smirk. "Thanks."

His smile is small. "I didn't mean... it's just... well." He gives a huge sigh. "I had to put Leroy down today."

It takes me less than a second to remember Leroy is Finn's dog that he couldn't bear to be apart from for six months so spent a small fortune to fly all the way to New Zealand. "Oh no, Finn." I can't stop myself. I throw my arms around him and place my head against his chest. "I'm so sorry."

He hugs me back. I can hear his heart throbbing fast and loud. "I can't believe it," Finn murmurs. "He just ran out onto the road... the car tried to swerve, but... I saw it happen... right outside my apartment... I... I can't seem to go home."

I feel a shudder through his body as he takes a deep breath. I remember his smell, his warmth. I remember how amazing it made me feel. It's something I've kept locked away inside me since he left. Letting Finn go, I step back. "Do you want to come in?"

He lifts his eyebrows slightly. "Really?"

"I've made slow-cooked lamb shoulder with ratatouille. If you want some... well, I made far too much."

Finn's dimples are still as sexy as ever. "I could smell it walking up the driveway." For a fraction, his eyes drop down the length of my body and my palms begin to tingle. "Would Freddie mind?" he asks.

I stare at him. Is this guy for real?

"N-no, he won't," I stammer. "He'll love it."

It's true. Freddie loves men. He looks at them everywhere we go like they're some kind of superhero; at the markets, the park, the beach.

"Well, okay. But only if it's not disturbing you." He clears his throat and crosses his arms.

Could this stupidly good-looking guy actually be nervous? I can't help it, I'm so thrilled he's here I want to run out onto the lawn and do a bloody handstand. I'm sad his dog died, but Finn's here, on my front doorstep. When he could be on any woman's doorstep anywhere in the world. He remembered where I lived and knocked on my door. It's inconceivable.

"No," I whisper. "You're not disturbing me."

I walk into the kitchen, Finn following like a warm breeze at my back. "Freddie," I say, trying to keep my voice calm. "This is a friend of mine, Finn. He's going to help us eat some of this food."

Finn sits down next to Freddie and nods at him. "Hey Freddie. Hope you don't mind sharing."

Freddie smiles up at him. "Don't mind," he says, his mouth full of food, and his eyes wide and adoring.

Finn gives a gentle laugh. "Excellent."

I dish up a plate of food for Finn, then myself. It's incredible how I manage to stop my hands from shaking. Outwardly, I might even appear relaxed. "So," I say, pulling a bottle of Chianti from the wine cupboard. I hold it up and raise my eyebrows at Finn. "Want some?"

"Thanks."

Pouring wine into two glasses, I continue. "Before you knocked I was filling Freddie in on my mildly adventurous day."

Sliding a glass of wine in front of Finn, I lock eyes with him and in that second I imagine throwing myself at him. Literally tackling him to the ground. Blushing, I look down.

Finn shifts in his chair. "That sounds intriguing."

I had been contemplating squeezing onto the bar stool next to Finn to eat, but now I know I can't get any closer.

Still standing, and grateful for the bench separating us, I pick up my knife and fork and carefully cut through the lamb. As it falls apart without a hint of resistance, I sigh. "It's good."

"Better than good, Emma," Finn says, swallowing. "This is amazing."

Now I really blush. "Oh, I didn't mean it like that. I was just… I wasn't sure it would have cooked for long enough."

Finn shakes his head and turns to Freddie. "You get to eat like this all the time?"

Freddie nods.

"You do realise how lucky you are, don't you?"

"I am?" Freddie's face is puzzled.

"Absolutely. Most other boys your age are eating over-cooked broccoli and burnt sausages right now."

"They are?"

Finn nods, his face serious. "They would be so keen to be in your place."

Freddie looks at me, then back at Finn. "Really?"

"Oh yeah. Once your friends find out what a great cook your mum is, they'll be wanting to come over all the time."

Freddie grins so wide I can see his tonsils. Finn has either just fluked it or he remembers me telling him how Freddie's struggling to make friends at crèche. I ache for some little boy to run up to Freddie and ask him for a play. I've tried suggesting Freddie ask someone over but he refuses. Maybe he's too shy, or worse, maybe his own mother already embarrasses him.

"I could invite Jake over. On Friday," Freddie says loudly. Sauce from the lamb is dribbling down his chin. "Mum makes the best pizza ever on Fridays."

"I bet she does," Finn says. "That sounds like a brilliant idea."

Freddie is so excited he's jiggling on his stool. I hope he's not going to slip off.

Finn clears his throat. "So, you were about to tell us about your adventure today," he says in his soft lilting accent.

Swallowing, I look up. He's got his head cocked to one side and an encouraging smile on his face. Oh God, he's trying to be nice. I should be the one supporting him right now, not the other way round.

"It's nothing really," I say. "I just caught someone trying to steal an old guy's car outside work."

"Cool," Freddie says, food once again in his mouth.

"When you say you caught them…" Finn's eyebrows draw together. He has very expressive eyebrows. They move about a lot.

"I literally caught him," I say, with a small grin. "He was trying to get the car started and when the old man called out, the guy jumped out of the car and I chased him down the street."

Finn smiles and shakes his head. "Course you did."

"He was really short. And slow. Otherwise I wouldn't have had a hope of catching him."

"How did you stop him, Mama?"

"I jumped on his back. Gave him a huge fright. And a big graze on his knee when he fell over."

Finn is still shaking his head. "Then what?"

"Well, then I made him walk back with me and apologise to the old man."

"He didn't try to fight you off? What if he'd tried to—" Finn glances at Freddie. "Fight back."

"He was only young. Fifteen maybe. He didn't really seem like the type. I could tell he wasn't a proper threat or anything."

"How could you tell?"

I shrug. "Dunno, I just could. He looked too… nice, I guess."

Finn's dimples are glinting at me like stars. "Do you do that kind of thing often, Emma?"

I frown. "What do you mean?"

"Superhero stuff."

"It's not… I'm totally not…"

"Mum's a superhero?" Freddie asks, his eyes wide. "Like Spiderman."

Finn looks at Freddie seriously. Then he leans close as if confiding something important. "A superhero who can cook," he whispers.

Freddie looks at me like I've turned into someone else. "Wow," he breathes.

I roll my eyes. "Oh, please. Don't listen to him, Freddie, he's trying to act all charming so I'll give him a second helping."

Finn holds up his empty plate. "Did it work?" he asks with a wink.

———

I relax after that. Finn helps me with the dishes, and seems happy to sit on the floor in Freddie's room and play trains with him while I have a shower. After that, I'm sure Finn will leave, but he suggests a walk to the park instead.

It's a gorgeous evening. There isn't a whisper of wind, and the dimming blue sky is streaked with thin pink clouds on the horizon. It's as if summer has decided to return for one last party before disappearing.

"You must know the area pretty well already," I say. We're walking side by side along the footpath, Freddie jumping around in front of us. "Not many people know about this park."

I'm acutely conscious of his hand swinging next to mine. As if reading my thoughts, he takes my hand, acting as if it's the most natural thing in the world. "I only discovered it last week on one of my walks with Leroy. I spent ages there throwing the ball for him."

I squeeze his hand. "Bet he loved that."

Finn squeezes back and there's a long pause before he speaks. "Yeah. He was ball obsessed. Every morning and night, he'd wait at the front door with a ball in his mouth till I was ready to take him out."

We're walking even closer to each other now. Our shoulders keep brushing together. Freddie has reached the park and is running towards the slide. "What happens to Leroy's body?" I've never been allowed a pet before, so I have no idea how these things work. "If you don't mind me asking."

Finn lets out a long, ragged sigh. "He'll be cremated tomorrow."

I lift his hand, which is still in mine, and give the top of it a soft kiss. "Will you take his ashes back to Scotland when you go?"

Finn abruptly lets go. "Maybe." He glares at the ground.

"Did I say something wrong?" I bite my lip.

"No." He stops walking and takes a deep breath.

I wonder where to look, what to say. "You can go home anytime, Finn. You don't have to be here. Don't feel obliged just because I fed—"

"Do you want me to go?"

"That's not what I said. I haven't been showering you in support over losing Leroy. And I'm sure the last thing you want to do is hang out at a park with some frazzled single mother and her son who wears a Spiderman T-shirt a hundred sizes too big for him."

Finn relaxes his shoulders and walks through the open gates into the park. Freddie is having the time of his life running up the slide, flopping onto his stomach, and sliding back down.

I follow Finn, confused by his erratic mood. He slows down till I'm walking beside him. "What's with the T-shirt dress anyway?" he asks.

"Freddie insisted on the T-shirt when we saw it in the shop. The smallest size was a men's small, which as you can see, is not small on a four-year-old boy at all."

"It's cute," he says quietly.

I snort. "Not when it's the only thing he'll wear. If it needs a wash, I have to sneak into his room at night and wash and dry the bloody thing before he wakes up the next morning."

Finn laughs, then turns to me, his face stern. "Why didn't you want to give me your number?"

"Sorry?"

"I asked Darryl for your phone number, so I could ask you… I don't know, if you wanted to go out or something. But your friend who works for him wouldn't give it to him."

"Lily?"

"She said you didn't want to see me again." He's standing so close I can feel his breath on my face.

"I never knew that," I whisper. "Why would Lily say… I mean, she never even mentioned… I wouldn't have—" I'm at a total loss for words. He wanted to ring me. He's thought about me − obviously nowhere near as much as I've thought of him, but still…

"I would have given you my number, Finn." I stare into his green, searching eyes. "You know I would have."

"Mama!"

I jerk back and turn to Freddie. He's standing at the top of the slide with his hands on his hips.

"Watch me," Freddie yells, dropping onto his bottom. I watch my son lift his legs over the rim at either edge of the slide. As he propels himself forward, I feel Finn's hand lightly stroke on my back.

Freddie grins when he jumps off the slide at the bottom. "That was fast," I call out.

Finn's hand slowly glides down to my bottom. Then he walks towards the swings. "Hey Freddie, let's have a swinging competition. See who can go the highest."

"Cool," Freddie yells.

I can't move. All I can think about is the throbbing ache in my lower belly. I want to have sex with that man making a complete idiot of himself on a swing. I want it so much I can't breathe.

———

Freddie crashes within minutes of us getting home. As I kiss him goodnight, he throws his tiny arms around my neck. "That was the best night ever, Mum."

Turning out the light, I wonder why we've never walked to the park after dinner before. Even if Paul wasn't keen, I could have left him at home with his TV shows and his gold-fish-eating cat. I should have taken Freddie to the park and swung on the swing beside him. I should have refused to let Paul decide how we were to live our lives.

"Freddie just told me he had the best night ever." I sit on the couch next to Finn and he puts down the cookbook he's been flicking through.

"He looked pretty happy," Finn says.

Even though Finn is grieving for his dog, I get the sense he might respond if I was to make a move. I slowly lean in to kiss him gently on the lips. "Maybe I could help take your mind off Leroy for a while?" I whisper.

He laughs gently. "Would it be inappropriate for me to ask if I could take you to bed and strip you naked," he murmurs. His lips press on my neck and I reach up to run a hand through his hair.

"I think it would be entirely appropriate. Providing I can remove your clothing first."

Finn's breath tickles my neck. "Emma, you are incorrigible."

"I know," I sigh. "It's your fault. I'm not normally so direct."

Standing, I pull him to his feet, down the hall, and into my bedroom.

SEVEN

FOUR WEEKS BEFORE

"Sorry about this Jack, won't be long." I brush some dirt off my shirt. "I'll start on the parsnips when I get back."

"No problem, Emma. Hope everything goes okay." Jack is invisible behind a stack of half-packed boxes.

I wrinkle my nose, stepping over the crate of potatoes. "Just want to get it over with really." Grabbing my keys from the office, I head for the door. "See you soon."

Getting into my car, I spy a young couple walking down the footpath. They're totally engrossed with one another, their heads touching as they talk, their fingers entwined. I smile and picture Finn. For a moment, I imagine us doing the same. Even going to the lawyer's office and having to be in the same room with Paul can't dampen my mood.

Before I start the car, I check my phone. Finn has sent a text message wishing me good luck and asking if he can pop round after work. Grinning, I send a quick reply. I took some pork ribs out of the freezer this morning in the hope he might come over. I'm already looking forward to seeing him again, even though we spent practically all week together.

———

Finn got out of my bed very early the morning after he unexpectedly knocked on my door. He thought it was best if he was out of the house before Freddie woke. I didn't care if Freddie saw him, but it was clear Finn was uncomfortable, so I let it go. He asked for my phone number before he left. Which of course I gave to him, no doubt with a goofy smile on my face.

On Wednesday evening he rang to chat. Those were his words. I suggested rather than chat on the phone, we spoke in person. So he came over, I fed him, he played trains with Freddie, and I took him to bed.

Friday morning, Mum rang and asked if Freddie wanted to go and stay with them for the night. She suggested I organise a catch-up with some friends. As soon as I hung up, I sent a text to Finn. He replied with about a hundred smiley face emojis and insisted on taking me out for dinner as a thank you for the meals I'd given him already. He picked me up at seven and took me to an incredible Japanese restaurant. Which meant that all those times I blabbered on at him about food, he was actually listening to me. Not only did he remember how much I love Japanese food, but he told me he spent almost an hour researching online to find the best in town.

We planned to check out a wine bar down at the waterfront after we'd eaten, but ended up heading back to Finn's apartment and having sex on the carpet inside the front door.

———

"Emma!" There's a rap on my window. Jack is frowning at me. "You okay?"

Blinking, I realise I've been sitting in the driver's seat daydreaming about my week with Finn. "Shit," I mutter. Smiling hard, I open my window. "All good, Jack. I was just having a spacey moment." I glance at my watch. "Oh crap. Better dash."

Jack's still frowning as I start the car and pull away. My cheeks feel hot. I'm supposed to have matured by now. Not be caught fantasising about some cute young guy. *Harmless fun*, I tell myself. I'm having a good time with Finn, that's all. No commitment, no future, no ties.

When I arrive at the lawyer's office, my face has thankfully returned to its usual pale, lightly freckled self. Paul is sitting in the reception area reading a car magazine. He knows nothing about cars and drives a silver Corolla.

"Lucky the lawyer's running late," Paul says, without looking up.

My eyes are drawn to the bulges of fat from his hips spilling out beneath the armrests of the chair. I wonder when it happened; the transformation from muscly guy, to flabby and obese. It must have been gradual, because I don't remember thinking he had suddenly put on a lot of weight. It was as if the Paul I'd first met – the man I'd been so keen to get together with – had been swallowed up by fat and turned into someone else in the process. "Sorry, I got caught in traffic."

"Uh huh."

He doesn't believe me. Not that I care.

"What's this about you not working then, Paul? I thought you were indispensable to the mirror de-mister industry." Ever since I've known Paul he's worked on commission for the same company. He travels around the country selling some special thing that stops your mirrors from fogging up in the bathroom. Who knew there could be such a demand for something so unnecessary? Not that I've ever told Paul that. He believes he's improving people's quality of life, one de-misted mirror at a time.

Paul shrugs. His neck is flushed so I know he's not as calm as he's making out.

"Are you sure you're not trying to get out of paying child support?" I ask firmly. I'm determined not to be the meek little wife he had before.

His anger hits me like a mallet. "Are you accusing me of something, Emma?"

Till now, I thought we were the only two people in the reception area, but when I hear someone clear their throat loudly, I glance at the desk to see a thin woman practically hidden behind a computer screen. She stands up. "Mrs Tilssen, thank you for coming. Mr Travers can see you both now."

Shaking, I wait for Paul to go through the door the woman is gesturing towards. With a deep breath, I follow.

———

When Finn arrives that evening, I'm rubbing homemade barbecue sauce over the pork ribs.

"Smells amazing." He comes up behind me, lifts my hair off my neck, and kisses me on my collarbone.

"Trying to work here," I say, grinning.

"I was thinking on the way over, how about I take you and Freddie camping while the weather's good?"

I pause, my hands in mid-air. "Camping?"

"Yeah." Finn looks uncomfortable now, like he's regret-ting opening his mouth. "There are a couple of great overnight tramps near here. It could be fun. Pitching a tent, toasting marshmallows. Freddie's probably already done that sort of thing bu——"

"No. He's never been camping," I say sharply.

I start to rub the marinade vigorously, avoiding Finn's eye. Why am I so worked up about the suggestion of us going camping together? "Won't you be heading back to Scotland soon?"

His body freezes and he says nothing for a long time. Finally, he clears his throat. "Where's Freddie?"

I force myself to look at him and smile. At least I can try to pretend Finn's camping suggestion hasn't completely thrown me. My heart is racing out of control. "Out in the garden digging for worms."

Finn heads towards the back door. "I'll see if he needs a fellow digger," he murmurs.

Once I've got the ribs under the grill and washed my hands, I take a deep breath, and head out into the back garden too.

Finn and Freddie are crouched over the small herb garden, each with a stick in their hands. A worm is wriggling about on the end of Freddie's stick and he has a grin the size of Alaska on his face. Freddie would love to go camping with Finn. So would I. Only, we might enjoy it too much, love it even. Then Finn will disappear back to the other side of the world, leaving us – me – behind.

"Mama look," Freddie says. "We found one."

"Excellent."

"Can I take it to crèche tomorrow to show Jake?"

"Sure."

I find an empty glass jar in the kitchen and take it back outside. Handing the jar to my son, I sit down on the back step, enjoying the last rays of sun.

Finn comes to sit next to me. The silence between us is so

awkward I want to run to my bedroom and hide under the covers.

"How did it go at the lawyers?" Finn asks suddenly.

I glance at his stony face. "About as I expected. Soon I'll be officially divorced."

"Are you sad?"

"No," I reply without hesitation.

"So, this is… you're not wishing you'd tried harder or had counselling or something?"

Frowning, I turn to Finn. "You don't know anything about my marriage."

"You're right. I'm sorry." Finn looks towards Freddie who is in the far corner poking about in the grass. "It's none of my business."

I sigh. "Finn, the one thing I regret in life is marrying Paul. I wish I didn't have to get a divorce, because I'm annoyed I ever married him in the first place."

"So you married him because you were pregnant? Surely, there must have been something there, Emma. I mean, plenty of women get knocked up and don't marry the father."

I stand and fold my arms across my chest. This is not a conversation I'm ready to have, especially with Finn. All I want to do is hang out with him and feel happy and sexy. "I'll check on dinner," I say, going back inside.

I hear him follow me. "Emma, I don't want to upset you."

If only he didn't have such a beautiful voice. I can't risk looking at him in case I start to do something stupid, like cry. Instead, I grab the oven mitt and pull the tray of pork ribs out of the oven. The more I try to convince myself that Finn is just a short-term, casual – casual what? I don't even know what to call this. The terrifying truth is I feel far more for him than I should. It might be best if we cool things off now, before I run the risk of falling completely head-over-heels madly in love with the guy.

"Emma, I think we both need to be more open about—"

A knock at the door stops him mid-sentence. I frown and glance at my watch. "Shit."

"What?"

"It's Lily. She normally comes over on a Monday, but she had a work seminar. She said she'd pop round if it wrapped up early, but I figured—" I shrug.

He shoves his hands in his jean pockets and looks at the floor.

Sighing, I walk to the door and open it.

"Fucking PR wankers," Lily states, striding into the room. "All I did was—"

She spies Finn and pauses.

"You remember Finn, don't you?" I say quietly.

Lily glares at Finn. "Hi," she says quickly.

"Hello, Lily." His face is impossible to read.

"So what's this about you not giving Finn my number, Lily?" I might as well get it all out in the open. Rip off the Band-Aid so to speak.

Lily blinks at me. "I didn't… I figured it was the last thing you wanted… some guy to complicate your life."

"Don't you think that should've been up to me?"

"Em, I wouldn't have done it unless I thought it was for the best."

Finn walks towards the door. "It's fine, I think I should get going anyway."

I have a sudden sensation of vertigo, like I'm standing on the edge of a cliff. "No, don't go."

Lily's hand is suddenly on my sleeve. She squeezes my

arm. "Em, you have enough to deal with. You barely know—"

"It's fine, Lily," I say angrily. "I'm good here. Really."

Lily drops her hand. "I'll go." She glances at Finn as if she's about to say something, then she swears quietly, pushes past him, and walks out.

This sudden protectiveness Lily has for me must be a result of my recent breakdown. She's taken it too far – there was no need for her to be so rude.

"Do you want me to leave?" Finn asks.

"No, I don't. Lily was just—"

Freddie runs in, his bare feet leaving a muddy trail in his wake. "Whoa, buddy." Finn holds up his hand. "Stop right there."

Freddie freezes, one foot in the air. He wobbles about as Finn walks over and places a hand on his head. "Those feet are not ready to come indoors."

Freddie looks down, sees the mud oozing between his toes, then quickly glances at me.

I laugh at his guilty expression. "Back you go, little man. Use the tap and I'll bring you a towel."

Freddie sprints back outside.

Finn smiles at me and I move towards him as if a magnet is drawing us together. Placing my hands on his chest, I give him a long, slow kiss on the neck. He groans and slides his hands around my waist. Lily has nothing to worry about. I'm going to live in the moment and try not to think about anything else. Because I'm not ready to give up this guy. Not yet.

EIGHT
THREE WEEKS BEFORE

"Jack, it's only an idea – you can totally say no – but I was wondering what you thought about maybe putting a coffee machine in that corner." I point to the front left-hand side of the shop. "It's such a nice sunny spot, and with the concertina windows opened up, it could become like a service hatch. We could set up some crates or chairs outside for people to sit on."

I watch Jack chew on one of the orange and chocolate muffins I made last night. Maybe I've gone too far. Jack is probably fed up with me meddling in his business.

"It's not a bad idea," he says, reaching for his cup of tea. We've paused for a break, having already filled seventy boxes (the flyers I delivered were surprisingly successful). Only thirty-two more boxes to go. "Just coffee?" he asks over the rim of his cup.

"What do you mean?"

"Well, you've been bringing me delicious baking nearly every day, Emma. You're obviously an amazing cook. What about having some food on the counter? People never can resist a little something to have with their coffee."

I smile, wondering if Jack has been reading my mind. "I could do that. I mean… I'd love to, but it's your business, and I'm not sure it's the direction you want to be heading." I look down. What was I thinking trying to suggest Jack change things? Having a café is my dream, not his.

"What would you say to a business partnership?" Jack asks, placing his cup on the ground.

"Sorry?"

"I carry on running the fruit and veg side, and get someone to help me with packing and delivery. And you set up the other part of the business. A café within a grocery store. It's a good idea. It could work well."

I stare at Jack. "You want me to set up a café here?"

Jack shrugs. "Why not? This space is bigger than I need. There's no other café nearby. And I may be an old man, but I'd like to think I'm not completely stuck in my ways. My son, Peter, has been telling me for years I need to diversify. And you've already helped to grow the business. I trust your ideas, Emma."

Blinking hard, I try to stop the tears threatening to fill my eyes. "That's very kind of you, Jack. You've been so good to me."

"I've been lucky, that's what. Now what do you say?"

My mind whirrs. Only three days earlier, I met Paul in a real estate office and signed on the dotted line. We barely spoke as we sold the first and only house we've ever owned. Freddie and I have to move out in two weeks. So far, I haven't found us a place to live, but if we were to rent, I'd have about sixty thousand in the bank once the mortgage was paid off.

"I've got some money I could invest," I say quietly. "If you were really sure you wanted to go ahead."

"There's no need," Jack says. "I can borrow from the bank."

My heart is going crazy. "No, I don't want you to borrow. I'd rather we were proper business partners."

"I don't want you to get into any financial difficulty, Emma," Jack says sternly.

"I don't either. But, this is… well, it's something I've always wanted to do. Running a café is… well, it would mean everything to me. I need to be more than a soon-to-be-divorced thirty-three-year-old mother."

Jack studies me, his head to one side. "I'm game," he says. "If you are."

————

"You're going to what?" Lily asks. She brushes her hair off her face. "Are you crazy?"

I take a sip of wine. "I don't think so." This is the first time I've spoken to Lily since last Monday and I can see she's wary of me. I'm a little uncomfortable with her too.

"It's a fantastic idea." Mags leans forward and grabs a fistful of peanuts from the bowl. "Especially if your lemon cake goes on the menu." Mags stuffs the nuts in her mouth and crunches loudly.

"What did I miss?" Trish asks, placing a bottle on the table and shuffling into the booth beside me.

"Emma's going to open a café in Jack's and use up her money from the sale of the house to do it."

When Lily says it like that, I feel like it's the most reckless idea in the world.

Trish starts to refill our glasses. "Really? Wow. That's exciting. Brave, but exciting. Sounds a bit more like the old Emma actually." Trish gives me a wink.

"I thought you wanted to find an apartment for you and Freddie. Buy your own place. Not deal with a landlord." Lily is leaning back in the booth with her arms crossed.

"It's not like you to be so negative, Lils," Mags leans forward on her elbows and gives Lily the stare. "What gives?"

"What do you mean?"

"Why are you giving Emma a hard time?"

Lily glances at me and looks down. "I'm just worried she's rushing into it all."

I narrow my eyes at Lily. "Are we still talking about me opening a café, or is this about something else?"

Lily's silent. With her head bowed, I can't tell what's going on.

"Lily, is this about Finn?"

"Whoa, hang on," Trish states loudly. "Are we talking about Finn, the guy you had a 24-hour sexathon with?" She places her hand on my shoulder and leans in close to my face.

I nod, biting my lip.

"No way!" Mags yells. Then she lowers her voice. "Have you seen him again?"

"He stopped by my house a couple of weeks ago. He was upset about his dog being run over—"

"Oh no, that's awful," Mags says. "The poor guy."

"He said he was driving around because he didn't want to go home. It was probably just one of those spur-of-the-moment things."

Lily's head shoots up. "He asked me for her number."

"What?" Trish shuffles forward eagerly. "When was this?"

Lily stares at me. "A couple of days after the hen's night. Darryl asked me for Emma's phone number to give to Finn, but I said no."

I'm determined to hold Lily's gaze.

"Why?" Mags asks quietly.

"Because!"

"Because why?" I ask.

Lily sighs and finally breaks eye contact to take a large gulp of wine from her glass. "Because he's no fucking good for you."

"Shouldn't I be the judge of that?"

"Emma—"

My phone rings. Paul's name flashes on the screen and I instantly pick up. "What's wrong?"

"Nothing." Paul hesitates. "Freddie wants to talk to you before he goes to sleep."

This is the first time I've let Freddie stay with Paul and his new girlfriend. I wasn't keen on the idea, but Paul kept insisting. Apparently Clara has had a change of heart and wants to get to know Paul's son. Also, Paul thinks it's time for Freddie to understand his parents live in separate houses now. I've been sticking to the story that Daddy had to move out because he was working through some personal problems. I thought it was best to keep things vague until Freddie got used to Paul never being around. And now Paul and his new girlfriend want to suddenly spend time with Freddie and confuse him.

"Paul, it's nearly two hours past Freddie's bedti—"

"I know," snaps Paul. "He says he can't sleep. Just talk to him and tell him everything's fine."

"Is everything fine?" I still haven't clapped eyes on this woman, Clara. Maybe she's being mean to Freddie, making faces at him when Paul's back is turned.

"Yes, it's perfectly fine," hisses Paul. "I'll put him on."

"Mama?"

My heart jolts hearing my son's voice. I should never have let Paul pick him up earlier this evening. I knew Freddie was nervous, the way he kept twisting the hem of his Spiderman T-shirt around his fingers. I should have told Paul it was too much, too soon. Instead I sent Freddie packing rather than stand up to my ex-husband. "Hey, Fredster, why aren't you asleep yet?"

"Mama, I want to come home," he whispers.

I recognise the wobble in his voice. He's seconds away from bursting into tears.

"Oh sweetie, it's okay. I know it's strange being in a new place, but your daddy is with you."

"Please."

Tears well in my eyes. "Okay," I breathe. "I'll come and get you. Put your daddy on the phone for me again."

I wait, every muscle in my body tense.

"He's just tired," says Paul. "Tired and emotional."

"I'm coming to get him," I say softly.

"Emma—"

I hang up.

Trish is already putting on her coat. "I'm coming with you," she states.

"You don't have to." I rummage in my bag for my keys.

"Yes, she does," says Mags. "Call me when you get Freddie home."

Lily stands to let me out of the booth. As I brush past she grips my hand and gives it a squeeze. We stare at each other for a few seconds. "You got this," she says quietly.

"Thanks," I whisper before following Trish out the door.

———

Paul is standing outside the front door of his new living quarters when I pull up outside. It's a deeply unattractive concrete-block townhouse painted a repulsive mustard yellow.

"He's already back in bed," says Paul, his arms crossed over his ample belly. "You should just leave him."

I walk right up to Paul's hulking figure. "Move," I say firmly.

"Emma, he needs to learn."

"I said I would take him home and that's what I'm doing. You either move, or I call the police."

Paul snorts. "Don't be ridiculous. You're making a drama—"

"—Emma wants what is best for Freddie, Paul," says Trish loudly. She's standing right behind me. "I'm sure you do too."

Someone comes out of the house and puts a hand on Paul's shoulder. "Paul, Freddie needs time to get used to us. It was a big ask to expect him to stay for the night when he hasn't even been here before."

Paul shifts to the side and the woman I assume must be Clara stands before me. She's slightly dumpy, with frizzy hair and a sickeningly friendly smile. I've never seen a frumpier outfit. I thought twin-sets made from lampshade fabric went out of fashion with hair curlers.

"Hello," she says, holding out her hand. "I'm Clara."

I hesitate for a fraction then shake her hand. "I'm Emma," I say, though of course she knows who I am. "And this is my friend, Trish."

They shake hands in this suddenly quite civilised exchange, and I glance at Paul. He has a hand on Clara's lower back and is looking at her with a slightly startled expression.

Clara smiles up at him and takes his hand. "Come in," she says to us, pulling Paul into the house. Trish and I raise our eyebrows at each other and follow.

The décor is truly ghastly. Paul must really like this

woman to even contemplate sitting in the floral couch taking pride of place in the lounge. As for the lace tablecloth and matching curtains – I haven't seen the likes of those since I visited my grandma back when I was twelve.

"Freddie's in his room," Clara says, pointing to a door beside an ugly dark wooden dresser filled with antique china. "We tried to make it nice for him."

I open the door and spy Freddie deeply cocooned in a high brass bed under a thick patchwork quilt. The shelf above his head is lined with old teddy bears, their black beady eyes like an image from some horror movie. No wonder the kid was freaking out about staying.

"Mama!" Freddie throws back the cover and runs over to me. I lift him up and he squeezes his little arms and legs around me. "I'm sorry."

"What for?"

"I tried to go to sleep."

"Shhh, it's okay." I inhale his sleepy pyjama smell. "You've had a lovely time with your dad and his... and Clara. How about we head home and you come to visit them again soon, eh?"

Freddie hides his face in my chest and nods.

"We so enjoyed having you over, Freddie," says Clara when I walk out to the lounge, Freddie's head still buried.

I thought I was good at putting on the fake happy voice, but hers is impressive.

"I'll get his bag," Paul mutters.

I watch him gather up Freddie's things and wonder what happened to my husband. Where's the yelling, the put-downs, the accusations?

Silently, Paul hands the bag to Trish. He pats Freddie feebly on the back. "See you soon, buddy."

I'm careful not to make eye contact with Trish. It's hard enough keeping a straight face as it is.

I smile at Clara. "Thank you."

She smiles back. "It was lovely to finally meet you."

Once Freddie is safely in his car seat, we wave goodbye. I drive around the corner and immediately pull over.

I turn to Trish. She's clutching her sides, her face pinched together.

We dissolve into ear-piercing hysterical laughter.

"That was priceless, Em," gasps Trish. "Bloody priceless."

"What's funny?" asks Freddie.

Wiping my eyes, I swivel to grin at my tired little boy. "Your daddy, Freddie. He's one of the funniest guys I know."

Freddie frowns. "Really?"

"Absolutely," says Trish.

I can see Freddie battling with this concept, but really he's too young to understand. I can't quite comprehend it myself.

NINE
TWO WEEKS BEFORE

"Emma, we need to talk."

It's Sunday morning. I'm still in my pyjamas, having spent a busy few days at Jack's trying to get the café set up. I needed a well-deserved slow start. Freddie is watching cartoons and I'm standing at the front door squinting at my husband. "Last time you said those words you walked out on us."

Paul sighs. "Emma, you have every right to be angry with me."

I narrow my eyes even more. "Are you on drugs?" I ask.

Paul shakes his head. "Can I come in?"

I consider his calm blank face for a minute. "Okay." I step back and Paul walks into the house and straight up to Freddie. He gives him a kiss on the top of his head. "Hey, Freddo." He hasn't called our son that in over a year.

Freddie barely acknowledges him. Cartoons are far more exciting.

Paul gives me a small parent-to-parent smile and shrugs.

Now I'm scared. "What do you want?" I ask quietly.

"Can we talk somewhere?" He looks pointedly at Freddie.

I head to Freddie's room – there's no way we're going into my bedroom – and Paul follows. He shuts the door behind him. I stand in the middle of the room and cross my arms. "What do you want?" I ask again.

Paul fixes me with a vacant, slightly goofy expression. I swear he's got to be high on something. "I've been on a journey of self-discovery."

Here we go. Definitely hallucinogens involved.

I bite my lip. "Bet that was a shock."

"It was, actually. I should never have abused you verbally the way I did during our relationship."

My entire body contracts. "Sorry?"

"I've learnt a great deal about myself over the past few weeks and I'm ashamed of my behaviour. I'm here to apologise and ask for your forgiveness."

"You're what?"

"Emma, our relationship was toxic, unhealthy. We should never have married. I realise that now. We ignored God's signs."

"*God*'s signs?"

"Clara says my anger towards you blinded me to God's love."

"Oh please."

"It's true." Paul takes a step towards me and I quickly move further away. "I have prayed for God to forgive me, and I believe he has. He led me to Clara, to a more fulfilling way of life."

"Okay, you know what, I've heard enough." I stride past Paul and open Freddie's door. "Goodbye, Paul."

"God loves you too, Emma. If you let him in, you'd be happier, I promise."

My head roars. "Don't give me that crap, Paul."

"Emma, please."

"Have you forgotten, Paul? Would you like me to remind you?" I realise I've raised my voice and I lower it to a whisper. "You had to have everything your way. If I ever did anything without checking with you first, you'd go through the roof. Nothing I did was right."

"I got angry, yes, but you never showed me love, Emma. You'd look at me like I was a piece of shit. You'd make a joke or come up with some sarcastic comment rather than have a serious conversation with me. And when I tried to be intimate with you, you'd go on about how fat and disgusting I was. I couldn't get anything from you. The only way to make you react was to… you drove me mental. Why do you think I ate all the time? Put on all this weight?" he gestures at himself.

I'm gripping the door handle so tightly my hand is hurting. His apologising can never make up for how he treated me, how I lost part of myself for years because of him. "I want you to leave," I hiss.

Paul closes his eyes. "I hope you will find it in your heart to forgive me one day, Emma. For our son's sake."

When he opens his eyes and smiles, I want to spit in his face. I've never felt a rage like it. I'm burning with fury. "Get out."

He nods and walks serenely past me towards the front door. He turns on the threshold and looks from me, to Freddie, and back to me. "You are in my prayers. Both of you."

Then he's gone.

I've always blamed Paul for everything. He was the reason I became a pathetic, hollow excuse for a person. He was an arsehole to me, made me hate myself. He was a control freak. Everyone saw it. My parents and friends were always telling me I had to stand up to him. But the things he said about me, they're true. I don't want to admit it, but I did always go on about Paul's weight, make snide comments, look at him like he was a piece of shit. It was so much easier to blame him for how miserable I felt. Why did I let our poisonous marriage fester?

Ten minutes later, I'm still shaking. I can't deal with this. I'm so on edge I feel as if I'm going to snap in half. Phoning Mum, I put on the calmest voice I can muster and ask if she'll have Freddie for the night. She's been on at me for a few days, worried I'm taking on too much, trying to open a café and pack up and move out of the house at the same time. She practically purrs down the phone when I tell her I'm struggling and need some time on my own to get sorted.

"I'll ask Eric to come and get Freddie shortly, and I'll drop him at crèche tomorrow for you, Emma darling. You take some time out."

Thanking Mum, I hang up, and ring Jack. "If your offer still stands, Jack, I would like to take the day off tomorrow. I'm really behind on my packing and it would be great to get a clear run at it while Freddie is at crèche."

"Of course," says Jack, as I knew he would.

Then I call Finn.

———

"What time is it?" I open one eye.

"No idea." Finn's face lies inches from mine. He's grinning at me and I immediately grin back. He reeks of alcohol, or maybe that's me.

Groaning, I force myself to sit up. "I think I'm still drunk," I say, holding my head in my hands.

"It wouldn't surprise me." Finn places a hand on my lower back. "You showed some impressive form last night."

With my hands still covering my face, I look at Finn through my fingers. "Please tell me I didn't actually stand on the bar and show everyone my G-string?"

Finn nods. "Yes indeed. To thunderous applause."

"Why did I *do* that?"

"You were dancing to ABBA as I recall."

I shake my head. "I hate ABBA."

"So you said a number of times."

"Why didn't you stop me?"

Finn laughs. "Emma, no one could have stopped you last night."

"I thought pubs were supposed to close early on a Sunday night," I say, gingerly lifting the covers and putting my feet on the floor.

"They did ask us to leave at midnight, but you refused."

I glance back at Finn. "Really?"

"You had everyone in the bar chanting 'hell no, we won't go'. So they stayed open another hour before they kicked us out."

I shake my head. "I have no memory of that whatsoever."

Picking a crumpled T-shirt off the floor, I carefully pull it on and stand up. "Whoa." I put a hand on the wall to steady myself. "Definitely still drunk."

Finn's face turns serious. "I'm a little worried about you, Emma," he says gently. "You seemed determined to drink a lot and, well, you didn't seem quite yourself. Is there anything you want to talk about?"

"I'm fine," I say, wishing he'd stop looking at me with such concern.

Stumbling out to the kitchen, I drink a large glass of

water. My mouth feels furry and the water tastes like metal. I wander into the lounge and frown at the coffee table. There's a half-empty bottle of vodka, two glasses, and an open crisp packet, with crisps scattered all over the table and the floor. I don't remember getting the vodka. I don't remember much of last night at all.

Thank God Freddie is at crèche.

I return to the kitchen for another long drink of water. Just as well Mum didn't witness my version of time-out last night.

"You're a bad influence on me, Emma." Finn yells from my bedroom. "I should be at work right now."

"Thank God I don't." Swaying back towards the bedroom, I narrow my eyes at Finn. "Why don't you look like crap?"

Finn shakes his head. "Must be because I'm younger," he teases.

I leap onto the bed and whack him in the face with a pillow. "Bastard!"

Laughing, we both roll onto the floor. I crash into one of the boxes filled with shoes and clothes: so much for getting some packing done. Not that I'm upset right now. There's far more interesting things to occupy my time.

My cell phone begins to ring from the pocket of my jacket lying by the wardrobe.

Finn pulls me towards him. "Leave it," he whispers, kissing my neck.

We let the phone ring.

Ten minutes later, the phone rings again.

"I have to get it, Finn." I push him off and scramble for my phone. It stops ringing before I can answer it. There are two missed calls from Freddie's crèche. "Shit."

I press buttons and wait for the recorded messages.

"Emma?" Finn says quietly.

He's holding his watch and giving me a mildly panicked look.

"What?" I mouth.

"What time are you supposed to pick up Freddie?"

My heart begins to thump loudly as I listen to Jill's voice on my phone. "Emma, it's Jill. I'm just wondering if there's been some miscommunication somewhere. No one has come to pick up Freddie yet—"

I drop the phone and stare at Finn. Freddie has switched to a shorter day at crèche on Mondays as he now does a full day on Fridays. I'm supposed to collect him at midday. "What time is it?" I ask.

"One o'clock," Finn whispers.

"In the afternoon?" I ask, incredulous. I've never slept in past midday in my life.

"We didn't get to bed till 5 a.m.," Finn murmurs. "I should have set an alarm."

It wasn't up to Finn to set an alarm. I'm the mother. I should have been making sure I picked my son up on time. I'm the one who should have had Freddie in the back of my mind at all times.

I'm at the crèche in thirteen minutes.

"I'm sorry," I say, bursting through the door.

Freddie is sitting quietly on the floor doing a puzzle with Jill. He glances at me then quickly looks away.

"Fredster, I'm so sorry. I lost track of time." I stumble on a yellow wooden block as I cross the room. "I've been so busy and…" my voice trails off.

Jill stands and puts a hand on my shoulder. "Emma, have you been drinking?"

"What? No. I had a few wines last night, but I'm fine."

Jill wrinkles her lips at me. "Emma, I can't let you take

Freddie in the car with you if you're still under the influence."

"That's ridiculous. I drove here, didn't I?"

The door behind me opens and Paul walks in.

"Daddy!" Freddie leaps to his feet and runs towards his father. Paul picks him up. "Hey, buddy." My husband eyes me the same way a tiger would assess its prey. Gone is the goofy God-loves-you expression. "What happened, Emma?"

"Nothing, I lost track of time. I got stuck in—"

"Paul, I think it's best if you take Freddie home," says Jill firmly.

I glare at her, betrayed. "Jill, I said I'm fine."

She has the gall to look sheepish. "I'm sorry, Emma, it's my duty to put the welfare of the child first."

I snort. "Please."

Paul moves to stand beside me. "Emma," he says quietly. Freddie still won't acknowledge me. "I'm worried about you."

I want to hit him. No, I want to knee him in the balls. This mess is his fault. If he hadn't come to see me yesterday none of this would have happened.

"I think Freddie should stay with me tonight," says Paul. "Until you recover."

"There's nothing I need to recover from, Paul. Unless you're referring to your visit yesterday."

Paul glances at Jill and back at me. "That's a private affair, Emma. And not something I think we should be talking about in front of Freddie."

"Or Jill," I mutter.

"Emma, you've been under a lot of strain." Jill places a hand gently on my shoulder. "Why don't you let me drop you home?"

I shrug off her hand. "I don't need to be dropped home."

They're ganging up on me. If they'd just leave me alone

for a few minutes, I could get things straight in my head. Figure out a plan.

"Freddie." I lean in close to him and he shifts away. "I'm really sorry I came late today. It's not going to happen again. Let's go home and I'll make us pizzas as a treat."

"Emma, I'm sorry," says Paul. "But I can't let you take Freddie home. Not in your state. I'll drop him round to your place first thing in the morning."

I shake my head. "This is crazy. I'm the parent here, Paul. You've hardly been there for Freddie at all. You were constantly away at work, although now we know it was more likely you were off fucking Clara. And now you start acting like you—"

"Emma, that's enough." Jill takes my arm firmly and leads me to the office. "Paul is going to take Freddie, and you are going to sit in here while I call your mum."

It's too much. I sit heavily in the chair Jill guides me to and start laughing. I can't help it. "I'm not four years old, Jill. I don't need you to call my mummy."

I look out of the office door through watery eyes and watch Paul leave, carrying my son.

I wish I could remember when I started staying silent with Paul. When did I stop standing up for myself and voicing my opinion? Was it before we married? After? When Freddie was born? I only have myself to blame for allowing Paul to rule every aspect of my life. Maybe it was always that way. Maybe I let him take charge because I liked the comfort of him being in control. After Edward I craved safety, security. It's because I stayed silent that I became so resentful and angry. I turned into an awful, sneering, goading wife, and it made me hate myself almost as much as I hated him. I wanted to have a successful marriage for Freddie's sake, but how could I, when I could barely stand the sight of myself?

In a trance, I listen as Jill phones Mum. It feels like only a few numb minutes pass and then Mum is kneeling awkwardly before me. I stare at her stilettos. "Are those new?" I ask.

Mum frowns and looks down. "My shoes?"

"Yeah. They look new."

"Emma, I'm going to take you home now, okay?"

I nod. "I think I need a shower."

"Yes." Mum helps me to stand. "I think you do."

I can't tell from her expression if she's angry or disappointed. Maybe it's both.

TEN
ONE WEEK BEFORE

The café has become my focus. The café and Freddie. I've taken a mature step and decided to distance myself from Finn and all his sexy ways. This has been made easier by the fact he's been in Melbourne on some work trip for the past three days. We haven't even spoken on the phone I've been so busy with the café. Plus yesterday Freddie and I moved out of the house and into an apartment two blocks away, and about a third of the size. Paul never showed up to help and Dad hurt his back when he insisted on carrying Freddie's bed to the truck. Mum's convinced he's permanently damaged, of course. Something else she can be angry with me about.

I'm running on four hours sleep a night, adrenaline, coffee, and bananas – Jack keeps shoving them at me and telling me to eat.

I'm looking to atone for my sins and prove I'm still a responsible, caring, hard-working mother. That little episode last week was an anomaly. A blip. I will never, ever forget to pick up Freddie from anywhere ever again. Or drink vodka.

Or dance on a bar in my G-string. Like I said, a blip. Temporary insanity.

"You'll need an extractor, and a commercial dishwasher to bring it up to code." The council inspector is making no attempt whatsoever to be nice. He's far too busy trying to look and act important. I can play his game. My café is going to happen, no matter what.

"I have an extractor being installed next week." I smile sweetly at the pimply face of Mr Torley from Council. He looks about fifteen years old. "And the dishwasher arrives this afternoon." The small, stainless-steel, no-frills kitchen we stand in is already a world away from the pokey office and kitchenette it once was. It's hard to believe Jack, Dad, and I only started ripping the old, stained linoleum off the floor two weeks ago.

Glancing at his clipboard, Mr Torley ticks another box. "Well, assuming those two issues are met to my satisfaction, I should be able to provide consent for your commercial kitchen, Mrs Tilssen. Subject to a final inspection of course."

I bite my tongue, wishing I could snatch the word Mrs from his mouth and squish it like a cockroach under my shoe.

Mr Torley looks disappointed he couldn't find more things to complain about, but I have been meticulous in making sure everything is up to code. I don't want anything to stop my official opening day in two weeks.

Trish has been an angel helping to set up the business side of things – the business contract, GST, point-of-sale, insurance – and Jack is his usual unflappable self. He's taken on a lovely guy called Ben to help with packing and delivering boxes. Ben's fresh out of school and wondering what to do with his life. He's a hard worker and a fast learner. I hope he decides delivering fruit and vegetables is a valuable long-term career.

There's a girl out front painting new lettering on the glass window:

Jack's Grocery Store and Café
Food For the Soul

I was worried Jack would think the words were a bit too flowery, but he's happy with them. He seems to like everything I do. I'm still getting used to it. It's like I keep waiting for the balloon to pop and for him to realise he's made a big mistake taking me on as his business partner.

My phone rings as I'm saying my polite goodbyes to Mr Torley.

"Hello?"

"Hey Em, it's Lily. Howzit going?"

"Great."

She's rung me several times with the same question and I give the exact same answer each time.

"Glad you're feeling better. What was it, another tummy bug?"

I'm sick with self-hate remembering last Monday. Once I sobered up and Mum finally left, I was worried Lily might pop in after work as usual, so I'd sent her a text telling her I was unwell. "Not sure. Virus probably."

"Sorry I couldn't come and help you move yesterday. Okay for me to pop round after work? I'm keen to see your new place, and I can unpack some boxes or something."

I want to say no, but I don't want to upset Lily, or make her suspicious I'm anything other than great. She doesn't know about my blip last Monday, and I'm feeling too guilty to tell her. It's clear she doesn't approve of Finn already. I haven't exactly been avoiding her, but there's a tension between us at the moment. I'm not all that keen to deal with it right now.

The pause is going on too long. "Sure, love to see you," I say brightly. "Though it might have to be takeaways I'm afraid."

"Wow, never thought I'd hear you say that, Em. You sure you're alright?"

I force a laugh. "Yeah, just busy getting this café sorted. Speaking of which, the coffee machine has just arrived, I gotta dash, Lils."

I've never been so pleased to see a delivery van in my life. I've been waiting for this damn coffee machine all morning. You can't open a café without a coffee machine. It's like opening a hotel with no beds.

Jack comes out of the shop and stands beside me as they lift the gleaming silver machine off the truck. "She's a beauty," he says.

"Should be for the price," I grumble.

Jack frowns and I want to kick myself because I know what's coming next.

"Now, Emma. We agreed you weren't to spend too much. I don't want you going into any debt."

I throw my arm around his shoulder. "Relax, Jack. Everything is under control. I have Trish and Dad keeping a close eye on my expenses. There's—" I happen to glance across the street to see Finn climbing out of his car. My stomach somersaults as he grins and jogs over. He scoops me off the ground and kisses me hard on the lips, ignoring the fact my boss is right next to me. "Missed you," he says when he finally lets me go.

My cheeks are surely flushed an unflattering red. I dare not look at Jack's face right now. "Ah, Finn, this is Jack, my boss."

"Business partner," Jack says, shaking Finn's hand. "So you're the guy leading our Emma astray."

Oh God, I want to die.

"The very one," says Finn.

Jack slaps Finn on the back. "You're from Scotland, I think. My wife, Alice, she was born in Glasgow. Left when she was ten but never lost the accent."

Okay I can relax. Finn has officially been approved of.

"Is that right?" Finn says.

Shaking my head, I chase after the two guys carrying my precious coffee machine into the shop, leaving Finn and Jack to carry on chatting outside.

———

It takes several attempts to convince Finn I can't take an extended lunchbreak so we can go back to my place for a quick shag – he says for a bite to eat, but I'm sure that's a not-so-subtle ruse. I'm tempted, obviously, but I'm still making amends for last week.

"How about tonight?" Finn says. "Can you find a babysitter for Freddie? We could go to that Japanese place again?" His expression is strained. He seemed so excited to see me when he arrived, but now he looks stressed or mad, I can't tell. Maybe he's grumpy because I haven't asked him about his trip to Melbourne yet.

"Mum's already looked after Freddie most of the weekend." I continue stacking coffee cups beside the newly installed coffee machine. "I can't ask her to have him again."

"Why not?"

I must be tired. Why else would I be a little annoyed? Finn has never been this pushy before. A large part of his appeal is the way he's so relaxed about everything. Plus he's always asking for my opinion and listening to my answer, instead of making a decision on things as if my view doesn't matter. Now I feel pressured, and I don't like it one bit. "Because it wouldn't be fair," I snap. "Anyway, Lily's coming over tonight. It's Monday remember?"

Finn sighs, shaking his head. What is up with him?

"Okay," he mutters. "It's just I wanted to talk about... well, forget it, I'll catch up with you later in the week."

That's it. Finn wants to tell me all about his trip to Melbourne and he's disappointed I'm so busy. Fair enough. I have been acting very self-absorbed. He's studying me with those gorgeous green eyes and a vulnerable expression, I expect with the hope I'll have a change of heart. I'm already wavering. The guy's indecently good-looking and I've missed him more than I should have. "I could text you when Lily leaves?" I run a hand down Finn's chest. "You could pop round then? If you're not too tired." I expect I'll be exhausted but if anyone can help me find a second wind, Finn can.

"I won't be too tired," says Finn quickly. He lifts his eyebrows and dazzles me with his dimples again.

Smiling, I watch him leave.

Jack comes out of the storeroom and catches my eye. "Seems like a nice guy," he says, with a cheeky grin.

I turn away before he can see me blush.

———

I'm at crèche ten minutes early. Freddie is dressed in a spotty dog costume and is engrossed in chasing Jake (in a tiger costume) around the room.

I engage in adult conversation with Jill, eager to convince her I'm still reliable, trustworthy Emma. Then I cuddle

Freddie and listen enthusiastically to a blow-by-blow account of his day on the walk home.

I give Freddie some lunch and strike up a bargain. If he plays quietly in his room for thirty minutes, he can watch two episodes of Ninjago on the TV. He thinks it's a great deal.

I spend the afternoon organising the kitchen and working on more food ideas for the café. It's ridiculous how much I'm enjoying creating recipes. It'll be a million times easier once I can use the new kitchen at Jack's – the kitchen in our rental apartment is tiny – but I don't need a lot of space when it's just me experimenting. I bake a lemon slice with a thin meringue topping; something I've been mulling on for a few days. I'm hoping it will be a winner, though I doubt anything can top the macadamia and raspberry brownie I made recently. Mags was in complete raptures when she came over to test it. And Freddie begged me to save some for the much-anticipated sleepover he had with Jake the night before we moved. I'm relieved to say the sleepover appeared to be a big success, even if most of our house was packed into boxes. The boys played with Freddie's trains, had pizza, and watched a movie. They wolfed down my brownie then ran around in the backyard with torches, making strange noises and laughing almost continuously.

At 9 p.m., I went to check on them. They were both fast asleep, grass in their hair, teddies pressed against their cheeks. Freddie had insisted on pulling his mattress onto the floor so he could be beside Jake. For a fleeting moment I wished Paul could have seen how cute they both looked.

Looking at my new tiny kitchen, I feel guilt seep into my body like rising damp. Our apartment doesn't have a back-yard for Freddie to dig for worms in, or run around with his friends. I was expecting him to be more upset with the move and I'm worried he thinks we're simply on holiday and we'll be going back to our old house in a few weeks.

I hope Freddie isn't permanently scarred from me forgetting to collect him from crèche or by my somewhat inappropriate behaviour. He seems to have forgotten it, although a couple of times this week he's asked to ring his dad. I'm trying not to read too much into it. Paul has seen Freddie twice since dropping him at crèche the morning after the incident that shall not be mentioned. Both times he asked me politely if Freddie could go to their place for dinner. It's not an ideal arrangement and I'm sure Freddie is a little confused – this new version of Paul is confusing us both.

There's a familiar-sounding knock at the door.

"It's open," I call.

"Something smells yum," Lily says, pushing open the door. She holds up a bottle of wine in one hand, and a brown paper bag in the other. "I took the liberty of grabbing us some Thai."

Lily knows I love Thai, almost as much as I like Japanese.

"Thanks, Lil, I'm starving."

Lily ruffles Freddie's hair. "Hey little man." He's sitting cross-legged on the floor about a foot from the TV screen. I've twice asked him to move back, but he keeps shuffling his little bottom forward again.

"Hi Lily." His eyes remain fixed to the screen.

Lily steps over an open box of Freddie's toys I haven't managed to unpack yet, and follows me into the kitchen. There's not really room for her to come in and she hovers by the door. "The place is looking good, Em."

"It's small."

"True, but it's got a nice cosy feel. What's in the oven?" she asks.

"My version of a lemon meringue pie, only it's more of a thinner slice."

"Do I get to try it later?"

"Absolutely."

I pull out some plates and cutlery and hand them to Lily. She sets the dining table, which takes up way too much space in the lounge (mental note to get a smaller table) and opens the takeaway containers while I put the slice onto a rack to cool.

"Wine glasses?" she says, waiting again at the kitchen door.

I'm trying to cut back on the drinking. The only problem is, if I tell Lily she'll ask me why, and I don't want to go there. Better I hand over the glasses and take very small sips.

Freddie's programme is finished so I won't have to engage in a battle to get him to turn it off. He sits on his chair beside me and immediately makes a mess as he digs into his pad thai.

"Hungry boy," Lily says, smiling.

I smile back.

It's not too awkward so far. Fingers crossed she doesn't bring up Finn.

"I want to hear all about the café, Em. Are you still on track to open? Sorry I haven't been able to help more, I've been absolutely slammed at work."

In between mouthfuls of food, I fill Lily in. I feel as if I haven't eaten in days. Which is close to the truth. It's nice to have Lily here to listen to my babble.

I'm wiping Freddie's fingers clean with a napkin when my phone rings.

"Hello?"

"Emma, it's Ben."

It takes me a moment to remember that Ben is the young

guy working with Jack. I'm a little surprised to hear from him. I didn't think he had my number. "Hi, Ben."

There's a pause and I know without seeing Ben's face, simply by the way he draws in his breath, that something's wrong.

"Jack collapsed," says Ben in a rush. "I called an ambulance and he's gone to hospital."

"Oh no. What happened?"

"I don't know. We were cleaning up the backroom and he just—" The poor kid sounds terrified. "They think he might have had a heart attack."

In movies, when people get a shock and put their hand over their mouth it looks so contrived. But I'm doing exactly that.

Slowly I lift my hand away. Lily is staring at me and biting her lip. "Thanks for calling me, Ben. I'll head to the hospital now. Do you know which one?"

Ben tells me and I hang up. I can't believe it.

Freddie puts a hand on my arm. "Mama, is someone sick?"

I glance at Lily, then reach out to hold Freddie's hands. "You know our friend Jack?"

Freddie nods.

"He had to go to the hospital."

"Because he's sick," says Freddie.

The only time I've taken Freddie to the hospital was to visit my Dad when he got a bout of pneumonia last year. Dad gave Freddie the jelly and ice cream from his tray of otherwise inedible hospital food, and let him push the button to raise and lower the bed. Freddie thought the hospital was fantastic.

"Yes," I say. "Sort of."

"I can stay," says Lily quickly. "You go."

I straighten up. "You sure?"

"Absolutely. How about it, Freddie? Your mummy goes to check on Jack, while you tell me about that programme you were watching before. What was going on with those snakes and their eyes turning red?"

While Freddie launches into a garbled four-year-old explanation, I throw on some shoes and race out the door.

———

Once at the hospital, I head straight to the emergency department.

"Hello," I say to the receptionist. "I'm here to see Jack Wilson. He was brought in a few minutes ago."

"One moment." She types on her keyboard for a ridiculously long time, then without a word, stands and leaves her desk. I watch her talk to someone in a glass-walled room. I'm thinking it's a young doctor. He's got a stethoscope slung around his neck and he looks that usual mix of confident and clueless. He glances at me, then looks back at the receptionist and shakes his head. What does that mean?

They disappear down a corridor together.

Less than a minute later, a nurse strides towards me. She's one of those no-nonsense types. I'm scared of her already. "Are you a relative?"

"Sorry?"

"Are you a relative of Mr Wilson?"

"No, I'm a friend, and business—"

"I'm afraid we are unable to give you any details on his condition."

"What do you mean?"

"We are currently contacting his family." She gives me a pointed look. "I'm sorry."

"But they live miles away. He needs someone with him now."

"Would you have a phone number? Of a family member?" Again she stares at me, like I've got something on my face. I wipe my cheek and frown. "No," I mutter.

The big double doors leading into the emergency ward swing open and a man walks out with a small baby in his arms. He has a dazed expression, like he's just woken up. I peer past, hoping to spy Jack. "Could you tell him I'm here."

The nurse shakes her head. "Sorry, but I can't."

I feel a weird sensation in my palms. It's like pins and needles. The prickling, burning sensation spreads up my arms and into my head. My scalp is on fire.

"He can't be," I whisper. But I know from her expression, he is.

ELEVEN
ONE DAY BEFORE

"You sure you don't want me to come to the funeral?" Finn asks. I haven't seen him since he stopped by to see me at the café after his Melbourne trip. He met Jack for the first time that day. Ironically – is it ironic? – Jack dropped dead only a matter of hours later.

"No. It's going to be weird enough. I'll call you when it's over."

"Good luck," he says.

I hang up, climb into my car and pull out onto the road.

Lily and Trish both offered to drive with me to the chapel, but I told them I'd meet them there. There are only so many sympathetic hand-squeezes I can take. I'm in such a fog that I drive past Jack's store without thinking. I've successfully avoided the route all week, and I have to go and ruin my track record today of all days.

The store is closed, of course. There's a few empty wooden crates stacked outside. And the half-finished paint job around the window gives the impression something exciting is about to happen. Dad and Ben kindly went round on Wednesday and took all the vegetables and fruit to the Auckland City Mission. Jack would have hated seeing all his good produce going to waste.

I wish it wasn't such a bloody perfect crisp autumn day, full of tweeting birds and smiling faces. Sun glints off the new unused coffee machine sitting proudly inside the window as I drive past. I press the accelerator and fix my eyes on the corner ahead.

Jack's son, Peter is standing at the chapel door. He must take after Alice, as I can't spot a trace of Jack in his face at all. Thank God. Peter's been staying in Jack's house since Tuesday. I picked him up from the airport and offered to help with any arrangements, but he's done it all on his own as far as I can tell. I've had a couple of brief conversations with him over the phone. One about flowers – did I know if Jack had a favourite? A second about catering. I offered to bake a few things for the wake and Peter told me there was no need. The funeral director took care of all that. It was included in the price, he said.

Jack's daughter, Chloe couldn't fly in till last night. There aren't that many flights out of Venezuela. I'm assuming she's inside already. I hope she doesn't dislike me as much as Peter clearly does.

I spot her the second I enter the chapel. She's in the front row, presumably with extended family members. She's wearing a wrap-around tie-dyed dress and a ridiculous amount of jewellery. There's silver in her nose, hanging off her ears, around her neck and wrists, and covering her fingers. She's staring at the coffin, oblivious to the people and movement around her. I can see Jack in her profile: the deep-set eyes and thick eyebrows, as well as the slight tilt of the head. Jack used to tip his head to the side like that when he was worried about something.

I sit next to Mum and Dad in the pew third from the front. Ben is beside Dad, looking uncomfortable and on the verge of tears. Mum is already dabbing at her eyes. She must have only had five conversations with Jack in her life, but in true Mum style she's being all emotional and dramatic. Mum, Dad, and my friends hardly knew Jack at all. I suspect they're mostly here for me.

Scanning the other rows, I spot Lily, Trish, Mags, and a number of faces I recognise as customers. People I've delivered boxes to, or said hello to over the past few weeks when Jack proudly introduced me as his new business partner.

I look at the smiling face of Jack on the cover of the small folded paper in my hand. It's inconceivable to think the man in the photo is now lying in the narrow rectangular box lying at the front. I'm glad Freddie isn't here. For once I agreed with Paul when he suggested he collect Freddie from crèche and keep him for the night. It's far easier for me to hold it together without Freddie curling up on my lap, smelling all delicious and asking too many questions.

I want the day to be over.

We all mumble our way through a hymn then the chaplain gives a short, well-rehearsed speech. Jack's children say a few words, Peter suitably stoic, Chloe in tears. There's a reading from an old school friend of Jack's, another hymn, and the coffin is finally lifted off its marble plinth. I can't look at it as it goes past. I can't let myself imagine the weight of Jack's extinguished life inside.

Filing outside, we gather around the hearse. The coffin sits ready to slide into the boot of the long black car. A basket is handed around. When it reaches me, I take the smallest, saddest-looking carnation (Jack said to me several times they were Alice's favourite flower) and place it with the others on the polished mahogany lid. The person in front of me has placed their palm on the coffin and is murmuring something, tears dribbling down their cheeks. I quickly make my way to the rear of the crowd.

Lily comes to stand beside me. "Nearly there," she whispers.

I nod without looking at her.

Everyone is silent as the hearse drives away. Chloe and Peter get into the backseat of another black shiny car and leave for the cemetery. They'll watch as Jack is buried under the earth.

Lily lets out a big sigh. "Phew," she says. "Don't know about you, Em, but I need a drink."

Mags and Trish join us.

"What now?" says Trish.

"We go next door." Lily points to an attractive building adorned with trailing rose bushes opposite the chapel. "For tea, cakes, and respectful chit-chat."

"That could be a challenge for you, Lils," Mags mutters.

I catch Mum staring at me. Any second she's going to come over and ask me how I'm coping. Again.

"Let's get this over with," I whisper, heading towards the building. The last thing I want is tea and cakes. I want oblivion. I want to not think about Jack dying, my ex-husband, my son who I've let down, my disappointed parents, my dream café that is now in tatters. I want tequila, with a large shot of Finn on the side.

———

It's another two painful hours before I can make my escape. I thank my friends and parents for coming and manage to deflect their suggestion for a late lunch together. Convincing them I'm exhausted and want to have some time alone, I take the alternate route home to avoid another glimpse of the shiny new coffee machine. The second I enter my empty apartment, I phone Finn.

"What time do you finish work?" I ask.

"Reckon I could get away in another twenty minutes." He pauses. "How are you?"

"Glad it's over. Fancy meeting me for a drink or two? Freddie's away for the night."

"Is he?"

I've got Finn's attention now.

"I need a major distraction after today," I say. "I have a lot of pent-up… energy to get rid of. Any ideas?"

"Meet you at Galbraith's in fifteen minutes," Finn breathes.

"Don't be late."

———

I'm at the bar ordering a tequila when I feel Finn's arm slide around my waist. He kisses me lightly on the cheek. "Hi, gorgeous," he breathes. "Tough day?"

I nod, a lump in my throat. This caring, affectionate Finn is not who I need right now. I want the Finn I met at the club. The sexy guy out for a good time, nothing more.

"I might start with a beer," Finn says, as I slide a shot glass towards him.

"Come on," I say, downing my shot and ordering another. "You can't let me drown my sorrows alone."

He frowns and places a hand on top of mine as it grips the edge of the bar. "Emma, I'm not sure this is the right way to deal with Jack's death."

Scowling, I grab his shot of tequila and throw it down my throat. I gesture at the barman to pour two more. Why does

Finn have to be so bloody perfect? Why can't he get angry with me, or arrive late, or tell me I'm being pathetic?

Blinking back tears, I resist the urge to lean against Finn. He can't weaken me. I can't let myself get close to another man after Paul. I just can't.

"Please, Finn, let's get drunk and forget about everything. I promise tomorrow I'll be a better person."

"Emma, you don't need to be a better person, you deserve to be happy and—" he cuts off and runs a hand through his hair. "You deserve more than this." He takes both my hands and takes a deep breath. "I was going to wait a few more days, but there's something I need to tell you, only before I do—"

His expression is pained. He's going to tell me something I don't want to hear, I'm sure of it. He's leaving NZ, or he's married, or he's dying of some rare disease. I rip my hands out of Finn's. "No, Finn. Please don't. Whatever it is, I don't care right now. You're meant to be the young, fun one here."

Two more tequilas are placed in front of me. Again I slide one over to Finn and pick up the other. "All I want is to forget, just for tonight," I urge.

He sighs loudly, picks up his glass, taps it against mine, and drinks.

———

Two hours and a short taxi ride later Finn is on his back on my living room floor. I'm sitting on him, my dress hitched above my waist.

"More," Finn growls, his hands pressing my butt cheeks.

I stop moving. "Sorry? Did you say something?" Leaning over, I snatch the bottle of vodka off the coffee table. Finn's fingers squeeze harder as I take a sip, savouring the alcoholic burn in my throat as I swallow.

"Now," I say, placing the bottle back down. "Where was I?"

Finn smiles. "I believe you were tormenting me, Emma."

"Oh yes." I rock my hips forward and back and find a place of blank stillness in my mind.

———

By nine o'clock I'm starving. "Let's go grab a burger," I shout. "I haven't had a greasy burger in years."

Finn stops banging his head up and down and leaps off the coffee table to land beside me. "Seriously?" he yells.

I crawl on all fours to the stereo and turn the music down. "If I don't eat something, I'll pass out." I roll over onto my back and watch the ceiling swirl around and around above me.

Finn laughs. "Can't you whip something up?"

"Nope." I shut my eyes. As my world goes black, my stomach lurches and I open my eyes again. "I need a burger. And fries. Lots of fries."

"Well then," Finn grabs my hand and pulls me to my feet. "Let's get this woman a burger."

I pray I won't puke in his face. "Call a taxi," I say. "I'll get dressed."

Staggering to my room, I pull on a clean set of under-wear, jeans, and a sweatshirt.

Finn is waiting fully dressed by the front door when I return.

"Shoes?" he asks, pointing to my feet.

I close one eye and will the room to stop spinning. "Too hard," I say. "Let's go."

Thankfully the cooler air outside revives me long enough to survive the drive to Burger Heaven. When my burger arrives, I inhale it.

"God that was good," I murmur, moving onto my fries.

Finn sits across from me, grinning. He's barely started his burger.

"You gonna eat that?" I ask.

He nods. "Just enjoying watching you too much."

I throw a chip and it hits him in the cheek.

"Hey!"

Grinning, I throw another chip. This one hits him on the chin.

"Right, now you're asking for it." Finn takes the lid off his coke, pulls out a handful of ice and stands up.

"No fair!" I squeal as he wrestles with me, eventually getting the ice down the inside of my top. Gasping, I shake it out and glare at Finn who sits back down, a smug look on his dimpled face.

"Excuse me, I'm going to have to ask you to leave."

I stare at the skinny boy in Burger Heaven uniform. "Sorry?"

"As manager, I have to ask you to leave please."

"Why? Because this bastard threw ice down my top?"

"Because you are both clearly intoxicated – and yes, because you are throwing food."

"Jesus, you sound like my mother." I can't believe this kid is telling me off. It's ridiculous.

"Come on, Emma." Finn hauls me to my feet. "Let's get out of here."

I grab my fries off the table. "Gladly."

Sticking my tongue out at the idiot kid, I follow Finn outside. "What now?" I ask, shoving a handful of fries in my mouth.

Finn slaps his forehead. "My burger!" He disappears back inside and returns with a burger shoved between his teeth. "Kid was about to throw it in the bin," he mumbles.

We wander down the deserted street. I wish I'd grabbed a warmer jumper. And shoes. It's not exactly tropical. My toes are frozen. "Clearly not a popular night to be out on the town," I say, leaning against Finn. Walking in a straight line is proving harder than I thought.

Finn throws what remains of his burger in a bin and puts his arm around my waist.

"What now?" I ask. My head is pounding and I'm beginning to feel a twinge of sadness creep under my skin, but if I go home then I have to face tomorrow.

Finn stops walking. He stares up the sloping street beside us.

"What?" I ask.

He gives me a loud smack on the lips, grabs my hand and pulls me up the narrow street. It's ridiculously steep. "My legs can't take it," I pant. "What are we doing?"

"You'll see." Finn continues to drag me with him.

"I'm dying," I gasp.

"Nearly there."

I concentrate on getting enough air in my lungs and making sure I don't fall. When we reach the top, I collapse onto the concrete footpath and Finn doubles over next to me out of breath.

Eventually he straightens. "Ready for the ride of your life?" he asks, putting out his hand.

I place my hand in his and he hauls me to my feet. "What sort of ride did you have in mind?" Surely, Finn doesn't want to have sex here. There's nothing but an ugly assortment of warehouses clinging to the slope, and some wire fences.

There's also the high likelihood I would vomit my burger all over him.

Finn walks over to a giant metal dustbin on wheels propped against the streetlight. There's a picture of cardboard boxes painted on the side of the bin and the words, *please fold flat*.

Finn pulls hard at the bin and it rolls towards him briefly before rolling back and banging against the light. He turns to me and raises his eyebrows. "What do you think?"

I frown. "About what?"

"A ride." He glances down the hill. "It flattens out at the bottom. There is literally no one around. Come on, Em. It'll be awesome."

"You're kidding? You want us to hop inside?"

Finn nods. "Let's do it. Tomorrow we'll be sensible adults." He gives me a weird look, like he's dreading the next day as much as I am.

A sad hollowness is beginning to clear my senses. I keep thinking of Jack, dead, underground.

Slowly I walk towards Finn and stand on tiptoes to stare inside the bin. A few pieces of cardboard line the bottom. It looks quite appealing; like one of the huts I used to build under the kitchen table when I was a kid. It would be nice to huddle somewhere out of the wind. The street isn't that steep, or long. There are no cars around. We'll be fine. I need to take risks again, be the carefree Emma I used to be.

"Okay." I bend my leg and Finn puts his hands on my shin and lifts me up. With my stomach on the top, I fling my legs around and land on the bottom with a loud metallic thump. Finn scrambles in beside me.

"Ready?" he says, reaching out over the rim of the bin to put his hands on the concrete pole of the streetlight.

I nod, and with a grunt Finn pushes hard. The perfectly

defined muscles on his arms shine in the soft glow of the light and my heart beats faster as the wheels beneath me begin to clatter. We move slowly. Finn sits beside me and grins. Then we are suddenly moving fast. Too fast. It's loud and terrifying. I don't want to be here. What am I doing? *This is a death-trap*, I think as the bin tips and my head slams into the metal side.

It's the last thought I have.

PART TWO
AFTER

TWELVE

ONE WEEK AFTER

Three Weeks After

I don't know where I am.

I'm in a bed, in a room I don't recognise, and yet it's familiar. I know before I carefully turn my head that I'll find a window with a leafless tree outside; its silver branches sometimes scrape against the window and keep me awake. I have no idea how I know this, but I do. If I sit up just a fraction more I'll see a car park beyond the tree… how can I know these things when I've never been here before?

I understand it's early morning from the light coming in through the window, casting a well-defined triangle of sunshine onto the industrial-looking carpet.

My hair is wet. Why is my hair wet? I smell of the soap my mum likes to use. I can't recall the name of the soap. It has pale purple wrapping with a picture of lavender fields.

This bed I lie in has metal sides, like a hospital bed. It tilts the top half of my body slightly upright, though I'm slumped to one side. But there's a nice soft blanket spread out over me and the walls aren't white like hospital walls, they're a lemon yellow. This room doesn't have the feel of a hospital room; no polished vinyl floor and complicated-looking equipment. I'm reminded of the rest home I used to visit my grandfather in on Sundays. This place smells like a rest home; stuffy air laced with the aroma of decaying bodies.

My right leg feels too heavy. I lift the yellow blanket to look at my leg, only… only I *don't* lift the covers. My brain is saying lift the covers but my arm doesn't respond. *Lift the covers*, I tell my arm. I stare at my arm for a long time. Finally it moves, slowly and with difficulty.

A huge white cast runs from my foot to my thigh. I'm wearing a blue cotton dress I've never seen before, scrunched up to the waist. Mum would call it a frock. I've never owned a frock. Never wanted to. Frocks are for old people.

I replace the blanket.

By the door is a large whiteboard on a stand.

Your name is Emma Tilssen the board tells me, in loopy green writing.

Today is Monday.

At 7am you will have a shower.

At 8am you will have breakfast in the Dining room.

At 9am Alison your Occupational Therapist—

"Morning, Emma." A woman walks into my room. She has brown skin and dark hair pulled back into a ponytail. Giant silver hoops hang from her ears. Who is she? How does she know my name?

"Nice to see the sun out after all that rain." The woman smiles and sits down in the small plastic chair beside my bed. She opens the top draw of my bedside table and pulls out an exercise book. It's like the ones we used to write in at school. "Shall we start with your room number?"

I blink at the woman, my head suddenly pounding.

The woman frowns and puts the exercise book back in the drawer. "Emma?" she says. "Do you know where you are?"

I'm too scared to move, too scared to respond.

"Emma, I'm going to go out of the room and come back in again. When you see me come back in, I want you to nod, okay?"

I don't move.

"Here I go, Emma. All you need to do is nod once when I come back in, got it?"

She leaves the room and shuts the door. Seconds later, the door opens and she walks towards my bed. She stops and waits.

I nod once.

The woman grins. "Welcome back, Emma."

Where did I go? She was the one who left the room.

I want to ask her how she knows my name. Opening my mouth, I tell myself to speak out loud the words in my head. "Owdaanaa." That's not right. What happened to the words I meant to form?

"Emma, my name is Alison. I'm your Occupational Therapist. You were in an accident. You have a brain injury. You're currently in a rehabilitation hospital." She speaks clearly, concisely. Like I'm an imbecile. "You are safe and being well cared for."

I can't remember being in any accident. I remember being at Jack's funeral, trying not to cry, glad Freddie wasn't with me—

Freddie, I scream in my head. *Where's Freddie?*

Speak, I tell my brain. Ask about Freddie. What if he was in the accident with me?

I don't know how to make my voice work but try to force sound out between my lips. It's a crackle, like logs on a fire.

"Fffee."

This woman, whose name I can't remember leans closer. "Sorry?"

Damn it. It's just one word. I can say his name. I have to. "Fffred."

"Freddie?"

I nod, my vision blurry with tears.

The woman nods back. "He's just fine, Emma. Lovely boy. He's staying with your parents until you improve. He brought this in for you yesterday." The woman picks up a piece of paper from the bedside table and holds it before me. It's a painting. There's a blob of green, a thick line of red, and lots of small yellow dots. "Freddie told me the yellow dots were rain." The woman gives a wry smile and puts the painting back. "There's been a lot of rain."

I close my eyes. Now I know Freddie's okay, I'm strangely calm. And tired. Really, really tired.

"I'll let you rest, Emma while I contact your family. We can do some tasks later."

I nod without opening my eyes.

"If you need the nurse press the green button on this cord." She lifts my hand and places something under it. "Your family will be very excited to hear you're awake. Properly awake I mean."

I'm not awake. I'm somewhere between awake and asleep, and sleep is winning.

———

I open my eyes as Lily's black hair tickles my face. I can tell instantly it's her from the smell of the perfume she always uses. Plus, I'd know Lily anywhere.

Lily pulls back, a hairbrush in her hand. "Hey," she says.

"Your hair was a fucking mess." She studies me carefully. "'Bout time you came back from whatever world you've been hanging out in." Her smile is shaky.

I stare at her. *Tell me*, I beg with my eyes. *Tell me what's going on.*

"Oh, Em," Lily says quietly. "Do you remember anything from the past three weeks? Anything at all?"

Three weeks?

I slowly shake my head.

Lily bites her lip and perches on the bed. She picks up my hand and rubs her thumb across the top. I feel like she's done that before. The sensation is comforting and familiar.

"Em, your dad will be here soon. Alison was on the phone to him when I came by for my morning visit. She told me you had come out of your amnesia thingy. How about we wait till Eric arrives, eh? Then we can both fill in the blanks."

It makes sense. I'm in no hurry. It's nice lying here, Lily's thumb on my skin. I feel all floaty, like I'm in a warm bath. "'K" I croak.

Lily grins. "Hey, that was brilliant. You're improving, Emma. I totally understood that."

My head is foggy, confused. If I'm improving, I must have tried speaking to Lily before. How could I have been awake and talking and have no memory of it?

I close my eyes and let myself float. Lily mentioned amnesia. Isn't that something to do with loss of memory? Everything will be clearer soon.

———

My throat is blocked. I need to cough. *Cough*, I tell my brain. It considers my request. I feel the message chug from my brain to my lungs. Finally, I cough.

"Emma?"

Opening my eyes, I find Dad in the chair beside my bed. The plastic one Alison sat in when the sun was painting a triangle on the floor. *Alison.* I remembered her name.

Dad sits forward and strokes my hair. "Welcome back, beautiful girl. I've missed you."

It's not like Dad to get all soppy and sentimental. I must be in bad shape.

Lily is still perched on the bed stroking my hand. "You nodded off," she says. "Just for a few minutes."

I feel like I've been asleep for hours.

"I dropped Freddie at crèche on the way here," Dad says brightly. "He told me to give you a big hug. Mum will bring him by later today."

I smile. At least I think I smile.

"He's been staying with Mum and I, and had a few sleep-overs with Paul and Clara. He's fine, Em."

Paul. I talked to him recently. About God. Why would I talk to Paul about God?

"You had us worried," Dad says in a rush. "Promise me you'll get through this."

I wish I knew what *this* was.

Lily clears her throat. "So before you go falling asleep again, I thought I'd give you a run-down." She exchanges a quick look with Dad and he nods briefly.

"You were in a crash," says Lily. "You broke your femur in three places, punctured a lung, cracked two ribs, and hit your head. Hard." She takes a deep wobbly breath. "You were unconscious for fucking ever."

"Six hours," says Dad softly, his eyes downcast.

"You were put on a ventilator to help you breathe," says Lily, her voice firmer. "For the first few days you weren't

126

really aware of anything – or anyone. You'd look at us some-times, but I'm not sure you knew who we were."

"We didn't bring Freddie in while you were in intensive care," Dad says. "We thought it might upset him. He started to visit when you were transferred here about two weeks ago."

Lily carries on. "There was some swelling and bleeding in the brain, but that's almost gone now. Your brain just needs time to heal. Rewire, the doctor said. Your speech will improve, and once you get the cast off you'll be able to move around."

Dad grips my hand. "Emma, you need to focus on getting better. Don't worry about anything else."

I nod. There are a thousand questions I want to ask, but I don't trust myself to speak. Or be understood. I must have been in a car accident. Where? Why? What happened? Did anyone else get hurt? Was it my fault? Was I on my way to pick up Freddie and never got there? Was he afraid, waiting for me? Was I… oh shit, was I drinking?

Alison walks in pushing a wheelchair. "Right then, Emma. It's time for your physio session." She wheels the chair around the bed and backs it in so the handles are close to my shoulder. "Sorry, Eric, but Tamara waits for no one."

Dad stands. "It's fine, I should go." He takes my hand and squeezes it tight. "You okay?"

I nod. What I want to do is shake my head and tell him I'm hopelessly confused and scared, but it seems physically too hard. Impossible, actually.

"Mum and I will bring Freddie in after lunch." Dad gives my hand a final squeeze and lets go.

Lily blows me a kiss. "I'll bring Trish and Mags round after work. We can celebrate your return to the land of the living."

I'm about to open my mouth to say 'bye', then I realise I might not get the word out. I nod because it's all I can do.

Dad and Lily are still walking out the door when Alison throws the blanket off and shoves her hands under my armpits in one fast and furious movement.

In a flash I'm reminded of Finn. I wonder if he's been to visit. Then again, I've been laid up here for weeks. He's probably moved on. Found someone else already.

"Right." Alison plonks me in the wheelchair and puts a complicated seatbelt around my body. "Reckon you won't need to be strapped in much longer. A few more days and you'll be sitting upright all by yourself."

She wheels me into a corridor, my white leg sticking out the front. Suddenly there's a loud commotion from the room beside mine. A man yells, "*Getyermotherfuckinclawsoffmebitch!*" Something smashes to the ground. Alison pushes me past the room quickly. "That's Pat," she says calmly. "He was in a car crash six months ago. Crushed his skull. Has some behavioural issues to work through."

Great. I miss a chunk of my life and move in next to a psychopath.

"Here we go." Alison wheels me into a large room with mirrors and Swiss balls lined along one wall. "Emma, this is Tamara, the physiotherapist on your team."

My team? When did I get a team? What are we training for?

A tiny Indian woman with jet-black hair pulled back into a thick plait strides towards me. "Emma, you can sit up straighter than that, what have we been working on?"

Alison places a hand on my shoulder. "Easy Tamara, she's just come out of her PTA this morning."

Tamara frowns and leans in close to peer at me through bushy eyebrows. She smells of cumin and menthol throat lozenges. "Should mean you'll have better recall on the exercises we've been working on."

Alison's hand on my shoulder disappears. "I'll leave you to it," she says.

I have an overwhelming urge to ask her to stay. Instead I watch her go, like a life raft leaving me behind.

Tamara grabs a tennis ball and puts it in my lap. "Let's see you pick that up with your right hand and hold it out to the side."

My eyes lock on the ball. You'd think it would be easy. A simple task. I tell my fingers to wrap around the ball but they aren't listening. There's a block between me knowing what I want my body to do, and my body understanding how to do it. I begin to sweat. I feel dizzy. *Pick up the stupid ball, Emma.*

I do it in the end. Once. The left hand is slower, harder. I'm exhausted afterwards, but Tamara doesn't seem to notice. She heaves me onto a special chair with high sides and tells me to sit as straight as I can without tipping backwards, forwards, or sideways. She times me, one finger hovering above the stop button on her phone, the other hand poised ready to catch me if I start to fall towards her. I last twenty-eight seconds.

"That's ten seconds better than yesterday, Emma. Well done."

Wahoo, I think. Even if I wanted to say it out loud – which I don't – I doubt I could.

Alison returns a few minutes later and wheels me back to my room. She manoeuvres me into bed and I'm asleep before she leaves the room.

———

I've spent the last forty minutes watching the car park. They should be here by now. I haven't seen Freddie in three weeks. I've missed almost a month of my son's life.

I think I'm going to throw up.

Fumbling for the cord lying next to me, I press the big green button on the end.

In less than ten seconds my nurse, Joey, is by my bed. He introduced himself a short while ago. If I wasn't so fucked in the head – literally – I'd probably be feeling a tad self-conscious and awkward with him. Joey is not your stereotypical nurse. He's goddamned gorgeous, with olive-skin, big brown eyes, and biceps so huge they strain against his T-shirt. Trish would eat the poor guy for breakfast. "What's up?" he says softly. I hate the way he's looking at me: like I'm some three-legged dog living on the street.

I place a hand over my stomach and groan.

He nods slowly. "Could be a side effect of the medication." Instead of leaping to action, he stands there, frowning.

My God the man is slow. Whenever Freddie announced he felt sick, I had approximately three seconds to get a vomit receptacle ready. I glare at his stupid bulging arm muscles.

"Emma, I want you to take a deep breath in for me."

Jesus the man is an idiot; I don't care how good-looking he is. I need a fucking bowl.

He sits on the bed and lifts my hand off my stomach. It's shaking like mad. Why is it shaking?

Joey places my hand on his chest and covers it with one of his warm unshaking ones. I shouldn't be impressed with his giant pectoral pressing against my hand, but a little voice in my damaged head says *whoa*. Suddenly I think of Finn. I need to ask if he's been to see me. If he has been in, it might mean I'm more than just a casual fling. God, why am I thinking about this at all when I'm about to see my son?

The simple act of breathing has never seemed so bloody hard.

"Tell you what, Emma," Joey says, squeezing my hand. "I'm going to take deep breaths and you try to follow. Feel my chest move and see if you can match your breath to mine."

I try to pull my hand away, but he holds it gently against his pale blue T-shirt. "Try it, Emma."

I look into his serious dark eyes and the nausea recedes a fraction. Closing my eyes, I put all my focus on the movement beneath my hand. Once I can feel the rhythm of Joey's breath, I try to slow mine to be in sync with his. Nothing else exists except our breathing, perfectly in time.

Joey releases my hand and places it carefully on my lap. I open my eyes.

"Better?" he asks quietly.

I nod. The nausea has gone.

He gives me an encouraging smile. "Something worrying you, Emma?"

I hesitate. "Ffff."

"Freddie?"

I nod and blink rapidly to stop from crying.

"You must be shitting yourself about seeing him."

I stop blinking. Are medical professionals supposed to talk that way?

"Freddie told me he was four," Joey says. "Do you remember much about being four?"

I shake my head.

"Me neither. I'm pretty confident this will turn out to be a fairly minor episode in his life." Joey winks. "Sorry to disappoint."

If I could talk I'd tell him he's got it wrong. Sure I'm worried about how Freddie is coping without his mum, but

I'm mostly worried about how I'll react when I see him. The last time I felt all emotional like this was when I was pregnant. I hated it then, and I hate it even more now.

Joey assesses me for several long seconds. "Patients tend to feel very fragile after a head injury."

I turn back to the window. I will not cry.

"It's okay," says Joey, "Crying in front of your loved ones is allowed, Emma."

I suck in air like I've been stung by a bee. I've just spied Mum's car circling the car park.

Joey moves to look out the window. He's careful to stand to the side so he doesn't block my view. "Freddie arrived, has he?"

We watch silently as Mum's red car pulls into a park. Dad gets out first. Then Mum in her stupid inappropriate heels. She adjusts her coat tighter around her body then opens the back door and Freddie springs out. He's wearing an over-sized green sweatshirt I don't recognise. Freddie's never owned a green sweatshirt. He doesn't like green. Plus he's had a haircut. It's too short. I never let the barber take off that much because it makes him look older. Freddie starts to run, splashing through some puddles and wetting the bottom of his track pants, then Mum must call out to him, because he stops and jiggles up and down. When Mum catches up to him, he takes her hand and drags her towards the building.

"Looks in a hurry to see you," says Joey.

I try to sit up straighter. Joey grabs a pillow off the puffy chair in the corner and stuffs it behind my back. "Better?" he asks.

I nod.

"I'll come check on you soon. And—" Joey picks up the box of tissues from the table by the window and puts it on my lap. "I expect to see a smorgasbord of blubbering going on. Okay?"

This Joey guy is growing on me. Especially now he's no longer looking at me like I'm an abandoned stray. Instead I get the impression I've somehow earned his respect.

———

It feels like an hour passes before my door slowly opens and Dad pokes his head in. "You've got a special visitor, Emma."

Mum appears next to Dad and gives me a nervous smile that's not really a smile. Her lips are in a smile shape, but there's no crinkle at the corner of her eyes, no brightness in her face. She looks older than I remember.

I try to open my mouth to say hi, only I can't. Not because talking is physically a monumental challenge, but because I can't speak over the lump in my throat.

Mum pushes the door wider and Freddie appears. He's holding onto Mum's trousers with one hand and biting the thumbnail of his other. His head is lowered and he sneaks a quick glance at me before looking down again.

Dad puts a hand on Freddie's back and guides him towards me. I reach for Freddie's hand and slowly bring it to my mouth. With concentration, I kiss the top of his hand, the palm, and each individual finger. The effort it takes is gigantic.

Freddie's eyes widen with recognition, then he launches onto the bed. He crawls onto my lap and clings to me. His body vibrates as he cries. "I didn't think you were going to wake up, Mama."

Tears stream down my face. I hold Freddie as tight as I can, wishing I could fuse him to me. When I look across the room, Mum's crying too. She hasn't moved from her position in the doorway. Her head rests against the frame as she sobs in silence. Dad has one arm around her and the other covers his face.

I wave them closer. Mum straightens up, wipes her face, and wobbles towards us. It's the first time I've seen her unbalanced in those shoes. She perches on the chair beside the bed and pats my arm. Dad sits on the bed and wraps his arms around Freddie and I.

Pulling some tissues from the crumpled box by my hip, I wipe the tears and nose dribble from Freddie's beautiful face. Mum dabs at her eyes. "Look at us," she whispers. "A bunch of blubbering messes."

Movement at the open door catches my eye. Joey stands outside. He smiles and gives a thumbs-up before moving away.

Freddie stops crying and wriggles about to get comfortable. I'm careful not to react as he knocks my cast and presses my still tender ribs. "Grandpa says you were hibernating, Mummy, like a bear. Even when you had your eyes open, your brain was still sleeping."

I nod and stroke his soft hair. "But now you're awake," he states.

Here goes. I have to try. "Yeth," I breathe. It's not much more than a whisper, but Freddie hears it and grins.

A few minutes later, Joey strides in. "Hello Emma, how are we doing?"

Mum has suggested to Freddie that it's time to leave, but he is reluctant to let me go. Or maybe it's the other way around. If only he could stay here curled up with me while I sleep. I'm so tired I can't keep my head up anymore. It's glued to the pillow. And the physical struggle involved in keeping my arms around Freddie is monumental.

"Now then, Freddie." Joey points to the whiteboard.

"Emma has an appointment with her clinical psychologist shortly. You'll need to say goodbye."

My heart begins to pound. I don't want Freddie to go, but I also need him to go before I pass out. I'm starting to shake with the strain of holding him.

"Come on, Freddie," says Dad. "We'll come back and see Mum tomorrow. Maybe you could do some baking this afternoon with Nana? I bet Mum would love some homemade muffins."

Freddie clings to me tighter. There have been some serious changes while my brain has been off duty. Mum baking with Freddie is a new development. She's not well known for her prowess in the kitchen.

"Tell you what." Joey gives Freddie a wink. "If you bring some muffins in tomorrow, and I'm allowed to have one, I'll let you use this." He pulls a permanent marker from his pocket. "You can draw all over your mum's cast."

"Really?" Freddie looks at me.

"Yeth," I say again. It's been the limit of my vocabulary but it's better than nothing.

"I could draw a tree. Or a flower. Or a dog. I've been practising drawing dogs at crèche."

"Maybe you could draw all of those things," says Joey. "There's plenty of room."

Freddie gives me a big kiss on the cheek and hops off the bed. "What flavour muffins do you like, Mr Joey?" he asks.

"Just call me Joey, buddy. Now let me think." He rubs his forefinger and thumb over his chin. "Nope, I can't decide. How about you surprise me?"

Mum gives me a quick kiss on the top of the head and makes for the door.

My eyes close.

"Love you, Emma." Dad kisses me on the cheek.

The old Emma would have hassled him for being too mushy and sentimental. The new Emma can't even open her eyes in reply.

Joey's voice travels to me from across the room. "You've got twenty minutes to rest before your next appointment, Emma."

I soak up the silence and the softness of the pillow under my head, then nothing.

———

"Definitely a hottie." Trish runs her tongue across her teeth and lifts her eyebrows.

I'm sure Joey must have heard her. He hasn't even made it out the door, but thankfully he keeps going. Poor bugger. He looked a bit gun shy when he came in a few minutes ago to clear the whiteboard and draw up my schedule for tomorrow. Trish instantly bombarded him with a gazillion questions, and Lily must have said fuck about a hundred times. Mags kept smiling and nodding like she was on drugs.

"Trust you, Trish," says Mags. "Emma doesn't want to think about hotties right now, do you, Hun?" She's on the end of my bed in an awkward cross-legged position and leans forward to pat my leg.

"How old do you reckon he is?" asks Trish. "Thirty? Forty?"

"Hard to tell," says Lily. "And what's with the goatee?"

I never really got the whole goatee thing, but Joey carries it off extremely well.

"Definitely getting the gay vibe," states Lily. "He is a nurse remember."

Mags whacks Lily on the arm. "That's sexist, or gayest, or whatever it is. Just because he's a nurse."

"Oh, keep your knickers on. The hot ones with well-groomed facial hair are always gay." Lily takes a big sip from her plastic champagne glass and grimaces. "This stuff is disgusting."

"It was the most expensive sparkling grape juice they had," says Trish.

Lily sniffs. "Doesn't exactly encourage someone to give up the booze." She picks up my glass and holds it out. "On that note, want another go?"

I shake my head. I tried drinking from my glass after Trish popped the cork to toast my new state of wakefulness, but the grape juice kept spilling from my mouth. The last thing I want is this lot watching while Lily holds a glass to my lips like a baby. It's bad enough I can't say anything comprehensible. Though if it was real champagne, I might be prepared to waiver my dignity rights. God, I'd love a proper drink. Apparently alcohol is a no-go zone after a brain injury.

"So I brought you this, Em." Trish rummages in her huge leather handbag and pulls out an iPad. She places it on my lap. "I never use it now I've got my new phone. Thought you could borrow it for a bit."

I stare at the iPad, unsure what to think. I've just woken up from three weeks of nothing; the last thing I want to do is look at Instagram and see what amazing things everyone else has been up to. I bet Harriet Galway is churning her own butter by now.

"It's for you to type stuff. Ask questions. Until your speech gets better," says Trish. "Which it will," she adds quickly.

I open a page in Notes and type 'thanks' slowly and with a shaking hand.

Trish bites her lip. "You're welcome," she mumbles.

"Hey, no crying, we all promised," says Mags.

"I'm not crying, there's something in my eye."

Lily laughs. "Alright you guys, let's give up on this fucking awful excuse for a drink and let Emma have a rest." She gives me a wink. "Mags will be anxious to feed her cats."

Mags gasps and puts a hand over her mouth. "They'll be starving." She clambers off my bed, knocking my cast. "Sorry, sorry," she says.

It didn't hurt. Much. My head is worse. A headache has been building all day and I don't think I can hide it much longer.

I delete 'thanks' and type 'bye losers'. They laugh and then Lily and Mags erupt into tears. I was hoping to lighten the mood but instead my friends leave with a tissue in each hand.

I've just closed my eyes when the door opens. With tremendous effort, I lift my heavy eyelids.

"What did you do to that lot?" Joey comes to stand by the bed. "Usually visitors don't—"

Joey stops mid-sentence. "What's wrong?"

My head pounds so painfully I don't have it in me to respond.

"Emma, do you have a headache?"

I shift my head a fraction towards my chest.

He frowns. "I told you to press the green button if you started to develop a headache. You do remember that conversation, don't you?"

Why does he have to sound so annoyed with me? I look up and hope the message in my eyes says something along the lines of 'sorry and bugger off'.

"I'll get you some medicine." Joey strides from the room.

Doesn't he have a home to go to? An adoring wife and cute little children to lavish with attention? Or – if Lily's right – a boyfriend who is waiting to rip off his shirt and run his hands over that ripped – and I'm suspecting hairless – chest. God, I wish Finn was here. Not to talk to. Or have sex with. I'm too tired to contemplate either. I just wish I could curl up and fall asleep with him beside me. But he's not here. It's not as if I was expecting him to be anxiously pacing about outside my door, or sleeping every night in the puffy chair in the corner. Okay, maybe a small part of me was hoping he might. I stare at the whiteboard until my eyes blur over. I've had enough of today and my sad pathetic self.

THIRTEEN

FOUR WEEKS AFTER

Alison strides in. "Morning, Emma. Looks like it's going to be a cracker out there."

I reluctantly stop staring out the window. "Yahoo," I say sarcastically. If I have to listen to another chirpy health professional tell me how lucky I am to have missed the last month of rain, I'll throw something in their face.

Alison ignores me and pulls the exercise book from my drawer.

"Now then." She opens the book, slides it onto my lap, and hands me a pen.

"Let's start with the basics. What is your room number?" Alison asks. She sits in the chair, leans back, and crosses her arms.

I roll my eyes and write *17*. It's messy, but I can tell it's a one and a seven, even if no one else can.

"Good. Now where are you?"

I write *Fairstone Rehabilitation Centre*. It takes me forever, and still looks like a three-year-old wrote it.

"Excellent. Can you tell me what month it is, and the day?"

July. Monday, I write.

"Brilliant work, Emma. Okay, one more."

"Can I ask you a question?" Yes, I managed that whole sentence without slurring or stumbling. Every person I see now says how incredible it is the way my speech is coming along. They have no idea how effortful every word is. How anxious I feel every time I open my mouth.

Alison pauses. "Go for it."

"Do you know what happened? With my accident, I mean." She's silent.

"Dad said people would tell me more when I was feeling better. But no one has." My words are slurred but Alison seems to be the best at understanding me.

"I've suggested several times that you should be told," she murmurs.

"Told what?"

"I'm sorry, Emma. It's not up to me. I'll have another word with your doctors about it."

I sigh. "Thanks for nothing."

Alison stands. "How would you like to go for a walk?"

"Is that meant to cheer me up?" I look from her face, to my cast.

"Well, I'll do the walking obviously. You must be itching to get outside and breath in some fresh air. I know I would be. How about I get the wheelchair and we go for a spin?" Alison is smiling at me encouragingly and I have to work hard to resist the urge to hold up my middle finger and tell her to fuck off. I don't know what's wrong with me. She's been nothing but lovely all week.

"How did you get into this?" I ask.

"What? Occupational therapy?"

I nod.

"I was supposed to become a doctor, or a lawyer – at least that's what my mother had planned," Alison says brightly. "But I wasn't interested." She hesitates and the smile slides from her face like the sun disappearing behind a cloud. "We have a challenging relationship."

"Join the club," I mutter. Mum has only been to visit once this week. She hovered by the window, refusing to meet my eye, let alone get within a foot of my bed. If she hadn't been responsible for bringing in Freddie, I wonder if she would have come in at all.

"Thought we could go check out the vegetable garden," Alison says, in an obvious attempt to steer the conversation back to me going outside.

"What?"

"Well, I can tell you're a bit of a foodie, and there's an impressive row of silverbeet going to seed."

"I've never mentioned food."

"Apart from the rubbish you have to eat in here," states Alison.

It's fair to say I haven't been complimentary of the meals I've been served while taking up unfortunate residence in the Fairstone Rehabilitation Centre. Makes airplane food look positively scrumptious. "I can't be the only one who finds it nausea-inducing."

Alison laughs. "Emma, the only time you show any interest in anything, apart from Freddie, is when there's a cooking show on the TV, or when someone brings you in something interesting to eat. It's not every day I walk into a patient's room to find a bunch of kale in a vase instead of flowers you know."

I look at my kale sitting by the window. Mags brought it

in as a bit of a joke. She claims I'm the only person in the universe who genuinely loves the stuff.

Joey pokes his head in. "You've got a visitor, Emma. It's Paul."

"Can you get rid of him?" I ask quickly. Joey and Alison exchange a glance as Paul steps into view. "Morning, Emma."

I don't want to see Paul. I'm not ready to see Paul. "Hi," I croak.

Alison frowns and leans forward to place a hand on my arm. For a second I think Joey is going to push Paul back out of the room, but it's probably wishful thinking.

Paul moves closer as I shrink into my pillow. "I thought it was important I pop in." He holds up a little wooden frame. Inside is a piece of cream fabric embroidered with *Get well soon*. It's hideous. Something you'd see at a street market or second-hand store that sits gathering dust on a dark corner shelf. "Clara made this for you," says Paul proudly.

"Of course she did," I mutter.

Paul's nostrils flare. I notice the exercise book I'm holding is wobbling and slap it down on my lap.

Alison stands abruptly, blocks Paul from getting closer, and holds out her hand. "I'm Alison, Emma's Occupational Therapist and lead carer."

When Paul shakes Alison's hand the flabby rolls beneath his chin wobble.

"Paul. Ex-husband." He gives me a fake smile. "Recently separated."

Alison looks at me and I try to ask her with my eyes if she could whisk me a million miles away from this room. Joey marches over and stands beside my hip. "Paul, this isn't a good time I'm afraid. I was about to take Emma to an appointment with the physio." He points to the whiteboard.

"Oh, right. Well, another time." Paul looks around the room and eventually walks to the windowsill to prop up his repulsive so-called gift. At the end of my bed, he pauses. His body casts a giant shadow across me. "I wanted to discuss Freddie, but it can wait."

I nod.

"He's very happy staying with us now," Paul continues. "He's slept over several times. Clara is very good with him."

What is the man trying to do? Destroy any semblance of self-belief I have left?

"Great," I murmur.

"Bye, Emma."

I listen to him leave, my eyes riveted to the messy words I've written in my stupid child-like exercise book.

Picking up the pen, I run black ink back and forth across the words until they're obliterated. I'm never going to be the Emma I was before the accident. The doctors keep saying, as part of my recovery, I need to accept she's gone. I'm supposed to get to grips with the new Emma I have become.

I miss the old Emma. I knew the old Emma.

This Emma who slurs her words and forgets how to brush her teeth scares me. I don't understand this new version of me who cries for no reason, and who can't multiply seven by eight anymore. I don't want anything to do with this inferior, damaged Emma.

I want to go back. I want to be playing trains with Freddie, or baking brownies, or drinking wine with my friends.

"Emma, we've talked about this." Joey picks up the exercise book and shoves it in the drawer. "You have to stay positive."

I roll my eyes. Joey says depression is a major concern after a brain injury. Any sign of me getting down on myself has him shoving another pamphlet in my face.

"Right." Alison grabs the wheelchair from the corner of my room. "Let's get out of here."

"I don't want to go and look at silverbeet."

"Fine. We'll just walk to the end of the drive and I'll tell you about my current obsession with finding the perfect taco."

"Great idea," Joey says, hoisting me into the wheelchair before I can think of a way to get rid of them. He kneels in front of me and waits till I meet his eye. "Keep going, Emma. Just keep going forward, even if it's tiny fucking steps."

I close my eyes.

"For Freddie," he whispers.

He's got me there and he knows it. I open my eyes, swallow over the lump in my throat, and fix him with an evil glare.

"At-a-girl," he says, winking and stepping out of the way. "She's all yours Allie."

Alison pushes me towards the door. "I must have tried twenty different places in the past month," she says, pushing me down the corridor. "So far the front runner is the fish taco from Loco Moco."

I clasp my hands on my lap and stare at my cast. "I'll have to try it one day," I mutter. The old Emma made pretty epic pulled pork tacos, according to everyone who ever tasted them. Finn went totally crazy the time I cooked them for him. Said he'd died and gone to heaven. It's been a week and he hasn't been to see me. I want to ask if he's been to visit while I was asleep, but for some reason I'm afraid to bring up his name. More than that, I'm afraid of the answer.

As Alison propels me towards the main doors, I have a sense of dread so overwhelming my vision goes black. I don't want to go outside. I don't want to go anywhere. I'm not even sure I want to exist.

———

"Okay so I slept with fucking Darryl a couple of weeks ago," says Lily. She's kicked off her work shoes and is reclining in the hideous puffy armchair with her feet on my bed. Her thick black stockings have a huge ladder in them from her toe to her thigh.

"You didn't!" I stuff another piece of dark chocolate filled with peppermint crème in my mouth.

She nods.

"Isn't he your boss?" I ask. It comes out sounding like 'both' instead of boss, and I wince.

Lily gives me a funny look. "Yeah. He is."

I feel like I've met Darryl, but I can't be sure. I know I've seen photos of him. "How was it?"

Lily grimaces and leans forward to grab a handful of pretzels from the packet on the bed. "Not what I was expecting."

"Oh dear."

"He's one of those guys who moans all the time. The second I touched his dick he was like 'ah Lily, ah, oh, oh'." Lily's demonstration is loud and with feeling. Pretzel crumbs shoot from her mouth. "It made me feel like I had to make noises too. Seriously, we sounded like a couple of fucking gorillas."

I'm laughing so hard chocolate dribbles out of my mouth. My black mood has lifted a little after going for a walk with Alison. It was good to get out of my musty room. Plus Alison talked about tacos for a full twenty minutes. Any conversation involving food tends to cheer me up.

"What are you going to do now?" I ask, still laughing.

"What do you mean?"

"Is it awkward at work? Are you trying to avoid him?"

146

Lily looks confused. "I'm going round to his place later tonight to have hot sex in his spa pool."

Of course, Dad chooses that moment to walk in the door. With Dr Terrance and Joey. They all must have heard Lily's last statement. Joey's trying so hard not to laugh I'm sure he's going to burst a blood vessel. I'm mortified, but Lily doesn't even stop talking. "It's got easier, the whole moaning thing. I reckon I'm getting more natural at it." Lily glances at the three men standing at the foot of my bed. "Oh hey, Eric. Want a pretzel?"

Dad raises his eyebrows, his cheeks red. "Not right now. Thanks, Lily." He looks at me. "Emma, you remember Dr Terrance?"

Of course I know Dr Terrance, I saw him yesterday. He's my neurologist, who is obsessed with showing me the same picture cards over and over again and making me touch my nose. I don't dislike him, but I don't like him either. "Yes, Dad. I do."

Dad nods, and keeps on nodding like one of those little squat dolls with the bobbing heads that sit on people's desks. Seeing him so anxious is making me nervous. Why are they here? I thought Dad had left for the evening. He stopped in earlier to give me a couple of cookbooks he got out of the library, and when he put them on my lap, I swear he was seconds away from bursting into tears. I'm seriously worried about my father. What happened to the laid-back, keep-your-emotions-in-check Dad I knew so well?

Lily recognises it's probably not the best time to go on talking about her sex life. She sits up and clears the food she brought in off the bed. "I'll head off," she says.

"I'd like you to stay for this, Lily," says Dad quickly, "If you don't mind."

Lily widens her eyes, looks at me, then back to Dad. "Are you sure?" she asks.

Now I'm really freaking out. "What's going on?" I look at Joey and he meets my eye for a second before looking away. My scalp starts to prickle.

"Emma," announces Mr Terrance. "As we've discussed, you have no memory of your accident or the hours leading up to it, as well as the days afterwards." He's talking more to Dad than to me. "Post Traumatic Amnesia, or PTA, is common with a serious brain injury such as you experienced."

"I can remember Jack's funeral," I say, "but that's it." I'm not entirely telling the truth, but close enough.

"It's quite likely you won't recover that part of your memory," states Mr Terrance. "Brains are very clever things. They can act as safety nets, protecting you from traumatic recall."

I've decided I don't like Dr Terrance now. His eyes are too close together. And he has off-putting grey horsehair eyebrows. Aside from that, he's a sexist pig. We've discussed his type several times over a glass or two at Morellis. Trish would agree the signs are all there:

1. Over sixty years old. Check.
2. Makes eye contact with males in the room only. Check.
3. Pretends to be interested in what you have to say, while not listening. Check.
4. Interrupts you and carries on talking to the males as if they're more important. Check.

"Actually, I do remember something else." Bugger him

and his sexist doctoring ways. "I phoned Finn when I got home from the funeral. I met him at the pub for a drink."

Dad looks like I've punched him in the guts. What's going on?

"We are here to discuss the accident, Emma." Dr Terrance gives me a condescending smile. "Your family thought it best I help explain what happened."

Lily leans over and takes my hand. I'm surprised how pale and serious she is. "Emma, you can't blame yourself for this. It was an accident."

Blame myself? What have I done? I've been asking all week for more details about the accident and none have been forthcoming.

Dad comes to sit on the bed and takes my other hand. This isn't good.

"Emma." He looks at me with sad old man eyes. "After Jack's funeral you met up with Finn and had a few drinks. We don't know exactly where you went, but you ended up at Burger Heaven together around ten that night."

"Burger Heaven?" I frown. "Are you sure?" That place has the greasiest, least-appealing burgers on the planet.

Dad takes a deep breath. "The manager said he asked you both to leave as you were throwing food and being... disruptive."

I grimace. "I must have been drunk." I smile at Lily, but she doesn't smile back.

"For some reason, when you left Burger Heaven, you decided to... to—" Dad clears his throat. "Emma, you know those large metal recycling bins that are used for cardboard? There's one outside the supermarket."

I nod slowly. "Yes." Where on earth is this going?

"You and Finn decided to hop in one and ride it down a... a steep street."

"Oh." I bite the inside of my cheek to stop from smiling. "What a couple of idiots."

Everyone is silent. Dad looks down and pats my hand. "Yes," he murmurs.

"So we crashed into something and I hit my head and broke some bones. How's Finn?"

Dad looks up. "Emma, Finn was hurt too."

"Is he okay now?"

He hesitates.

I get the creepy pins and needles thing again. Like I did when I went to the hospital to check on Jack. "He's not... he can't..."

Lily squeezes my hand. "Em, he's not dead."

I let out my breath. "Thank God. You had me—"

"Emma," Dr Terrance interrupts. "Finn received extensive injuries to his spine, and he is currently unable to walk. He also sustained a punctured lung, deep lacerations to the legs, and severe concussion."

My eyes blur. "Oh God."

"There's one other thing we discovered while you were in ICU." Dr Terrance sounds annoyed now, like he'd rather not be having this conversation.

Lily clears her throat and glares at the doctor. Then she leans in close and places a warm hand on my cheek. "Emma, sweetie." I can smell pretzels on her breath. "You're pregnant," she whispers.

I look at Dad. Tears pool in his eyes. He tries to smile but fails.

"Pregnant?" I whisper.

Dr Terrance reaches for the clipboard hanging on the end of my bed and puffs up his self-important chest. He probably wants to go home and have his wife pour him a whisky and tell him how wise he is. "Luckily you haven't experienced any seizures," he states. "They're quite common after a brain injury and can require intensive drug therapy. We've been able to limit the foetus's exposure to medication." He nods at the clipboard in confirmation.

I stare at Lily, my mind screaming. *But I was on the pill*, I want to say, *how could...* then I recall the weekend Freddie and I had that vomiting bug. Ever since I was an eighteen-year-old nervously asking my doctor to prescribe me the pill, I've been careful: if I vomited or took antibiotics, I took extra precautions. But I didn't think I'd be seeing Finn again, or having sex for that matter. I thought there was no way...

"Pregnant?" I say again.

Lily opens her mouth to speak, then closes it and nods.

———

It's nearly nine o'clock but I haven't shut the curtains yet. I like looking out at the black night knowing I've made it to the end of another day. I'm tired, and my headache is getting worse, but I don't want to sleep. I can't sleep.

Instead I stare at my iPad. I'm catching up on Harriet Galway's blog and Instagram posts. Over the past few days she's been busy picking the apples and pears from her little orchard, and learning to crochet blankets for her precious little cherubs. I, on the other hand, have been re-learning how to tie shoelaces. I also have a large, hard poo stuck in my bowel, which – since I'm pregnant and there are only certain drugs it's safe to take – is proving a challenge to eliminate. What an exciting blog post that would be.

Joey startles me by suddenly appearing by my side. I didn't even hear the door open. "You should try to get some sleep," he murmurs.

"I will."

"Emma?"

I look up.

"I'm sorry. About the accident. We all do stupid, reckless things at least once in our lives. Most of the time we get away with it."

I'm trying not to think about Finn. Since the others left, I've been numb.

"I didn't."

"Didn't what?"

I place a hand on my stomach. "Get away with it."

"It's not my business, but is Finn the father?"

"Yes."

"Had you been trying to start a family together?"

I give a short, bitter laugh. "We barely knew each other."

"Oh."

I glare at my iPad.

Joey is silent. Why doesn't he just go already? Surely his shift has finished by now.

"You have a strong network of family and friends, Emma. You aren't alone."

"I know," I snap, still unable to look up.

He fills my water glass. "I'm off home. Jenny will be caring for you during the night."

Nodding, I wait for Joey to walk out and shut the door. Then I stare at the screen of my iPad without seeing it. Because of me, Finn is in hospital, unable to walk. I wonder if anyone has been to see him. I should have asked Dad. Surely no one would have told Finn I was pregnant, would they? At least now I know why Finn hasn't been to visit, or tried calling. It had to have been me who suggested we do something as stupid as climbing in that bin. Finn must hate me right now. The thought is so painful, it takes my breath away.

FOURTEEN

FIVE WEEKS AFTER

"What did you have for breakfast this morning?" asks Alison.

I roll my eyes. "Dry white toast, cornflakes, and canned peaches. A gourmet treat."

Alison looks pointedly at my pen, and I write it down.

I know what the next question will be. It's been the same one for the past three sessions. I begin to write down *chicken* when Alison laughs. "Actually, I was going to ask something other than what delicious meal you had last night."

I look up. "You're not interested in the flabby white chicken breast floating in a heavily-salted packet gravy, with a mound of grey beans on the side I forced myself to eat?"

Alison cringes. "Disgusting. Actually, I have good news on that front."

"The head chef has resigned?"

"No. But I am allowed to take you out for lunch."

I frown. "Sorry?"

"Doctors say you can venture out into the real world. I thought you might like to go visit Freddie at your parents' place. Maybe stay for lunch? It's time to start doing that sort of thing."

"I would love to." Oh no, I think I'm going to cry. What is wrong with me? Any little thing will set me off. At least now I know it's not just the brain injury that's upset my emotional state. There's also a cluster of cells in my uterus I can blame. I clear my throat. "Thanks."

"So my question to you, Emma, is this... what food are you craving more than anything? And please make it something we could stop and buy on the way to your parents' house," she adds in a rush.

I hold the pen to my lips. This is a difficult question to answer. I have spent a ridiculous amount of time daydreaming about food over the past week. "I would give anything to eat slow-cooked beef cheek on carrot puree with a prune and port sauce—"

"Well shit, so would I," Alison says shaking her head. "Where can you buy that?"

I shrug. "I'd have to make it," I murmur. "Which isn't happening, so my answer is—"

I write three words in my exercise book and hold it up.

"Bread and butter," Alison reads. "Seriously?"

I nod. "Fresh potato sourdough from the bakery on the corner of Ferry St, and proper organic butter from the deli next door. That is my wish."

"Okay then." Alison stands. "Today, Emma, I will make your wish come true."

Already today is a thousand times better than the weekend just gone. Apart from a visit from Dad and Freddie on Saturday, and a short chat with Lily on Sunday, I spent most of the time sitting in a poorly-lit lounge playing Connect Four with my psychotic neighbour, Pat. He only called me a bitch twice and told me to suck his dick once, so there are definite signs of improvement. Underneath all that sexual aggression and name-calling he's a nice guy – at least that's what his wife tells me. She visits him every day and takes his constant verbal abuse with amazing grace. That's true love right there.

"I'll phone your father and organise the visit," says Alison. "Then I'll sort out some paperwork and see my other patients. All being well, I'll come and get you around eleven thirty, okay?"

"Okay."

Alison races over to the whiteboard and changes my timetable for the day to include 'home visit for lunch'. All the staff here are fans of that whiteboard; apparently writing down a daily schedule is the best way to keep a patient progressing on track. At the door, she turns to face me. "I think that's the first smile I've seen out of you all week, Emma. It's a pleasant change."

"There hasn't been a lot to smile about," I grumble.

"Well, as part of my job, I'll have to figure out a way to make you smile more often. I like a good challenge." She gives me a wink.

I roll my eyes. "Good luck."

Alison clutches at her chest and staggers from the room.

I bite my lip to stop from laughing.

If it wasn't for her and Joey, I think I'd be curled in a ball in the corner, banging my head against the wall. There I go again. I think I've taken self-pity to a whole new level of awful this week. If only I could find a way to snap out of it.

———

"All set?" says Alison.

"Yep."

She steps to one side and Joey pushes a wheelchair towards me.

"Can't I use crutches or something?" I say.

Joey raises his eyebrows. "I'd like to see you try. You can't balance on one leg yet."

"Yes I can. I managed ten seconds this morning."

"Fantastic!" Joey looks genuinely ecstatic for a millisecond, then super serious. "Now sit."

Sighing dramatically, I heave myself out of my bed, grip the edges of the wheelchair and manoeuvre into place. Joey and Alison watch without assisting. They are both regularly adding to a list we started in my notebook of all the everyday things I need to relearn and become confident in performing. Getting dressed without help is one of them. As is being independently mobile – their speak, not mine.

After I receive a short, encouraging pep talk from Joey, Alison pushes me out of the building and parks my wheelchair next to a white station wagon. She opens the passenger door. "I've put the seat as far back as it goes. Hopefully we can squeeze you in."

"I could always stick my leg out the window."

"And if that doesn't work I could strap your chair to the roof with you in it."

"Ha, ha." I'm doing my best not to smile.

Alison grins. "Worth a try."

After a small amount of cursing – mostly from Alison when I accidently kick her in the head – I make it into the seat, my cast wedged beneath the glove box. Alison folds down the wheelchair and slides it into her boot. Then she gets into the driver's seat and revs the engine. "Ready?"

I nod. "Let's get out of here."

Alison shoves a folded white paper bag onto my lap. "You might need this."

"What for?"

She accelerates down the driveway. "Motion sickness is a bitch after a brain injury."

My stomach flips inside out as we swing around a corner. Groaning, I unfold the bag and open it up. "Thanks for the heads-up."

While I get close to chucking up my breakfast – there is serious acid mouth and overzealous saliva production – I manage to keep my stomach contents in check as far as Ferry St, where Alison leaves her car idling and dashes in to buy the bread and butter of my dreams.

The drive to Mum and Dad's is less nausea-inducing, especially with the delicious aroma of fresh sourdough in the car. I'm even able to engage in limited conversation.

"When do you think I'll be able to drive again?" I ask.

"Usually there's a six month stand-down period after a brain injury like yours."

"Six months!"

"Afraid so. Then you'll sit a driving test with an OT trained to assess driving skills."

"So not you then?"

"No. Not me. And before you ask, I have no influence over their decision."

I laugh and Alison smiles, though her eyes don't leave the road.

"Assuming you pass the test, the OT will recommend to your GP that you have your driver's license reinstated."

"So much to look forward to," I murmur.

Alison clears her throat and taps her finger on the driving wheel. "Can I ask you something personal?" she says lightly.

I'm guessing this is about my pregnancy. I have stead-fastly refused to talk about it, even though everyone keeps asking me how I feel. Even Lily, who I can normally rely on to see from my expression when a topic is not up for discussion, keeps pestering me. I don't want to talk. I don't want to think. I especially don't want to tell anyone that I spend nearly all night awake picturing Finn lying in some hospital bed unable to walk. Is he improving? Is there a chance he'll walk again? Does he think about me? Does he miss me as much as I miss him? What will happen when he finds out he's going to be a father? Will he wish he'd never laid eyes on me? Of course he will. He's probably cursing the day we met. Thoughts swirl round and round my head for so long I end up turning on the iPad Trish loaned me and playing solitaire till the sky grows light.

Alison must take my silence as consent and continues. "Are you glad you're pregnant?"

I'm silent. It's the one question I know I should have an answer for, but don't.

I shrug. "Still getting used to the idea."

"How does the father feel?"

"I don't know."

"So you haven't seen him since the accident?"

I shake my head.

"Would you like to?"

Biting my lower lip, I nod. "Yes," I whisper. It's not until the word is out that I realise how much I do want to see Finn. I need to see if he's okay. If he hates me or… or not. I can't imagine how he will react when he finds out I'm pregnant with his child. I don't want to imagine in case…

We turn onto my parents' street and all thoughts of Finn fly from my head. I'm instantly nervous at the thought of seeing Mum, Dad, and Freddie. Mum especially. "Will you stay?" I ask. "For lunch?"

"Yes. I always stick around for the first visit. After that, you're on your own."

I try to return her smile, but I can't.

We pull into Dad's driveway and I stare at the front door. Alison turns off the engine and shuffles around in her seat to face me. "Emma, home visits are an important part of the recovery process, but they can be difficult."

"In what way?"

She opens her door. "Everyone has to make adjustments. It's challenging."

"That's hardly the most inspiring pep-talk."

"We can leave as soon as you want to, Emma. Just give me the word."

"Alison?" I put my hand on her arm to stop her climbing out. "Thank you. What you've done for me – it makes a difference."

"Thanks," she says softly. "Now let's go see your little boy."

———

"Where's Mum?" I stroke Freddie's back as he jiggles in the seat beside me. My cheeks are still flushed from the embarrassment of trying to manoeuvre a wheelchair through the house. For a while there, I didn't think Alison would be able to pull me up the front steps. It was all the more mortifying having my son and father watch.

Dad places a plate of rotisserie chicken on the table next to the salad. "Sorry, love. She'd already arranged to have lunch with some friends from her book club. She felt it was too late to pull out."

"Oh." I watch Alison slice the bread. We should probably add that one to the notebook. I can't imagine what kind of mess I would make trying to use a bread knife.

"She sends her love," Dad adds with false enthusiasm.

I can't decide if I'm relieved or disappointed. I'm used to Mum getting in a complete flap during a crisis, but she's been strangely absent. Every day I expect her to turn up at rehab and be all over me like a hysterical rash, but she only brought Freddie in once last week and barely said a word. Every other day it's been Dad bringing Freddie to visit. I'm relieved Mum is the one person who has made no attempt to bring up my pregnancy, but I'm also surprised. "Is she avoiding me?" I ask.

"What? No. Of course not." Dad sits opposite me. "It's so great to hear you talking like this, Emmie. There's hardly any difficulties with your words at all now."

"She's working hard on her recovery," Alison says, sitting next to Dad.

God this is awful. I feel like I'm on display. Any wrong move and I'll have lost the game. Also, I'm slightly appalled Dad has reverted to calling me Emmie again. He hasn't called me that since I was about ten years old. Not quite the vote of confidence I was after.

"Mama can I draw another dog on your plaster?" Freddie asks.

"Sure. After lunch." My voice slurs on the word 'sure'. My speech is always worse when I'm anxious.

"Well, Emma." Alison holds out the wooden board of neatly sliced sourdough. "How about some bread? I hear it's very good."

"Thanks." I take a slice and squeeze it lightly before nibbling a crusty edge. Blinking away the tears that threaten yet again for no obvious reason, I ask Freddie to pass me the butter.

He slides it over the table and I stare at the slab of butter on the dish. What am I supposed to do next? I've got the bread and the butter but how am I supposed to get them together?

Alison coughs. "Let's have a day off working on your knife skills, Emma." She picks up her knife. "How about I butter your bread?"

I feel my cheeks grow hot yet again and glance at Dad. He switches from looking completely miserable, to smiling. "So great to have you here, Emmie," he says again.

"Thanks, Dad," I murmur.

Freddie picks up a piece of bread and holds it out to Alison. "Can you butter mine, too?"

"Please," I remind him.

"Please," says Freddie, producing the only genuine smile in the room.

FIFTEEN

SIX WEEKS AFTER

"Well done, Emma." Joey holds my elbow while I sink onto my bed, exhausted in every fibre of my being.

I screw my face up. "I got lost three times," I mutter.

We've returned from an arduous 'path-finding session' as Joey calls it. Now that my cast is off, we're on a mission to get me moving, even if it is at a snail's pace, wearing a clumpy moonboot and leaning heavily on crutches. I had to find my way from my room, to the dining room, to the gym, and back to my room. Sounds easy, but I kept losing track of where I was, why I was there, and where I needed to go. My mind would go blank like a large sheet of white paper and Joey would have to prompt me to get my brain functioning again.

"A week ago you'd have got confused trying to find your bathroom," says Joey. "Give yourself some credit. It's important to recognise the huge achievements you've made so far."

Some days his positive attitude is really annoying. Especially when my throbbing leg is reminding me how far I still have to go.

With the last sliver of strength I can muster, I shuffle back and rest against my pillow. Joey lifts my legs onto the bed and removes my moonboot. When his fingers brush against my skin, an image of Finn flies into my head and I get an ache behind the ribs.

"You okay?" Joey asks, putting my moonboot beside my bed.

"Yeah. I guess."

"You don't sound all that convincing."

I stare out the window. Funnily enough, I can talk to Joey better than anyone at the moment. He makes me feel like it's okay to be vulnerable. "I never thought I'd end up a solo mother," I murmur. "I guess no one does."

Joey perches on the edge of the bed. "I grew up without a Dad. He and Mum got divorced when I was two and he moved to Australia and started a new family."

"I'm sorry."

"Don't be." Joey shrugs. "Anyway, when I was a kid, I loved soccer. It was all I did at lunchtimes, and after school I'd beg Mum to take me down to the local soccer fields so I could practise. My sister would complain about it but Mum ignored her tantrums and would drive us down there every single day." Joey shakes his head, smiling. "Mum was a demon on defence. She made it pretty tough for me to get past her. We'd take turns playing one-on-one with my sister as goalie."

"That was nice of her," I say quietly.

"Yeah. It was. At the games it was always Mum on the sideline surrounded by a gaggle of dads yelling advice from the sideline. I was so jealous of the other boys, and embarrassed by Mum."

"This isn't exactly making me feel better," I say.

Joey stands. "When I look back on it now, I realise how tough it must have been on Mum, but she did it because she loved me and needed to step up and be a mother *and* a father."

I wince. "Still not filling me with warm fuzzies."

Laughing, Joey strokes his goatee. "Far be it from me to gloat, Emma, but I was the best player on the team. The dads may have liked to make a big song and dance about watching the games and calling out unhelpful comments, but Mum was the only parent taking time to drive me to the field and practise with me. She was a better Dad than the rest of that lot combined."

I take a few moments to process Joey's story. "I bet she was secretly gloating herself on the sideline."

Joey nods. "Sure was."

"Thanks," I whisper. "Good pep talk."

"Anytime."

Someone clears their throat loudly. I look towards my open bedroom door and Trish gives me a small wave. "Hey, is this a good time?"

"Absolutely." Joey gives me a quick smile. "See you this afternoon."

Trish steps out of the way as he leaves, then comes to sit in the small chair beside me. "He seems attentive," she says with raised eyebrows.

I ignore her comment. "How did it go?" Last night Trish rang and said she had an appointment with Paul's lawyer today. She'd promised to come and fill me in afterwards.

"Usual stuck-up wanker," she says. "I can see why Paul picked him."

"What about the child support stuff?"

"Oh, I knew he didn't have a leg to stand on. It was stupid to even try the 'self-employed, not taking a wage from the company' angle. The lawyer was fairly quick to back down once I pointed out the facts. Your child support will be backdated to the day Paul moved out."

"Really?" I relax my shoulders. "Thanks Trish. You're awesome."

"I am actually, because I have more good news." She leans forward and takes my hand. "I've been talking to Jack's lawyer too."

My heart gives a painful thump. "Jack?"

Trish nods. "He left his half of the business to you. You're the sole owner now."

"What?"

"The lease is paid-up until the end of next year too. No pressure, Em, but once you're well enough, you could get the café up and running. I'm sure Ben would help with the grocery part, and you could get someone else in too."

"No," I say quickly. "That's the last thing I want to do."

Trish frowns. "I thought you'd be pleased," she murmurs.

"Sorry. It's just… I'm not the Emma I was before the accident, Trish. I don't have some great dream to open my own café anymore. I don't even want to go near a kitchen."

Trish studies me for a few seconds. "Okay, so would you like me to look into selling the business?"

"Yes," I nod. "Please. If you could, that would be great."

Trish leans forward to give me a hug. "You feeling okay?" she whispers.

I know she's referring to my pregnancy. "Not too bad."

She sits back. "Have you thought about… what you're going to do?"

I shake my head and my brain knocks against my skull making me woozy. "I'm still trying to get through each day."

"Fair enough. I'm here for you, Em. We all are."

"I know."

"Is there anything I can do?"

I want to ask Trish about Finn. Has anyone seen him? How is he doing? But at the same time, I don't want to mention him. No one has brought up his name. It's like we're all scared to go there, me most of all. "I'm fine, thanks, Trish."

"Well." Trish stands. "I'd better get back to work. I'll let you know how I get on with the business."

After she leaves, I lie on my side and watch cars enter and exit the car park. I've let Jack down. Getting drunk after his funeral and having that accident – it was irresponsible and disrespectful. "I'm sorry," I whisper. "I'll do better, Jack. I promise."

I wish I could see Finn, hear his voice, feel his body pressed up against mine. I keep reminding myself we hardly knew each other, that whatever went on between us was probably a rebound thing for me, and a bit of fun for him. But I'm pregnant with his baby. And I miss him. Desperately.

Closing my eyes, I wait for Tamara to arrive and drag me to the gym for my physio session. Somehow I have to keep going. I can't give up. I need to carry on, for Jack, and Finn, and Freddie. And for myself.

————

Everyone is here to see me off. They line up before me; soldiers about to be relieved of their duties.

"Keep up with your exercises," Tamara commands. I can tell she wants me to hurry up and go so she can get on with tormenting her patients. "Remember: the more repetition, the faster you'll lay down neural pathways."

"And don't expect miracles. Be grateful for small victories," says Francis, my clinical psychologist. She's about a hundred years old, with an extremely off-putting moustache, and completely lacks any sense of humour. I've had daily sessions with her from day one, and I'm confident she understands me less now than when I came in. She presses me to 'talk about my feelings' and is convinced at the end of every session we're 'on the verge of a breakthrough'. No doubt she's disappointed that we never did break through.

"Your brain needs to rest to heal," says Alison.

Joey nods, while maintaining a firm grip on Pat, my psycho neighbour for the past two months. Pat scratches his balls and says something along the lines of '*Gofuckyourself*'. He's grown on me, though his verbal abuse keeps me from getting too close. Plus he has a rather alarming exhibitionist streak. He's shown me his erect penis four times, and sadly has a way to go till he can function in the outside world. But he's a legend at Connect Four.

Dad can sense I'm keen to escape. He picks up my duffle bag and hoists it onto his shoulder. "Ready?"

I nod and bite my lip. They're watching me, smiling, waiting. Except for Pat, who is still scratching his privates and looks increasingly confused.

"Thanks so much for everything," I say dutifully.

Alison gives me a quick hug as I move towards the door. "Good luck," she whispers. Then Joey lets go of Pat, reaches for my hand, and pulls me into a hug too. "Take care, Emma," he says before letting me go and lunging at Pat who is attempting to pull down his pants.

I head down the now-familiar corridor: past the nurses' station; the bathroom; Room 15, which smells of fish and contains a woman who had a stroke at the age of fifty, and as far as I can tell hasn't moved a muscle; past room 14, with the guy who was in a car crash and has to be in restraints; past the gym where I have spent all week kicking a soccer ball around small orange cones, and through the door marked 'EXIT'.

I exit.

"Need a hand?" Dad asks as I stop at the top of the four steps I must conquer before I can get to the car park.

"Nah." I shuffle to the left, put my hand on the rail, and tell my legs what to do. The muscles are slow to respond, but after a few seconds I place my right foot on the first step and bring my left foot down to meet it. We negotiate the next three steps in a similar fashion and, without looking at Dad, I walk at as fast a pace as I can manage towards his car.

———

Twenty-five minutes later, we pull into the driveway of my parents' house. It's not the home I grew up in – that house was sold when Freddie was born so they could move closer to me. Dad said it was time to move into a smaller place anyway, but we both know the real reason. Mum wanted to be more involved – to come over and help me with Freddie – especially when it came to giving me advice or telling me how other mothers did things. Neither Paul nor I were all that encouraging and Mum eventually got the message and visited less and less.

There's nothing wrong with Mum and Dad's current house. It's nice, in a comfortable, no frills kind of way, but I still miss our old place; the one with the sloping kitchen floor and the giant basement full of Dad's tools and bits of wood he'd collected over the years. Dad got rid of all of the wood when they moved and his tools have been reduced to a single shelf in the tiny garage.

"I still can't believe no one told me about my apartment until yesterday." Turns out a week after my accident Mum and Dad decided to give notice to my landlord and move all my stuff into storage.

Dad sighs and turns off the engine. "I'm sorry Emma. I should have told you earlier, but we... at the time... we just didn't know how long you would be..." He trails off.

"It's okay," I mumble. Not that it is okay. I'm annoyed but I'm also conscious Dad looks very close to tears. "The rent was pretty steep and there was no way of knowing when I'd be able to move back in. I can start looking for a new place tomorrow."

"You know one of the conditions of your leaving rehab was that you live with us for a while. Going straight into being on your own again with Freddie, it's too much. Your mother insists you ease into things."

I wrinkle my nose.

He sighs and stares out the windscreen. "And me."

"I won't last a day without upsetting Mum."

Dad looks at me. "Give her a chance. She's worked hard to make sure you'll be comfortable here."

The front door opens and Freddie runs out. "Mama," he yells.

I reach for the door handle.

"Emma?" Dad places a hand on my leg. "Don't push yourself too much, okay?"

I meet his eye. "'K," I whisper.

As soon as I'm out of the car, Freddie takes my hand and drags me inside. "Come see your room. Nana and me got it ready."

I frown. "I thought I'd be sharing with you, Fredster?"

"Mama says you need your own space so you can rest your brains," states Freddie.

He pulls me through the lounge. The couch has been pushed closer to the TV, and the mahogany dining table –

handed down through the generations – is now wedged into the corner by the window.

The second Freddie opens the double glass doors into the dining room, I can see why.

"Tada," he announces with a huge smile.

"Wow. What a…" I want to say a particular word but I can't quite reach it in my brain. It's like trying to get something off a high shelf. I can get a finger to it, but can't manage to take a proper hold. "What a change," I gush. "It looks just like a bedroom now." Apart from the fact that Mum's best china still fills the cabinet on the wall, and my makeshift wardrobe is a piece of sagging rope with a few coat hangers gathered in the middle. The single bed is quite possibly the same one I slept in as a kid.

Transformation. That was the word I was trying to say. What a transformation.

"I made the curtains over the glass doors using block-out fabric." Mum stands behind me drying her hands on a tea towel. She's wearing purple slippers over her stockinged feet; old lady slippers. I wonder when she started wearing those?

"It's great, Mum. Thanks." I try to inject some enthusiasm in my voice. "You didn't need to. I would have shared with Freddie." Truth is, I was looking forward to having Freddie sleep in the same room as me. I've been awake a lot in the night. It would have been nice to have some company.

"I thought you'd want your own room." Mum's lower lip shakes.

Shit. I've gone and upset her already.

"I do. It's really nice, Mum."

Dad puts an arm around Mum. "Something smells delicious," he says.

Mum gives him a distracted smile. "I made bacon and egg pie."

"Mama's favourite," says Freddie.

It used to be my favourite. When I was Freddie's age. Over the years I've developed a strong aversion to Mum's signature dish. I've eaten a lot of bacon and egg pie in my life. "Yum." I clutch my stomach. "I haven't had a decent meal in weeks."

Mum's smile is fragile. "You're probably sick of my pie."

"No way." My head is beginning to pound. I glance at my bed and wonder how many hours I need to get through before I can collapse. "I've missed your pie, Mum. Reckon I'll want a double helping."

Freddie bounds towards the kitchen. "Me too," he yells.

I follow Mum, stumbling as the carpet transitions to wood in the hallway. Dad's hand grasps my elbow. As soon as I've regained my balance, he lets go and we both pretend my moment of weakness didn't happen.

I sit down at the kitchen table next to Freddie, a smile plastered on my face. I feel it drain away when I spy a large whiteboard on the wall behind the door. "What's that?" I ask.

Dad sits opposite. "It's for you. To keep track of things." He busies himself with spreading his napkin on his lap.

"Oh." I follow his lead, spreading out my napkin slowly and with great dedication. "Thanks," I say, without looking up.

———

"I won!" Freddie's grin is wide and innocent. "That's four times in a row, Mama."

"Is it?"

"Yep."

We've been playing this stupid memory card game I received as a leaving gift from the rehab centre for the past hour. I thought Freddie would be sick of it by now, but he loves it. How he can remember the dog is on the card third row down, two across when I turned it over ten moves ago is a complete mystery to me.

"I better give up now before you make it five."

Dad's newspaper rustles as he folds it up and puts it on the small table beside his armchair. "Come on, Freddie, time to get ready for bed."

Freddie looks at me. "Can we play one more?" His legs haven't stopped banging against great-great-grandmother's table leg since he sat down.

I open my mouth to speak but Dad gets there first. "Afraid not, buddy. It's past your bedtime."

I was going to say we could play one more round. After all, this is my first night back under the same roof as my son in over two months. But I'm in my parents' house now. Their house; their rules.

Mum went to bed half an hour ago. She's always been an early-to-bed, early-to-rise type, but seven o'clock is bordering on ridiculous. I'm suspicious she wanted to avoid further awkward interactions with her pregnant, brain-damaged daughter, but I could be reading too much into it. Maybe she's just exhausted from taking care of her grandson for so long.

"Come on, Freddie." I get to my feet. "I'm going to clean my teeth too. If we're quick there might be time for me to read you a story in bed."

Dad stands up. "I can do that if you like?"

"Dad, I haven't been able to read my son a story in weeks. I'd like to do it, if that's okay?"

He holds up his hands. "Just trying to help."

Ignoring him, I take Freddie's hand: in part because I love my son desperately and want to hold his hand, but mostly because I don't back myself to get to the bathroom without falling or getting lost.

Freddie's hand is hot and sweaty in mine. He looks up at me, his pupils wide with excitement. "Dad says I can go camping with him and Clara in the summer."

"Does he?" Paul hates the great outdoors. Once we went to a concert in a park and left during the interval because the grass got too damp. "Where are you going to go?"

"Clara wants us to camp at the lake where she used to go with her family. She's got four brothers, Mum."

"Wow, that's a lot of brothers."

"Will I get more brothers too?"

I wonder if Dad can hear our conversation as we climb the stairs. "I don't know, Freddie. Maybe."

I'm remembering a conversation with Finn. He talked about taking Freddie and I on a tramp, camping overnight and roasting marshmallows. Finn loved tramping. Being in the outdoors, he once told me, brought him the same joy as creating in the kitchen brought me. And now he can't walk. He might never go tramping again, and it's my fault.

———

"You've got a lot to deal with, Em. Do you want to have a baby right now?"

I pull the covers up higher and roll on to my left side. Lying on my right is hopeless. After five minutes my leg aches. The orthopaedic surgeon tells me I could have pains for months while the bones and surrounding tissue regenerate. The phone slips from my hand – why does every little thing have to be so difficult? I haul it back to my ear. "It's hard enough focussing on this conversation, Lily. How am I supposed to make a decision?"

"Fuck knows."

I'm glad I have a room downstairs now, away from Mum and Dad and Freddie. I'm talking as quietly as I can, but I'm still worried Mum will march down the stairs and tell me off.

"I feel like I'm sixteen again, waiting for my parents to go to sleep so I can sneak out of the house."

"Where did you sneak off to at sixteen?"

"Nowhere. I just liked to sit at the end of the driveway and eat chocolate biscuits."

"Wow, you were seriously rebellious."

We both laugh quietly. I have to keep my voice down; I don't know why Lily is whispering.

"I'm too wired to sleep," I mutter.

"I thought you wanted to sleep all the time."

"I do. Two hours ago I would have done anything to go to bed. I think I'm over-tired."

"Do you want me to come over?"

"No. Thanks anyway."

There's a long pause. "You don't have to decide just yet," Lily whispers.

"Yes I do."

"They said you can terminate later if necessary. It will be a different procedure, that's all."

"Yeah."

"I'm sorry, Emma. I wish you didn't have to go through all of this."

"Lils, can I ask you a favour?"

"Shoot."

"I know you weren't keen on Finn, but I was wondering if you could take me to see him. Tomorrow maybe?"

"Em—"

"I feel like I need to. That it will help me to decide. Please."

Lily sighs. "I didn't like him because he wasn't honest with you."

"In what way?"

"Remember we met him at that bar and Darryl said Finn was the guy having the fake stag do?"

"Yes."

"It wasn't fake. He was engaged."

"Sorry?"

"He left Scotland to have a break from his fiancée, according to Darryl."

"I don't get it." I have to put one hand on top of the one holding the phone to stop it slipping.

"Finn organised a job transfer to New Zealand for six months. His plan was to get some action before he had to return to his home country and settle down into wedded bliss."

"He has a fiancée? In Scotland?" My tongue feels thick and foreign in my mouth.

"He did. I guess he still does. Who knows? I'm sorry. I should have said something as soon as I found out. I tried to, but then Jack had his heart attack, and then there was the accident, and then… well, you were working hard on your recovery, and no one was really talking about Finn – you especially. I just… it's no excuse, Em, I should have told you."

I giggle. I can't help it. Then I'm laughing a loud, demented laugh that is bound to wake everyone. "He got what he came here for," I gasp.

"What?"

"There was no shortage of action, Lils," I howl.

"Oh, Emma. Are you sure you don't want me to come over?"

I stop laughing as abruptly as I started and take a deep shuddering breath. "Will you still take me to see him?"

"Em, did you hear what I just said?"

It's fine, I tell myself. I was only in it for a bit of fun with a sexy guy. So he was engaged and didn't tell me. Big deal. Even as I try to convince myself, I know I'm losing the argument. The weight of a giant rock presses on my chest. At least it's clear where I stand. Where I've always stood with Finn. "I still need to see him," I whisper.

Lily sighs. "If you think it will help."

"Thanks." There's a creak from the dining room doors. I hide my phone under the covers and lift my head to watch the curtains part. Mum pops her head in. "I heard voices," she murmurs.

"I think it was people walking down the street."

Mum looks unconvinced. "Sorry to bother you."

"It's fine, Mum."

"Night, then." Her head disappears and I retrieve my phone.

"I think Mum's disappointed in me."

"Cause you're pregnant?"

"Maybe. Dunno. There have been a few options for her to choose from recently." I can feel the familiar headache – my faithful companion – crank up another notch. "I'm gonna try and sleep now, Lily. Night."

"Night, Em."

I put my phone on the small stool acting as my bedside table and lie flat on my back. I hated being in the rehab centre. I was desperate to get out. Now I'm out and nothing has changed. If anything, it's worse.

I wasn't the love of Finn's life. We weren't set to embark on a life-long, loving, highly sensual relationship where he would become the second – and vastly improved – father to Freddie. He was after sex. I was the idiot who thought there might have been something more. For the first time I acknowledge this fact. I let it hover in the room, judging me. The dreadful truth is I liked Finn. A lot. I thought… letting my breath out in a rush, I make my mind go blank. It doesn't matter what I thought. I have to face facts and stop deluding myself.

Quietly, I climb from my narrow bed, walk out of the house, and down the driveway. My bare feet slap on the concrete like fish flapping in a bucket. The last time Dad and I went fishing together was when I was in my last year at school. I liked getting up early with him and putting in the boat with morning mist wet and salty on my face. It's a shame Dad sold that little boat. Freddie has never put a rod in the water, or scraped off fish scales with a big rusty knife, a parent's strong hand on top for support.

At the bottom of the driveway I stop and stare at the small rectangular metal box with a narrow opening on the front and a lift-up roof. It rests on a slim wooden pole.

"Emma?" Dad hurries towards me. "What are you doing? It's freezing out here."

I point to the box. "What's that?"

Dad frowns. "The letterbox?"

That's it. I knew what it was the second Dad said the name. Letterbox. A box for letters. No one writes letters anymore.

"Come back inside, Emmie." Dad puts a hand on my back. "I'll sit with you for a while."

"Why does Mum hate me?"

"She doesn't hate you, she loves you. Desperately."

"I think she hates me."

"She's scared."

"Of what?"

Dad takes my elbow as we walk back into the house, down the hallway, through the lounge and into the dining room, which is now my bedroom. "Your mum wants you to be happy, Emma. It's all both of us want."

"So why is she scared?"

"She doesn't know what to do. If we could fight this battle for you, we would. But we can't."

"I wish I could sleep, Dad. I'm really tired."

Dad lifts my legs onto the bed. He helps me to lie down and kneels on the floor. Clasping his hands on the mattress, he lowers his head as if to pray. "If you have this baby, Emma, we will support you, and love you, and love the baby, that's a given." His voice is muffled against the sheets. "But you shouldn't have this baby if you can't put yourself first." Dad lifts his head and reaches up to stroke my head. "You have to believe in yourself, Emmie. In the incredible future you still have ahead of you."

"I don't know how," I whisper.

Dad's hand pauses to rest like a warm compress on my forehead. "Yes. You do."

———

Finn's body is hot. He's pressed up against me. We're spooning, naked, sweaty. "You smell so good," Finn murmurs, his lips brushing my neck.

It's late. We're tired but neither of us wants to sleep. "Probably the duck I was roasting before you distracted me," I mutter.

Finn inhales deeply. "Maybe. Think it's just you. You and me together. We have a smell."

"Of sex?"

His breath is warm on my skin. "And something else."

I press my body back into his and he presses forward in response. "Are you getting all poetic on me, Finn?" He can't see my face, but even I can hear my smile.

"Must be my romantic Scottish blood."

"Do you miss it? Scotland?"

He is silent. His hand touches my shoulder and slides down over my ribs, to rest on the curve of my hip. "I'm happier here."

"What do you miss the most?"

"Shortbread."

"That's it? Your stomach really does rule. What about family?"

He pauses. "I hardly have anything to do with my parents, or my sister. I haven't seen them since I left home at seventeen. It's one of the reasons I spent so much time hiking and camping in the highlands as a kid. The more I could keep away from the tension and constant fighting between my parents, the better. The only one in the family I see now is Audrey."

"Who's Audrey?"

"My grandmother."

I'm so sleepy I can feel myself starting to nod off. "You call your grandmother, Audrey?" I slur.

Finn's hand slides forward and rests on my belly. "She doesn't want any reminders she might be getting old," he says softly.

———

I wake lying on my side. The wrong side. My right leg throbs. I roll onto my back. It's still dark. Fumbling for my watch on the stool, I check the time. Four thirty-six. Damn. There's no way I'll fall back asleep now. I flex my right foot forward and backwards as the physio taught me, waiting for the pain to reduce.

My hands move to rest on my stomach. I imagine Finn's hand beneath mine, his body beside me. I ruined the duck that night. It sat in the cooling oven till morning, though Finn insisted on eating some for breakfast. He had a hard time chewing the tough, dried-out flesh. I laughed at his expression. Laughed so much I cried. We went out for breakfast after that. I had corn fritters. Finn had scrambled eggs... or was it the pancakes? I can't remember.

I wish I knew how Finn was. I can't bear the thought of him never walking again. I don't even care if he's engaged. I need to see him.

SIXTEEN

SEVEN WEEKS AFTER

"You sure about this?" Lily asks.

I stare through the windscreen at the tall grey building. For ten days I lay inside the walls of this hospital and I remember none of it. Not one tiny thing.

"What was I like?" I ask. "When you came to see me here."

Lily sighs. "You hated it. It's like you were desperate to get out. You kept pulling at your ventilation tube. They had to restrain you because you were going to damage your vocal cords."

"Really? I thought I just lay there looking stupid."

"You were agitated all the time. Your eyes would follow me everywhere I went. I swear you were trying to talk to me; to tell me something." Lily closes her eyes briefly. "It was awful, Em. Everyone was terrified. It's like you were trapped and trying to find a way back to us."

I put my hand on Lily's leg. "Sorry."

She shakes her head. "Don't be sorry. Not for any of it."

I lift my hand and turn to open the door. "Let's get this over with."

An overly helpful man at the information desk gives us directions to Finn's room on the third floor.

"Your dad went to visit him," Lily says as the lift doors close.

I frown. "Who? Finn?"

Lily nods, her eyes on the flashing ascending numbers. "Your mum was fucked off. I've never seen her so mad."

I think of earlier, when Lily turned up to bring me to the hospital and Mum tried to talk me out of coming. It was the longest interaction she'd had with me all week. Dad didn't say a word. "I wonder why he hasn't mentioned it? He didn't tell, did he?"

"About the pregnancy? No way. I think he just came to check on him."

The lift doors open and we walk down an empty corridor until we find Finn's room. It's eerily quiet. Where are the nurses?

Lily pauses. "I'll come in if you want?"

I'm betting she'd rather go without alcohol for a year. "It's okay. I'd prefer to see him on my own."

Lily's smile is wan. "I'll wait down there." She points to an alcove with a huddle of chairs.

We hug briefly and she moves away.

I wonder if I should knock before entering. Hesitating, I tap lightly with my knuckles. There's no response.

I turn the door handle and enter.

Finn faces me, propped on a gentle incline. He's lost weight and he's pale. I never knew he had so many freckles. His closed eyelids looked bruised, and his face is clean-shaven. Finn hates the freshly shaved look. He boasted to me once that stubble was his thing. The ladies love it he'd said, grinning, till I punched him on the arm.

"Are you Emma?"

I startle and spin towards the sound. I've moved too quickly for my fragile brain. My vision becomes wavy at the edges, black in the middle. I grab the door to steady myself. Blinking slowly, my sight returns. "Sorry?"

"I'm thinking you might be Emma? Am I right?" Her accent is unmistakably Scottish.

The elderly woman doesn't smile or frown – her expression is unreadable. She holds herself like a ballet dancer; erect and poised, her white hair pulled back tightly into an immaculate bun. In her hand is a mug with the tag of a teabag hanging over the edge. She strides to the window and places her mug on the sill. Then she turns to me and waits.

"Yes," I whisper. "I am." Finn hasn't moved. It's like he's frozen.

"How are you recovering?" the woman asks, clasping her hands in front of her smart buttoned cardigan. "I understand you had rather serious head injuries."

I glance at Finn's barely recognisable face. "I'm okay," I croak.

"I'm Finn's grandmother, Audrey."

"Yes." I look at her and try to smile. "I guessed you might be."

"Would you like me to wake him? He sleeps deeply but —" She frowns and looks towards the window. "I expect he would like to be woken."

"I… I'm not sure." I clear my throat. "Only if it's okay."

She walks up to Finn and places a hand on his shoulder. The way she looks at him, I feel like I'm intruding. "He said you have a son," she says, her eyes still on Finn's scarily inert body.

For a second, I think she's referring to the embryo hidden within my body, then I realise she's talking about Freddie. "Yes."

"I have two daughters." Audrey pauses. "Finn is my only grandson. He and I, we have a special bond. I have three granddaughters, but Finn…" her voice trails off.

Machines beep around me. The air conditioning hums. Muffled footsteps pass by outside the door.

"How did you know who I was?" I ask.

Audrey assesses me, her expression once more inscrutable. "Finn has mentioned you a few times. He wanted to come and check on you… only he couldn't."

"Is he… Are his legs…?"

"The doctors say he's making good progress," says Audrey. "There is already some movement in his legs, though it continues to be an arduous and painful process of recovery."

There is a long silence while we both stare at Finn.

"I don't remember it," I whisper. "I keep wondering if I made the suggestion to get in that bin. If it was me who…"

"Finn says he is entirely to blame," she snaps. Her hand that has been resting on Finn's shoulder begins to shake him vigorously and his eyes fly open.

I take a step back as his eyes lose their glazed, bewildered look and focus on me.

"Emma?" Finn croaks. He tries to sit up and winces.

Audrey still has her hand on his shoulder and pushes him back down. She mutters something I can't hear and he nods a fraction, his eyes still locked with mine.

I've missed you, I want to say. But of course I don't. Because he's engaged, I tell myself firmly.

"Hi, Finn," I whisper. Then my throat clogs up and I

can't say anymore. I drop my head and study my shoes trying to blink away tears.

Audrey shakes her head. "I'll leave you for a moment." She looks pointedly at Finn. "To talk," she says firmly.

I listen to her walk past me and out the door before lifting my head. Finn is still staring at me.

"I'm sorry," he whispers. "Emma, I'm so sorry."

I rub my eyes and take a deep breath. "I don't think it's been a picnic for either of us recently." My attempt at a smile is almost as poor as his.

"I wanted to come and see you," says Finn, "But... the doctors still won't let me out of here. I tried ringing you at home, but your mum... she didn't." He pauses. "Are you... are you okay?"

The cocky confidence I've always heard in his voice has vanished. Replaced by a nervous wobble.

I straighten and take a deep breath. "I will be," I state.

When Finn smiles faintly I see a glimmer of the Finn I used to know. The dimples, the glint in his green eyes.

"How's Freddie?" he asks. "I've been worried about him."

"He's fine." Anger flushes through me. How dare he ask me about my son like they had some special relationship. Seeing Finn is bringing back memories and feelings I've tried to suppress. I want to pick up the vase of flowers on the table beside me and throw them at his cute, lying face. "How's your fiancée?" I snap.

Finn closes his eyes briefly and opens them again. "Emma—"

"It's fine." I hold up my hand to stop him saying more. "We had sex a few times, I'm not going to get all jealous girlfriend on you."

"That's not—" Finn hesitates as the door behind me

opens. I turn to see a blonde goddess enter the room, smiling like an angel. When she sees me, her smile falters for a fraction before returning.

"Sorry, I didn't realise you had a visitor, Finn."

She might as well be singing an aria her voice is so golden. I want to run out of the room, grab Lily, and make for the nearest vodka and tonic.

"Hello," the woman glides towards me holding out her hand. "I'm Siobhan."

As we shake, I look down at her ivory, smooth, unblemished hand gripping my flaky-skinned, splotchy, nail-bitten monstrosity.

Obviously this is the elusive fiancée, come to hammer another nail in my already pounding head.

"Emma," I whisper.

Siobhan lets go of my hand and throws her arms around me pulling me into her bosom and forcing me to inhale her perfect, innocent aroma. I'm reminded of a plum tart fresh from the oven with vanilla ice cream; that heady mix of sweet fruit, buttery pastry, and cream.

"I'm glad you've come to see Finn," she breathes in my neck. "He's been desperately worried about you. We both have." Siobhan gives me an extra tight hug before releasing me. What the hell is going on? The woman should be kicking me out of the room for sleeping with her soon-to-be husband. She should be yelling and throwing things. Not giving me a bloody hug.

My thoughts must show on my face. Siobhan nods. "It was a shock to learn of your… relationship, but I knew there was a risk when Finn came to NZ. We even discussed the possibility of one of us wanting to… but we have to move on, concentrate on your recoveries after such a ghastly accident." She stares at my forehead as if there's a little door about to open and spew brain cells everywhere. "How are you recovering from your head injuries, Emma?"

"Siobhan," Finn says. I glance at him lying there with deep, anxious lines on his forehead. "Emma has just arrived. Would you mind leaving us to talk, just for a minute?" He bites his lip and tilts his head to one side with a gentle smile as he looks at his fiancée.

My chest hurts. I can't take more of this. "It's fine," I mutter, shuffling towards the door. "I'd better go."

"No," Finn says loudly, panicked. "Stay. Please."

Siobhan places a hand softly on my shoulder and guides me to the bed, her smile a little less confident. "Stay and talk to Finn, Emma. It's important for you both." She leans over Finn and places a palm on his cheek. "I'll do another lap of the gardens. Take your time."

For a brief moment she glances at me and I see fear in her eyes. How can she be afraid of me? Then she glides to the door and exits.

Crossing my arms, I glare at the pillow next to Finn's head. "I need to get going," I mutter.

"Emma, I'll never forgive myself for what I did. It was the stupidest, most idiotic... I understand if you can't stand the sight of me. I can't stand the sight of me either." I risk a quick look at his face and there are tears in his eyes. "Emma, you were the last person in the world I wanted to hurt. After everything you went through with Paul, and Jack. You were being so brave and I was some idiot coward running away from life. I should have been open with you from the start." He takes a deep breath. "And it wasn't just sex, not for me anyway."

I close my eyes so I don't have to see his face. "We have to get on with our lives now, Finn. The best we can."

Silence stretches between us. "I couldn't have got this far

without Siobhan," Finn murmurs. "She's been so forgiving, and supportive... and I've put her through hell. As for Audrey, she's been her usual never-take-no-for-an-answer self. If it wasn't for her, I'd be lying here with one leg instead of two."

Inhaling, I cling to the pain in my head and open my eyes. "We've both been lucky then. To have people around to help us."

"Emma," Finn whispers, his green eyes as beautiful as always. "I wanted so desperately to get out of here to come and see you. I... I missed you."

My body hurts everywhere. I should yell. Tell Finn he can't say things like that when he's engaged to someone else. He can't look at me with those beseeching, melt-into-me eyes. It's too painful. Reaching down, I pick up Finn's hand, kiss it lightly on the top, and let it go.

I'm not going to tell him I'm pregnant. He doesn't need to know. It's time to put myself first. I need to leave this room and never see Finn again. Cut all ties with him, no matter how hard it will be. The sooner I have an abortion, the faster I can put him in the past. "Goodbye," I gasp.

No longer able to look at him, I stumble to the door. Even as I fumble with the handle, I'm hoping he will call out, but there's nothing – not a sound other than my uneven breath as I leave his room.

Lily is waiting for me, her arms opening wide as she sees what state I'm in. I fall into her, sobbing. "It's not about him," I gasp.

"Alright," she murmurs, squeezing me tighter.

"It's everything, Lils. Everything in my stupid brain-fucked life."

"Come on, let's blow this joint." She puts an arm around my shoulder and guides me towards the lift.

"Emma."

Audrey has appeared behind me like a ghost. "I was hoping to have a word," she glances at Lily. "In private."

I can feel Lily stiffening beside me, getting ready to fight. I catch her eye and give a slight shake of the head. Scowling, she lifts her arm from my shoulder and slumps down the corridor.

Wishing I had a tissue, I sniff heavily and rub my eyes. "What is it?"

"Finn made me fly his dog over here. It cost me a small fortune, but he said he couldn't live without Leroy for six months. Leaving his fiancée was fine, but not the dog."

It was a mistake for me to come. I know this from the fierce glow in Audrey's eyes. "Siobhan has barely left his side. Neither of us have. When he's discharged in a couple of weeks we can finally take him home to Scotland."

I'm not sure how or if I'm supposed to respond, so I say nothing.

"Finn needs to come home, Emma. He needs to put this behind him and settle down."

"I'm not stopping him," I splutter.

Audrey's eyes are narrow slits. "He's feeling very guilty, Emma. His mood is… is volatile at the moment."

"It's been a difficult—"

"It is my understanding you were both very drunk."

"Sorry?"

"When the accident occurred. There's no way of knowing for sure, is there?"

"Knowing what?"

"Who influenced who? Especially – as you've just admitted – you can't remember anything."

Finally, it clicks. "You think I was a bad influence on him," I state, my heart beating faster. "You think I'm some deviant little minx who led your precious grandson astray." I'm raising my voice now. "Are you demented?"

Lily charges towards us, grabs my arm, and pulls me away. "Fucking leave her alone," Lily growls, making herself as tall as possible (which is sadly not that tall).

Together we stride to the lift and I bang the button with my fist. "Bitch," I mutter.

"Fucking cow," Lily whispers. We step into the lift and I spin around to glare at Audrey before the doors close, but when I look back down the corridor, she's gone.

———

Dad walks into the kitchen. "Couldn't sleep again?"

I've been sitting at the kitchen table waiting for the black sky to brighten into day.

Dad flicks the kettle on. "You made yourself a cup of tea. Well done."

"Yes." Believe it or not this is a big achievement. "Reckon you could probably take the pictures down now."

There's a row of poorly-drawn diagrams on the wall behind the kettle with instructions for making tea. Above the toaster is another unique picture display. I drew them with Alison's help during one of our sessions. There are many mortifying moments in my new life. Having someone help me work through the simple process of making toast with butter and jam is one of them.

I watch Dad prepare a cup of tea with infinite ease.

"Why didn't you tell me you went to see Finn?" I ask quietly.

He leans back against the sink and takes a sip, eyeing me over the rim of his mug. "Thought it was best not to mention it."

"Why?"

Dad shrugs.

"Was Audrey there? His grandmother?"

"Yes."

"Did you speak to her?"

"A little."

I get the feeling this conversation is going nowhere. "She doesn't like me."

"She doesn't want you to get in the way."

"Of what?"

Dad puts down his mug and crosses his arms. "Finn asked me to go and see him."

"Why?"

"He wanted to say sorry. I'll admit I went to the hospital with the sole intention of telling him to never go near you ever again but... he was devastated, Emma. He kept going on about how it was all his fault and that you were the last person in the world he wanted to hurt."

"Finn didn't force me into that bin, I could have—"

Mum walks in, Freddie behind her. "Morning," I say brightly, hoping she hasn't heard our conversation.

Freddie climbs into my lap for a morning cuddle. I pull him close, inhaling his familiar smell. "Thought I'd come with you to crèche this morning. You can show me the new baby chickens."

"Cool!" Freddie lets me go and climbs onto the chair beside me. "You might be allowed to hold one, Mama, if you sit really still."

"Is that a good idea, Emma?" Mum talks to the inside of the fridge rather than my face.

I try to keep my voice calm. "Why wouldn't it be?"

I watch Mum take out the milk and smile at Freddie. "The usual, Freddo?"

At some point in the last few weeks Mum has started calling my son Freddo. I hate it. She never used to call him that. Paul is the only other person who uses Freddo, and thankfully it isn't very often. I want to tell Mum not to use the name but I'm scared she'll overreact. Truth is, I know she will.

"Mum?"

She sighs heavily. "Oh Emma, it's a very loud and busy environment. Alison says you're to avoid that sort of situation."

I've never wanted to throw my mug at the wall more than I do right now. "I'm not going to stay all morning. Just for a few minutes. And I am capable of making my own judgements on things."

"Emma," Dad warns. "Your mother was—"

"—oh, don't *you* start!" I say loudly.

Freddie claps his hands over his ears, his eyes wide and panicked.

"Freddie, it's okay," I murmur, trying to pull his hands away. "We were just talking."

"I don't want to go to crèche," he says quietly. "I want to stay home with you."

Freddie hasn't wanted to go to crèche since I moved in. My dear mother takes every opportunity to inform me he never complained about going before. Each morning has been a battle to get Freddie out the door. I had hoped by going with him today he'd be happier about staying. The last thing I want is for Freddie to feel like no one is listening to him. He's had an unsettling time recently. I owe him. I'll owe him forever.

"Okay. You can stay home with me, Freddie. Maybe try crèche tomorrow, eh?"

"Kkkh." Mum lets her breath out. "Really, Emma?"

I glare at Mum. "What?" My teeth grind together.

Mum ignores me, puts Freddie's bowl of cornflakes with yoghurt in front of him, and leans in close to his ear. "Remember what we talked about last night, Freddo?"

Freddie frowns.

"About making sure your mum gets the rest she needs," Mum whispers loudly.

Freddie glances at me, instantly worried.

"I don't recall any conversation last night," I say as lightly as I can.

Mum straightens and ruffles Freddie's hair, her eyes fixed on his head. "Now, how about I take you to crèche this morning, and Mum comes to see the chickens in another week or so?"

Freddie gives me another worried glance. "Okay," he says.

My hand shakes as I run it through my hair. My chest is so tight I'm struggling to breathe. "Mum, I am quite capable of making decisions regarding my son."

Mum's eyes flick to mine. "Are you?" she hisses, before turning away and striding from the room.

My cheeks burn. I clench every muscle in my body trying to stay contained.

"Emma." Dad sits down opposite me. "She's trying to do the right thing."

"No, she's trying to punish me," I mutter.

Freddie picks up his spoon and starts to eat. His free hand sneaks across the table, rests on my arm, and squeezes softly. Goosebumps rise on my skin. Can a person die from guilt? "How about after crèche we walk to the park, Freddie?" My voice cracks. "We haven't done that in ages."

Freddie instantly looks happy. "Can we play the letterbox game?"

"Of course."

Dad puts some bread in the toaster. "I'll join you," he says cheerfully.

I close my eyes and take a deep breath. While Mum has been noticeably absent from whichever space I happen to occupy, Dad has been my permanent shadow ever since I left rehab. He makes me feel even more useless than I am. "Thanks, Dad," I murmur, "But Freddie and I will be fine, won't we buddy?"

Freddie grins and nods, his mouth full.

Dad hesitates. "Okay," he says finally. Then he walks to the whiteboard and writes, *Walk to park with Freddie, 2 p.m.*

———

It's good to be out of the house. Just me and Freddie doing a regular mother and son activity. After ten minutes of walking in the fresh air, my headache is only a faint whisper at the base of my skull. I need to get outside more.

"Four, one," chirps Freddie. He jumps and hops along in front of me. "Four, three." Hop, jump, run. "Four, five."

"Wow, you are really good at this," I say. "What are the numbers on that one over there?" I point to the grey letterbox across the street.

Freddie squints. "Four, six."

I smile and nod. My brain may have turned to mush, but at least I still know my numbers from one to ten. To Freddie at least, I'm not a total flake.

When we turn in at the entrance to the park, I'm relieved to see it's not busy. I was nervous the playground would be teeming with screeching toddlers and earnest chatty parents. There's a little boy clambering around the base of the slide and a girl about Freddie's age on the swings.

Both their mothers are intent on staring at the screens of their phones.

"Watch this, Mama." Freddie sprints to the steps leading to the suspended wooden tunnel. He clambers up with ease and crawls inside the tunnel. Giggling, he peers out at me through the small gaps between the planks. "I'm hiding," he yells.

I know this game. With my hands on my hips, I wander around the playground pretending to search for my son. "Now, I wonder where Freddie is?" I say loudly.

He giggles again.

I love the sun warming my back, and the silver branches of tall trees stripped of leaves. My chest expands and I breathe more easily. There's no one watching me or keeping tabs. Something inside me shifts and my limbs feel lighter. I place a hand on my lower stomach and take another deep breath.

I thought it would be hard coming back to this park. I have such a clear image of Finn swinging next to Freddie. Both of them looking at each other and laughing. It was the first time I'd seen a grown man content and happy doing something so simple. Finn's childlike sense of fun and joy was almost a bigger attraction than his body – and that's saying something.

After a couple of rounds of a fairly simplistic version of hide-and-seek, I sit on the bench and watch Freddie pick up small sticks, place them in the swing and push the swing higher and higher, until the stick falls off.

Finn may have been the one to suggest we hop in that bin, but I was the bigger idiot. Right from the moment I laid eyes on him. As I sit here smiling at my son, Finn is lying in the hospital with a face devoid of the relaxed, playful Finn I fell for, and I'm to blame. He should never have got involved in my screwed-up life. I'm pissed at him for being engaged to that goddamn Scottish princess, but I'm more annoyed with myself. How could I have contemplated – even if it was only in tiny bursts of enthusiastic daydreaming – a future life where Finn and Freddie would unwittingly compete to draw out the happy, carefree girl I started to bury the day I married Paul.

"Freddie," I call. "We better head back now. Alison will be arriving soon." Today we get to go on a 'fieldtrip' as she calls it. Alison is taking me to the supermarket so I can attempt to navigate the aisles, ticking off items on my shopping list. I'm bracing myself for it to be the worst game of hide-and-seek a thirty-three-year-old can play. It was hard enough finding the tomato paste when my brain cells were fully intact; now the task is going to be monumental.

We leave the park with Freddie's sweaty hand encased in mine. At the end of the block, I stop walking. Freddie stops too. He's waiting for me to turn us towards home, only I don't know how to get there. I recognise the corner we stand on, but I have no idea which direction to head. I've only walked to the park from Mum and Dad's place a couple of times before. Usually I come at it from another direction. Not that I could find the way to my old house either.

Freddie looks up at me and I force myself to smile. "How about you see if you can remember the way home, Freddie. Do you think you can?"

He hesitates for a fraction then points across the road. "That way," he says standing up straighter.

"You sure?" I hope he is, because I honestly don't have a clue.

Freddie nods, his face serious.

"Right then, let's go."

We cross the road and continue to follow Freddie's

instructions. After several blocks, Freddie's voice becomes less confident. He slows down.

I wish I'd brought my phone, so I could look on Google maps. I stubbornly left it beside my bed, knowing Dad would try to ring and check on me.

"Mama, I'm not sure." Freddie's lip wobbles. "Sorry."

"That's okay." I bend to give him a hug. "You did really well. We must be really close to home now."

Glancing around, I will myself to recognise something, anything. "Come on. It's not far." I walk purposefully down the street to my left, my heart racing.

"Emma!" Mags waves from across the road. She waits for a car to pass then jogs over to join us. "Hey," she says. "Thought I'd come find you. Your dad was looking a tad worried."

"Mags." I can't decide if I'm thrilled to see her or mortified. "What are you doing here?"

She frowns. "I rang you yesterday to ask if I could pop round. I haven't seen you since you moved home."

"Oh," I hesitate, a niggling ghost of the conversation we had coming back to me. "Sorry, I forgot."

Mags gives me a small, concerned smile and turns to Freddie. She crouches down and holds her palms out to Freddie who slaps them as hard as he can. Freddie turns his hands over and Mags slaps back in return. It's their routine. "Hey, little man. Did you have fun at the park with your mum?"

Freddie grins. "Yeah."

Mags straightens. "You okay?" she murmurs.

"Sure."

"Where were you off to?"

"Sorry?"

"Where are you headed?"

I cross my arms, knowing my hands are shaking. "Nowhere."

"I was trying to remember the way home, but I got stuck," says Freddie, sticking his finger in his nose and having a good pick.

"Is that right?" says Mags.

I stare at the ground.

"Well, you did pretty well. Come on, I'll show you how close you are. Wanna ride?"

Freddie's finger exits his nostril and hovers in the air. "In what?"

Mags turns Freddie round to face away from her, lifts him under the armpits and puts him on her shoulders. Freddie grips my friend's hands, his eyes wide with wonder.

Mags neighs like a horse and hops down the footpath back the way we have come. I follow quietly, wishing it was night-time and I could crawl into bed.

When we reach the bottom of Mum and Dad's driveway, Mags lowers Freddie to the ground and Freddie sprints towards the front door.

Reluctantly I meet her eye.

"Is that the first time you've been to the park since the accident?" she asks.

Biting my lip, I look away. "Yeah."

"Your Mum says you insisted on going on your own with Freddie."

I sigh and begin to walk up the driveway. Mags puts a hand on my arm. "Em." I stop walking but keep facing away from her.

"The doctors said improving your memory takes time."

"I know," I mutter.

"Sometimes you have to let your friends and family help – even if you silently want to strangle us."

"It's not *you* I want to strangle," I whisper.

"Oh sweetie." Mags wraps her arms around me. I lean against her – my big, strong, kinder-than-Mother-Teresa friend.

"Everything okay?" Dad calls. Mags releases me and I turn to see him standing at the open front door with his eyebrows pressed together.

"It's fine," I say, my throat sore. "We lost track of time."

He doesn't appear to believe me. "Alison's here," he says before disappearing inside.

Mags tucks her arm in mine and we walk up the driveway together. "What's all this rubbish about you going to the supermarket?" she mutters. "You hate the place."

Alison doesn't know about Jack, or my almost café. She thinks I used to shop at the big supermarket in town. She has no idea everything on my list – written slowly and with a sense of growing loss as each item was scribbled on the page – is food Mum likes to have in her kitchen. Pre-made soups, pasta sauce, frozen veg, and pizza bases. Apart from toast, I haven't made a meal since my accident. And I'm not planning for that to change anytime soon.

"It doesn't matter anymore," I say.

Mags nudges me and I stumble sideways. She smiles at me like I'm some confused toddler and shakes her head. "Em, that's like me suddenly saying cats don't matter anymore and I want to give them away for a dog."

Snorting, I nudge her back. "Impossible."

"Exactly." She loops her arm back in mine and we continue up the front steps. "Now let's go tell this Alison, before you end up with a trolley full of dogs."

Alison appears in the kitchen doorway, a cup of tea in her hand. "I didn't think they sold dogs at the supermarket."

Mags nudges me again. I'd forgotten how much she likes

to elbow people in the ribs. It drives Lily nuts. Right now I'm not a huge fan either.

"Em?" Mags says. "Want to tell Alison, or will I?"

I clear my throat. "I'm not sure I'm up to the supermarket visit today, sorry."

I step out of the way to avoid the elbow heading my way. "Tell her why?" Mags says.

"I'm tired," I snap. "And since I'm clearly not even capable of taking my son to the park without getting lost, I'm unlikely to find the canned peaches in a hurry."

Mum descends from the stairs in a floral crossover dress designed for twenty-year-olds, and shiny pale-blue stilettos. She talks to Alison as if I'm not even there. "I wasn't comfortable with Emma taking Freddie to the park on her own."

"I think it's great for them to spend more time together," Alison says.

Mum makes no comment as she retrieves her handbag from the hook by the front door. "I have an appointment at the hairdresser," she says to the invisible person standing behind me. "Your father is having a lie-down." She glances at Mags and narrows her eyes as if she's never seen my friend before. "He's under a lot of stress."

Mags frowns. "I'm sorry to hear that."

Silently we listen to Mum click-clack out of the house. I wonder if she will ever like me again.

Alison and Mags exchange a look. "Well, how about we leave the supermarket for another time and work on something easier," Alison says brightly. "We can—"

"I'm not up for it." I choke.

Pressing past Alison, I stumble down the hall, through the lounge, and into my room. I should go and find Freddie and check he's okay. Instead, I lift the covers, and climb into bed.

After a short time Mags comes to stand at the end of my bed.

"What?" I mutter.

"Alison's gone and I called Lily. She's on her way over. Trish is stuck in some meeting, but she'll be here later this evening."

"I really want to be alone, please Mags."

"Tough shit."

"I'm exhausted, and I know you all mean to help but—"

Mags holds up a hand. "I'm going to show Freddie funny cat videos on YouTube and then we're going to practise cartwheels. The first idea was mine, and the second was his. I haven't attempted a cartwheel since I was eight, and even then I was useless. Then, when Lily arrives, we're going to drag you out of bed and force you into doing something fun."

"You don't have to—"

"Enough, Em. You're not dealing with this on your own, so get used to it."

Mags strides out of my makeshift bedroom and I curl into a tight ball on my side, one hand pressed against my pregnant stomach. With a groan, I close my eyes, and let the blackness take me.

———

It seems only a second passes before I'm woken by a hand shaking my shoulder.

"Hey," says Dad, leaning over me. "You okay?"

I feel calmer now. "Just more of the usual," I mumble, slowly sitting up. "How long have I been asleep?"

Dad shrugs. "Not too long. Freddie was getting worried though, so I said I'd come and wake you. Sorry."

"It's fine." Scrambling out of bed, I'm hit with a wave of light-headedness and grip Dad's arm.

"Easy, Emmie." Dad pats my arm.

"Sorry, just got up too quickly."

"Take your time." His patting is firm and rhythmic, as if he's soothing a baby.

I pull my arm away and walk quickly into the hallway. I can hear Freddie's voice in the kitchen and head in that direction. Mags is sitting at the kitchen table with a large graze across her cheek. Freddie kneels on a chair beside her eating a mini packet of crisps. When he catches sight of me, he smiles and gives me a tiny wave. "Mags fell over," he says.

"Don't ask," Mags says, rolling her eyes.

"Cartwheels still a challenge eh?" I head to the bench and flick on the kettle.

"We saw a video of a cat drinking out of a toilet," Freddie says excitedly, crisp crumbs flying from his mouth. "It was so funny, Mama. And there was another cat who did wees on the toilet too. I thought he was going to fall in."

Freddie's giggle is delicious, and for a moment my heart bursts with love. "Sounds highly educational."

There's a loud knock on the front door before I hear it being opened. "Halllooo," Lily calls. "Any limpets around who want to give their Aunty Lils a giant hug?"

Freddie leaps off his chair and charges out of the room. "Oomph, who is this elephant?" Lily gasps, staggering into the kitchen, Freddie firmly wrapped around her waist.

I brush the tears which have appeared out of nowhere from my eyes.

Lily gives me the once-over. "Shit day, eh?"

"That's a bad word," announces Freddie, clinging to Lily so tightly, I'm sure she can't breathe.

"So is 'fuck', little man. Never use it." Lily gives me a

wink. "Now, I have brought a little something to brighten your afternoon, Emma Dilemma."

"It better not be another one of those mindfulness colouring-in books." There's a pile of them beside my bed from well-meaning types. Colouring-in books are for children, not adults recovering from brain injuries.

Lily grins. "Way better." She tickles Freddie in the ribs until he lets her go and drops to the floor. "I'd better run for it before he turns into a limpet again."

Lily sprints back out with Freddie in hot pursuit. I turn to Dad who is slumped in a chair yawning. "Tea?"

"Good idea," he says. As he leans forward and attempts to stand, I push him back down. "I'll make it."

His hesitation is brief, then he nods and relaxes back in his chair.

Weirdly, I want to fist-pump. It's the first time Dad's let me do anything for him since I moved home.

I'm placing a mug in front of him when Lily enters with a large present in her arms. The wrapping paper – which I can't stand – is bright yellow with smiley-face emojis all over it.

Freddie jiggles about beside Lily like he's busting for the loo. "Lily says it's for both of us, Mama. Can we open it?"

I glance at Lily. "What's the occasion?"

She shrugs and places the present on the table. "I ordered it last week."

"You ordered it?"

She smiles. "Yep."

I sit beside Freddie and provide nominal assistance as he tears off the paper. "Wow!" he yells. "What is it?"

Lily ruffles Freddie's hair. "It's an ice cream machine. I thought you and Mum could make ice cream together."

Freddie's eyes widen. If he could eat ice cream for breakfast, lunch and dinner, he would.

"Thanks, Lily," I murmur.

Lily smiles gently. "Thought it was time to get back on the horse."

"What horse?" Freddie asks.

"It's a figure of speech," I say, swallowing hard. "It means I should get back into the kitchen and have some fun making ice cream with my cheeky limpet son."

"Yay!" Freddie surely must have wet his pants by now with all the jiggling. "Can we make some?"

"Absolutely, though we might have to go to the shops for some ingredients."

"Sorted." Lily retrieves a supermarket bag from beside the door. "I think I've got everything we'll need."

SEVENTEEN
EIGHT WEEKS AFTER

"Don't forget your meeting at ten." Dad points to the whiteboard.

Next to 10 a.m. it reads: *Meeting. Paul.*

"Yep." How could I forget? I've been dreading today all week. My meeting with Paul is only the beginning.

What Dad hasn't written on the board is my appointment at the clinic this afternoon. He knows Mum's taking me to get the abortion, yet he hasn't written it down, and I've been too embarrassed to ask him why. I wonder if he thinks Freddie will read the word 'abortion' and ask what it means.

I focus on buttoning Freddie's raincoat and try to block the upcoming day from my mind. It's bucketing down but I'm determined to still take Freddie to crèche. On Saturday Mags took me to the mega toyshop next to the mall so I could purchase Freddie his first ever scooter. All day yesterday he practised going up and down the street. He's already turning and balancing with ease.

I may not be able to drive yet, but I'm determined to take Freddie to crèche from now on. If that means I have to walk for thirty minutes with Freddie beside me on his scooter, then that's what we'll do. I was prepared to fight to the death when I brought up my intentions over dinner last night, but Mum and Dad both accepted my proposal with infinite grace and went back to eating.

As I explained to Lily on the phone last night, my parents and I have reached a precarious state of equilibrium. Politeness is our new middle name. Never in the history of man has a family been more intent on civil interaction. Yesterday I apologised for sneezing, for fuck's sake.

———

Freddie and I are soaked by the time we drip our way through the cloakroom, remove our waterlogged jackets, and enter the zoo.

Correction: a zoo is an oasis of tranquillity compared to the noisy chaos of thirty pre-schoolers in a confined space with nowhere to run on a miserable day. A pneumatic drill sounds like a purring kitten in comparison.

Jill walks over to greet us. "Hello, Freddie," she yells. "Got a bit wet, eh?" She hands him a towel. "Give yourself a rub down with this."

Freddie takes the towel. "Good to see you, Emma," Jill says. She hugs me and whispers, "Welcome back, sweetie."

"Thanks," I mouth.

A child roars past pushing a plastic bulldozer. Four girls screech some tuneless song behind me. On the low table a metre to my left, a boy bangs a round peg into a square hole, and Jake leaps out of nowhere in a dog costume to bark repeatedly in my face.

Every single cell in my body needs to escape. It's like I'm Alice, slowly falling down a hole. Into hell.

I grip Freddie's shoulder and crouch down to speak in his ear. "I better dash while the rain isn't so heavy."

He glances at the torrents of water landing in the sandpit outside but miraculously falls for my story. "Okay." He locks his arms around my neck. "Bye, Mama."

"Bye, Fredster. I'll be back to pick you up, okay?"

He pulls back, his face serious. "Have you set your alarm?"

I nod. "Sure have. The second it goes, I'll be on my way here."

He smiles, satisfied I won't forget him. This time.

Don't cry, I tell myself as he runs after Jake growling.

Three mothers ask me how I'm doing on my way through the cloakroom, their curiosity barely tempered by their concern for my wellbeing. I think I fend them off well enough, but by the time I get outside I can't remember a word I've said to them. I'm sweating and shaking and my head is pounding worse than the worst hangover of my life. I stagger down the street, rain pricking my face, and manage to make it round the corner before I sit with a thump on the curb. Wearily I place one white sneaker, then the other into the raging current running down the culvert. The water runs over and through my shoes, chilling my feet even further. A car surges past, spraying my already soaked body. I left my raincoat behind. It has my phone inside with the Google map I was going to try not to look at as I attempted to find my way home. This afternoon, I'm getting rid of Finn's baby. *No*, I tell myself, *it's a foetus, a group of cells; it's not a baby yet. It's not.*

A car pulls up across the road. Through my dripping eyelashes I watch Dad cross the road with an umbrella over his head. He puts out a hand and pulls me to my feet. "Thought you might want a lift home," he says softly.

Without a word, I let him lead me to the car.

An hour later, Mum taps on the glass doors of my temporary bedroom.

I look up from my screen. Harriet Galway has posted a photo of the cake she made for her son's second birthday. It's a beetroot chocolate cake with raw cacao, coconut oil and avocado frosting; no refined sugar, no wheat, everything organic and fair trade. She helped her son to pull the beetroot from their garden the day before.

"Paul's here," Mum says, avoiding my eye.

"Thanks." I unwrap myself from the thick blanket I cocooned myself in to warm up. Even a thirty-minute hot shower when I got home from crèche wasn't enough to get the chill out of my bones.

Mum disappears and I make my way into the lounge, where Paul stands.

I quickly close the doors to my room behind me. My sleeping quarters are none of his business.

"How's it going?" he asks, lowering himself into Dad's armchair. He's wearing the light grey suit that makes him look like an elephant in a tie. Only he's not such an elephant anymore. He's lost weight. Quite a bit of weight.

"I'm fine," I say, sitting on the couch and clasping my hands on my lap. Paul came to visit me once more when I was in the rehab centre. Thankfully it was a short visit. He was very polite, to the point where I wondered what had happened to the old Paul. Apparently Clara had been the one to suggest he come by and check how I was.

"Good. Good. You look well." I've never seen the man nod so eagerly about anything before.

I can hear Mum vacuuming upstairs. When Dad and I got home from crèche, we found her cleaning the grout above the stove with an old toothbrush. Neither of us said a word to her about it and for a split second it felt like old times – Dad even gave me a conspiratorial wink. "Did you want to talk to me about something, Paul?"

"Ah, yes. The thing is Emma, I've been seeing a therapist about... about our marriage."

"We're separated," I state.

He ignores my comment and sits up straighter. "I behaved poorly."

I know that look. Here comes the 'but'...

"But I believe it's important you acknowledge your own part in the breakdown of our marriage."

"Sorry?"

Paul licks his lips and I'm gripped with a fear so powerful I want to yell for Mum.

"You were verbally abusive, Emma," he declares.

"You're exaggerating."

"No. I'm not."

My head is heavy, sore. "Paul, in case you haven't realised, I've been through a fairly traumatic accident."

Paul sits forward. "You know what you used to say. You'd say I was a poor, fat excuse for a father."

I roll my eyes. "Because you were, Paul. You never helped me with Freddie—"

He frowns and opens his mouth to speak but I cut him off.

"You were a control freak who made me feel invisible, Paul."

"I knew what was best for you—"

"No, you didn't. How could you when you never listened to me, or asked my opinion?"

The vacuum cleaner is no longer going. I glance at the

door hoping Mum hasn't heard my raised voice. "Paul," I whisper. "What do you want?"

He clears his throat and sits up straight. "I want you to admit you had a drinking problem. I want you to accept the destruction of our relationship was not solely my fault. I want you to see that because of your drinking, you failed to take proper care of our son, and you turned some guy you were casually fucking into a cripple."

"Get out," I gasp.

"Not until—"

Mum runs into the room. "You heard her," she yells grabbing his tie and dragging him to his feet. "Get out of this house!"

Paul yanks his tie from Mum's hands. He turns his shiny red face towards me. "I came here to tell you I'm applying for full custody of Freddie. As far as I'm concerned, you are an unfit mother."

Mum gives a high-pitched wail and launches at Paul. I scramble to my feet, my head rushing. "Stop." As I move towards them my vision goes black. My foot catches on the edge of the coffee table. I stumble and shove my hands out in front. My fingers slip off the edge of the table and my head smashes into the glass top.

I hear Mum call my name. Then nothing.

———

I squint one eye open. Mum is kneeling beside me holding an icepack to my forehead. "It's going to be an impressive lump," she murmurs.

"Has he gone?" I ask.

Mum nods.

I'm lying on the carpet in front of the couch. The coffee

table has been pushed away. "At least I didn't break the glass," I mutter.

"I've rung an ambulance," says Mum. "And your father."

I consider this carefully. "How long was I out?"

"A couple of minutes maybe."

I expect another knock to the head was not what the doctor ordered. "Someone needs to get Freddie from crèche."

"I will."

"Okay."

"And I'll have to cancel my appointment at the clinic," I whisper.

"I'll do it."

We are silent.

"I'm such a failure," I whisper.

Mum's eyes fill with tears. "I think it's the other way around," she says. Her hand takes mine and she squeezes hard. "I hate him," she spurts. "I should have said something before you two married, but you were pregnant and we didn't… I thought I'd lose you altogether."

"It's not your fault I married him, Mum. And he's not getting custody."

Mum meets my eye and doesn't look away. "Not while I'm still breathing, he isn't."

"I'm sorry," I say, praying Mum doesn't turn away from me. "For everything."

Mum sniffs. "So am I."

The front door flies open with a bang. "Emma," Dad yells. I wince at the panic in his voice.

Mum gives my hand an extra hard squeeze. "In here," she calls.

He charges in and stops abruptly. I push myself upright,

Mum still holding the frozen peas to my head, and lean against the couch. "I'm okay, Dad."

His shirt's untucked, his hair's a mess, and his eyes are wild.

"Breathe, Eric," Mum says. "Just take a second."

Dad inhales and lets a fountain of air from his lungs. "What happened?" he asks.

Mum and I don't have to look at each other.

"She slipped," says Mum.

There's a loud knock at the door. "That'll be the ambulance. Can you let them in, Eric?" Mum asks.

Dad dashes out. "Best keep it to ourselves for now," Mum whispers.

A few months ago, Dad would have been the one calmly holding frozen goods to my face, while Mum launched into hysterics.

"Can you come with me in the ambulance?" I ask quietly.

Mum picks her phone up from the couch. "I'll ring Lily and see if she can get Freddie."

I wish I didn't have to let Freddie down. Again. Maybe Paul's right. Maybe I am an unfit mother.

———

"You were lucky, Emma." A female doctor – who must be fresh out of medical school, with her lack of frown-lines and perky breasts – addresses me with barely-concealed disgust. To be fair, my resume is less than glowing: thirty-something jobless solo mother with a brain injury, incurred while being drunk and stupid (let's not forget she's also pregnant to a man engaged to someone else), is re-admitted after a fall during an argument with her ex-husband over custody of their child.

I'm one of those types people whisper about. It's clear from the doctor's expression I've somehow created this shameful mess. If I was a more level-headed grown-up, I would never have allowed my life to get this ugly.

"Your recent knock will set back your recovery a little, but there's nothing of concern from the scans and tests."

Mum sits beside me, patting my hand. "And the baby?" she asks.

My eyes flick to Mum like she's given me an electric shock.

"The baby is fine. Like I said, Emma was lucky." This woman doctor, who I'm willing to bet hasn't had to trip over an obstacle in her life, clearly thinks I'm anything but blessed with good fortune. "This time," she adds. "It will take me a while to fill in your discharge forms, but once they're ready, you can go home. Your occupational therapist will talk you through the next couple of weeks. As concussion has a compound effect, you will need to re-assess your capabilities."

It's obvious she is placing my 'capabilities' at a level on a par with an amoeba.

"Thanks," I mutter as she leaves.

Mum pushes back her chair. "I'm going to ring your father and see if he can come and collect us." She looks at me carefully. "Okay?"

I nod.

The moment she's out the door, I want to call out and tell her to stay. If I'm alone, I'll re-live Paul's words. I can't lose Freddie. I can't think about losing Freddie. I can't breathe or exist if he's not with me… I can't—

Trish and Mags burst through the door. "Emma Dilemma, you have got to stop doing this to us," states Trish.

Mags hurries to my side. "Oh Em, when Lily rang, I couldn't believe it. What happened?"

Mum slips in. I realise she's not wearing stilettos. She's in simple black flats. For some reason, this makes me want to cry. Again. "Dad's on his way," she murmurs.

Mags and Trish give Mum an awkward wave. "Hi, Sylvie," they say in unison.

Mum's smile is fragile as she backs out the door. "I'll go chase up the paperwork."

We are silent as she leaves. "What's up with Sylvie?" Trish asks.

"Not really sure," I say.

"Maybe her doctor has put her on something," says Mags. "My friend Tom is on lithium. It's really helped even him out."

"I don't think so." The lump on my head is starting to throb and I touch it lightly. "Can I borrow your phone, Mags? I want to call Freddie. Check he's okay."

While Mags fishes in her handbag, I climb off the bed.

Trish puts a hand on my arm and leans in close to my ear. "Your mum told me about Paul and the custody threat."

I blink rapidly. "Yeah."

"He's all talk, Em. No court would let that prick take Freddie from you."

I can't reply. If I tried to speak I'd turn into a blubbering mess.

Trish crouches down and helps me get my shoes on. I even let her tie my shoelaces. It's exhausting enough just staying upright. Sometimes dignity isn't worth the effort.

EIGHTEEN

NINE WEEKS AFTER

"Bye, Mama." Freddie climbs onto the bed and kisses my cheek, careful not to knock the iPad on my knee.

"Have a good time." I give him a quick kiss and get back to my scrolling.

Freddie sits still for a few seconds, then gets off the bed and walks slowly towards the door. I look up in time to cop a disapproving look from my mother. "You can do better than that," she murmurs.

Ignoring her, I turn back to my iPad and continue to read Harriet Galway's post on making kombucha.

"Right. Up you get." Mum strides to the window and opens the curtains, then the window. "There's no air in here."

"My appointment isn't for another hour, Mum."

She pulls the iPad out of my grasp and slams it on the end of the bed. "I thought you had a shower this morning?"

"I did." I lean forward. "Can you give that back? I wasn't finished."

Mum picks up the iPad and slides it defiantly under the bed. "Why are you in your pyjamas then?"

"Because."

Mum is silent, considering her next move. "Get dressed," she says at last.

I've no intention of moving. "I'm not seven, Mother."

"You're acting like it." She begins to pick up clothes from the floor. "We do have a washing machine, Emma."

"I'm going to re-wear them."

Mum throws the clothes on the ground. "You were desperate to take Freddie to crèche last week. Now you hardly have two words to say to him. This isn't like you, Emma."

"Dad said he wanted to take him."

"Because you expressed no interest whatsoever."

"I'm on doctor's orders to get lots of rest, remember?"

"Since when does that have any influence on what you decide to do?"

Why can't the woman leave me in peace?

"Get up," Mum says again. "And put on something that doesn't smell of bacon."

I've fried a lot of bacon this past week. Bacon sandwiches are hands-down the best invention on the planet. I should have appreciated them earlier. It makes spending time in the kitchen worthwhile.

My phone begins to ring. It's sitting on my pile of unopened mindfulness colouring-in books. I ignore it and reach for a piece of white chocolate.

"Are you going to get that?" Mum asks.

"No."

Mum storms around the bed and answers my phone. "Lily, it's Sylvie. Emma won't speak to you because she's too busy lying in bed feeling sorry for herself."

I roll my eyes and take another bite of chocolate.

"Yes," Mum says. "Thank you." She hangs up and eyeballs me. "Lily is coming over. She wants to go with us to the surgery."

"What if I don't want her to come?"

"Tough. I want her there."

"It's a simple procedure, Mum. They just—"

"I know what they do," Mum snaps. She closes her eyes. "You could wait a bit longer," she whispers.

"I don't want to have Finn's baby, Mum. I don't want to have anyone's baby."

When Mum fixes her gaze on me, I have to look away.

"You've got a good lawyer on this, and Trish is doing everything she can. Paul is not going to take Freddie, Emma. He's not."

"I'd rather not think about it on the day of my abortion, if that's okay with you."

Mum throws her hands up in the air. "Jesus, Emma, you're killing me."

"What do you want from me?"

"I want you to get dressed," she yells.

"Fine." I slip off the bed and glare at her putrid purple slippers. "I'd rather do it without you watching."

I wait for the purple slippers to leave, then retrieve the iPad from under the bed.

———

"I know you don't want to hear it, but I have to say this, just once," says Lily.

She's sitting beside me in the waiting room. Mum's standing at the fish tank watching a couple of sad-looking skinny black fishes swim in listless circles.

"What?" I ask.

Lily puts a hand on either side of my face and makes me face her before narrowing her eyes. "Are you sure about this?" she asks, her breath warm and sweet.

I pull back. "You're supposed to be on my side."

"I am. It's just, I know you, Em, and you're not in a good headspace. You're not yourself."

"This is what I want," I say, my teeth clenched.

"Okay," she says. "I'm sorry."

On the wall behind the reception desk is a large digital clock with the date displayed underneath the time. There's something about that date. Something I should be remembering.

"Shit, Lily." I turn to her so quickly she jumps. "It's your birthday."

Lily shrugs. "Doesn't matter."

"Course it does. I can't believe I forgot. Why didn't you say anything?"

"Em, it's no big deal."

Oh God, when will I stop failing at everything. "It is a big deal. I'm so sorry. I'll make it up to you. We'll go out this weekend. Celebrate with the others."

Lily grimaces. "Actually, we can't."

"Why?"

"Darryl wants to take me somewhere this weekend. It's a surprise."

"Wow."

She bites her lip. "Yeah, I guess."

"Have you gone off him?"

"Fuck no." She says it so loudly the old man with the hearing aid at the far end of the reception room looks at her and scowls.

"So what's the problem?" I ask.

Lily sighs. "It's the opposite."

"Oh."

Lily nods. "Exactly."

"Emma Tilssen?" A tall nurse who reminds me of Mags looks around the waiting room.

I lean forward to stand and freeze. There's a faint flutter in my lower belly. It's too early for me to be feeling the baby kick, yet I feel as if it's swimming around in a sea of amniotic fluid trying to get my attention.

Damn you, Finn. I'm not listening. A tiny growl escapes from my lips as I get to my feet and follow the nurse down a corridor and into a small room, Lily and Mum close behind.

We sit, and I'm careful not to look at anyone. I swear a sea otter is having a dance in my guts.

"Emma, before we go any further, there are a number of questions I'll be asking you regarding the termination."

I nod.

"This is what we call a late termination at 14 weeks gestation. I need to ensure you are fully comfortable with your decision. From your records, I understand you were in a serious accident a short time ago."

"Yes."

"With the baby's father."

"Finn," Mum says loudly.

Finn. Finn with his dimples, and his sexy accent. Finn who hunted for worms with Freddie, who ate my food, and took me to bed, and for a short time made me love myself.

A guitar string snaps inside my heart.

"Mum," I gasp. "I need to go home."

Lily and Mum grab one arm each as I scramble to my feet. "I'm keeping it," I mutter to the nurse. "I'm keeping the baby."

Without a word we leave the surgery. Mum and Lily

won't let go of me, even when we have to shuffle out the door sideways. I keep tripping as I walk to Mum's car. By the time we get there, Lily and Mum are half-carrying me. The moment I sit in the passenger seat, I lean forward to put my head between my thighs.

"Em?" Lily leans over me. "It's going to be okay."

"I know," I gasp.

Mum gets into the driver's seat, shuts her door, puts the key in the ignition and grips the wheel. She sits immobile and when she speaks, her voice is flat, emotionless. "Emma, I'm sorry you got lumped with me as your mother," she says.

I lift my head. "What?"

"I'm not a natural at it. Not like you with Freddie. I don't… I've never…" She leans forward and puts her head against the steering wheel. "I wanted to be a good mother, but it was so hard, all the time. It's why we didn't have more children. I just… I just couldn't face it."

I stare at Mum, stunned. "I can't believe you've never told me this before."

Mum lifts her head, her bottom lip shaking with emotion. "I didn't want you to think it was your fault. Because it wasn't. You were such a bubbly, happy child, you hardly ever cried, but I could see you… you worried I didn't love you. You were so anxious around me, and the complete opposite when you were with your dad. You'd follow me around, trying to get my attention, and I… I couldn't handle it. I'd shut myself in my room to get away. Eric was always taking you out fishing or to the park because I… I felt like you were so much happier with him. It wasn't until I went back to teaching that I started to feel normal again, but I felt so guilty." Tears pool in her eyes. "I'm so sorry," she whispers.

"You were a great mother, and you've been amazing with

Freddie. Since my accident, you've been an incredible support. I don't know what I would have done without you."

Mum presses her lips together and shakes her head. "I've been so angry with you, when really I was angry with myself. I thought if you hadn't been drunk, the accident wouldn't have happened. I thought Jack's funeral tipped you over the edge, and if I'd been a better mother, I could have caught you somehow. If our relationship had been better, you would have opened up to me more, talked to me about your problems with Paul. I should have helped you, but instead I just stood back and let you deal with everything… and you nearly died." Mum's face is stricken. I wish she'd look at me, but her gaze is fixed to the windscreen.

"Mum, my marriage, the accident, they were my decisions, my mistakes, you shouldn't blame yourself. That's just insane."

Mum's laugh is harsh and bitter. "If only I could believe you."

I'm shocked to think Mum blames herself for my actions. "You're my mum, but it's not up to you to fix me. I'm an adult, and I take full responsibility for my life."

Mum finally turns to look me in the eye. "Your father understood. He kept telling me I was trying too hard, with you, with Freddie. But I didn't know how to back off. Whenever I got overwhelmed or hypersensitive, he'd calm me down; tell me that just because you and I were different, it didn't mean I was a bad mother. Since your accident he's not been there for me in the same way, and it's a good thing. I'm better at coping with situations – with you and Freddie – than I thought." She puts her hand on top of mine. "And I've been sorely tested," she says smiling a little bigger.

"Well fuck, Sylvie," says Lily loudly. "You aren't the only one. Emma had better start leading a boring ordinary life soon, or I'm gonna have to find a more low-maintenance friend to hang out with."

I smile, blinking back tears. "I promise from now on, I will try to be as boring as possible."

"Good," Mum and Lily say in unison.

"Can we go home now?" I lean forward and give Mum a peck on the cheek. "I want to tell Freddie he's going to be a big brother."

Clearing her throat, Mum sits up, takes a deep breath, and starts the car. I look at her profile and realise I've spent my whole life on the defensive with my mother, worried about what she thought of me, convinced I wasn't good enough. I never considered what effect keeping her at arm's length might have had on her. "Love you, Mum," I whisper, putting a hand on her arm.

She pats my hand and looks at me with so much love in her eyes she doesn't even have to say the next words for me to believe them. "Love you too."

———

"I'm going to have a brother?" Freddie bounces on the couch beside me.

"Or sister," I say.

Freddie stops bouncing. "Can I choose?"

Dad laughs. "No, Freddie, you don't get to choose. None of us do."

Freddie leans towards me. "Mama?"

"Yes?" I put an arm around his waist and he shuffles closer. "Can it hear me?"

"The baby?"

His face is solemn. "Yes."

"I reckon if you get really close it might."

Freddie considers my stomach, then he kneels down and bends over so his lips hover over the button of my no-longer-loose-fitting jeans. "Hey, baby," he says loudly. "I'm your big brother, Freddie."

He sits back satisfied. Then he throws his arms around my neck and goes very still. "Will he like me, Mama?"

"He or she is going to be the luckiest baby in the world," I whisper. "Because they've got you."

"And you," says Freddie.

"That's right," Mum says, walking in with a tray of hot chocolates and a bowl of marshmallows. "Now let's get cracking on this puzzle."

Slowly, I get to my feet, pause for a few seconds as my doctor suggested I do whenever I stand, and head to the table where Dad is sorting through puzzle pieces. "There's a corner," I say, grabbing the piece and squeezing into the seat beside him.

"I was leaving it there for you to find," Dad says, winking at Freddie, who is shuffling about in the chair opposite me.

Freddie giggles. There's a dusting of cornflour from the marshmallow he's chewing on his cheek. I brush it off, and Mum, Dad, Freddie, and I bend over the puzzle in the centre of the table. Tomorrow I'll get hold of Finn and tell him about the pregnancy. The sooner I get it over with, the better. I expect he's returned to Scotland by now, but I'm sure there's some way I can reach him. Then again, if he's gone, maybe I can get away with never letting him know about the pregnancy at all? Could I really do that? No, I tell myself. He deserves to know.

———

My phone rings and I lift it to my ear. "Emma, it's Finn."

Dad pulls up at the main doors of the rehab hospital for my physio session, and I grip the phone tighter. "Hello," I murmur.

Dad leaves the motor running and glances at me. "Who is it?" he mouths.

I hesitate for a second. "Trish," I whisper.

"Can you hold on, just a sec?" I say to Finn. Holding the phone to my chest, I open my door. "Thanks, Dad."

"See you in an hour," he says.

I give him what I hope is a smile, though my face feels frozen, climb out, and shut the door. As he pulls away, I lift my phone back to my ear. "Sorry about that."

"Emma, I got your message... I'm finally out of hospital, and I... I head back to Scotland soon." He clears his throat. "I wanted to contact you but I thought..." his voice trails off. "I'd love to catch up."

My hand is shaking and his voice is just as I remember – only more sexy, because it's vulnerable sexy instead of his usual confident sexy. I'm mad at myself for thinking this way. My heart feels like it's being squashed into a little box. It's my turn to speak, but I can't.

"Emma?"

"Yes."

"Where did you want to meet? I could... I could come to you?"

"No," I gasp.

Finn is quiet for a few seconds. "Okay, well, there's a café on Albert St. Maybe we could meet there tomorrow morning?"

"Okay," I mutter.

Finn offers to text me the name and address of the café and we agree to meet at ten.

"See you tomorrow," Finn says softly.

I hang up without replying.

———

He's waiting outside the café, leaning heavily on a pair of crutches. It looks like he could be in the middle of a goddamn photoshoot – hair tousled, jeans and T-shirt fitted to accentuate his trim, athletic body. On closer inspection, he's slimmer and less tanned than the Finn of old. But his sexy stubble is back. Damn it.

Being a Saturday morning, the footpath is packed with people going about their weekend business. I'm able to duck behind a couple of fifty-something women intent on a shop window display and take a second to remember what breathing feels like before I expose myself and cross the street.

I can feel his eyes on me as I approach, but wait until the last second before I look up.

"Hi," he says, shifting his crutches and trying to stand more upright.

I stop walking, cross my arms, and make it very clear he's not to touch me. The hesitant smile on Finn's face disappears.

He sighs loudly. "I reserved us a table." He limps slowly towards the café entrance, and leaves a crutch dangling from his arm as he pulls the door open. Hopping to one side, he indicates for me to enter ahead of him. I get a whiff of his smell as I move past, and I want to turn around and run. Instead we are shown to our table. Finn leans his crutches against the table and grimaces as he lowers himself into a chair opposite me. The way he sits, I can tell the position is uncomfortable.

"I thought you might like it," he says warily.

"Like what?" I ask.

"This place." Finn casts his arm about the room. Frowning, I look around. When Finn had sent me the text with the name of the café and directions, I hadn't taken much notice. The name hadn't rung any bells, but it wasn't like I was one of those Lycra-clad thirty-something women who flitted from one café to the next while their husbands earned squillions. I hardly came to the city centre at all.

"It's nice," I offer. Which is an understatement. This is the café I wish I owned. Well, the café I had hoped to turn Jack's into – right down to the pots of fresh herbs hanging from the walls, and the comfy couch in the corner. The carrot cake on the counter is so gorgeous, I want to pin a picture of it on the fucking ceiling above my bed.

"I was going past a while ago – before the accident – and something about it… well, I thought of you." Finn shrugs as if he can't quite comprehend why on earth he was thinking of me at all.

"You're walking," I blurt. "That's good."

Finn nods but stays silent. I feel so awkward and nervous, I don't know where to look. How the hell am I ever going to tell him I'm pregnant?

"I mean you're looking better," I stammer. "You are, aren't you? Better?"

"The doctors say I should get close to 95% mobility," Finn states flatly. What is wrong with him? He's acting like we're having some boring business meeting. He won't even meet my eye.

"And you, Emma. You look…" Finn hesitates and I'm assuming he can't find a category to put me into. Suddenly his green eyes bore into me. "Beautiful," he whispers. And for a second I see that he means it. The way he's looking at me tells me he believes, honestly, that I am beautiful. It scares the shit out of me.

I narrow my eyes. "I swear to God, Finn, if you start fluttering your cute green eyes, I'll pick up this bowl—" great, even the dusky pink ceramic sugar bowl is gorgeous – "and throw it in your face."

He looks as if I've slapped him.

"Emma, I'm sorry. I want to make sure you're going to be okay, and I... I want you to know that I cared about you. That I still care about you. I have to go back to Scotland. I *am* going back. But it doesn't feel right. I don't know why... well, maybe I do know why, but there's no point in... Emma, I'm just so sorry. I'll never forgive myself. Ever."

"Finn, you're engaged. I get that whatever was going on between us was some casual—"

"I'm not talking about Siobhan," he snaps.

I jerk backwards.

Finn groans. "Oh God, I didn't mean it like that. Of course, I'm sorry about the Siobhan thing. I'm a horrible, deceitful person, but Emma... the accident... if I hadn't made you climb into the bin... if I hadn't acted like some stupid loved-up teenager trying to impress..." Finn pauses and runs a hand through his hair.

When I notice there are actual tears pooling in his eyes, I have to resist the urge to reach across and comfort him. "You didn't make me do anything, Finn. We were drunken idiots. I don't blame you for what happened."

Finn leans forward to take my hand, which has been gripping the edge of the table. "Emma—"

"Good morning," chirps a young man in a black apron who has appeared beside Finn. "What can I get you?"

I snatch my hand out from under Finn's and scrape my

chair back so abruptly it tips backwards and crashes onto the floor. Everyone in the room turns to stare and my head begins to roar as the world goes black. "Emma," I hear Finn call, panic in his voice. Then I'm falling. I'm Alice in the rabbit hole. It's dark, and I'm reaching out for something, anything to catch me, but there's nothing. I'm alone in my endless black hole.

———

A warm hand is stroking my hair and I'm lying on something that is cushioning my head. There's a strong smell of bacon, and I can hear the unmistakable hum of an extractor fan.

"I've called an ambulance," says a male voice. "They'll be here shortly."

With a single thump of my heart I remember what's just happened and my eyes fly open. Finn's face is above me, his eyes fixed on mine. "Emma," he whispers, leaning closer. "You okay?"

His lap is my pillow. He's leaning against a pile of boxes and cradling me with one arm. I risk a quick glance around the room and discover I'm on the floor of a kitchen. The waiter who came to take our order is hovering nearby and a chef in a white hat pauses from chopping celery to give me a quick glance before resuming his duties.

My hip is on fire. It's like someone's holding a flame to the bone. "Are you hurt?" Finn asks.

Heat rushes to my face. "I'm fine."

Finn shakes his head. "Course you are," he murmurs.

Some sick pathetic weak female part of me is actually enjoying this moment of being helpless in Finn's arms. Oh God, where's my inner Michelle Obama when I need her? No, make that Gloria Steinem. I could do with a ball-busting feminist attitude right now. If Finn could just disappear and my hip stop throbbing, I'd start right now by telling the grinning waiter who is having the time of his life dining out on my dramas to shove a celery stick up his arse.

"Do you think you could go and keep an eye out for the ambulance?" Finn growls at the waiter before I can open my mouth.

The guy nods and trots away.

"Did you carry me in here?" I blurt.

Finn nods. "With a bit of help."

"What about your legs?"

He shrugs but his lips are white and there's sweat on his forehead. I must be killing him, my lying on his legs like this. I try to lift my head, but he gently pushes it back down. "Easy, Emma. Just take a few minutes."

"God, the whole bloody café would have been watching."

Finn tries not to smile by biting his lip. "Someone clapped."

"No."

"Actually a fair few clapped, until I told them to piss off."

I try not to smile too.

Annoying Waiter comes tearing back in. "It's here," he squeals. "The ambulance is here!"

I roll my eyes and attempt to sit up. "Tell it to go away."

Finn puts a hand on my back and with his assistance I manage to stay semi-upright. "No chance, Emma."

"I'm fine now." Truth is, I think I'm going to throw up.

A woman in uniform walks in with a large black bag. She crouches beside me. "Hello, my name is Belinda. Are you Emma?"

"Yes."

"I understand you blacked out."

I don't reply.

"Emma, can you tell me where you live?"

I hesitate. "With Mum and Dad," I mutter.

"And the address is?"

Oh God, my mind's gone blank. "I'm fine."

"I'm sure you are. Do you remember your parents' address, Emma?"

I can't look at her. Or Finn. I stare at the jumble of gleaming saucepans on a low shelf ahead of me.

"Emma?" Belinda prompts.

"She was in an accident with me," Finn says. "A few months ago. She hurt her head badly."

"How badly?" Belinda asks, taking something out of her bag.

"She was unconscious for several hours, in Intensive Care for about ten days, and in a rehab centre for several weeks. Since then she's had ongoing treatment from occupational therapists and physios. Unfortunately she had another knock to the head a couple of weeks ago, which I understand may have exacerbated things."

How the fuck does Finn know all this?

"Right. Emma, I'm going to start by taking your blood pressure, okay honey?" Belinda looks at Finn. "Will you be riding with us in the ambulance?"

"Yes," Finn replies quickly.

"No," I snap. "He won't."

Belinda acts as if she hasn't heard me and wraps a black strap around my arm. "Can you tell me your birthday, Emma?"

"He's not coming in the ambulance."

"We can discuss that in a minute."

"He's engaged to someone else. He's going back to Scotland."

"Do you know what month you were born in, Emma? Let's start with that."

The strap tightens painfully around my arm and I hold my breath until it releases its stranglehold.

"Do you often have low blood pressure?" Belinda asks.

"I don't know."

"Have the doctors mentioned it to you recently."

"No."

Belinda frowns. "It's very low, Emma."

I shrug and stare at the saucepans again. The only other time I had low blood pressure was when I was pregnant with Freddie, but I'm not about to mention that with the father of my unborn foetus rubbing his hand up and down my back. I know I'm supposed to tell Finn I'm pregnant, but not here. Not like this.

Belinda pulls out a stethoscope, puts the buds in her ears and places the cool, round metal end on my wrist.

"Finn," I whisper. "Please. I don't want you to come to the hospital."

"Emma—"

"Please, Finn." I still can't look at him.

He sighs and takes his phone out of his pocket. "Who can I call?"

"What do you mean?"

"Someone needs to know where you are right now." His voice is clipped and tense.

"Mum," I mutter. "She's going to find out anyway."

NINETEEN

TEN WEEKS AFTER

"How's the ice cream coming along?" Mum asks.

Freddie's face is a sea of concentration as he slowly pours the mixture we've made into the metal bowl. This is the fourth time we've made ice cream together since Lily gave us the machine. I can't be sure who enjoys the process more; Freddie or me.

"Almost there," I say, my hand supporting the bottom of the bowl.

"What flavour did you make this time?" Mum peers over Freddie's shoulder.

"Banana," says Freddie. "It's going to be super yum."

"Sounds super yum." Mum pauses. "Alright if we make a quick detour before we drop Freddie at crèche?" she asks. "I need to pick up a book from the library."

"Sure thing."

Mission accomplished, I place the bowl in the sink and point to the correct buttons for Freddie to push. Then he jumps off the chair and heads to the bathroom to wash his hands. "Don't forget to brush your teeth too," I call.

"You still okay to take me to see the apartment this afternoon?" I ask, rinsing the dishes. There's a shift in the air at the mention of my request.

"I hadn't forgotten," Mum says quietly.

A few nights ago I informed Mum and Dad I'd started looking for a place for Freddie and I to rent. I was very polite about it, careful with my words. I could tell they weren't thrilled with the idea, but I tried to make it sound as if it was better for all of us if Freddie and I had our own space.

As we finish getting ready and I wrestle to get Freddie's too-small shoes onto his feet – mental note to take him shoe shopping – I get the distinct impression Mum is working up to telling me something. She keeps picking up her keys and putting them down to rearrange a picture on the wall or move some Lego left on the floor. Twice she's been up the stairs with one of Dad's jumpers, only to come back down with it still in her hands.

By the time we clamber into the car, I'm as nervous as she clearly is about whatever it is she wants to say. Even Freddie has picked up on the tension. The three of us sit like mute statues as Mum drives towards the library. My mind is so busy mulling over what is going on inside Mum's head, I don't realise we're going past Jack's store until she slows down and stops in front of it.

Frowning, I glance at the papered-over windows. *Jack's Grocery Store and Café: Food For the Soul* is still written on the glass, and I wonder when it will be scraped off by the new lease-holder. Trish hasn't told me who took over the lease, she just mentioned it was all sorted and changed the subject. Probably afraid I'd bite her head off again.

"Why are we stopping?" I growl.

Mum clears her throat. "I wanted to show you something."

Dad – who is supposed to be at work – suddenly appears from the side of the building. Smiling, he walks over and opens my door.

"Surprise," he says.

"Surprise what?" I make no attempt to move from my seat or smile back.

He holds out a hand. "Come and see, Emmie."

I glance at Mum who gives me an anxious smile. "It was mostly Lily's idea."

Now I'm utterly confused. "What was Lily's idea? What's going on?"

"You need to actually get out of the car to find out," Dad says, still smiling, though it's not the confident smile he wore a few seconds ago.

"Can I come?" chirps Freddie from the backseat.

Dad gives up on me and opens the back door. "Absolutely buddy, this is a surprise for you too."

My head starts to pound. "We're not going anywhere until—"

"Emma." Mum puts a hand on my leg. "This is giving you an option. Something to think about. You still get to choose. Okay?"

The front door to Jack's opens and out pile Lily, Trish, and Mags. "For crying out loud, Em. Get out of the car," Lily yells as they head towards me. "We haven't got all day to hide in there."

"What's going on?" I call.

She stops walking and puts her hands on her hips. "You need to have some faith."

"In what?"

Lily shakes her head. "In life," she says softly.

Trish hands me a manila folder. "Jack didn't just leave you half the business. He left you the whole building too."

"What?"

"When you and Jack decided to go into business together, Jack approached the landlord and asked if he could buy the building. He wanted to make sure your investment was safe."

"Safe?" I whisper, staring at the folder.

"He didn't want you to spend all your money on setting up the café, only to have the landlord knock the building down – which was on the cards, by the way. We think Jack had got wind of it and thought he'd better act."

"Oh my God," I mutter. Frowning, I place the folder on my lap and put my shaking hands on top. "I can't believe it."

"Jack's wanker son must have contested the ownership, so I only discovered it was yours a little while ago," Trish continues.

"There's more," Lily chirps. "We were going to wait and spring this on you once you had recovered some more, but then you started talking about finding your own place to live and… well, the building is yours now, Em, and there's an apartment upstairs you could live in – no rent to pay—"

"And the café," Mags blurts. "It wouldn't take much to get it open. I mean, you're pregnant, and you've got all that brain stuff happening, but you could get help." She waves her hand around the group gathered on the footpath. "We'll help."

I stare at Mags wordlessly.

"The café is basically all ready for opening," says Trish firmly. "And we could add in some extra tables and chairs, or you could keep selling fruit and veg if you want. I know you said you didn't want anything to do with the café, but I thought, well, maybe you might have changed your mind."

"You're spending more time back in the kitchen now," says Lily. "And food has always made you happy, Em. You shouldn't turn your back on that."

"It's not going to be easy with a baby on the way," says Mags. "But I'm sure you'll find staff. Plus you don't have to be open all the time, you could pick the hours to suit. I mean, Freddie will be starting school soon, and you could close at 3 p.m. or whatever—"

Lily throws an arm around Mags. "I think she's listening, hon, but it's taking a moment to sink in."

"Yeah," I mutter. "Sounds like you've been rehearsing your speeches for a while."

"Actually it's all impromptu," smiles Lily. "We're just so amazingly in tune with each other."

I roll my eyes and give her a wavering smile back. My armpits prickle and my legs keep twitching. I can't believe this is happening.

"Why don't we go and look upstairs," says Dad, taking Freddie's hand. "At least have a look at the apartment."

"Okay." Numbly, I get out of the car and we trail down the side of the building and up some wooden stairs.

Trish inserts a key in the door and pushes it open, then steps back so I can enter first. "They say it's three bedrooms," she says, entering the dark hallway behind me. "But to be honest it's more like two and a half."

There is one small room off to the left. It looks to be a sunroom or veranda that's been closed in at some point. A long row of windows line one wall, and I expect if I was to reach my arms out wide, I could touch the walls on either side.

"A cot could fit at the end," says Lily. "And with a new coat of paint, some blinds instead of those ugly curtains. It would make a cute baby's room."

"True," I croak.

We back out, bumping into each other and enter the room opposite.

"This could be your room Freddie," says Dad. "Look, it's got stars on the ceiling that will glow at night when you turn the light out."

"Cool," Freddie breathes, staring up at the stickers someone has left there.

The dark curtains with silver crescent moons continue the astronomy theme. *They need to go*, says a voice in my head, and I'm shocked with myself for thinking this way already.

A little further along the hallway lies the bathroom with bathtub, sink, and toilet, all in matching salmon pink the likes of which I haven't seen since I was ten. "It's a tad dated," mutters Trish.

Not that Freddie notices; he just loves the handmade shell ceiling light and the shower curtain covered in fish.

Opposite the bathroom is another bedroom, with a double wardrobe and a small built-in seat beneath the window. Outside is a view across the road to the big plane trees in the small park where Freddie and I used to stop and eat our ice creams.

"It's nice," I say quietly, staring at the view.

"Come see the rest," says Lily. She takes my hand and pulls me back into the hallway and through some double doors into an L-shaped room with a little living area, space for a table and chairs, and – as we move around the corner – a giant U-shaped kitchen which looks like it came from an American farmhouse. White tongue-and-groove cupboard doors with iron handles, a thick wooden bench top, and a huge Aga oven.

"Apparently the owner had visions of living here and fixed up the kitchen, but then she got a job in London so she had to rent it out. She's a real food lover apparently."

I stare at the kitchen until my eyes blur.

Mum takes my hand. "Like I said, Emma, it's an option for you. There's a lot to think about and—"

"It's perfect," I whisper, meeting her eye and giving her a watery smile. Then I glance at Dad and smile even more. "Pretty amazing, eh?"

He smiles back, tears in his eyes. "It is," he says softly.

Crouching in front of Freddie, I look into his beautiful eyes. "What do you think, Freddie? Do you want to make this our home?"

Freddie bites his lip. "But there's nothing here, Mama."

I pull him close. "That's because we need to put all our stuff in it. Everything that's been in storage while we've been at Nana and Grandad's. Remember your bed with the drawers underneath? And all your books and games?"

Freddie nods frantically. "And my train set."

"Yes, your train set too."

Freddie puts his arm around my neck and squeezes tightly. "Okay, Mama."

Blinking back tears, I hug him, then stand and look at my parents and friends. "Thanks," I say, incapable of another word.

"It's a lot to take on," says Mum.

Lily laughs and throws an arm around her. "Lucky she's got all of us to help out then."

"I am," I choke. "Very lucky."

Mags wipes her eyes. "Alright, that's enough, now let's get organised. I have to head to work, but I say we have a working bee here this weekend."

"Good idea," says Trish.

"I'll bring Darryl," Lily states.

Trish, Mags and I give her the stare.

"What?" she says, her cheeks going pink. "He can move stuff."

"Absolutely," says Trish, trying not to laugh.

Mags snorts, and it's enough to set me off. I laugh until I cry, and Freddie laughs too – though I'm betting he has no idea why. Mum is the only one in the room who is struggling to find humour in the moment. I look at her pinched anxious face and stop laughing. "I'll be okay, Mum," I say, pulling her into a hug. "We all will."

TWENTY

ELEVEN WEEKS AFTER

I'm going to tell Finn today. He's been texting and leaving messages ever since the debacle at the café, and I've been ignoring them. But his text this morning said he flies out tomorrow, and he deserves to be told. Reluctantly, I pull out my phone.

"Hi, Emma," he answers. "How are you?"

"Sorry I didn't reply to your messages. I meant to but… I didn't know what to say." The reality is, I have something so big to say that I don't know how to start.

Finn breathes heavily. "Look, Emma——"

"I'm pregnant," I blurt. *Oh shit.* I stop walking and stare at the numbers on the letterbox beside me. *Four seven. Four seven. Four seven.*

"Sorry?" Finn breathes.

Clearing my throat, I force myself to speak. "I'm pregnant," I croak. "It's my fault. I mean, I told you that I was on the pill, so we didn't use condoms, but I forgot about this vomiting bug I had – Freddie gave it to me – anyway, it meant the pill wasn't effective. I should have told you at the café but then... well, it didn't go as planned, and then—"

"I'm the father?" Finn asks.

I take a deep breath. *Here goes.* "Yes," I whisper. "You are."

"Jesus, Emma," he says, his voice raspy.

"Look, I'm not expecting anything from you at all. You should go back to Scotland, get married, get on with your life. You can decide if you want to—"

"Could I come and see you?" Finn interrupts.

"What?"

"I'd like to come and see you, so we can talk about this properly not... not over the phone."

"Now?"

"Yes, now. This is big, Emma."

"I know... it's just—" I can hardly tell him that the thought of seeing him again is making me want to throw up.

"Where are you?" Finn asks.

"I... I've just dropped Freddie at crèche."

"What about the park where we went with Freddie, that time after dinner? Could I meet you there? In ten minutes?"

Ten minutes. Holy crap.

"I don't know."

"Please, Emma. I can't... you can't expect me to just hang up and walk away from this."

Gulping over the giant lump in my throat, I struggle to speak. "Okay," I manage. "See you soon."

Hanging up, I turn in the direction of the park. I wish I'd worn something nicer than jeans and an old jumper. Not that it matters what I'm wearing, I tell myself. I was going to shower and wash my hair this morning, but I lost track of time making pancakes with caramelised bananas for breakfast.

I'm so nervous about seeing Finn, I'm starting to sweat even though it's overcast and cold.

When I reach the park, I check my watch. I have no idea how much longer—

"Emma!"

Turning, I see Finn getting out of a car by the park entrance. He walks towards me, his gait stilted and awkward. One leg doesn't look like it can even bend. His hair is longer, and he's still very pale.

"Hi," I say, half-looking at his face, and half-looking at some invisible person behind him.

He stops walking and leans close. For a second I think he's going to put his arms around me, but he straightens and gives a weak smile. "I should have suggested somewhere warmer to meet."

"It's fine."

Finn glances over at the park bench. He looks as nervous as I feel. "Should we sit?"

Nodding, we make our way to the seat. I'm acutely conscious of his body next to mine and my hand closest to him tingles. A picture of Siobhan flashes into my head and I step away, creating more space between us. When we sit, I make sure I'm sitting as far away from him as possible.

He gives me a hurt look, then leans back and crosses his arms. "I take it the pregnancy came as a shock," Finn says, staring straight ahead at the swings.

"Yes," I say. "It's taken me a while to get my head around it."

"How—" Finn's voice cracks. "How far along are you?"

"Sixteen weeks."

Finn sucks in his breath and spins to face me. "You've known for four months?" he says loudly.

Biting my lip, I nod. "I wasn't sure I was going to keep it."

His eyes widen. "You… you thought…" He looks back at the swings, his jaw tense. "Right," he mutters.

"I don't expect anything from you Finn. Nothing. You can go back to Scotland, get married, you don't—"

"That's a ridiculous thing to say," Finn snaps.

I look down at the ground, blinking back tears.

Suddenly Finn reaches over and grabs my hand. "Emma, I'm sorry. It's all so… I can't seem to process this. After everything that's happened to us, I never imagined—"

"I didn't mean to get pregnant." I wish I didn't sound so meek and pathetic. If only Finn would let go of my hand. When he touches me, I want to throw my arms around him and beg him to love me instead of his gorgeous, thoughtful, kind fiancée. Who am I kidding?

"Emma, please look at me." Slowly I raise my head. His smile is fragile. "You are going to be an amazing mum," he murmurs. "And I'll do everything I can to be a good dad."

"I don't expect—"

"You keep saying you don't want me involved, but I'm the father, Emma. I know you'd rather I buggered off and left you alone, but you have to let me be part of this. Somehow."

I'd forgotten how gorgeous he is, how much I love his voice. Yanking my hand out of Finn's, I stand. "I thought… I thought you'd want nothing to do with this baby."

"You thought wrong."

I stare at a crack in the paint on the backrest beside Finn. "I'm not sure I can—"

"You can't stand the sight of me, I get that."

"No, I just… I need some time to think about everything."

"So do I," Finn says, suddenly getting to his feet. He's so

close I take a quick step back. Finn shuts his eyes for one second, two, three, then opens them again. His eyes are hooded now. Wary. It's almost as if he's afraid of me. "You must be freezing," he says flatly. "You should go."

I open my mouth to speak, but can't figure out what I want to say. "Okay," I croak. Turning, I walk out of the park, conscious Finn is watching. At least I've done it; I've told him. I wish I felt more relieved, and less like I'm going to be a lonely single woman forever.

———

"Okay, so I've got a plan," Trish says, flopping into the seat next to Mags. I look on enviously as she takes a huge gulp from her vodka and lemonade. My lime and soda is not slipping down with quite the same ease. It's been four days since my conversation with Finn, and apart from very little sleep the first night and a smattering of tears, I'm feeling surprisingly positive. The fact he hasn't made any contact means he's probably lost interest in being a father already. Either that, or Siobhan has forbidden him from having anything to do with me. Now he's back in Scotland, I feel a space opening up in my chest. An acceptance and a loss all in one.

"This better not involve another fake hen's do," I say.

"Never again," Lily says solemnly.

"Has Tina had her roots done?" Mags squints at Tina behind the bar.

"I think she has," Trish says. "Wonder if she's got herself a man."

"She doesn't have to have a man to decide to improve herself," Mags says.

"Absolutely," Lily says, "But by God they come in handy."

"Oh shut up," we groan. Lily has spent the past half hour talking us through her weekend with Darryl. There was the bath with rose petals and champagne he organised, a two-hour post-coital massage he gave Lily, claiming he enjoyed every minute of it, and an evening yacht cruise – just the two of them because, what do you know, Darryl used to be a professional sailor. They dropped anchor in some secluded bay and swam naked in the freezing water. Bastards.

"So what's your plan?" I ask Trish, relaxing into the booth. It's so good to be sitting here. Almost like old times, except I'm a very different person to the Emma of old. Funnily enough, I'm starting to like this new Emma more and more. She's kinder to herself, and to others. Less bitter. More appreciative of simple joys. Like catching up with friends.

Trish shuffles forward. "Okay, hear me out first before you all start yelling."

"Can't promise," Lily mutters. She's a tad fragile, having barely slept all weekend. Plus she's decided to try and swear less. Darryl told her she was sexier when she didn't say fuck in every sentence.

"I was talking to a lawyer friend of mine who deals with quite a number of custody cases and she mentioned something I think you should consider, Em."

"Alright," I say slowly. "Hit me with it."

"Well." Trish clears her throat and glances at Mags and Lily. "I think you should suggest, since Paul wants full-time custody of Freddie, that he has him for a trial period of, say, two or three weeks."

"What?" Lily screeches. "Are you insane?"

Trish holds up her hand. "Wait. Let me finish."

I'm so stunned by her suggestion I can't even speak.

"You know what Paul's like, Em. He's bloody hopeless

with Freddie. He can be a doting father for all of ten minutes and then he has to lie down and recover – or disappear on work business for a week. How do you think he's going to handle three weeks with his son? You've always done everything for Freddie."

"True," I say.

"What about little Lady Grey?" Mags asks. It's our new name for Clara.

"She works full-time and I'm guessing she's not going to volunteer to take time off. Plus I've heard through the grapevine – okay, from Emma's mum – that she's going to look after her sick mother for a week. I thought we could make sure her absence coincided with Paul's trial period with his precious son."

"It's insane," Lily states.

"Em." Trish grips my hand. "He's making a big song and dance because he wants to prove he's some model citizen and not the complete plonker we know he is. Also, let's face it, he's bitter and twisted towards you. I know you want to avoid going to court and dragging things out. What have you got to lose?"

"Freddie," I state.

"If anything, this shows the court you're willing to share custody, and that you're not being unreasonable or getting in the way of Paul seeing his son."

"Even if the idea did have some sliver of merit, I don't think I could do that to Freddie. He might think I'm fobbing him off." My stomach flips imagining Freddie's distress.

Trish eyeballs me. "I hope it never comes to this, Emma, but if the courts ask Freddie who he wants to live with – and that's a big 'if', because they try hard to keep children out of it – wouldn't it only be fair for him to spend some time with Paul, to see what it would be like? My guess is, after living with his father for a short time, it'll be a no-brainer. He'll choose you in a second, and he won't be so resentful when he becomes an angst-ridden teenager and thinks you stopped him living with his father."

"Have you been working on this speech for a while?" Lily asks.

Trish nods. "There's one other part to the plan, which involves all of us."

Mags frowns. "I'm not doing anything illegal."

Trish laughs. "There's no need to resort to that yet." She bites her lip. "Emma, when was the last time you had a holiday?"

"What?"

"A holiday. A proper holiday with no responsibilities. No husband or children. Just you doing something completely for yourself."

"I haven't even contemplated a holiday in years."

"Exactly." Trish reaches into her handbag and pulls out a glossy brochure. "Okay, ladies. Emma has been through hell and back recently. She needs a damn good break and a chance to really focus on herself and her recovery before she opens her café and adds a second sprog to her family." She slides the brochure in front of me. "A ten-day retreat in Bali. Yoga every day. Healthy meals provided. No alcohol," Trish winces dramatically. "Massages and swims in the ocean. Maybe a surf lesson or two."

The four of us stare at the brochure hypnotised. "Bali," I murmur.

"It's women-only," Trish states. "No men to deal with."

Mags's eyes are wide. "Only women?"

Trish nods. "What do you think?"

Lily slams her palm on the table making us all jump. "If

we don't do this, I will never forgive us." She glares at me. "You deserve this, Emma."

On the cover of the brochure is a picture of a beach with sun loungers spaced along it. An attractive woman is having a massage on one of the loungers as the sun sets over the ocean behind her. I'm so jealous of that woman I start to salivate. "It sounds amazing, but I move into my apartment next week and it would be too unsettling for Freddie to suddenly leave him with Paul and disappear to another country hundreds of miles away."

"Sylvie and Eric will keep an eye on Freddie. I spoke to them a couple of days ago. They want you to take the trip, Emma. They'll make sure Freddie is okay. And it's only two weeks. Occasionally, you can put yourself first."

"I'll have to find someone to take care of my cats," Mags mutters.

Lily and I lock eyes and start laughing. "You will, Mags," I say, wiping the corner of my eye. "It'll be the longest you've left them for."

Mags doesn't find it amusing. "They're my family," she says softly.

We all leap up and throw our arms around her. "We are too!"

"Okay, okay," Mags laughs. "Get off me."

Collapsing back in our seats, my vision wavers and wobbles. Blinking and breathing, I wait for my fragile brain to recover its equilibrium.

"So, we do it?" Lily asks.

They're watching, waiting for me to give the final word.

"We do it," I whisper. "Assuming Paul will have Freddie."

"He won't feel like he can say no," Trish says. "I'm sure of it."

Lily picks up the brochure. "No alcohol, eh?"

Trish nods.

"Holy fuck," Lily states. "This is going to be huge."

"Yep," I whisper. There's a familiar ghost of a flutter in my belly. *That's right, little one. We're going on an adventure.* Then I picture Freddie and begin to immediately have second thoughts. While the girls chat excitedly about Bali, I feel the guilt begin to ooze from my pores. Am I really an unfit mother, as Paul believes me to be? Or am I, for the first time in a very long time, putting myself first?

TWENTY-ONE

TWELVE WEEKS AFTER

"Emma Tilssen, put that down!" Dad charges up to me. "It's far too heavy."

I shift the box containing Freddie's toys and books higher onto my hip. "Dad, it's fine. I'm good, remember?"

Dad hesitates then steps back. "Okay."

Last night I sat Dad down in his favourite armchair and told him straight up he had to stop treating me like I was an invalid. I said now that I was moving into my apartment, we all had to settle into a new kind of normal. It was important Freddie and I developed our own daily routine independent of other people.

Striding up the stairs at the side of my building (I keep saying those words 'my building' in my head, like a mantra), I squeeze through the front door and into Freddie's newly-painted bedroom. I had given him the option of three different colours, and he'd chosen my least favourite. But in the end I think he made the right choice. The khaki green looks great against the grey-striped curtains. "Hey, Fredster. Here's some more things to unpack."

Freddie is taking his job of transferring his clothes in neat piles from his bag to his drawers very seriously. He grins. "Thanks, Mama."

I'm not sure who is more excited about finally being back in our own place again. I'm pretty sure I know who is more nervous. I place the box on the carpet and lie down next to Freddie. There's a niggle in the base of my skull and I've learnt if I make myself rest – even if it's just for a few minutes – a headache won't develop.

Propped on an elbow, I watch my son unpack. It's hard to believe he'll be starting school soon. "We're nearly all moved in. I thought we'd have some lunch, then get a taxi to the supermarket and do a shop. You could help me make pizzas tonight."

"Cool." Freddie ducks his head and nuzzles it into my neck, then returns to his task.

I stroke his back. "You sure you're okay about going to stay with your dad next week?"

Freddie frowns. "I guess."

We've talked about it every day this week, and Freddie goes from being excited about staying with his dad, to crying and saying he doesn't want to go. It's been a rollercoaster few days and I'm pretty sure I've reached mother-guilt saturation levels. I'm prepared to do anything to alleviate the situation, which is why I blurt out, without any forethought or planning, "You know, it's your birthday soon, and I thought you might like a puppy?"

Freddie freezes, a pile of socks slipping from his hands. He gapes at me, his cheeks flushed.

"What do you think?" I ask, smiling. Sure, it's complete bribery and Mum will go mental when she finds out I'm taking on the responsibility of a pet, with a baby on the way, no income, and no man to support me, but stuff it. I'll manage. Somehow.

"Yes!" Freddie throttles me with a hug. "Can it sleep on my bed? Can Jake come for a sleepover when we get it?"

"Absolutely," I choke.

"What's this?" Mum stands at the doorway holding the vacuum cleaner.

"I'm getting a puppy for my birthday," Freddie yells, bouncing off me.

Mum's eyes widen. "Are you?"

I bite my lip and wait for the reprimand.

"Wow," Mum says through clenched teeth.

I get to my feet. "Mum, you don't need to vacuum."

"I'll just do a quick run around. We've been traipsing dirt in and out all morning."

I feel a little bubble of laughter swell in my chest watching Mum walk away in her stilettos. There can't be many sixty-five-year-olds who would happily vacuum in heels so thin you could stab a steak with them.

"Hellooo!" Lily calls. Freddie runs past me towards the front door. "Guess what, Lily!" He launches himself into her arms. "I'm getting a puppy."

Lily staggers down the hall and spies me on the floor of Freddie's room. "You're getting too heavy, little man," she says collapsing onto his freshly-made-up bed. Freddie giggles and rolls off her. "Now what's this about a puppy?" She narrows her eyes at me.

I grin. "As soon as we get back from Bali."

Lily shakes her head. "Em, you are a fucking write-off."

Freddie puts his hand over Lily's mouth. "No swearing," he says sternly. Lily has got Freddie onboard to help curb her language. She's been trying really hard, which is a sure sign she's feeling more for Darryl than she's letting on to me – or to herself.

Lily lifts Freddie's hand from her mouth. "Thanks, buddy," she says. "Lucky I've got you, eh? Now," Lily gets to her feet. "I've got an hour before I need to be back at work and a delicious array of lunch options from the deli on the backseat of my car. Who's hungry?"

"Me," Freddie says.

"Me too." Dad stands at the door with Freddie's scooter. "Where do you want this?" he asks me.

"In there, thanks Dad." I point to the hall cupboard.

"Lil, you are my saviour," I say, slowly getting to my feet. "I was wondering what to get us for lunch. Want a hand bringing it in?"

"Sure." Lily jumps to her feet and I follow her out to her car. "Tickets are all booked," she says, opening the car door. "A week today."

I gasp and collapse against her.

"What?" she says alarmed.

I clutch at my face. "I'll have to go shopping for a swimsuit."

Lily pushes me off her and punches me in the arm.

"Oww. You gave me a dead arm." Grinning, I rub at my throbbing bicep.

"Serves you right."

We gather up the food from the backseat. "Em," Lily says, following me back to the apartment.

"Yeah."

"Have you heard from Finn at all?"

My heart beats erratically. "No."

"Darryl reckons…" Lily trails off.

I pause on the top step and turn to face her. "What?"

Lily wrinkles her nose. "I wasn't sure if I should say anything."

"About what?"

"Well, Darryl told me…" Again Lily trails off.

"Spill."

She eyes me carefully. "Finn's not getting married. Apparently the bride-to-be called off the engagement."

A sudden ache grips my chest. "Are you sure?"

Lily nods. "But don't worry, it happened long before you dropped your little baby bombshell."

"So they broke up before I told Finn about the baby? Are you one hundred per cent sure because if—"

"—Emma, they broke up about an hour after our little visit to the hospital," Lily says quickly.

I stare at her, stunned. "But that was weeks ago," I whisper.

Lily frowns. "Please don't get mad at me. I only found out from Darryl last night. But it doesn't change… I mean Finn's still back in Scotland, isn't he? Emma, the whole Finn-and-you thing has been so… I'll be honest, I don't know how to deal with it. I was furious with him when I found out he was engaged, and then after the accident, well, I hated him Emma, I really, truly hated the guy. But he's the father of your baby whether I want him to be or not. God, I don't know what to say, Em. I'm rambling…"

"He never said anything. I even mentioned the fact he was engaged and he didn't deny it. He made me think… why didn't he tell me?"

Lily bites her lip and tips her head to one side. "Remember Finn had that work trip to Melbourne?"

I frown. "Yes."

"He didn't go for work. He'd arranged to meet Siobhan there."

"What?"

"Would it have changed things?" she asks. "I can't read where you're at with Finn."

"I've been trying not to think about him," I say.

"He made you glow," says Lily.

"Sorry?"

"I never saw you happy with Paul. Not the way you were with Finn. He brought out a spark in you."

Frowning, I remember back to the first night I met Finn. The moment he looked at me I felt like a better version of myself. "What are you saying?"

Lily shrugs. "Nothing."

I follow Lily into my apartment and we unpack food onto the kitchen table without speaking. I wish Lily hadn't mentioned Finn's news. And I really wish the ache in my chest would disappear.

"Em, this is going to sound really cheesy," Lily mutters, "but I think you're amazing. Just so you know."

I give her a quick smile. "It helps having friends who are prepared to whisk me off to Bali next week."

"True, we are pretty awesome."

Freddie, Dad and Mum start to crowd into the kitchen and I hunt out some plates.

"This looks delicious, thanks Lily," Dad says.

I pause to stare at the inside of my cupboard, take a deep breath to banish Finn from my thoughts, let the air out slowly, and turn back to the table.

———

By mid-afternoon, nearly all the boxes have been unpacked and I finally convince Mum and Dad to bugger off home. It's the first time Freddie and I have been alone together in our own place since my accident, and it feels indescribably, fantastically normal. After a quick trip to the supermarket we make our pizzas and eat facing one another at the table. In between mouthfuls we discuss what type of dog we want to get, then Freddie watches TV while I clean up. I can't remember the last time I felt this relaxed.

There's a knock at the door as I dry my hands on a tea towel. I was hoping no one would stop by tonight, but both Trish and Mags said they might pop in so I'm expecting it'll be one of them.

Unfortunately, it's Paul.

"Hi," he says. "You've moved in then."

I keep my hand on the door and my face as calm as I can. "It appears so."

Paul glances behind me and sees Freddie watching TV. "I wanted to talk to you about the holiday you want to take," he whispers.

"I am taking it, Paul. It's booked and paid for."

"Yes, but it's really not good timing, Emma." Paul keeps his voice low. "Clara will be away and I'm very busy at work."

I'm determined not to react. I'll be civil and polite or die trying. "It will take a bit of rearranging, Paul, but I'm sure you're looking forward to having Freddie come stay. He's very excited."

Freddie takes that moment to look over and give Paul a quick wave. "Hi, Dad," he says, before gluing his eyes to the TV again.

"We haven't spent an extended period of time together before," Paul whispers. "He's a very… busy boy."

"Four-year-old boys are."

"Perhaps it might be better if he stays with your parents?"

"They're happy to help if needed, of course. But they're planning to do some maintenance jobs around the house now that Freddie and I have moved out. They could do with a break from caring for Freddie, having done so much of it recently."

"You don't think it's a tad irresponsible taking off on holiday? How will it come across in court?"

"As I said last week, Paul, I'm hopeful we can make custody arrangements we are both happy with, without having to go to court."

"I want what's best for Freddie," says Paul.

My jaw hurts and I'm strongly resisting the urge to shove my fist up the man's nostrils.

"So do I." My voice is so soft and gentle it scares me.

It obviously scares Paul too. "You've clearly made up your mind about going," he says, taking a step back.

"I have."

He sighs. "I guess I'll see Freddie next week then."

"He can't wait."

Paul calls out a quick goodbye to his son and heads down the steps.

The baby does a somersault and I rest my head against the wall. A familiar weariness, which Alison tells me might last for months, presses down on my head. I'm glad I'm not in a relationship, even if I am pregnant. I don't need a man. I've got family and friends and a future I'm no longer dreading. Things could be better – especially with Paul's threat of custody permanently hovering over me – but they could also be infinitely worse.

You've got this, Emma, I tell myself. *Keep going.*

TWENTY-TWO

THIRTEEN WEEKS AFTER

"Hello?" I say breathlessly.

"Emma, it's Joey."

I sit heavily on the bed, surrounded by a mountain of clothes. "Hi, how are you?" Even though he said he would be in touch after I left the rehab centre, I'd not really expected him to call. I mean, surely nurses tell all their patients they'll check in on them some time?

"Good. I'm good," says Joey. "Sorry I haven't been in touch till now. I've been keeping up with your progress through Alison though. Sounds like you've had a setback or two, but she thinks you're really improving. Well done."

Oh God, could his speech be any more rehearsed? It's probably part of his job description to make an obligatory follow-up phone call. "Thanks," I say.

"Actually, we've missed you around here," he says, clearing his throat. "Me especially."

He must realise that's going too far. I'm almost embarrassed for him. As if I'm going to believe Joey the Muscle thinks I'm special.

"I was wondering… well, I wanted to ask if maybe you felt like getting a bite to eat together? I've got this Saturday night off and… well, we could maybe try that taco place Alison's been banging on about."

Is he seriously asking me out? With my history? Stunned, I stare at my bombsite of a bedroom. Lily will be here any second with Mags and Trish, to take me to the airport. I'm still recovering from dropping Freddie at crèche and the guilt and tears have left me unable to concentrate on my last-minute packing. I've got the woozy head too; I can go days now without any hint of my brain injury and then it whacks a punch. A task as simple as packing becomes as monu-mental as running a marathon. How can I leave Freddie with his father for twelve days? I'm feeling like the worst mother in the world.

And now this.

"I'd love to, Joey, but I'm heading off on a holiday today. To Bali." I'm not sure I would like to eat tacos with Joey, or any other guy for that matter, but I'm sure he's never heard 'no' from a female in his life.

"Wow, that's fantastic. I've heard Bali is amazing."

"Yeah."

"Are you… Who are you going with? If you don't mind me asking."

Surely that's not a hint of jealously in his voice? "It's a girls' trip with friends. You've met them. Lily, Mags and Trish."

"Ah yes, I remember them."

There's a bang on my front door, as if my friends have been summoned. Oh shit, I'm nowhere near ready.

"I'd better finish packing," I say quickly.

"Sure thing. Maybe when you get back we could… you know, hook up?"

Did he just say 'hook up'? "Sounds good, bye Joey."

"Bye Emma, have a great trip."

I throw my phone on the bed and race down the hallway. "You won't believe what just happened," I say, flinging open the door.

Finn looks at me like a startled rabbit. "You could try me," he says.

I lose all sensation in my legs. "You're supposed to be in Scotland," I blurt.

Keep me upright legs. Just keep me standing.

Finn shakes his head. "I couldn't get on the plane." He shoves his hands deep into his jean pockets and gives a wry smile. "I ended up hiring a campervan and touring round the South Island. I needed to get out, clear my head, think about... everything." Glancing down, he notices the bump beneath my singlet. It's popped out practically overnight. One minute you wouldn't know I was pregnant, the next I've got a bloody cantaloupe sticking out in front.

"Emma," Finn breathes. "Oh my God." His eyes glow with a soft, green light. I want to melt into his warm gaze. He didn't go to Scotland. He's no longer engaged. Maybe he—

He's not here for you, you idiot. He's come because of the baby. I have to stay calm, rational. I grit my teeth. "I'm quite capable of being a single parent."

He frowns, and the light in his eyes dims. "I'm sure you can do anything you set your mind to – but don't I get a chance? Not with you: I know there's no hope there, but I want to have a relationship with our child. I want to at least be able to discuss this whole situation. I can't believe you thought I'd go back to Scotland and forget about it."

Finn's here. In front of me. I'm not prepared for this. "Do you... do you want to come in?"

"Yes," he says. "Please."

I step back and he brushes past me into the narrow hallway just as a car charges down the street blasting its horn. I look to see which juvenile idiot is driving so dangerously when Lily's car comes into view and I realise it's her. She pulls up in front of the shop and Trish winds down her window. "Let's get the hell out of here, Emma Dilemma," she yells.

I turn to Finn, my cheeks burning. "Sorry, I—"

"You've got plans," he says quickly. "We can talk another time." He tucks his hair behind his ears, causing my palms to ache.

Like a herd of bulls, my friends charge up the steps. "You better not be fucking freaking out on us," Lily says, pushing past me. "Where's your bag?" She spies Finn and stops so quickly Mags knocks into her.

"Hi Lily," says Finn.

Lily narrows her eyes and looks from Finn, to me, and back to Finn. "We okay here?" she asks me.

I can't even nod.

"I thought you went home to Scotland," Mags says, planting her feet and squaring her shoulders. Trish looks like she's going to karate-chop his nuts.

"Not yet," Finn says in a low, raspy voice.

"Why?" Lily demands, as she places a hand on my arm and squeezes.

"I wanted to..." Finn shuffles awkwardly and I wonder how his legs are healing. They must be better if he managed to walk up the stairs to my front door without crutches. "I wanted to talk," he finishes.

Clearing my throat, I fix Finn with a look I hope is blank and emotionless. "I'm going to Bali on a holiday with my friends right now, Finn. We're actually on our way to the airport."

"Sure," Finn says. "Sorry." My friends move aside as he walks out the door. He's about to start down the steps when he stops and turns back. "I hope you have a great holiday, Emma. You deserve it." I have no idea what sort of expression is on his face, as I can't bring myself to look at any part of him. Instead I focus on the chipped paint on the door and listen as his footsteps carry on down the steps and fade away.

"Emma?" Mags says softly. "You okay?"

Blinking, I turn to my friends. They deserve a break from my constant dramas. I owe them that at least. Letting my breath out in a rush, I smile as best I can. "Wait till you see my room. There's more shit on the floor than there is in my bag."

Lily puts an arm around my waist and propels me into my bedroom. "Lucky we're here to sort your fucking mess out, eh Em?"

I can't wait to get to Bali now. If I stay here, I'm doomed to replay the last few minutes in my head over and over. Why-oh-why didn't Finn go back to Scotland like he was supposed to? My hands fly to my belly. Oh God, what if he wants to suddenly make a claim on my baby. Is that why he turned up? He's got all excited about sowing his seed and growing his little highland clan? Bugger him. Bugger Paul. I'm going to go on holiday with my friends, and I'm going to pretend men don't exist.

———

"I can't believe I'm doing this." I stare out of the small window at the wing of the plane.

Trish leans her head back against the seat beside me and closes her eyes. "You weren't the only one who needed to get away," she murmurs.

I study her face. She's still flawless, her skin like silk, but she's different. It's as if tiny silken threads have snagged on the thirty-plus years of her life and made her more fragile. It's a word I never thought I'd associate with my friend. Trish is the tough, independent ball-breaker. We never worried about her, because nothing got to her. Unlike the rest of us, who spent much of our late twenties wondering why we hadn't met the man of our dreams, and blaming our parents for the flaws we'd inherited, Trish was quite happy to try out different boyfriends the way you'd try on bikinis in a changing room. Some she refused to even look at in the mirror, they were clearly such a bad fit; others moulded to her body as if made for her. She's had three proposals of marriage and turned them down so casually she could have been passing on a second helping of lemon tart. She claimed she was happier not being in a relationship, until she met Pete. For a year they were inseparable. Lily even came up with a Brangelina-style name for them: Petri-dish, which we used at every opportunity. Two years ago, Pete got a job offer in Sydney and left Trish without so much as a goodbye. He claimed it was better that way. Clean break or some such rubbish. Trish was miserable for a week, then got on with getting over him. Occasionally I wonder if she ever did.

"What are you needing to get away from?" I ask.

When Trish opens her eyes, I'm stunned to see her eyes are wet.

"Trish? What's going on?"

She blinks quickly. "It's nothing, Em."

"Bollocks it's nothing." I lean across Trish and whack Lily on the leg. She pulls her earphones out. "What?"

I flick my eyes to Trish and raise my eyebrows. "Trish is *crying*," I hiss.

Lily stares at Trish, who wipes her eyes and gives a sheepish shrug.

"Fuck," Lily mutters. She takes the magazine off her lap and hits Mags on the head. Mags drew the short straw and had to sit in the row in front of us. She unclicks her seatbelt and swivels around. Putting her knees on her seat, she peers over. "What?" she demands.

"Trish is crying," says Lily.

"Ha, ha, very funny—" Mags stops when she sees Trish's face. "What the hell?"

"I have cried before, you know." Trish attempts a smile.

"When?" Lily demands.

"When I first saw Em in the hospital. I just waited till I got home first."

"Wow. I must have looked like shit."

"You did," states Lily. She picks up Trish's hand. "Spill."

"Excuse me." A stern, heavily-made-up woman in uniform taps Mags on the shoulder. "The seatbelt light is on. We are taking off shortly."

"Sure," Mags says, "Sorry." She makes no attempt to move.

"Now," the woman says.

"Absolutely." Mags sits back down, waits three seconds for the woman to move off, then spins around again. "What's up, Trish?"

"I can deal with it," says Trish. "I'm just being unusually emotional."

There's a prickling in my legs. "How are your boobs?" I blurt.

"What?"

"Are they sore? Tender?"

Trish looks at me, her face impassive. "Emma—"

"Wait!" Mags leaps out of her seat and squeezes onto Lily's lap. "Are you pregnant?" she squeals.

Trish shakes her head, tears on her cheeks. "You'll get us kicked off the plane, Mags."

"Answer the question," Lily demands.

Trish glances at me, hesitates, and looks at her hands. "I'm sorry, guys. I wasn't going to say anything until after our holiday, because it's supposed to be for Emma and—"

"—I can't believe you thought you had to wait to tell us." I'm still trying to get my head around it. Trish. Pregnant. I'd be less shocked if she announced she was joining Greenpeace.

Mags starts to sob noisily. "This is amazing."

"Who's the father?" Lily demands.

"I'm not sure." Trish hesitates. "It might be Elliot."

"The pie man?" I ask.

Trish nods.

"Or?"

Trish takes a deep breath. "Or Pete," she whispers.

"Petri-dish Pete?" Lily yells.

Trish nods. "He moved back here a few months ago and got in touch."

"And you never told us?" Mags says. "What the hell?"

"I was going to, but then Emma had her accident and…"

"Great. Another thing that's my fault," I mutter.

Everyone ignores me.

"Do they know you're up the duff?" Lily asks loudly.

"Excuse me." The woman in uniform is back, and looking so icy she could freeze a pork chop. "I have asked you to put your seatbelt on. If you don't comply immediately, I will have to speak to the captain."

"Give me five minutes," says Mags.

Trish sniffs. "Mags, sit down. We can talk about it once we get to the resort."

Mags hesitates, then slowly extracts herself and returns to her seat, the woman glaring at her the whole time.

I take one of Trish's hands and Lily takes the other. No one speaks as the plane taxis to the end of the runway and takes off.

It's not until the plane levels out, that we let her hands go.

"I hate the way it makes me feel so *fragile*," Trish grumbles. "I thought you were being a little pathetic when you were pregnant with Freddie," she says to me. "Sorry."

"How many weeks are you?" I ask.

"Nine."

"I thought you were on the pill?" Lily asks.

Trish smirks. "I haven't been on the pill for a while. It pretty much made me feel suicidal for a decade."

Lily and I look at each other. How could Trish have kept this hidden from us?

"I feel like the worst friend in the world," I say.

"Yeah," Lily says. "I bore you senseless with every detail of my mundane sex life for years, and you keep the fact that you want to end your fucking life from us."

"I'm sorry," says Trish. "I blame my parents."

Trish grew up in a household with a father in the military and two older brothers. There wasn't a great deal of affection going on.

"Well of course it was your fucking parents," says Lily. "It always is."

The seatbelt light goes off and Mags dives back onto Lily's knee. "What did I miss?"

"Trish has been suicidal for years and never let on." Lily shakes her head.

Mags gasps and her eyes well with tears. "I bet it was her parents," she chokes.

Suppressing an urge to laugh, I bite my lip and look at Lily, which is a bad idea because she's clearly trying hard not to explode too.

Trish giggles. "I can't believe I could be pregnant to pie-boy."

"Or Petri-dish," Mags says.

"My boobs are already about a size bigger and they hurt like buggery in the shower. The baby will freak out trying to latch onto these boulders." Trish shakes her breasts up and down.

"Wait till they start leaking milk," I splutter. "Plus, with a bit of luck, you've got cracked nipples to look forward to."

Trish's laughter turns to tears. "What am I doing?" she gasps.

The three of us throw our arms around her, Mags unbalancing and falling headfirst into her lap.

"You're having a baby, that's what you're doing," I murmur.

Trish grips my hand. "Will you help, Em? I don't know how I'm supposed to navigate this pregnancy thing."

I squeeze her hand so tightly she winces. "Try to stop me."

TWENTY-THREE

FOURTEEN WEEKS AFTER

"I'm never leaving." Mags flops beside me, her plate piled high with pawpaw, pineapple, and mango. She's wearing a bright apricot sarong over a black swimsuit – practically the only outfit she's worn all week. I wonder why we bothered packing clothes at all.

"How was yoga?" she asks, chewing on a piece of mango.

I watch the juice dribble down her chin. "Great. I think I'm starting to get the hang of it. Though I still lose my balance more than anyone else. Did you sleep in again?"

"I don't know how you can get out of bed that early."

"If only I could start every day with yoga on the beach and a swim in the ocean."

"Did the others make it?"

"Lily did. Trish wasn't up for it." Since our arrival at the resort Trish has suffered increasingly severe morning sickness. It takes her till midday before she can eat. At least she's able to lie on the beach sipping ginger tea and doesn't have to sit in an office pretending she feels fine.

"Lily gone up the hill?" Mags asks.

I nod. The only way to get decent cell phone coverage is to walk twenty minutes through rice paddies up a short, steep hill. Lily has gone there every morning to phone Darryl. We've been very mature and refrained from giving her a hard time, but it hasn't been easy. Especially when she returns looking like a naughty schoolgirl who's been caught flashing her underpants at the boys behind the bike shed (okay that was me, and I only did it the once).

"He's got to her," Mags says, sucking from the straw of her freshly-made-to-order vegetable juice. I don't know if it's the sun, or the staggering amount of salads, or a combination of the two that has us glowing, but I for one feel like I've got liquid chlorophyll flowing through my veins.

"Seems pretty serious." I take a mouthful of my acai bowl, passionfruit seeds bursting in my mouth. "I haven't heard her swear once since we got here." Lily announced when she arrived that since we were detoxing from alcohol, sugar, coffee, and meat, she was going to go cold turkey and give up swear-words once and for all.

Mags waves to a fellow retreat-goer leaving the open-air restaurant. I think her name is Annabel and she's escaped here on her own to recover from a recent relationship breakup. Mags would know. She's been very social since we arrived. While Lily, Trish and I have been content to sit at our designated dinner table and chat among ourselves, Mags has been working the room; sitting down at the table of Danish women staying here for a friend's thirtieth, or at the bar getting to know the German girls celebrating their graduation from medical school. I never knew Mags to be so extroverted.

"Thought I'd sign up for another surf lesson this afternoon," I say. "Want to join me?"

"Sure, why not."

Yesterday we both managed to stand up on our board and ride the friendly (in other words, minuscule) wave all the way to the shore. We were so pleased with ourselves, we stopped there and then, so we couldn't possibly sour the moment. We lay on the beach drinking virgin pina coladas until Lily and Trish found us and dragged us to a meditation workshop.

It's funny how Mags and I find the whole meditation thing ridiculous, and Trish and Lily absolutely love it. I would have sworn it would be the other way around.

Lily rushes in and sits in the seat opposite me; her face flushed and her skin covered in a thin sheen. I haven't warmed up enough for my layer of sweat to develop yet, but it won't be long. For the first couple of days, I found the humidity and heat oppressive. Now I love its securing warmth.

"Jesus, Lils," says Mags. "Were you having phone sex up there?"

Lily shakes her head and leans across to steal Mags's juice. She takes a long sip. "Worse," she croaks.

Mags slaps at Lily's hand as she tries to sneak a piece of pineapple. "Get your own."

Lily leans back in her chair and takes a deep breath. "He says he wants to marry me."

"What?" I stammer.

"He proposed?" yells Mags.

Lily shakes her head in disgust. "No. Thank God. He said he was thinking of asking me soon and that he wanted me to get used to the idea first. Reckons I'd run a mile if he just sprung it on me."

"Sounds like he knows you pretty well."

Lily looks at me in horror. "I know," she says, cringing. "It's awful."

"Come on." I stand up and pull Lily to her feet. "Let's go find Trish vomiting in the toilet. She needs to hear the latest."

Trish isn't in her room. Or on the beach. We eventually find her in the day spa having a pedicure. She looks like a Queen; two small Balinese women crouch at her feet as she sits on a raised chair overlooking hibiscus bushes and one of the three swimming pools at the resort.

"Hey, guys," she says, as we flop on the over-sized massage chairs either side of her. "Want to join in?"

"You had us in a complete panic," Lily says, wiping the sweat from her forehead.

Trish smiles apologetically. "Sorry. Thought I needed something to make me feel more human."

A gorgeous young Balinese woman enquires if we would like to join our friend, and we fairly quickly find ourselves with our feet in bowls of warm, fragranced water filled with floating frangipane blossoms.

"Darryl just told Lily he wants to marry her," announces Mags.

Trish shifts in her chair. "You're kidding?"

"It's true." Lily looks devastated. "The idiot thinks he's in love with me, and we've barely been together three months."

Instantly I recall my fake hen's do and the first time I met Finn. When he looked at me that night, with admiration and lust, I became a worthy person again. After I married Paul, all sense of my genuine self vanished. Finn brought me back. I went from being lost, to being someone who had something to offer.

"Do you think he's confusing love with sex?" Mags asks.

Lily rolls her eyes. "Please. Do you want to know what I did the day before we left to come here?"

"What?" asks Trish.

"We had a meal with his parents. At their house."

I can't speak. Mags has her jaw open in horror.

Lily hangs her head in shame.

"You refused to meet Johnny's parents for over a year," I whisper. "Lils, this is serious."

Lily covers her face with her hands and groans. "Why did he have to bring up the M word?"

"He's a bastard, Lils." Trish pulls a bowl onto her lap and hunches over it. "Thinks he can get away with anything," she mutters, before bringing up some well-digested curry from the night before.

We wait until she's stopped retching and one of the friendly staff members has removed the bowl and handed Trish a small damp towel to wipe her face.

"Why don't you just pretend you never had the conversation and carry on like normal?" Mags asks. "He might not bring the whole marriage thing up again for months. Years, even."

Lily's head snaps up, her face bright. "Great idea, Mags. It never happened."

"Never happened," Trish and I echo loudly.

We settle back into our seats and are content to stare at the view as our feet are rubbed in oil. Beyond the pool, a group of older women are attempting to play volleyball on the beach. They're struggling to get the ball over the net. It's always embarrassing watching women let the female sex down. If it was a bunch of guys out there, they'd be leaping about shirtless, their tanned abdominals covered in sand, their fists smashing the ball over the net with ease. I'm kind of wishing they *were* out there now, instead of a pack of fifty-something unfit Americans. "Can't believe we have to go back in two days," I murmur, closing my eyes.

"Thought you'd be desperate to see Freddie," says Trish.

"I am, but I've thought about him less and less as the week's gone on. I've realised there's nothing I can do when I'm miles away, so I might as well make the most of this rare, probably never-to-be-repeated holiday. Does it make me a bad mother?"

"Hell, no," Lily says. "It makes you normal."

"Any emails from Paul?" Mags asks.

I shrug. "Haven't checked today." I told Paul there was no cell phone coverage here, and if he really needed to contact me he could email or call the front desk. He's only sent one email, outlining the difficulties with having to take care of his son and hold down a job while I'm gallivanting about being neglectful and selfish. The only surprise is that I haven't had more of the same. He's been surprisingly quiet, but Mum reassures me every day by sending a brief text to let me know Freddie's fine. She hasn't rung, or asked me how I'm coping a thousand times over. Hard to believe it's my mother – but I'm realising more and more how the people closest to me are the ones who mystify me the most.

"This is totally left-field, but you could always marry him, Lils," I say quietly.

My three friends lift their heads and yell. "It never happened, Emma!"

"Okay, okay." Grinning, I take one of the bliss balls being offered to us on a golden tray and pop it in my mouth. It's good. I think I'll find the chef and ask for the recipe. I could place a jar of them on the counter beside the coffee machine. Freddie could be my helper, rolling the mixture into balls. Here I go again, thinking about Jack's café. I can't help calling it Jack's, even though the place is mine now. I have no intention of changing the name. It will act as a small reminder of the wonderful, generous man Jack was.

Before we came to Bali, I was hesitant about re-opening

Jack's, but with time to relax and think, the more excited I get at the prospect. I won't go crazy. I'll start small. Keep it manageable. Open maybe four days a week, 9 a.m. to 2 p.m. When the baby's born, I might even close for a few weeks. I need some income, but only enough to get by. At least I don't have to worry about paying rent. And I still have money left over from the sale of our house. With Freddie starting school soon, the café should be workable. I hope.

For the first time since I arrived at the resort, I feel homesick. It's like this space deep inside my ribs has been hollowed out and the only way to fill in the gaping hole is to go home. The faintest whisper of a headache niggles behind my eyebrows. Frowning, I concentrate on the stranger's fingers kneading and pulling at my toes. For five days I haven't had any headache whatsoever. I've been steady on my feet, no slurred words, fuzzy vision, or forgetting what I'm meant to do next. With my hands on my belly, I take a deep breath, hold it for several seconds, and slowly let it out. One of the women making a fool of herself trying to play volleyball face-plants in the sand. Smiling, I relax, and the human growing inside me does an impressive version of an Irish jig — or should I say a Scottish highland fling?

———

"Since this seems to be the week for us to reveal our secrets, there's something I wanted to tell you guys." Mags's voice is hushed.

We're sitting on the beach watching the sun go down on our final evening in Bali. The water is flat and calm, the sky a pastel spectacle of pink, orange, and yellow.

"It's unlikely to match Trish and Lily's recent news," I

murmur, my toes digging into the cool sand. "But let's have it, Mags."

"I've been meaning to say something for ages. The thing is, it's only since being here I've felt confident enough to admit it to you, and to myself."

Lily lets a trail of sand run through her fingers. "Now I'm intrigued."

Mags uncrosses her legs, then crosses them again. "You remember when we were at university and you asked me if I was keen on girls?"

Lily and I exchange a look. For months we'd been convinced Mags was batting for the other team. She had loads of boys who were friends, but there wasn't any connection or sexual energy between them. When Mags was around certain *girls*, on the other hand, she'd mumble and blush and giggle till one of us pinched her.

"You got grumpy and refused to speak to us for the rest of the night," I say.

"Yeah, I was pretty upset. Mostly because… well, it was kind of the truth."

No one says anything. The lapping of waves was barely audible a minute ago. Now it roars in the still, muggy air. "It's not that I don't like guys." Mags stares out at the horizon. "I think I just prefer girls."

"I can't believe you didn't think you could tell us," whispers Trish.

Mags clears her throat. "You thought about killing yourself and never said anything."

"True."

"You're a lesbian," states Lily. It's like she's sounding out the idea.

"Yeah. I guess."

"Are you…?" Lily pauses. "Are you, like… I mean, is there anyone in particular who…"

I bite my lip. It's not often Lily is lost for words.

"If you're asking if I'm secretly lusting after one of you, the answer is no way, never have, never will."

"Fuck me," Lily whispers.

"No thanks," Mags says loudly.

Trish snorts and clamps her lips together.

I'm laughing as quietly and discretely as I can. I'm hoping the fading light is enough to hide the tears leaking down my face.

"Are you laughing?" Lily accuses.

I nod. "S-sorry," I stutter. "It's great, Mags, really. I'm glad you told us, it's just… well… you must be really enjoying this resort…"

Trish snorts again and covers her face.

Mags gives a faint smile. "It has been pretty special."

"Lots of girls in bikinis," I murmur.

"Emma!" Lily whacks me on the arm.

"It's okay," Mags says starting to laugh.

Lily grips her sides and howls at the last remnants of a glowing cerise sun.

"You realise there's no way we're going to be all PC and decent about this, Mags?" I announce.

Mags nods. "I figured you'd want to hassle me about it for a week or so."

"Six months at least," says Trish.

"So you're cool with me being gay and lying for most of my life?" Mags asks.

"Absolutely," Lily says. "I mean, you should have told us earlier, but it's your life. You get to make your own rules."

"Thanks."

I stand, brush the sand off my backside, walk over to

Mags, and lean down to give her a hug. "We won't hassle you too much," I say, breathing in the sunblock on her skin.

Straightening, I put my hands on my hips. "If we weren't in an alcohol-free zone with two of us pregnant, I'd be suggesting we have a toast to Mags and get drunk on exotic cocktails, but that's not an option, so how about chai tea all round?"

Trish stands and pulls Mags to her feet. "Love you," she whispers.

"You too," Mags says softly, wiping her eyes.

Lily scrambles to her feet and throws an arm over Mags's shoulder. "You realise I'll be trying to set you up with half the girls from my work now?"

Mags shakes her head. "No thanks, Lils."

"Why? Have you got your eye on someone?" Lily asks.

"Maybe." Mags giggles. "I'm meeting up with Lisa from Australia later for a drink."

"Margaret Beatty, you dark horse, you."

Together, we make our way up the deserted beach to the open-sided bar. The air is rich and heady with the scent of tropical plants. Unfortunately it's also vibrating with the sounds of Bob Marley's 'Redemption Song'.

Mags leads us into the bar area.

"It's been quite a week," I murmur to Trish.

She shakes her head. "Quite the revelation."

TWENTY-FOUR
FIFTEEN WEEKS AFTER

I hear the café door open and Mags calls out. "Helloo?"

"In here," I yell, drying my hands and grabbing the oven mitts.

"It's looking fantastic," says Mags, entering the kitchen. "And smells even better."

I pull a muffin tray out of the oven and place it on the counter. "Thanks, I was pleased to find those chairs second-hand. Dad had to tighten the bolts, but now they hardly wobble at all."

"What's this?" Mags points to a tart resting on a cooling rack.

"Goat's cheese and leek tart with roasted tomatoes. I thought we could have a slice with salad for lunch."

"Sounds amazing."

"Alison said she'd drop in and have some lunch with us too. I had my last session with her yesterday."

"Really?" Mags spies the chocolate chip biscuits I made yesterday stacked in a jar next to the coffee machine. She raises her eyebrows in question.

I nod and she pulls off the lid, snatches one up and takes a large bite. "That's good, right?" she says through a mouthful of biscuit.

"I guess so. I'll see Alison again in six months for a follow-up, but she thinks I'm doing well."

"That's because you *are* doing well. Is she coming to the opening party?"

I thought it would be a nice gesture to have a small gathering to celebrate the café opening next week. But now that Mags is calling it a party, I'm starting to think it was a bad idea. "She's hoping to."

"How did the date go?"

"It wasn't a date," I mutter, my cheeks glowing.

Mags grins. "Sure, Em."

Joey rang the night after my return from Bali to remind me about our 'taco mission', as he called it. Since I'd already agreed, I felt I couldn't really back out, and so the previous night I'd endured a not-entirely-unpleasant evening eating tacos and drinking sparkling water with Mr Muscle, as the girls call him. Joey had shown his chivalrous nature by drinking sparkling water too, though at one point I practically begged him to drink a jug of sangria like nearly everyone else in the tiny restaurant – at least then one of us would have been able to talk more freely.

"It was just plain weird," I say, removing the muffins from the tin and placing them on a rack. "I felt like everyone there was staring at us, trying to work out what a hottie like Joey was doing with me."

Mags sniffs. "You need to accept that you're actually still a bit of a hottie yourself."

"Whatever. I think part of the problem was that I couldn't get it out of my head that he was my nurse. He's held me on the toilet while I've peed, for God's sake."

Mags laughs as I continue. "At least the tacos were good. Alison was right, they're better than anything I've made. The salsa was amazing."

"I have a date myself, actually."

I widen my eyes at Mags and smile as her cheeks begin to glow. "Who's the lucky woman?" I ask.

"Someone I met at the vet a few days ago. Remember I had to take Misty in for her annual check-up? There was this gorgeous woman, Phoebe, who had brought in her tabby, Silky, who'd been in a cat-fight and had a nasty wound on her leg."

"Did this Phoebe pick up on your lesbian vibe?" I ask.

Mags whacks me lightly on the arm. "I guess I kind of picked up on hers, and I took the plunge and asked if she'd like to go out, like, on a date, and she said yes."

"That's great, Mags. Well done you."

"Thanks. I'll probably be nervous as anything."

Someone knocks loudly at the café door.

"That'll be Alison," I say.

Mags nods. "I'll let her in."

"Thanks." I finish removing the muffins from the tray and start to stack some dishes.

"Em?" Mags says softly.

I turn with a smile. "Hey Ali—" My voice dies as I see Finn walk into the kitchen behind Mags.

"Hi, Emma," he says quietly.

"H-hi," I stammer.

"If it's a bad time, I can come back?" he says quickly.

While on holiday I'd received a text message from Finn asking if he could come by to talk about the baby when I got back. I'd sent a breezy I'm-in-Bali-and-nothing-can-phase-me reply saying I would be busy getting ready to open the café, but he could stop by if he was in the area. I never expected he would be in the area quite so soon.

"I'm just going to make a phone call," says Mags, practically diving out the door. While lying by the pool in Bali, my friends and I had a long discussion about what to do regarding Finn. Eventually we agreed that, since he was the baby's dad, I should probably allow him to be involved. He had a right to know his child, Lily said. The flaw in this approach, I now realise, as Finn stands before me, is that it's a lot easier to *talk* about being a level-headed responsible adult than it is to *be* one.

"Would you like a muffin?" I ask, pointing. "They're raspberry and white chocolate."

Finn gives a weak smile. "Tempting, but no thanks."

Biting my lip, I look around the kitchen, hoping Finn will say whatever it is he needs to get off his chest.

He clears his throat. "I realise it is difficult for you to see me, but I'd like to help out with our baby and be a part of his or her life."

I meet his serious green eyes and for a split second entertain the idea of stepping across the room and throwing my arms around him. Instead I take a deep breath and let it out. "Okay," I say softly. "That seems reasonable."

Finn starts to move, and I think he's read my thoughts and is going to hug me, but he stops abruptly and crosses his arms. "Thank you," he says. "I don't know the first thing about being a father, but I'll do the best I can."

"You'll be fine," I say quickly. "You were amazing with Freddie." I'm about to say he was better at interacting with Freddie than Paul was, but thankfully stop myself.

"How is Freddie?" Finn asks uncrossing his arms. "He must be due to start school soon."

I nod. "Next week."

"Wow. How do you feel about that?"

I shrug. "Okay, I guess. Nervous."

"And Paul… is he… are things okay there?"

I'm not sure if this is any of Finn's business. "Not really." Before I can stop them, tears rush to my eyes.

Finn re-crosses his arms and frowns. "What's he done?" he says.

"Nothing you need to concern yourself with."

"Darryl said Freddie stayed with Paul while you were in Bali," Finn states. "I thought maybe things had improved on that front."

I narrow my eyes. "I'd appreciate it if you and Darryl didn't discuss my pathetic little life, thank you Finn."

Finn spreads his hands wide. "I can't help it if I still care for you, Emma," his voice has risen to the point where I'm sure Mags must hear him.

I'm annoyed at that look of pity in Finn's eyes. He still cares about me because I'm carrying his child. I'm fragile property to be delicately dealt with.

"It was an experiment," I mutter. Then I grimace, wishing I'd never used the word 'experiment' in relation to my son.

"What was?" Finn asks.

"That sounds terrible. I didn't mean… it's just… Paul has applied for custody of Freddie."

"You're kidding?" Finn looks genuinely horrified. At least it means he's no longer staring at me like I'm an injured puppy.

"I don't think he really wants to have Freddie, he just wants to prove a point; that I'm an unfit mother, or something along those lines."

"Which you aren't," Finn says firmly.

"The thing is, he's never been a hands-on dad. I think it's

been good for him to be solely responsible for Freddie. He realises how much is involved."

"Did it work? Does he still want custody?"

"I don't know. He certainly looked relieved when I collected Freddie last week, but he hasn't said anything about it."

"I can't believe it, Emma. You're a fantastic mother."

"When I'm not getting drunk and being reckless and selfish."

"I was the reckless, selfish one, Emma. Not you."

"No, Finn. We both were."

Finn sighs, his eyes downcast. "I'll leave you to get on with things. Thank you for agreeing to let me be involved with the baby."

My palms suddenly ache as I note the change from 'our baby' to 'the baby'.

"My visa runs out soon," Finn says. "I won't be able to stay in New Zealand much longer, so…"

"I understand. I'll let you know when the baby's born, though I don't expect you to fly all the way back from Scotland. I'll… I'll send photos or something."

Finn nods. "Thanks," he says flatly. "Good luck with the café, and… and the rest of the pregnancy."

"Thank you." It's like we're strangers talking about the weather.

"And give Freddie my regards. I hope school goes well."

Would he just hurry up and go? "Okay."

"Bye, Emma."

"Bye."

Finn opens his mouth as if to speak, then closes it, turns and strides out of the door.

I stare at the spot where he was standing and it's like I

can see a faint outline of him still there in front of me. Then I blink, and it's gone.

———

"So, how was lunch with Mags?" Lily dips a carrot stick in the tub of hummus and shoves it in her mouth. I'm craving hummus right now, and have made three batches since we returned from Bali.

Freddie crunches happily on his celery stick filled with peanut butter.

"Good." I know I should mention Finn's visit – Mags will spill anyway – but I don't want to bring Finn up in front of Freddie. Or maybe that's my excuse for not wanting to talk about him at all.

"Mags tells me you had a visitor."

Bugger. "News travels fast."

Lily assesses me for a few moments. "Anything you want to talk about?"

"Not really. How's Darryl?"

Lily smiles. "Good."

I raise my eyebrows. "Sounds serious."

"He wants us to move in together."

"And?"

Lily's eyebrows draw together like she's confused. "I told him I'd consider it."

I scoop up the biggest dollop of hummus possible onto my cucumber baton and shove it into my mouth. "What happened to my friend?" I ask through my mouthful of food.

"Honestly, Em, I don't know. I'm worried she's matured or something."

"Oh my God, you could be right. I haven't heard a swear-word out of you since you arrived."

Lily nods, her expression grave. "Exactly."

"Jake is coming for a sleepover next Friday for my birthday. We're going to pick up Kai." Freddie states.

Kai is the three-month-old puppy we fell in love with at the animal shelter. He's a mix of Jack Russell, Cocker Spaniel, and something else I can't remember. I'm nearly as excited as Freddie about bringing him home.

"Is that right, Fredster? Are you having Mum's famous pizza?"

Freddie nods. "And we're going to make ice cream in the special machine you bought."

"Wow! Lucky," Lily says. "Wish I was invited."

Freddie considers this for a second. "You can sleepover too, but you'll have to share Mama's bed. There's not enough room on my floor."

"Well thanks, Freddie. I'm not sure if I can make it, but I'll get back to you."

There's a brief knock on the door and Dad pokes his head in. "Anyone home?"

"Hey, Dad. Come and have some hummus."

Dad rolls his eyes. "Not again."

"This baby is thriving on chickpeas right now."

Dad sits at the table and stares suspiciously at the bowl of hummus and surrounding vegetable sticks. He warily picks up a carrot stick, considers the hummus, and puts the untainted carrot in his mouth. Dad is not a big fan of exotic flavours.

"Is this your dinner?" he asks.

I can practically read the worried thoughts on his face.

"We're having an omelette after we get back from the park." The days are getting longer and I've decided a walk outside with Freddie is needed for us both. I've even agreed to play a game of tag when we get there.

"So your day went okay? You're not trying to do too much?" Dad asks.

"Dad," I warn. He's been trying to treat me like normal, but it doesn't come naturally. Not yet.

"Sorry," he mumbles. Standing, he heads back to the door. "I'll grab my toolbox from the car and then you can show me the leak."

Freddie rams the rest of his celery into his mouth and chews quickly. "Can I help Grandpa?" he asks.

Before I can nod, he's off his chair and running to the door. Freddie loves helping my dad fix things. Mum told me during my time in hospital and rehab they spent many hours together in the garage "knocking things around". While I want Dad to take a step back from watching over me, I know how much he likes to be useful, and I think it's a great way for Dad and Freddie to connect. Plus I tried to fix the tap last night and only made it worse.

Once the boys are happily settled with their boy's toys in the bathroom, I re-join Lily at the table again.

"How's the new position going?" I ask, reaching for more hummus.

Lily wrinkles her mouth. "Okay. I get why it was probably best to move to another department, but I kind of liked sleeping with the boss."

"The job with benefits," I grin.

"Exactly. Plus, it was sexy as hell, working with him and having secret gropes in his office."

"Maybe you've developed a sexual fetish and you'll start flirting with your new boss. Has Darryl thought of that?"

Lily laughs. "You know I think he has! My new boss is a tall, skinny, sixty-year-old woman with three divorces behind her and no children. She's the first to arrive and the last to

286

leave, and she thinks out of the seven staff on her team, I'm the most hard-working and driven."

"Wow. What did you spike her coffee with?"

"I'm working so hard because I want to finish on time and get out the door. I think I need a career change."

"Any thoughts?"

"Nah. Although it would be awesome to be a fitness instructor."

"You don't even go to a gym."

"Because I lack the incentive. This could be a way to start exercising and get the hell-toned body I always dreamt I should have."

"Never give up on your dreams, Lils."

She briefly raises her middle finger at me.

I pretend to look shocked. "Hey, no swearing, remember?" My phone rings and I leave a smear of hummus on the screen when I answer. "Hi, Trish."

"You home?"

"Yep."

"Good, I'm outside."

"You could have just come up."

"Yeah… is anyone there? Apart from Freddie I mean."

I wonder what's going on. "Lily's here. And Dad's fixing a tap in the bathroom."

There's a pause. "Right," Trish says.

"Do you want me to come out?" I ask.

"No. It's okay. I'll… I think I'll come in."

"Great."

There's another long pause. "I've got someone with me."

So that's what this weird conversation has been about. "Okay."

"It's Clara."

"Oh."

"She wants to talk about Freddie."

I'm instantly on high alert. I can feel my body temperature rise. "What about Freddie?" I snap.

"Em, it's fine. I'll bring her in," Trish says softly. "Just tell Lily to keep a lid on it."

The second I hang up, Lily is on her feet. "Who the hell does Trish think she is?"

"You heard that?"

"Every fucking word."

"Lily, Clara isn't a bad person."

"Anyone connected to Paul is public enemy number one, Em. Let's keep this in perspective."

There's a knock at the door and I put a hand on Lily's arm. "Calm, okay? Let's at least hear what Lady Grey wants first."

Lily shakes her head. "This pregnancy is making you soft," she mutters.

When I open the door, Trish is looking so uncomfortable I give her a hug. Clara stands behind her, equally ill at ease.

"Hello, Clara."

"Hello, Emma."

"Come in." I step back and they file inside.

Lily glares at them both from the table. "Hey, Lils," Trish says. "You remember Clara?"

Lily assesses Clara for a full five seconds. "Yeah," she says.

"Hello, Lily," Clara croaks. She glances at me, then away.

I'm nervous now. "Have a seat." I wave to the couch.

Trish sits first, and Clara perches beside her.

I sit opposite them in an armchair I bought from a second-hand shop last week. I loved its worn, lived-in Seventies vibe. Plus I reckoned I could splash out, since it was only twenty bucks. "Trish says you want to talk about Freddie?" I keep my voice low and firm.

Clara shifts about. "Yes, if that's okay?"

"It depends what you want to discuss."

Trish gives me a warning look. "Clara has a proposal for you. Regarding custody."

Lily scrapes back her chair and comes to sit on the arm of my chair. "Freddie is staying with Emma," she states.

"Yes," Clara stumbles. "I think that is for the best." She shoves her hands between her thighs and takes a deep breath. "Emma, Paul has no idea I'm here. I asked Trish if she would help me because she's been involved with the custody situation, and I thought she could give me some advice."

I narrow my eyes at Trish. "What advice?"

Trish doesn't speak.

"I love Paul," says Clara. "But I recognise he has some... faults."

Lily snorts and I slap her hand. "Don't," I mutter.

Clara blushes. "Paul loves Freddie, and I've grown fond of him too. He's a lovely boy, Emma. You've done a wonderful job with him."

"Get to the point," I growl.

"I think Paul would find it very difficult if he was to gain full custody of Freddie. He's a good Dad, but perhaps not the hands-on type. When we had Freddie staying with us, Paul expected me to... help out quite a lot."

"What a surprise." Lily says sarcastically.

I slap her hand again. "What are you saying?"

Clara clears her throat. "I'll be blunt here, Emma. I can't have children, and I'm glad. I've never felt the urge to be a mother. When I told Paul we couldn't have children together, I thought he'd be upset, but he wasn't. I think... I think he was kind of relieved." She grimaces. "Sorry."

I shrug. "It sounds like Paul."

Clara shifts again on her seat. "The thing is, Emma," she bites her lip. "Paul is… a proud man. I don't believe he actually wants full custody of Freddie, but he doesn't want to back down either."

I glance at Trish, thinking about her suggestion to leave Freddie with Paul while we went to Bali. Perhaps her plan *did* work.

Trish gives me a small smile. "Clara has come up with an idea, but wanted you to know about it first."

"Okay," I say. Clara is looking so close to tears that I almost feel sorry for her. "What's your idea?" I ask softly.

Clara blinks rapidly. "I thought if I told Paul that I wasn't prepared to continue our relationship if Freddie came to live with us, then he would be able to let you have custody without… without—"

"—without losing face," states Lily.

"Emma, I enjoy Freddie's company, I really do," says Clara, "And I think it's important Paul spends time with his son. I don't want you to think that I'm trying to separate Freddie and Paul. It's really why I'm here. I want you to know that I'd be making this ultimatum to help get Paul out of this… situation."

"What makes you think Paul will go for it? He might tell you to take a hike," says Lily.

Clara frowns. "I hadn't thought… I didn't think…"

"You're safe on that front, Clara," I say. "He's completely besotted with you."

She turns even redder. "Thanks," she mumbles.

"So what do you think, Em?" Trish is trying to contain her obvious excitement. "Worth a go?"

"Sure. Go for it, Clara. If I don't have to go through a custody battle and get to keep Freddie, I can't see any problem with your plan at all. In fact, I think it's brilliant." I stand. "You understand Paul better than I ever did."

Clara stands too. "He told me you tended to bring out the worst in each other," she says. "But that's still no excuse for him… for us…" She stops, her cheeks pink.

I don't reply. I've been opening up to my friends and parents a little more over my difficult marriage to Paul, and I've started seeing a psychologist once a week. I was cruel to Paul, though I have a hard time admitting it. When I should have sat down with him and talked things through, I let emotions fester. I should have told him we didn't make each other happy. I should have left him, long before he left me. Paul looked for love outside our marriage. Can I really blame him?

Freddie comes running in and launches onto my lap. "All fixed, Mama." He looks at Trish and Clara. "Hi," he says cheerfully. "Grandpa let me help him fix the tap."

Oh, for the ignorance and innocence of youth, I think, pulling Freddie close.

Clara and Trish produce matching smiles.

"Cool," says Trish.

Clara doesn't say anything. She meets my eye then looks away. I'm glad Paul found her. She may be stuck in a time warp, with the worst interior décor known to man, but she's growing on me.

"Well, I'll get going," Clara says with a fake cheeriness I've come to recognise. "See you soon, Freddo." She pats Freddie on the head as she walks past.

One day I'll have a word with Clara about calling my son 'Freddo'. But not today. For the foreseeable future she can do and say whatever she wants, if it means I'll get to keep my son.

TWENTY-FIVE
SIXTEEN WEEKS AFTER

"Em, it's Trish, got a sec?"

I shift the phone to my other ear and give the tomato chutney a stir – it's my second go, as I accidently burnt the first batch while I was stacking jars of my peach and lime jam on the new shelves. Dad built them for me along the back wall of the café. "What's up?"

"Paul has withdrawn his request for custody."

I let go of the wooden spoon and grip my cell phone. "Say that again."

Trish gives a small laugh. "He doesn't want custody of Freddie," she says in a high-pitched voice. "I wish I could be there to tell you in person, but I'm slammed at work, and I knew you'd want to know straight away."

I walk slowly out of the kitchen and slump into a café chair. "Thank God," I whisper.

"Isn't it fantastic! I mean, he didn't have a hope of getting custody anyway, but now you don't have to go through some drawn-out battle."

Tears dribble down my face. "I was so worried," I whisper.

"I know."

"Are you sure?"

"Completely."

I wipe my eyes. "I think that's about the best news I've ever had in my life."

"It sure is. I'll let you go," Trish says. "You can finish your crying in peace."

"Thanks, Trish."

"See you soon."

After I hang up, I stare about the café like it's the most beautiful space in the world. Wooden crates line up beneath the shelves of preserves, ready to be filled with fresh, spray-free, lovingly-grown vegetables. Vases filled with wildflowers on the tables seem to be just waiting for someone to sit down to admire them, cup of coffee in hand. Glancing out the window, I marvel at the light hitting the trees across the road. How could I not have appreciated the vibrant colour of those new spring leaves until now?

An old man shuffles past. He peers into the window and I give him a gentle smile and a wave. When he waves back, I feel as if I'm going to explode with joy.

There's a weird sensation in my belly and I place a hand on my stomach. Does the baby sense my happiness? I hope so. "There's more to come, little one," I whisper.

I quickly type up a text and send it to Mum, Dad, Lily, and Mags, letting them know the big news. Then before I even think about why or what it might mean, I send a message to Finn.

Paul no longer wants custody. So relieved. Em

I remember the chutney and race back into the kitchen to

give it a stir. Thankfully, it's only just starting to catch on the bottom of the pot.

My phone pings and I go back out to the café to grab it. There's a message from Finn.

Fantastic news! Thanks for letting me know. How is the pregnancy going?

I stare at the screen. Tomorrow is my pregnancy scan. Mum was going to go with me, but last night she sprained her ankle and said she couldn't walk to the front door, let alone up two flights to the radiology floor. I told her I was happy going on my own.

Again, before I overthink, I send another message.

Good. I have my scan tomorrow. If you want to come and see a half-formed baby on the big screen, you can. Either way fine

For all I know Finn might have already left the country. Before I can start to berate myself and question what on earth I'm doing, he replies.

Love to. Thanks

I shake my head, smiling. This is a good start. If I can interact with Finn and still feel as happy as I do now, maybe this whole platonic father-of-my-baby thing will work out.

My phone pings again and there's a message from Lily with about twenty fist-pump emojis, followed by another ten kiss emojis.

I stir the chutney and hear my phone ping again. This time it's Mum expressing a similar sentiment, but with actual words instead of symbols.

I check the consistency of my chutney by allowing some to cool on a spoon. Then turn off the stove, pour the chutney into sterilized jars, and lock up the café. After a quick change of clothes upstairs, I walk to crèche, responding to texts on the way. As I enter the cloakroom, I spy Jake's Dad, Rick. "Everything okay?"

"Yes, fine, I just forgot to bring this in earlier." He hands over Jake's overnight bag. "Sometimes I worry about my mental capabilities."

Grinning, I take the bag and put the strap over my shoulder. "I know that feeling well."

Rick widens his eyes. "Sorry, Emma, I didn't mean—"

"It's fine," I laugh.

He grins back. "So, a puppy eh? Jake hasn't stopped begging us to get a dog since the day he turned three."

I grimace. "Sorry, we're probably not helping. But he can come and play with Kai anytime he likes."

"Thanks."

The doors open and children stream into the cloakroom in various states of disarray. Freddie has a pirate hat made out of newspaper on his head.

"Mama," he yells, even though he's now right next to me. "Can we go and get Kai now?"

I crouch down and give him a giant hug. "Yes, Fredster, we can. Where's Jake?"

"Washing his hands. He was painting."

Jake runs in, his T-shirt covered in paint, and spies his dad. He stops, frowns, and plants his hands on his hips. "I'm going with Freddie, Dad," he states.

Rick and I exchange a smile. "I know, Bud," Rick ruffles his son's hair. "I was just giving Emma your bag. Remember I forgot to bring it in this morning when I dropped you off?"

The frown dissolves and Jake stares up at me. "Can we go and see Freddie's new puppy now?"

"First we'll go home, change out of that T-shirt, and have some afternoon tea."

"Yay!" Jake jumps about excitedly. He's a big fan of my

baking, and I've made his favourite banana chocolate muffins as a surprise.

"Let's go, boys." We wave goodbye to Jake's dad and the boys trot off down the street ahead of me.

"Wait at the corner," I call, even though they're already slowing down. I watch my son chatting with his friend. A strand of hair is plastered across his face, but he makes no attempt to shift it. I realise his hair is almost back to the length it was before my accident. Before I became this new version of myself. A version I'm beginning to think is not so bad. Possibly even an improvement.

———

I pick up my phone, my hand shaking. I've snuck into my bedroom, leaving Jake and Freddie eating pancakes in the kitchen. Kai has finally passed out and is prone on the floor beside the front door.

Finn answers on the fourth ring.

"Morning, Emma," he says.

"Hi." I take a deep shuddering breath.

"What's wrong?" Finn asks, concern in his voice.

"Nothing, it's just, I'm not going to be able to make the scan today." I wasn't going to mention my hellish night, but now I have Finn on the phone, I'm desperate to talk about it. "We picked up a puppy yesterday. He's called Kai. And I thought… I mean, I know a puppy is hard work, but Kai is… he's out of control. He's bitten me God knows how many times, and Freddie, and his friend Jake who came for a sleep-over, and he's peed on just about every surface that exists in my apartment, and I tried to get him to sleep in the baby's room, but he howled basically all night. It kept the boys awake, so I ended up lying on the floor next to Kai, which meant I didn't sleep a wink, and this morning he chewed the leg on my armchair and ate a hole in one of Jake's shoes. Honestly, Finn, I can't leave him alone here while I go to the scan. Who knows what he'll do." I'm panting from talking so fast.

Finn says nothing for several seconds. "I can't believe with everything going on, you decided to get a puppy." Is that humour in his voice or anger?

I put my head against the wall. "I don't know what possessed me."

"Have you got a crate? Any chew toys?"

"What are they?"

Finn makes a sound that could be a snort or a weird laugh. "I'll be there in less than an hour," he says, then hangs up before I can convince him not to come.

Freddie yells out. "Mama, Kai's eating Jake's hair."

I throw my phone on the bed and race back to the kitchen.

———

"Finn!" Freddie races to the front door I've just opened and pushes past me. "We got a puppy."

Finn crouches down and Freddie wraps his arms around him for a hug, just as Kai barrels towards them and makes a break for freedom. In one swift movement, Finn stands up with Freddie still in his arms, steps inside and slams the door closed. Kai slides into the door, flails about on his back for a few seconds, before finding his feet and charging at Finn's leg.

Reaching into his pocket, Finn drops a red plastic thing onto the floor. It rattles and rolls about. Kai immediately lets go of Finn's jeans and sniffs what I assume is some special dog toy.

"It's called a kong," Finn says, lowering Freddie to the ground. "You stuff it with dog biscuits and the puppy has to work out how to get them out by rolling the kong around. Keeps them busy and gives them something to chew."

I stare at Kai nudging the toy with his nose. "Thanks."

We all watch Kai silently as he begins to attack the kong with more gusto.

"He's pretty cute," says Finn.

"When he's not being a monster."

Creases appear at the corners of Finn's eyes. I've never known someone could smile so much without moving their lips. "Emma, I have to ask. Why on earth have you got a puppy?"

I'm so exhausted and emotional from the past twenty-four hours and the fact Finn is standing in front of me cuddling my son that I want to cry. But I don't. "It's a birthday present for Freddie. Seemed like a good idea at the time," I mutter.

Finn glances at Jake still stuffing his face with pancakes at the table. "This must be your friend, Jake," says Finn, putting Freddie down and following as Freddie races back to sit in his chair. Finn still has a limp, I notice.

"Hey Jake," says Finn, pulling out a chair. "I'm Finn."

"Hi," Jake says through a mouthful of mush.

Wearily, I cross to the kitchen, retrieve a plate, and place it before Finn. "Help yourself," I say, slumping into the seat beside him. "I made far too much."

Finn stares at his plate. "You sure? I didn't expect—"

Freddie picks up a pancake and throws it onto Finn's plate. "Not too much maple syrup," he says seriously.

I can't help but smile.

"Thanks," Finn says. "What about you?" He looks at me with a frown. "Have you eaten?"

Nodding, I reach for the pot of coffee. "I've had a couple but I'm more interested in this right now." I fill my mug, then lift it towards him. "Want some?"

Finn stops drizzling the maple syrup and stands abruptly. "I'd love some. Where are the cups kept?"

I start to stand and his hand shoots out to press my shoulder gently. "I'll get it. Take a second to just sit, Emma."

I'm distracted by his hand and take a moment to remember where the cups are. "Top drawer," I murmur, pointing.

Within minutes, the stack of pancakes has disappeared, and Freddie has filled Finn in on his birthday, including the fishing rod he received from his Nana and Grandad when they came over last night to sing 'Happy Birthday' and eat cake. Dad has decided he wants to teach his grandson to fish, so he's looking at buying a second-hand boat. I told Dad he'd have to make sure the boat was big enough to take me too, because I didn't want to miss out on the fishing fun, and when Mum said she wanted to come too, I don't know who was grinning more, Freddie, me, or Dad.

Kai is still intent on his new toy, and I'm finally able to take some deep breaths, alternating with large gulps of coffee.

Finn has been so busy chatting with Freddie and Jake he's barely even acknowledged me. Which is good. It means I can lean back and surreptitiously observe him. There's a different energy around him now. I remember Finn being so relaxed and chilled: life was for enjoying. Whenever I was in his presence, I'd feel not just sexy, but calm too. Now I feel anxious. The way he's sitting, it's like he can't relax. *He's in pain*, says a voice in my head.

"How's your leg?" I blurt.

Finn flicks his eyes at me, then back to his empty plate. "Good," he mutters. "Most of the time."

"Does it hurt more when you sit?" I ask.

Finn frowns. "A little. Nothing major."

"Well," I push back my chair. "How about you boys wash your hands, clean your teeth, and then you can start to pack up Jake's things."

Finn stands and his face contorts for a brief moment. I'm getting the feeling 'nothing major' is an understatement. As the boys rush off, Finn and I begin to clear the table. "You didn't have to come over," I say, avoiding his eye.

Finn ignores my comment, turns on the tap and starts to rinse the dishes. "Have you cancelled the appointment?" he asks. "For your scan?"

"Not yet."

"Then don't."

"But—"

"I'll sort Kai," he says.

This slightly bossy side to Finn is new to me, and I'm not sure how to take it. The rebellious, don't-go-telling-me-what-to-do reaction is simmering just below the surface, but I'm already a couple of weeks overdue on my scan, and I was looking forward to seeing a grainy image of my baby. I wanted the reassurance things were all on track before I faced the not-insignificant hurdles of opening a café and Freddie starting school. Plus Finn did turn up with the miraculous kong and stop Kai from destroying my sanity. Maybe he has further tricks up his sleeve to tame my wild animal.

"I don't know."

Finn dries his hands and limps quickly down the hallway. "I'll be right back."

Kai looks up from his toy and chases Finn to the door. Finn picks up Kai and holds him firmly under one arm. "You need to stay here, mister." He gives Kai a brief stroke, then puts him down, nudges him out of the way, and slips out the door. Kai stares at the door forlornly for half a second, then careens back to his toy.

When Finn returns, he's carrying a large rectangular box and a bulging bag. "Right," he says, ripping open the box on the lounge floor. Of course, this sends Kai into complete raptures as he starts to tear apart the cardboard. "This is a crate." Finn pulls out a black metal cage and quickly erects it. "It's going to be Kai's favourite place to sleep and chill."

"Yeah, right."

"And since it's his home, he's not going to want to ruin it by peeing or pooing inside."

I raise my eyebrows. "I think you are overestimating this puppy's intelligence."

"Kai will tell you when he needs to go out. Your job is to pick up on the message early and get him outside as fast as possible. He'll learn pretty quickly that toileting is done outside, not on the kitchen floor."

I cross my arms. "I've been taking him over the road to the park constantly, and he's never done anything."

"He will." Finn pulls out a thin foam squab covered in a soft, fluffy fabric and lays it inside the crate, then he pulls out a blanket and places it inside. Next comes a plethora of toys, some soft, some round, some downright weird; like the skinny plucked rubber chicken with a ridiculously long neck. "One of these will become his favourite. Once he chooses, you want to go to the pet shop and buy three more exactly the same."

"You make it sound so straightforward."

Finn stiffens as he stands and I know he's trying hard to hide the pain any movement seems to cause. "Trust me, things will get easier, fast."

Kai runs into the crate, picks up the deformed chicken toy, and begins to shake it from side to side. The chicken emits high-pitched squeaking sounds as it flays about. Finn grins. "Let's hope that one doesn't turn out to be the favourite."

It's a relief to see the grin on Finn's face. For the first time, I see a hint of the relaxed and sexy man I knew. "Thank you," I say.

Finn shuts the crate door and locks it. "You're welcome," he says.

"Are we just going to leave him in there?" I ask. "Won't he get upset?"

"He's exhausted. Puppies need a lot of sleep. There'll be occasions when you just put him in here so he can take some time out. That's something you should tell Freddie. Kai's still a baby. He needs to have quiet time. Play is good, but too much can make him a little crazy."

Sure enough, as we watch, Kai spins around in a couple of tiny circles, then drops onto the blanket, and shuts his eyes.

"Wow," I murmur. "You're like one of those dog whisperers or something."

Finn grins again and my heart gives a giant thump. "I've just had a little bit of experience in this area, that's all."

Freddie and Jake appear, and Finn explains to them what the crate is for. They keep blinking at Finn and grinning as if he's a glowing orb of ice cream. Then we gather up our things and head out the door.

"I'm dropping Freddie at Jake's house for the afternoon," I say to the back of Finn's head. "You could come in my car if you want. Saves us both driving to the scan."

Holding my breath, I wait for Finn to respond.

"Sounds good," he says over his shoulder.

———

Finn stays in the car while I drop off Freddie and Jake, then we drive in awkward silence to the radiology centre.

"Thanks for letting me come to this," Finn says as I pull into a park.

I turn off the ignition and face him. "Look, this is weird for me, okay. I'm still getting my head around the fact I'm having another baby, and I know you're the father, but it's not easy having you… the situation we're in is challenging. I'm trying to be all adult and level-headed but… well it's hard with you here."

Finn looks away, his face stony. "I know you don't want to be around me, Emma. I can appreciate how difficult this is."

"It's not that—"

Finn opens his door. "I can wait outside the room if it's too much having me there."

"No!" I take a deep breath. "I want you to have the opportunity to see your child, Finn. If that's what *you* want."

His eyes are expressionless. "I would like to, very much."

We go into the reception and I give my name. Then we sit beside each other without touching. Finn clears his throat. "Do you… do you feel anything yet?" He glances down at my bump.

"Little movements, like a flutter, that's all."

Finn nods. "And how are you feeling?"

I give him a gentle smile. "I feel good. Less tired than I did when I was pregnant at this stage with Freddie."

"That's good."

"And I'm craving different things. With Freddie, I wanted to eat peanut butter all the time. I would literally stick my finger in the jar and scoff down giant globules of the stuff every hour on the hour."

Finn smiles.

"But for this one," I give my tummy a pat. "I want hummus. All the time. Sometimes I'll dip carrot sticks or crackers into it, but I'll also just eat it by the spoonful."

"Not sure I could do that," Finn grimaces.

"I'll probably never want to eat hummus again once this baby is born."

"Emma Tilssen," calls a woman in a white coat.

Startled, I stand up quickly. Finn gets to his feet more slowly. "Are you sure it's all right for me to come in?" he murmurs.

I nod once and follow the woman into a room. We exchange a few pleasantries, then I lie on the bed and wait.

"Right then, if Finn would like to take a seat next to you there, Emma, we can get started." The woman sits in a swivel chair close to my hip and starts pushing buttons on a machine. I happened to mention to her that Finn was the father, but that we were not in a relationship together, and she's been pretty cold with him since. I expect she's been burnt by the opposite sex and holds a grudge against all good-looking males.

Finn perches on the edge of his chair as the woman lifts the hem of my T-shirt and bunches it beneath my breasts. The air feels cool on my bare skin. "I understand you want to confirm how far along you are?" she says.

I nod.

"And what about the sex of the baby? Are you hoping to find out, or keep it a surprise?" The woman squirts gel on my lower abdomen and onto the end of a probe attached to a cord. She presses the flat surface of the probe gently against my skin and begins to move it around, focussing intently on the screen beside my head.

"I'm not sure." I glance at Finn who has his hands stuffed tightly between his thighs. "Would you like to know?"

He looks at me like I've asked him to strip naked. "What?"

"Do you want to know if we're having a boy or a girl?"

"I… I don't know. It's up to you, Emma."

I shrug. "I was thinking maybe we could find out? If that's okay?"

He stares at me without speaking.

"There," says the woman. "Say hello to your baby."

I look at the screen and see the unmistakable image of a little being curled up in a C shape, with an overly large head and tiny arms and legs. My breathing stops.

"There's its heartbeat," the woman says, pointing to a small round dot that blips on-off rapidly.

I hear the air leave Finn's lungs in a rush and turn to look at him. He's lost all colour in his face and leans towards the screen, his hands gripping the bed. On instinct I reach out, place my hand over his, and squeeze. "You okay?" I ask.

He blinks rapidly and puts his free hand on mine. "It's amazing," he breathes.

We smile at one another.

"Now I'm going to take a few measurements," says the woman briskly. She shoots me a warning look like I'm fraternizing with the enemy, but I ignore her.

Finn and I watch the screen silently, my hand pressed between his. It's like a spell has been cast over us both. If I move so much as a muscle, it will break.

"So, Emma," the woman says. "You're twenty-two weeks along, according to my measurements. And everything looks fine."

Blood rushes to my head. "Really? Are you sure?"

The woman nods.

Finn reaches up and strokes my hair from my face. Then he suddenly sits back as if he regrets what he's done and tucks his hands back between his thighs.

I blink away tears and look at the frozen image of a foetus that is somehow, incredibly, inside me. Well, I know how it got there, obviously, but how can something so sensuous and freeing as sex result in something as massive and mind-blowing as *this*? "Is it a boy or girl?" I ask, my voice hoarse.

The woman smiles and begins to wipe the gel off my stomach. "It's a boy," she says softly.

I bite my lip and will myself not to cry. Freddie's going to have a little brother. I try desperately not to look at Finn, but I can't help it. He's rocked forward and put his head down like he's about to be sick. Pulling down my top, I clamber off the bed.

"Thank you." My voice wobbles.

"What about a photo?" The woman holds out an envelope to Finn. "You can put it on your fridge," she says sternly.

Finn takes the envelope and I hurry ahead of him out of the building towards my car.

Without a word, I put on my seatbelt, wait for Finn to get in, start the car, and pull out onto the road.

"Emma—"

"Don't." I hold up a hand, then place it back on the steering wheel. "You didn't have to come."

"What? It was incredible. I can't believe what I just saw. There's a little boy – our little boy – growing inside you."

"You acted like you were at the dentist."

Finn chokes. "What was I supposed to do? That woman clearly pinned me as the young prick who was dragged in against his will and wants to get the hell out of there so he can find another woman to knock up."

"Are you?"

"Jesus, for real?"

I glare at the road ahead. "You were engaged to a gorgeous young woman who loved you, and yet you were quite comfortable shagging me and making me think—" I cut myself off.

"That's why I looked like I was at the dentist," he mutters.

"Sorry?"

"After what I've done to Siobhan and to you, I didn't deserve to be allowed that moment. To sit beside you, and hold your hand, and look at our child and smile at each other like I was some caring, loving husband, when I'm anything but."

"You're not the devil, Finn. When you turned up this morning and helped me with Kai... truthfully, it was one of the kindest, most thoughtful things anyone has ever done, and I've had a string of kind people do incredible things for me recently."

"It was nothing." Finn slumps against his seat and stares out his side window.

He looks so miserable I'm reminded of myself. The sad, depressing me who wallowed about in rehab thinking her life had ended, when I was actually being given a chance to become a better version of myself. "You need cake," I say firmly.

Finn lifts his head and looks at me.

"I made a ginger cake with lemon icing yesterday," I continue, watching the road. "You need a big slice with stewed plums and cream on the side. I happen to know of a place. It's not open yet, but I'm close to the owner. I'm confident she'll let you in."

"Emma, why did you ask me to the scan?"

"Because you're this baby's father." I give my stomach a quick pat. "And you wanted to be involved."

"Do you want me here? Or would you rather I went back to Scotland and sent a postcard each year on his birthday?"

I frown. "It's not about what I want. I can do this without you. But I'm sure our son would like to know his dad. If you want to spend time with this baby, we'll work something out. I haven't got the answers, but I'm sure we can sort it, Finn. For his sake."

"I'm not sure I... what makes you think we can do this?"

"We had a relationship together. It was mostly about sex, but not completely. Not for me anyway. We got on, we laughed, we had fun, we didn't drive each other up the wall." I pause and take a deep breath. "I liked being with you. So I reckon we have a chance of being good parents. If we can get through this awkward phase we're in now and maybe become friends, it will turn out to be easier for both of us."

"Pull over. Please, Emma."

"Why?"

"I need you to stop the car."

I indicate, and pull to the side of the road.

Finn unclicks his seatbelt and then mine. "Turn off the engine," he says gruffly.

With a shaking hand, I reach for the key.

"Look at me," Finn says, putting a hand on my cheek and turning it gently towards him.

I stare at his chest rather than his face.

He puts a finger under my chin, and tilts my head up. His breath is warm on my skin as he leans close. "It wasn't just about the sex for me either," he says kissing me lightly on the lips.

Goose bumps spring onto my neck and arms. I can't move. "What are you doing?" I finally whisper.

Finn sighs and takes one of my hands. "Okay, it's time for my speech and it's going to be longer than yours, so brace yourself. When I ran away from Scotland, from the life that had been planned out for me, right down to the house Siobhan and I would live in and the school our wee bairns would attend, I was looking to escape. I needed to get away, and I told Siobhan I couldn't marry her. That it wouldn't be fair. I suggested we break off our engagement, but she told me to go, do what I needed to do – even if this included having sex with other women – and to come back to her when I was ready."

"Sounds like a saint," I mutter.

Finn shakes his head. "We'd been together since we were eighteen years old. She knew everything about me and I'm sure she thought I'd be back within a couple of months. I probably would have been, but then... I hadn't bargained on meeting you. At all. Everything about you was a surprise. You were married, you had a child, you had... things you were working through—"

"I was a mess."

"No, you weren't. I loved being part of your life. You were fierce, Emma. About Freddie, your parents, your friends, your food. Especially your food."

"Fierce?"

Finn shakes his head and squeezes my hand even tighter. "Passionate. Brave."

"Half the time you and I were together, I was drunk, Finn. It's easier to be passionate and brave when you're pissed."

"That's not true. There were plenty of times we were together and we weren't drinking. You were just you. And I loved it." Finn clears his throat. "Then I convinced you to ride in a death-trap—"

"It's not your fault."

"You say that, but the truth is, you nearly died because of me, and I have to live with that every day."

"I've recovered. I'm better than before."

"And I'm so incredibly glad about that, I really am. But I'm miserable. Which is a weak thing for a male to say, but it's the truth."

"What happened with Siobhan?" I ask.

"She wanted to see me, and I arranged to meet her in Melbourne because I needed to talk to her face-to-face. I told her I'd been seeing someone, and she was... she was upset."

He told his fiancée about me. Was it to get out of marrying her, so he could be a free agent, or because he wanted to be with me? Or did he feel guilty about sleeping with me and wanted her to take him back? My pulse is pounding so loudly in my head, I'm sure Finn must be able to hear it. I stare at his hand gripping mine. "Did she... did you break up?" I whisper.

Finn groans. "She cried for two days and I felt so terrible. She'd come all the way from Scotland to see me and I couldn't... she wanted us to try and work it out... and I agreed. I shouldn't have done it, but I did."

He lets go of my hand. "I was going to tell you about her when I got back, and then Jack died and..."

"And we had the accident."

Finn is silent for so long I have to look at him. He's pale, wide-eyed, and gaunt. "I should have told you straight away. I should have stopped you from drinking the night of Jack's funeral. I knew you were suffering, but when you said... when you said I was the fun, sexy one, I realised you didn't think of me the way I... you didn't want a serious relationship with me, you wanted something casual, and it made sense. You'd just got out of an awful marriage, the last thing you wanted was… anyway, I thought I might as well get drunk too, try to have a good time, and deal with…" Finn sighs. "Like I said, I hadn't planned on meeting you, Emma."

"I bet you wish you never had," I murmur.

Finn shakes his head and looks out the window. "Not for a minute."

My stomach lurches. "What happened with Siobhan?" I ask quietly.

Finn blinks, glances at me, then looks at his hands. They're gripping his legs so tightly, his knuckles are white. "She could see I wasn't in love with her. I was trying really hard to be, but she knew I wasn't."

It still doesn't mean he cares about me or wants to… "Why did you kiss me just now?" I blurt.

He leans a fraction away from me and looks at me with eyes devoid of emotion. "I'm sorry. I know you don't want to go there. I promise I won't do it again. I'll try to be friends and I'll try to be a good parent. I'm just not sure I can do either."

That was his moment. And he didn't take it. Which makes things pretty clear.

"You'll do fine," I say flatly. Straightening, I put on my seatbelt, and start the car. *It's good*, I think. *For the best*. If only my brain could convince my thumping heart.

Neither of us speak until I pull into the small carport behind the café. As I open my door, I can hear Kai yelping. I'd forgotten all about Satan upstairs. "Oh no," I groan.

"He's probably only just started up," says Finn softly.

The thought of going back up to my apartment to deal with Kai brings a wave of exhaustion. It takes all my willpower to get out of the car.

"Emma, I've been thinking." Finn moves around the car to stand beside me. "My work visa has expired, and I managed to get a holiday visa for three months, but the truth is, I'm not sure what I'm doing... with my life. I thought maybe I'd do some travel for a bit but even that... well, you're so busy with the café, and Freddie about to start school. I wondered if I could help with Kai? Take him for a walk in the morning and again in the afternoon. I could start to train him on the lead and to come when he's called."

"That's a nice offer, Finn, but—"

"Please. I would really like to. I miss having a dog. Plus, my doctor keeps telling me I need to walk more."

Kai hasn't stopped yelping throughout our conversation. He's like a flashing neon sign telling me I'd be mad not to take Finn up on his offer, even if it does mean I'll have to see more of him. "Are you sure you want to?"

Finn nods. "Positive."

I think of the list of jobs still to be done before I can open the café. I try very hard *not* to think about Finn kissing me. "Okay," I say. "That would be a big help. Thank you."

Finn claps his hands together. "Great, why don't I start right now?"

"Now?" I want to cover my ears so I don't have to hear the puppy cries piercing the air.

"I'll come up and grab him. Take him to the park for a run around."

"I'm sold," I say, throwing up my hands. "Let's go and release the beast."

Finn gives a short laugh which doesn't reach his eyes, then hands me the envelope in his hand. "For the fridge," he says quietly.

I take the envelope and head towards the stairs. Being a responsible adult thing is growing on me. I can do this. It's not so hard.

"Emma," calls Finn.

I stop and turn.

There's a half-smile on his face. "Any chance I could take you up on that offer of ginger cake when Kai and I get back? I haven't eaten all morning."

Why does he have to have such goddamned luscious lips? And those bloody dimples… "Sure," I shrug. "Consider it payment for dog duties."

TWENTY-SIX

SEVENTEEN WEEKS AFTER

"Mama," Freddie yells.

I can hear him running up the stairs outside. "Don't open the front door!" I scramble to my feet but it's too late. Freddie bursts through, knocks me backwards, and I land on my bottom in a pile of gooey shit. Literally.

"What's that smell?" Freddie says, holding his nose.

"Kai pooed by the door. I was taking him out but he clearly couldn't hold on."

Freddie backs away from me and throws his bag in his bedroom.

"How was school?" I call, shutting the front door with my foot. Mum picked Freddie up today, and even though I've collected him the last four days, I'm feeling guilty I wasn't there waiting outside his classroom for the bell to ring like all the other perfect mothers.

Freddie emerges from his room and stares at me. "Are you sitting in Kai's poo?" he asks.

I lift one butt cheek off the floor and expose the mess on my jeans and the floor. Freddie grins. "Yuck!"

Kai charges down the hallway and yaps excitedly. "Hey, boy," Freddie kneels down and gives Kai a stroke. "Did you miss me?"

"We both did," I say as brightly as I can when all I really want to do is yell at the goddamn puppy. With the café opening in two days I'm feeling a tad overwhelmed. "There's some pikelets on the table."

"Cool." Freddie thunders towards the kitchen, Kai prancing about beside him.

Gingerly, I press a hand against the wall and try to stand.

There's a sudden knock on the front door and I step back in fright only to place a bare foot directly onto the recently flattened poo. Stinking yellowy-brown crap oozes between my toes. "Who is it?" I shriek, my voice a warble.

"Me," says Finn. "Sorry I'm late. There was a crash at the lights and it took forever to get through."

"Can you come back in ten minutes?" I yell. "It's not a good time right now."

"Are you okay?"

All week Finn's been diligently taking Kai out for a walk twice a day and I've been diligently working hard in the café. Last night when he returned from walking Kai, Freddie begged Finn to stay for dinner. What could I do but nod? It was a little awkward, but at the same time, I loved the three of us sitting at the table chatting about harmless things, Freddie grinning at Finn with complete adoration, me trying not to do the same. I even managed to make Finn laugh a couple of times. After we'd eaten, Freddie wanted Finn to read him a story in bed, which Finn seemed happy to do. In fact Finn read to Freddie for over half an hour.

I didn't want Finn to leave. Before I even knew what I was doing, I asked if he'd like to stay and watch a movie. He gave me a weird look, and I was sure he was going to say no, but he didn't. I wish I hadn't opened my stupid mouth. For the entire movie Finn sat silently on the ground, his back against the couch, his eyes fixed to the screen. The moment the movie ended, he was out of there so fast you'd think he'd been trapped in a room full of poisonous spiders. I dreaded having to see him again. And now he's here, and I'm… well, I'm covered in shit.

"Emma?" Finn calls. "What's going on?"

Oh what the hell. "I'm covered in shit," I call.

"What?"

Leaning forward, I reach for the handle and manage to open the door. Finn pushes it open slowly and peers around the door. He takes time to assess the situation.

"It's all over my arse too." I swivel so he can get a good view of my soiled backside.

"Shit," he mutters.

"Exactly." I don't think I've ever been more mortified in my life. "If you laugh, I'll never speak to you again."

Finn bites his lip. "Okay."

Freddie races towards us. "Finn," he says through a mouthful of half-masticated pikelet. "Mum fell in Kai's poo."

Kai leaps at Finn in equal measures of excitement before running behind me, stepping all four of his paws in the poo, and taking off back to the kitchen leaving a trail of brown paw prints in his wake.

"Great," I mutter.

"Right, don't move," Finn says. He strides into the bathroom and reappears with a roll of toilet paper. Handing it to me, he avoids my eye and takes Freddie by the hand. "We need a bucket of warm water and some old cloths," he says. "And we need to catch that dog and give him his first bath."

"Cool," says Freddie.

I begin to unroll some paper and wipe my foot. The smell

is so repugnant I want to vomit. Why-oh-why did I have to be so impulsive? What possessed me to get a puppy? Mum and Dad should have been firmer with me. Told me what a ridiculous idea it was. And Lily. Since when does she hold back from telling me when something is a bad idea? Of course, I would have done it anyway.

Groaning, I add to the growing pile of poo-covered toilet paper I've created, and reach back to wipe my jeans. Why do I have to be so pig-headed?

Finn appears and places a bucket of foamy water before me. He drops two cloths inside and gives me a wink. "Having fun?" he asks.

Scowling, I crouch down and squeeze out one of the cloths. When I glance up at Finn, he's laughing silently. "I'm sorry, Emma," he gasps. "I'm trying not to."

"Sure."

"You'll laugh about it one day."

"That seems unlikely."

He tries to look serious and fails dismally. "I'd better go help Freddie give the delinquent a bath."

Ignoring him, I return my attention to my smelly arse.

———

"Whose idea *was* this?" Lily pulls her sweatshirt off, shoves it in a locker, and tugs at her Lycra pants.

"Mine." I pick up my mat. "Come on. Let's go in before I change my mind."

Leading my three friends into the yoga room, I inhale deeply. The smell of incense is heavy and cloying in the air, and I'm grateful for its intensity. I've had two showers since the poo incident earlier today, but I still get sudden whiffs of excrement in my nostrils. Several women are on their mats in the cosy room lit with candles. They look so peaceful lying on their backs, a bolster beneath them, their eyes closed. I wonder if they're trying hard to look serene when all they want to do is pull their G-string out of their bum crack the way I need to.

"What are you doing?" Mags hisses. "Stop touching your bottom."

Trish gives her little girl giggle and lays out her mat. "Since we're pregnant, do we get to spend most of our time in child's pose?" she whispers to me.

"I hope so," I whisper back. I want to have another go at my G-string but I'm worried about Mags telling me off again. She's been seeing quite a bit of Phoebe, the woman she met at the vet, and she's a tad sensitive with us. I think she's worried we'll start hassling her. We're tempted, but we're trying to be mature.

Lily lays her mat out in front of Mags. "You better not start checking out my arse," she mutters fairly loudly.

Red spots appear on Mags's cheeks and she glares at the wall.

"Behave," I hiss.

Lily grins and sits on her mat. She's in a ridiculously happy mood since she told Darryl she'll move in with him. If anyone deserves to be hassled more, it should be her.

"I won't be able to do half the postures with these puppies getting in the way." Trish glares at her boobs.

"Maybe avoid down dog," says Lily. "You don't want to accidently knock yourself out."

"Lily," I warn. "Stop."

A couple of the women on their mats in the front row have opened their eyes and turned to check us out. I smile apologetically and attempt to settle into a look suitably calm and yoga-like. Closing my eyes, I press my thumb and forefinger together and place my hands, palm upwards on my knees.

"What are you doing?" Mags elbows me in the ribs. "You look like a doofus."

I was on such a self-improvement high after we returned from our holiday, I thought rather than meeting at Morellis we could get together to do something more rewarding. Selfishly, I didn't enjoy going to Morellis now I couldn't drink alcohol. I figured yoga followed by a herbal tea at the café next door was a far more sensible, grown-up option. I'm beginning to think it's not one of my best ideas to date. Even Dad looked at me like I'd grown another head when he came over to babysit and I told him of my planned evening with the girls.

Our yoga teacher appears and sits on the small raised platform before us.

"You've got to be kidding me," Lily mutters.

The woman looks about sixteen. She's short and toned, tanned and beautiful. There's not even a faint whisper of stomach fat on her, and her silken black hair drops to her waist in perfect sheets. "I hate her," whispers Trish.

"I shouldn't have had that curry for lunch," murmurs Mags.

Lily snorts quietly and the teacher joins her palms together at her heart and nods in our direction. "Welcome, everyone. It's wonderful to see some new faces. Thank you for joining me on the mat this evening, and for allowing yourself this time to settle into the here and now."

I double over, laughter rippling through me. Scrambling to my feet, I dash for the door, making it to the changing area only a split second before I begin to howl.

Trish, Mags, and Lily burst in. "What's wrong?" Mags asks.

"You won't believe what happened today," I gasp.

Lily puts her hands on her hips. "Try us."

I collapse on a seat and clutch my stomach. Surely this much laughter can't be good for the baby.

"You'd better tell us because there's no way I'm going back in there now." Trish plonks herself on the seat beside me. "You should have seen the looks those women gave us."

"Sorry." I try to calm down. "I don't know what came over me."

"I do." Lily begins to gather up her things. "You've lost the plot. Come on."

"Where are we going?"

"There's a pub on the corner. Emma can enlighten us over Virgin Bloody Marys."

I shouldn't have been so severe with Finn. He was right. This poo story is going to go down in history. That's if I can stop laughing long enough to tell it.

———

"Night, Mama."

I turn off the light and blow another kiss across the room. "Night, Fredster. I'll be back in ten minutes to get Kai." Freddie has Kai's furry little black and white neck in a fairly severe headlock and the poor pup is giving me a plaintive look as if to say, *rescue me, please.*

For a moment I pause to take in the incredible sight of my son curled up happily in bed with his new puppy. Maybe this owning-a-dog thing will be worth it. Eventually.

Pulling the door shut, I wander down the hallway and sit in the lounge. It's been a long time since I've thought about Paul. I wonder what he and Lady Grey are up to right now. Are they out to dinner or at a movie? When you don't have a child and a puppy and a new business to take care of, those are the sorts of things you can do easily. I don't miss Paul. Not for a second. But I miss having *someone*.

After a few minutes of staring at nothing, I pull out my phone and look at Finn's number. Realising how sad and pathetic that makes me, I click on Instagram so I can at least rub salt into the wound and see how everyone else is going with their perfect lives.

Harriet Galway hasn't posted anything in days. Not since before I went to Bali. Normally she posts two or three times a week. She's probably been too busy making kombucha or sewing clothes for her wee cherubs.

Scrolling down, I stop on a photo. It's Harriet, but not as I've ever seen her before. She looks terrible. Her hair is a mess, her face is splotchy, and there's a raised red pimple on her forehead. She's standing in front of an ugly building with graffiti along the wall.

I read her comment:

This morning I left my husband. I bundled my children into the car and drove away from my gorgeous little cottage, and my wonderful garden. I came here and moved my beautiful children into this ugly building, which is the only place I can afford to rent. I don't know what I will do now. Or tomorrow. I'm sorry to all my followers. I showed you my life through a lens. It was a filtered life. A lie. A sham.

I click the button on the side of my phone and the screen goes black. My baby moves and I place a hand on my stomach. "You're okay," I whisper, closing my eyes and resting my head back.

A couple of minutes later, I dial Finn's number.

He answers on the third ring. "Hi," he says.

"Hi." My voice is croaky. "Sorry to ring so late."

"It's seven o'clock," Finn says.

"Yeah, well, it feels like it should be midnight."

"Are you all set for the big opening?"

"Actually that's why I rang. We're having a little get-together at the café, tomorrow night at five. A casual pre-opening celebration, I'm not sure if you're free but you'd be welcome to come along."

There's a long pause. "Thanks for asking, Emma. I would love to come, only I'm not sure your family and friends would be very happy about it."

"They'll be fine." Truth is, I'm not sure how they'll react to seeing Finn. Everyone's aware he's still in NZ. They know he's walking Kai for me. And of course they're privy to the news he wants to be involved with the baby – though I haven't told them he went to the pregnancy scan. But not even Mum has asked me what's going on. It's like they've all had this secret little meeting and agreed not to discuss him under any circumstances. I can't decide if I'm relieved or disappointed.

"I think it's probably best I don't come," Finn says. "I don't want to add any stress—"

"Okay." It was stupid to ring him. I should have resisted the urge. The problem is, even though I know I should get off the phone and go and deal with the load of washing in the machine, or do some other grown-up responsible job, I don't want to. I want to hear Finn's lilting Scottish voice. I want to talk to him. About anything.

"Emma—" Finn starts.

"I'm sorry I was grumpy with you about the poo incident yesterday. You're right, it was very funny… in retrospect. It's just, at the time I was mortified."

Finn's taking so long to respond I wonder if he's distracted. Oh God, he's with someone. Why didn't I think of that? He's lying naked in bed with some saucy vixen.

"I'll let you go," I blabber.

"Emma, I miss you so much it's ridiculous," Finn says loudly.

Would he say that if saucy vixen was sprawled out next to him? I think not. But maybe she's in the bathroom, admiring her young, tanned, non-pregnant body.

"You don't have to respond," Finn says softly. "I know where things stand. It's just hard for me."

"Is there someone with you?" I stammer.

"Sorry?"

"Do you have someone there? And by someone, I mean an overly-attractive female."

Finn gives a short laugh. "No, Emma. There is no female here with me, attractive or otherwise."

"Good."

Neither of us speak. Instead I listen to Finn breathing fairly heavily down the phone. This is hopeless. I'm hopeless. I don't understand. He said he misses me, but what does he miss? The sex? My cooking? My warped sense of humour? The Emma I used to be before the accident?

"I've been offered a job," Finn says abruptly. "A dream job, actually."

I steel myself. The job could be anywhere in the world. "Really? What?"

"A park ranger on the Kepler Track. It's near Te Anau in the middle of the South Island. I'd live in one of the tramping huts and be responsible for the trampers; checking people in, making sure they understand the weather, talking to them about the local flora and wildlife. I'd also be in charge of checking conditions on the track, keeping the hut clean."

I can hear the excitement in his voice. Why do I feel so

utterly devastated? Say something, I tell myself. "That sound's amazing. You'd be perfect."

"Yeah, it's not confirmed yet. I'm waiting to hear if my visa will be approved."

So he's moving on with his life. Fair enough. I almost wish he'd found a job in another country. It'll be harder knowing he's so close, and yet so absent.

"It means I could come and visit," Finn says brightly. "I'd get five days off every two weeks. I could fly back occasionally and see the baby, help out in some way. And the job's seasonal from November to April. I could be around more over the winter."

Oh God, how am I going to deal with that? It'll be torture having Finn visit, and yet, what can I do? He's entitled to see his baby.

"Great," I mutter.

"The issue is—"

"I better go," I say quickly. "Congratulations, Finn."

"Emma—"

"Freddie's calling me, bye." I hang up and throw my phone on the couch. Bugger him. Why can't Finn go back to Scotland and leave me to get over him? Because I'll admit it right here, right now: I'm not over Finn. If anything, I'm keener on him now more than ever. Before the accident, it was mostly about sex with a hot guy, but now I know Finn a little better, it's far worse. He's the guy I want to call at the end of every day. The person I want to share my life with.

———

"To Emma," Dad says, smiling broadly and raising his glass. "For her bravery and determination over the past fairly challenging year."

"That's an understatement," Lily yells, causing everyone, including me, to laugh.

"We know this café will be a huge success," continues Dad, "and we look forward to eating copious amounts of your delicious food, sitting at one of these tables surrounded by other satisfied customers."

"Here, here," shouts Mags.

"To Emma," everyone says, raising a glass.

"To Mama," I hear Freddie call. He's standing on a chair at the long table beside the window with a glass of water raised in my direction. Mum is close behind, a precautionary hand on his back. She sips her wine and blinks rapidly, her face quivering with emotion.

The fading evening sun casts a golden tinge over everyone gathered in my soon-to-be-opened café and my world slows down. I pause, suspended in a state of appreciation and love for this exact moment in time, surrounded by the most important people in my life.

Mags, a full head taller than Mum, throws her arm around Mum's shoulder and gives her an over-enthusiastic Mags-squeeze, causing Mum's head to practically disappear into Mags's armpit. Trish leans close to Freddie and whispers something while pointing at the plate of chocolate brownies, causing Freddie to grin and nod enthusiastically. Lily leans against Darryl, his arm tight around her waist and gives me an understanding wink. Alison stands near the coffee machine talking to Joey, whose bicep turns into a boulder as he takes a gulp from his beer bottle. And Dad is doing pretty much exactly what I'm doing. Looking around the room, taking it all in.

I step over to him, put a hand on his arm and lean close. "Thanks for everything, Dad," I whisper. "I couldn't have got this far without you."

Dad kisses me on the forehead. "Love you, Emmie," he whispers.

"Love you too," I croak.

We pull apart, embarrassed yet pleased with our newfound relationship, wherein our emotions are no longer confined to humour and flippancy.

"Did you invite Finn?" Dad asks, his voice abrupt.

"Y-yes," I stutter, surprised and alarmed that Dad would choose this moment to mention him. "But he's not coming."

Dad opens his mouth, hesitates, and closes it again.

"What?" I ask.

"Nothing. It's not up to me."

"What's not up to you?"

Dad sighs. "He's not all bad, this Finn character. I get the impression he cares quite a bit about you. And Freddie."

"Dad what's going on?"

Shaking his head, Dad looks towards the door. "Hear him out," he whispers, then he spins on his heel and strides into the kitchen.

Finn walks through the open café door wearing the exact same outfit he wore the very first night I met him. The same jeans, the same shirt, the same gorgeous face.

Suddenly Lily and Trish are flanking me. It's as if they've clicked their fingers and been transported to my side.

"It's fine," I mutter. "Stand down."

Spying me, Finn heads in my direction, but he's cut off by my mother. She speaks to him rapidly but I can't hear what they're saying. Whatever it is, they're both looking very uncomfortable with the subject matter.

"What's he doing here?" I hiss. "He said he wasn't coming."

"I asked him," states Lily.

"What?" I stare at Lily, stunned.

"I told him if he didn't come here tonight and tell you everything, I was going to tell you myself."

"Oh God," I groan. "It's got to be bad."

Lily shakes her head. "Not if he says what I'm hoping he'll say."

Trish nods too. "We figured we'd give him one chance."

"We?" I narrow my eyes at Trish. "What do you mean, we?"

"Blame Mags," says Lily. "It was her idea to go see him."

"Okay, hold up." I step back from them both and raise my palms. "You either tell me what the hell is going on or I disown you as friends."

Suddenly he's behind me. I sense him. Smell him. Hear his breath and feel the presence of his body close to mine. Lily raises her eyebrows briefly then turns to Trish. "Fancy another sparkling water there, Trish?"

Smiling, Trish glances at her barely touched, full-to-the-brim glass. "Why, that would be lovely Lily." They link arms, spin on their heels and walk into the kitchen.

"Hi Emma," says Finn, his voice low.

Taking small, careful steps I pivot on the spot to greet him. "Hi."

"I'm sorry to appear like this. I was going to wait for another time but—" Finn wrinkles his nose – "I wasn't left with a great deal of choice."

There are few things in life I find more infuriating than being kept in the dark about something. I put my hands on my hips and scowl. "Lily tells me you have something to say. Might as well get it over with."

Finn shuffles about and glances at the others in the café; most have their eyes glued on him. "Could we talk some-where else?" he asks.

"No," I state. "We can't."

"Okay." Finn crosses his arms, then uncrosses them again. "The thing is, your dad found out something recently and I asked him not to tell anyone, but then he told your mum, and she told your friends, and now… well, now I guess I have to tell you."

I'm so busy feeling betrayed by my nearest and dearest that I fail to notice Finn has reached out and taken my hand until he squeezes it softly. "Emma, do you remember meeting my grandmother, Audrey?"

I nod, recalling the intense look the woman gave me as she stood beside her grandson in the hospital.

"She was pretty pissed off when Siobhan and I broke up," Finn says. "She was convinced if I gave it more time I'd get over you, but I knew that wouldn't happen."

My heart, which is already thumping, begins to gallop. Did he just say something about not being over me?

"Audrey went home to Scotland in a huff, and then she must have felt guilty, because she sent me an email apology and deposited some money into my account so that I could, in her words, 'follow my instincts'."

"That was generous," I mutter.

"Not really, she's loaded. Anyway, I learnt that Jack's son was going to sell this building to some developer, and I knew it would spell the end of your café, so I offered to buy him out."

"Wait." I pull my hand from his. "Jack left me this building in his will."

"Well, technically he left you half. His son owned the other half, and he was an arsehole to deal with, but eventually I was able to purchase his shares and ensure the building went to you. I tried to make sure no one found out, but then your dad was talking to your family lawyer, and she let something slip, and so he came to see me and... well, it was your dad, Emma. I couldn't really lie to him—"

"You own half this building?" I whisper.

"No, you do. It's entirely yours."

"But you paid—"

"Emma, I wanted to do something to help you. And this all happened before I found out you were pregnant, so please don't think... well, that this was done out of a sense of fatherly duty or something."

"Was it because of the accident?"

"What?"

"You felt guilty and thought this would ease your conscience?"

Finn frowns and steps back. "I feel guilty about the accident. I've wished a million times I hadn't suggested we do something so completely stupid, but that's not what this is about."

"What is it about?"

"It's about you, Emma. It's about the very first time I saw you in your tiara and your bare feet."

"Finn, don't—"

"I thought you didn't feel the same way about me. I was convinced you wished I'd gone back to Scotland and stayed there. You kept saying how we needed to be responsible adults and figure out a way to be parents to our child but nothing more."

I stare at Finn's lips as they move. Is he really saying these things? I feel as if nothing around me is real.

"But then your friends came to see me," Finn continues, "and they said, well... they told me to stop being a typical male and to just come and tell you that I'm in love with you, and of course Lily insisted it had to happen immediately or else—"

"They knew," I say softly.

"Knew what?"

"That I wasn't over you."

Finn freezes. "Emma, I don't know what the future has in store for us. I don't even know if I can stay in New Zealand yet. If I take this job, I'll be away for weeks on end, and you—"

I quickly place my palm over his mouth. I'm about to do it. I'm about to tell this far-too-good-looking Scottish bloke that I'm crazy in love with him. I don't care that there is a room full of people watching. I don't care that we have no plans in place for the monumental months ahead. I know enough. I know I want to wake up tomorrow morning in Finn's arms. I want to take the risk and see where it leads, because I make my own rules now. And this – this crazy, messy life, this café, this roomful of family and friends, and this man standing before me – is all I want.

"I love you, Finn," I say loudly, before leaning in to kiss him.

The room erupts with cheers.

ACKNOWLEDGMENTS

Thank you to Rhea Kurien for seeing some semblance of talent in my work and sending me the email so many writers dream of. Thanks to the team at Aria Fiction, especially Hannah Todd, for getting this book out there for the world to discover and, with luck, enjoy.

Thanks to Alison for your OT advice – if I've stuffed up anywhere, the fault is entirely mine.

Thanks Brea and Rachel for stepping up so I could step back.

To my friends, especially the book club contingent, thanks for your encouragement, belly laughs, and constant support.

To my parents, sisters, brothers, in-laws, aunties, cousins, nieces, and nephews you are beautiful human beings and the very best supporters I could wish for.

To Mike, Grace, Sophie, and George…you're the best. Love you guys. Thanks for putting up with me.

ABOUT THE AUTHOR

OLIVIA SPOONER has been writing fiction for twenty years and still feels she is only at the start of her writing journey. She lives in New Zealand with her husband, three children, a big hairy dog, and an overweight cat. Olivia is the proud owner of an independent bookshop where she happily shares her love of books with everyone who walks through the door. When not surrounded by books or creating stories, Olivia is most likely to be found at the beach or simply out walking - the more remote the location, the better. She loves a good meal and to the disbelief of her children adores a massaged kale and avocado salad. And chocolate. Just not together.